COVERT WARRIORS

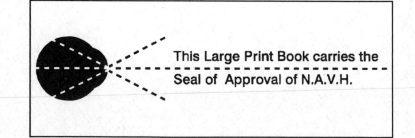

This Large Print Book carries the
Seal of Approval of N.A.V.H.

COVERT WARRIORS

W. E. B. GRIFFIN AND WILLIAM E. BUTTERWORTH IV

THORNDIKE PRESS
A part of Gale, Cengage Learning

Detroit • New York • San Francisco • New Haven, Conn • Waterville, Maine • London

GALE
CENGAGE Learning·

Thorndike Press® Large Print Core.
The text of this Large Print edition is unabridged.
Other aspects of the book may vary from the original edition.
Set in 16 pt. Plantin.

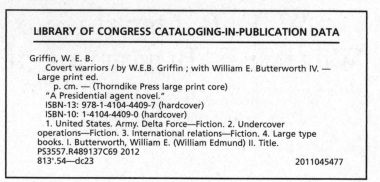

LIBRARY OF CONGRESS CATALOGING-IN-PUBLICATION DATA

Griffin, W. E. B.
  Covert warriors / by W.E.B. Griffin ; with William E. Butterworth IV. — Large print ed.
      p. cm. — (Thorndike Press large print core)
  "A Presidential agent novel."
  ISBN-13: 978-1-4104-4409-7 (hardcover)
  ISBN-10: 1-4104-4409-0 (hardcover)
  1. United States. Army. Delta Force—Fiction. 2. Undercover operations—Fiction. 3. International relations—Fiction. 4. Large type books. I. Butterworth, William E. (William Edmund) II. Title.
  PS3557.R489137C69 2012
  813'.54—dc23   2011045477

Published in 2012 by arrangement with G. P. Putnam's Sons, a member of Penguin Group (USA) Inc.

Printed in the United States of America
1 2 3 4 5 6 7 16 15 14 13 12

26 July 1777

The necessity of procuring good intelligence is apparent and need not be further urged.

George Washington
General and Commander in Chief
The Continental Army

FOR THE LATE

WILLIAM E. COLBY
An OSS Jedburgh First Lieutenant
who became director of the Central
Intelligence Agency.

AARON BANK
An OSS Jedburgh First Lieutenant
who became a colonel and the father of
Special Forces.

WILLIAM R. CORSON
A legendary Marine intelligence officer
whom the KGB hated more than any
other U.S. intelligence officer —
and not only because he wrote the
definitive work on them.

RENÉ J. DÉFOURNEAUX
A U.S. Army OSS Second Lieutenant

attached to the British SOE
who jumped into occupied France
alone and later became a legendary
U.S. Army intelligence officer.

FOR THE LIVING

BILLY WAUGH
A legendary Special Forces Command
Sergeant Major
who retired and then went on to hunt
down the infamous Carlos the Jackal.
Billy could have terminated Osama bin
Laden in the early 1990s
but could not get permission to do so.
After fifty years in the business, Billy is
still going after the bad guys.

JOHNNY REITZEL
An Army Special Operations officer
who could have terminated the head
terrorist
of the seized cruise ship *Achille Lauro*
but could not get permission to do so.

RALPH PETERS
An Army intelligence officer
who has written the best analysis of our
war against terrorists and of our enemy
that I have ever seen.

AND FOR THE NEW BREED

Marc L
A senior intelligence officer, despite his youth, who reminds me of Bill Colby more and more each day.

Frank L
A legendary Defense Intelligence Agency officer who retired and now follows in Billy Waugh's footsteps.

OUR NATION OWES THESE PATRIOTS A DEBT BEYOND REPAYMENT.

I

Highway 95
80 Kilometers North of Acapulco de Juárez
Guerrero State, Mexico
1110 11 April 2007

"Oh, shit! The fucking Federales!" the driver of the off-white Suburban said when he saw the roadblock ahead.

"Our esteemed associates in the unceasing war against drugs," the man sitting beside him said. "Try to remember you're a diplomat."

The driver of the car was Chief Warrant Officer (3) Daniel Salazar, Special Forces, U.S. Army. The man sitting beside him was Lieutenant Colonel James D. Ferris, also U.S. Army Special Forces. The two men in the back of the white Suburban were Antonio Martinez and Eduardo Torres, both of whom were special agents of the U.S. Drug

11

Enforcement Administration.

Lieutenant Colonel Ferris was an assistant military attaché of the United States embassy and Mr. Salazar was an administrative officer of the Office of the Military Attaché of the embassy. Both held diplomatic passports, and had been issued by the Mexican government a *carnet* — a plastic card the size of a driver's license — further verifying this status. Martinez and Torres did not have diplomatic status but had been issued a *carnet* identifying them as DEA agents working in Mexico with the blessing of the Mexican government.

Everyone was in civilian clothing. Ferris and Salazar were armed. Both carried Colt Model 1911A1 .45 ACP semiautomatic pistols in high-rise holsters concealed by their loose cotton shirts. They were also armed with fully automatic 5.56mm AR-15A3 Tactical Carbines, now resting on the Suburban's third row of seats.

The Mexican government didn't like at all the fact that Americans were running around Mexico armed with pistols and what were actually submachine guns. But the laws of diplomacy are immutable. Diplomats are not subject to the laws of the country to which they are accredited.

Martinez and Torres were not armed. The

theory was that because the DEA agents were working closely with Mexican law-enforcement authorities, including and usually the Policía Federal, these agencies would provide them with all the protection they needed.

The subject of weapons had been a bone of contention between Lieutenant Colonel Ferris and the Honorable J. Howard Mc-Cann, whom President Joshua Ezekiel Clendennen had six weeks before appointed as his ambassador plenipotentiary to the Mexican Republic.

Sympathetic to the feelings of the Mexicans, Ambassador McCann had told the military attaché — Colonel Foster B. Lewis, MI — to make sure that Lieutenant Colonel Ferris was made aware that he agreed with the Mexican position that American diplomats should not go about armed absent a clear situation in which they might be in genuine danger.

When Colonel Lewis had a chat with Lieutenant Colonel Ferris about this, Ferris replied in a somewhat blunt manner perhaps to be expected of a Special Forces officer.

"Fuck him. I have no intention of getting blown away by some drug lord's banditos without a fight."

"Colonel, you have been informed of the

ambassador's desires."

"Colonel, if you order me not to be armed, I will of course obey. I will also get on the horn to General McNab and request immediate relief."

Colonel Lewis's military superior was Major General Amos Watts, the Defense Intelligence Agency's commander. Lieutenant Colonel Ferris's immediate military superior was Lieutenant General Bruce J. McNab, the Special Operations Command (SPECOPSCOM) commander.

When Lewis reported the substance of his conversation with Ferris to Ambassador McCann, the ambassador considered the political ramifications of the impasse, the most important of these being that General McNab and Secretary of State Natalie Cohen were, if not friends, then mutual admirers.

It had been the secretary's idea — rather than a proposal from one of her subordinates — to have Army Special Forces personnel sent to Mexico to train the Mexican military and police forces so that they could better wage their war against the drug cartels.

Ambassador McCann's predecessor had protested the idea as best he could and had been overruled. The secretary was in love with her own idea.

Ambassador McCann's predecessor had reported the substance of that conversation to McCann during the turnover.

"She told me that she had learned from General McNab that the primary role of Special Operations — despite all the publicity that Delta Force and Gray Fox get — is the training of indigenous forces to fight their own battles, and their success in doing so is judged by the amount of fighting the trainers have to do themselves, with no fighting at all being a perfect score. She said that seemed to her exactly what the situation in Mexico required.

"She also told me that she had prevailed upon General McNab to send her the best trainers he could, and that he had — 'reluctantly, we're friends' — agreed to do so. So that's what Ferris and his people are doing here — they're on loan to the State Department for ten months. Ferris has been down here three."

Ambassador McCann had told Colonel Lewis, "I'll give this matter due consideration and make a decision about it later."

Although Colonel Lewis considered himself a loyal subordinate of Ambassador McCann, he could not help himself from thinking that that was the sort of response one could expect from a career diplomat: *Never decide today that which can be put off until tomorrow — or even later.*

Whenever Lieutenant Colonel Ferris knew that he and Danny Salazar would be traveling through what he privately thought of as "Indian Territory," accompanied by members of the DEA, or sometimes the FBI — the latter known as "legal attachés" and with *the* legal attaché afraid to defy Ambassador McCann, they also went unarmed — Ferris elected to arm himself and Danny with AR-15A3s in addition to their .45s. He had done so today when he headed for Acapulco.

He reasoned that if they were bushwhacked by drug scum, and the DEA or FBI guys happened to pick up the .45s that he and Danny happened to drop while grabbing their A3s, and that extra firepower kept everybody alive, he would hear nothing from Ambassador McCann.

The roadblock on the highway ahead consisted of six black-uniformed Federales operating out of a Ford F-250 6.4L diesel crew cab truck, which Colonel Ferris suspected had been paid for by U.S. taxpayers.

One of the Federales, an AR-15A3 slung from his shoulder, stepped into the road and held up his hand, ordering the Suburban to stop.

"There's a CD plate on this," Danny said. "Jesus H. Christ!"

A *corps diplomatique* license plate on a vehicle was usually enough to see the passengers therein waved through roadblocks.

"Make nice, Danny," Ferris said, "remembering that we are guests here in sunny Meh-hi-co."

Danny slowed the Suburban to a stop, simultaneously taking from his shirt pocket his diplomatic *carnet* and holding it up.

Ferris, doing the same, ordered: "*Carnet* time, guys. Smile at the nice Federales."

The Federale who had blocked the road approached the car.

"Good morning, Sergeant," Ferris said in Spanish, holding up his *carnet*. "What seems to be the problem?"

"Out of the truck, please," the sergeant said.

"Sergeant, I am Lieutenant Colonel James D. Ferris, an assistant military attaché of the U.S. embassy."

"Get out of the truck, Colonel."

"I demand to see the person in charge," Ferris said as he opened the door and stepped to the ground.

He saw a Federale lieutenant standing with the others.

17

"Over there," the Federale said, nodding toward him.

"Thank you," Ferris said.

"Everybody out," the Federale said.

Ferris walked toward the *teniente.*

"Good afternoon, Comandante," Ferris began.

Ferris knew that a *comandante* actually was a captain. But he had learned over the years that people are seldom offended by a promotion, even one given in error.

"Comandante, I am Lieutenant Colonel James D. Ferris, an assistant military attaché of the U.S. embassy."

The *tenientes* did not reply, but three of his men, two second sergeants and a corporal, walked toward the Suburban.

"This is my *carnet,*" Ferris said.

There was a burst of 5.56mm fire.

Ferris spun around.

Salazar and Torres were on the ground. Martinez, a surprised look on his face, was on his knees, holding his hands to his bleeding abdomen. Then he fell to one side.

"You murdering sonsofbitches!" Ferris shouted.

Another second sergeant struck Ferris in the back of his head with a pistol.

When Ferris fell to the ground, the second sergeant who had pistol-whipped him

18

quickly pulled Ferris's wrists behind him, fastened them securely with "plastic handcuffs," and did the same to his ankles.

The *teniente* pulled a black plastic garbage bag over Ferris's head and closed it loosely. Four of the Federales picked up Ferris and loaded him into the rear of the Suburban.

The *teniente* and one of the second sergeants then got into the Suburban, and with the second sergeant driving, made a U-turn and headed in the direction of Mexico City. The others got into the Ford F-250 and followed the Suburban.

[Two]

URGENT
SECRET
1615 11 APRIL 2007

FROM: AMB USEMB MEXICO CITY
TO: PERSONAL ATTENTION SECSTATE,
    WASH DC
CONFIRMING TELECON 1600 THIS
    DATE

SEÑOR FERNANDO RAMIREZ DE AYALA OF THE MEXICAN FOREIGN

MINISTRY TELEPHONED USAMB AT APPROXIMATELY 1505 THIS DATE RE-QUESTING AN EMERGENCY AUDI-ENCE. DE AYALA WAS RECEIVED AT THE CHANCELLERY AT 1550.

DE AYALA REPORTED THAT HE HAD BEEN INFORMED BY THE POLICÍA FEDERAL THAT THEY HAD FOUND AT APPROXIMATELY 1200 HOURS LOCAL TIME THE BODIES OF THREE MEN WHO HAD BEEN SHOT TO DEATH ON THE SIDE OF HIGHWAY 95 APPROXI-MATELY 50 MILES NORTH OF ACA-PULCO DE JUÁREZ.

THE BODIES HAVE BEEN TENTATIVELY IDENTIFIED BY DOCUMENTS FOUND ON THEM AS CHIEF WARRANT OFFI-CER DANIEL SALAZAR, EDUARDO TORRES AND ANTONIO MARTINEZ. THE BODIES HAVE BEEN MOVED TO HOSPITAL SANTA LUCÍA IN ACAPULCO FOR AUTOPSY AND TO VERIFY THEIR IDENTITY.

CWO(3) DANIEL SALAZAR, USA, IS ADMINISTRATIVE OFFICER OF THE

OFFICE OF THE MILITARY ATTACHÉ OF THE EMBASSY, AND EDUARDO TORRES AND ANTONIO MARTINEZ ARE SPECIAL AGENTS OF THE DRUG ENFORCEMENT ADMINISTRATION ATTACHED TO THE EMBASSY, AND I AM PROCEEDING ON THE PRESUMPTION THAT THEIR BODIES ARE THOSE FOUND BY THE POLICÍA FEDERAL.

ALL THREE ARE KNOWN TO HAVE BEEN EN ROUTE TO ACAPULCO DE JUÁREZ TO PARTICIPATE IN A MEETING WITH US AND MEXICAN LAW ENFORCEMENT AUTHORITIES. LIEUTENANT COLONEL JAMES D. FERRIS, ASSISTANT MILITARY ATTACHÉ OF THE EMBASSY, WAS TRAVELING WITH THEM IN AN EMBASSY SUBURBAN VEHICLE WHICH BORE A DIPLOMATIC LICENSE PLATE. THE WHEREABOUTS OF COLONEL FERRIS AND THE SUBURBAN ARE PRESENTLY UNKNOWN.

WHEN I INFORMED DE AYALA THAT I INTENDED TO SEND JONATHAN B. WILSON, THE EMBASSY LEGAL ATTACHÉ, TO ACAPULCO DE JUÁREZ TO

IDENTIFY THE BODIES AND ASSIST IN THE INVESTIGATION, DE AYALA MADE IT CLEAR THAT WILSON'S ASSISTANCE IN THE INVESTIGATION OF THE SITUATION WOULD NOT BE WELCOME. MR. WILSON IS PRESENTLY UNDER WAY TO ACAPULCO.

FURTHER DETAILS REGARDING THIS SITUATION WILL BE MADE AVAILABLE TO YOU BY SECURE TELEPHONE FOLLOWED BY MESSAGE AS THEY ARE LEARNED.

RESPECTFULLY SUBMITTED

J. HOWARD MCCANN
AMBASSADOR
SECRET

[Three]
Office of the Commanding General
U.S. Special Operations Command
Fort Bragg, North Carolina
1625 11 April 2007

There were two telephones — one black, the other red — and an open leather attaché

22

case on the desk of Lieutenant General Bruce J. McNab, the small, muscular, ruddy-faced officer who, sporting a flowing red mustache, commanded SPECOPS-COM.

The red telephone had both a buzzer and several light-emitting diodes (LEDs). The red one began to flash as its buzzer went off. When McNab grabbed it, a green light-emitting diode illuminated, indicating that the encryption system was functioning. Protocol required that persons privileged to have a Command Net telephone — one notch down from the White House switchboard network — answer the telephone within thirty seconds. A timer on the telephone base informed General McNab that he had done so in seven seconds.

"General McNab," he said.

"This is the White House switchboard. Please confirm functioning encryption."

"Confirm," McNab said.

"Go ahead, Madam Secretary," the White House operator said.

"Bruce, this is Natalie Cohen," the secretary of State said, then chuckled, and said, "who has just decided to call you later."

"Yes, ma'am," McNab said.

The LEDs had gone out by the time he replaced the handset.

He turned his attention to the attaché case, which held what looked like a normal Hewlett-Packard laptop computer and a device that looked like a BlackBerry. They were cushioned in rubber foam with a small row of buttons and LEDs. Neither the laptop nor the BlackBerry was what it seemed to be.

The attaché case was known as "The Brick," a term going back to the first cell phones issued to senior officers that had been about the size and weight of a large brick.

He picked up that device that looked like a BlackBerry. It was known to those who both were privileged to have one and knew the story as a "CaseyBerry." He knew that when Secretary Cohen said she would call him later, she would do so immediately using the CaseyBerry in her Brick.

As McNab looked at his CaseyBerry, a green LED indicating an incoming call lit up, as did a blue LED indicating that the encryption function was operating.

Those who believed the White House switchboard and its ancillary encryption capabilities were state of the art were wrong. State of the art was really what Aloysius Francis Casey, Ph.D., termed "Prototype Systems, Undergoing Testing."

When, for example, the encryption system in the "Prototype, Undergoing Testing" Brick that General McNab held had all the bugs worked out, it would be made available to the White House and to the National Security Agency at Fort Meade, Maryland.

In the meantime, even if NSA intercepted the signals transmitted — via satellites 27,000 miles over the earth — between the AFC Corporation's test facility in Las Vegas, Nevada, and the Bricks in the hands of a few more than a dozen people around the world, they would not be able to break the encryption. Dr. Casey was sure of this because AFC, Inc., had designed, installed, and maintained the decryption computers at Fort Meade.

Before he would turn over to the government McNab's "Prototype, Undergoing Testing" Brick with all the bugs worked out, Casey would ensure that McNab and others on the CaseyBerry network had a newer "Prototype, Undergoing Testing" Brick whose encrypted signals NSA could not crack.

General McNab pressed the TALK button.

"McNab," he said.

"Bruce, I just sent you a radio I just got from Mexico City. Do you have it?"

"Just came in," he said.

The monitor of the laptop had illuminated and was now showing the message the secretary of State had received from Ambassador McCann.

McNab pushed three buttons on his desk, simultaneously informing his secretary, his senior aide-de-camp, and his junior aide-de-camp that he required their services.

He still had his fingers on the buttons when the door burst open and Captain Albert H. Walsh, his junior aide-de-camp, who was six feet two inches tall and weighed 195 pounds, quickly walked in.

"Just you, Al," McNab said. Then he made a push-back gesture to his secretary and his senior aide, who were now standing behind Walsh. They turned and went away.

"Just got it," McNab said.

McNab pointed to a chair and pushed the LOUDSPEAKER button on his CaseyBerry. Captain Walsh sat down and took a notebook and ballpoint pen from the pocket of his desert-pattern battle-dress uniform.

General McNab finished reading Ambassador McCann's message that had been sent to the secretary of State.

"Shit!" he exclaimed, immediately adding, "Sorry."

"That was my reaction, Bruce," the secretary of State said.

McNab pushed one of the buttons in the attaché case. A printer on the sideboard behind his desk began to whir. McNab pointed to it, and Captain Walsh quickly went to the printer.

"Something about this smells," McNab said. "Danny Salazar is no novice. For that matter, neither is Ferris."

"You know everything I do," she said.

"Has the press got this yet?"

"They will half an hour after it gets to the White House."

"Can I call Roscoe Danton before that happens, give him a heads-up?"

Roscoe J. Danton was a member of the *Washington Times-Post* Writers Syndicate.

"Why?"

"Gut feeling we should. He's almost one of us. We owe him. And we may need him."

"Does Danton have a Brick?"

"No Brick," McNab replied. "A Casey-Berry. Aloysius likes him. Number fourteen."

"I'll call him and tell him to call Porky. But all he'll have, Bruce, is ten or fifteen minutes."

John David "Porky" Parker was President Joshua Ezekiel Clendennen's spokesman.

"That's a long time, sometimes."

"Bruce, I'm really sorry about this."

"I know," McNab said.

The LEDs went out.

McNab put down the CaseyBerry, picked up the black telephone, and pushed one of the buttons on its base.

"Terry," he announced a moment later, "I need you."

"On my way, sir," Major General Terry O'Toole, deputy commander of SPECOPS-COM, replied.

He was in McNab's office forty-five seconds later. He was trim and ruddy-faced.

McNab pointed to the printout. O'Toole picked it up and read it.

"Shit," he said. "And I gave Jim Ferris to you."

"What *you* did, General," McNab said, "was comply with my request for the name of your best field-grade trainer. What *I* did was send him to DEA so they could send him to Mexico. And *I* sent Danny Salazar with him to cover his back."

O'Toole looked at him.

McNab went on: "And what you're going to say now is, 'Yes, sir, General, that's the way it went down.' "

O'Toole met McNab's eyes, nodded, and repeated, "Yes, sir, General, that's the way it went down."

28

McNab nodded.

O'Toole said: "What happens now?"

"Do you know Colonel Ferris's religious persuasion?"

"Episcopalian."

"Al," General McNab ordered, "get on the horn to the Eighteenth Airborne Corps chaplain. Tell him I want the senior Episcopalian chaplain and the senior Roman Catholic chaplain here in fifteen minutes."

"Yes, sir," Captain Walsh said, and went to a telephone on a side table.

"And call my wife," McNab said. "Same message; here in fifteen."

"Yes, sir."

"What about your wife, Terry? Does she know Mrs. Ferris?"

"May I use your telephone, General?" O'Toole replied.

"Don't tell her who," McNab said.

"I understand, sir."

Neither Mrs. McNab nor Mrs. O'Toole would be surprised by the summons. Both had gone more times than they liked to remember to accompany their husbands when they went to inform wives that their husbands were either dead or missing.

McNab picked up the CaseyBerry and punched in a number.

It was answered ten seconds later in what

29

was known as "the Stockade." Delta Force and Gray Fox were quartered in what had once been the Fort Bragg Stockade. The joke was that all the money spent to make sure no one got out of the Stockade had not been wasted. All of the fences and razor wire and motion sensors were perfectly suited to keep people *out* of the Stockade.

The CaseyBerry was answered by a civilian employee of the Department of the Army, who were known by the acronym DAC. His name was Victor D'Alessandro, a very short, totally bald man in his late forties who held Civil Service pay grade GS-15. Army regulations provided that a GS-15 held the assimilated rank of colonel. Before Mr. D'Alessandro had retired, he had been a chief warrant officer (5) drawing pay and allowances very close to those of a lieutenant colonel. And before he put on the bars of a warrant officer, junior grade, D'Alessandro had been a sergeant major.

"Go," Mr. D'Alessandro said by way of answering his CaseyBerry.

"Bad news, Vic," General McNab said. "Danny Salazar and two DEA guys with him were whacked about noon fifty miles from Acapulco. They were in an embassy SUV with Colonel Ferris. The SUV and Ferris are missing."

"Shit! What happened?"

"I want you to go down there — black — and find out," McNab said. "You and no more than two of your people. By the time you get to Pope, the C-38 will be waiting to fly you to Atlanta. By the time you get there, you should have reservations on Aeromexico to either Acapulco or Mexico City. I'll try to confirm while you're en route."

In a closely guarded hangar at Pope Air Force Base, which abutted Fort Bragg, were several aircraft, including a highly modified Boeing 727 and a C-38, the latter the military nomenclature of the Israel Aircraft Industries Ltd./Galaxy Aerospace Corporation Astra SPX business jet. The C-38 had civilian markings.

"I'll take Nunez and Vargas."

"Your call."

"Who's paying for this?"

McNab, who hadn't considered that detail, gave it some quick thought.

There were two options, neither of which would cost the U.S. taxpayer a dime. In D'Alessandro's safe, together with an assortment of passports in different names, were two manila envelopes, one marked "TP" and one "Charley." Each envelope held two inch-thick stacks of credit cards, American Express Platinum and Citibank

31

Gold Visa cards, the names embossed on them matching the names on the passports, and two business-size envelopes, each holding $10,000 in used hundred-, fifty-, and twenty-dollar bills.

There had been a "TP" envelope in the safe for several years. TP stood for Those People. Those People were an anonymous group of very wealthy businessmen who saw it as their patriotic duty to fund black Special Operations missions when getting official funds to do so would be difficult or impossible.

The "Charley" envelope was a recent addition to D'Alessandro's safe. Charley stood for Lieutenant Colonel Carlos G. Castillo, Special Forces, U.S. Army, Retired. The Amex Platinum and Citibank Gold Visa cards in the Charley envelope identified their holders as officers of the LCBF Corporation.

During a recent covert operation — which went so far beyond black that McNab had dubbed it Operation March Hare, as in "mad as a March hare" — Castillo and McNab had learned that Those People had concluded that since they were making a financial contribution to an operation, they had the right to throw the special operators under the bus when it seemed to be the

logical thing to do, considering the big picture.

One of the results of that was the LCBF Corporation's decision to provide General McNab with the same sort of stand-by funding as Those People provided. It had not posed any financial problems for the LCBF Corporation to do so. The LCBF Corporation already had negotiable assets of more than $50 million when the director of the Central Intelligence Agency handed Mr. David W. Yung — LCBF's vice president, finance — a Treasury check for $125 million in settlement of the CIA's promise to pay that sum, free of any tax liabilities, to whoever delivered to them an intact Russian Tupelov Tu-934A transport aircraft.

Mr. D'Alessandro had written "Charley" on the LCBF envelope without thinking about it. D'Alessandro had still been a sergeant major when Second Lieutenant Castillo had first been passed behind the fences of the Stockade. And as good sergeants major do, he had taken the young officer under his wing. Both D'Alessandro and General McNab devoutly believed they had raised Castillo from a pup.

General McNab would have dearly liked to stick Those People with the costs of D'Alessandro's reconnaissance mission, but decided in the end it would not be the thing to do now. He would think of something else — a bayonet, maybe — to stick them with at a later time.

"Let Charley pay for it, Vic," he said.

"I'll be in touch," D'Alessandro said, and broke the CaseyBerry connection.

[Four]
The Machiavelli Penthouse Suite
The Venetian
3355 Las Vegas Boulevard South
Las Vegas, Nevada
1710 11 April 2007

Aloysius F. Casey, Ph.D., chairman of the board of the AFC Corporation, stepped off the elevator onto the upper-level reception foyer of the Machiavelli Suite, and then stepped to one side, graciously waving out the two females from the elevator.

The first woman was Mrs. Agnes Forbison, who was fifty-one, gray-haired, and getting just a little chubby. Mrs. Forbison was vice president, administration, of the LCBF Corporation. Previously she had been — as a GS-15 — administrative assistant to the Honorable Thomas Hall, secretary of the then–newly formed Department of Homeland Security, and after that, deputy chief for administration of the now-defunct Office of Organizational Analysis.

Second to get off the elevator was a stunningly beautiful woman with luxuriant dark red hair. Her passport identified her as a Uruguayan citizen by the name of Susanna Barlow.

Following Señorita Barlow off the elevator was Lieutenant Colonel Carlos G. Castillo, Ret. — a good-looking, six-foot, 190-pound thirty-seven-year-old — who was the president of the LCBF Corporation. Castillo was followed by an enormous black dog, a Bouvier des Flandres, who answered to Max.

As Castillo stood beside Miss Barlow, she said — hissed perhaps would be more accurate — "You remember I told you this was a mistake."

On Castillo's heels came Mr. Edgar Delchamps, a nondescript man in his early sixties, who was vice president, planning and operations, of the LCBF Corporation. He was retired from the Central Intelligence Agency, where he had served for more than thirty years as an officer of the Clandestine Service.

Delchamps was followed by thirty-three-year-old David W. Yung, Jr., who stood five feet eight and weighed 150 pounds. Despite

35

his obvious Oriental heritage, Mr. Yung could not speak any of the languages of the Orient. He was fluent, however, in four other languages. The vice president, financial, of the LCBF Corporation was an attorney and previously had been a special agent of the Federal Bureau of Investigation.

The final passenger stepped off the elevator. His Argentine passport identified him as Tomás Barlow. He was about the same age as Castillo and was built like him. He was Señorita Barlow's brother. In a previous life, they had been Colonel Dmitri Berezovsky, the SVR *rezident* in Berlin, and Lieutenant Colonel Svetlana Alekseeva, the SVR *rezident* in Copenhagen.

Castillo walked to the edge of the upper-level entrance foyer, rested his hands on the bronze rail atop the glass wall, and looked down to the lower level. Max went with him, put his front paws on the rail, and barked.

Four men — three of them well, even elegantly, dressed — were standing there, looking up at the upper level. One of them was a legendary hotelier who owned four of the more glitzy Las Vegas hotels, and three more in Atlantic City, New Jersey, and Biloxi, Mississippi.

36

Another was a well-known, perhaps even famous, investment banker. Another had made an enormous fortune in data processing. Castillo knew him to be a U.S. Naval Academy graduate. The fourth man was a sort of mousy-looking character in a suit that looked as if it had come off the final-clearance rack at Goodwill. All that Castillo knew about him was that no one knew exactly how many radio and television stations he owned.

Those People and the executive board of the LCBF were about to meet.

Castillo turned and walked back to the people by the elevator door.

"This is your show, Aloysius," he said, loudly enough for Those People to hear. "You get to choose who gets thrown off the balcony first."

Delchamps and Tom Barlow chuckled. Yung smiled.

Casey shook his head and walked toward the head of the curving staircase leading to the lower level. Max trotted after him, then turned to look at Castillo as if expecting an order to "stay." When that did not come, he went down the stairs ahead of Casey, headed directly for a coffee table laden with hors d'oeuvres, and with great delicacy helped himself to a caviar-topped cracker.

"Careful, Max," Castillo called. "They're probably poisoned."

"Enough, Carlito!" Señorita Barlow ordered.

She then started down the stairs. Everyone followed, Casey last, after Castillo, as if to ensure that Castillo didn't get away.

"Annapolis," as Castillo thought of him, waited at the foot of the stairs and put out his right hand.

"Thank you for coming," he said. "We have to get this straightened out between us."

Castillo took the hand with visible reluctance.

"For the good of the country," Annapolis added.

"We don't seem to agree on what's good for the country, do we?" Castillo replied.

"I thought champagne would be in order," "Hotelier" said, "to toast the success of the latest operation. What was it called?"

He snapped his fingers, and two waiters moved to coolers and began to open bottles of champagne.

"I understand some people called it March Hare," Edgar Delchamps offered.

"Well, whatever it was called, it was one hell of a success," "Radio and TV Stations" said.

The waiters quickly poured the champagne, and then walked around, offering it on trays to everyone.

"I give you . . ." Hotelier said, raising his glass.

"Whoa!" Castillo said. "Two things before we do that, if you please. One, why are we talking about such things with these fellows in here passing the champagne?"

"They work for me," "Investment Banker" said. "They are trustworthy."

"Somewhat reluctantly — I'm paranoid on the subject of who gets to hear what — I'll give you a pass on that."

"Thank you," Investment Banker said. "Anything else, Colonel?"

"One more thing," Castillo said. "Two-Gun, give the nice man the envelope."

David W. Yung had earned the moniker "Two-Gun" when he and Edgar Delchamps were about to pass through customs into Argentina. Yung was at the time a legal attaché — the euphemism for FBI agent — accredited to both Argentina and Uruguay, and thus immune to laws regarding the carrying of firearms. Delchamps enjoyed no such immunity; if found in possession of a weapon, he would have been arrested. The problem had been solved by his giving Yung his Colt Officer's Model .45 ACP pistol to carry through customs — thus resulting in Yung's immediately being dubbed "Two-Gun."

Yung walked to Investment Banker and handed him a large manila envelope. It was fully stuffed and held together with thick rubber bands.

"And this is?" Investment Banker said.

"I've been told it contains two hundred thousand dollars in circulated currency," Castillo said. "I never opened it."

"The funds we sent to you?"

"Correct. I wanted you to have them in case you were thinking your money had anything to do with the success of Operation March Hare."

"Did you really think you could put my Carlos in your pocket for a miserable two hundred thousand dollars?" Señorita Barlow demanded.

"Señorita Barlow," Annapolis said reasonably, "that was all that Colonel Castillo asked for."

"Score one for the Navy, Sweaty," Castillo said.

During her association with the Merry Outlaws, "Svetlana" had quickly morphed first to "Svet" and then even more quickly to "Sweaty."

Annapolis pressed his advantage.

"We stood willing to provide whatever was asked for," he said.

"Yeah," Aloysius Casey said, "but you thought you were buying something that wasn't for sale."

"It seems to me," Investment Banker said, "if I may say so, that our problem has been one of communication . . ."

"I just told you what our problem was," Casey interrupted. "You thought you were buying something that wasn't for sale."

"It seems to me, if I may say so," Delchamps said sarcastically, "that the Irishman has just put both thumbs on the problem. You thought you owned us for two hundred thousand."

There was silence for a moment, then Investment Banker said, "If I may continue, gentlemen?"

He interpreted the silence that followed to mean there was no objection, and he went on: "If either of us had, when suspicions arose, contacted the other . . ."

"You were suspicious of *us?*" Yung challenged sarcastically.

"Yes, indeed, Counselor," Investment Banker said. "Perhaps I was being paranoid, but when the Locator suddenly showed Colonel Castillo to be halfway between Budapest and Vienna — on a Danube riverboat that has the reputation of being a floating brothel — when last we'd heard he was on the Lopez Fruit and Vegetables Mexico property, I began to question Dr. Casey's data, and thought we might be having a problem."

"I thought putting Charley on the Love Boat was a nice touch," Delchamps said smugly.

Casey explained: "We were just a little worried that one of you might tell Montvale, or maybe even Clendennen, that Charley was in Mexico — and where."

President Clendennen recently had appointed Charles W. Montvale to be his Vice President. He had previously been director of National Intelligence.

"To be completely honest," Annapolis said, "that path of action was discussed. The phrase I used at the time was 'over my dead body.' And obviously I prevailed." He looked at Castillo. "I give you my word of honor, Colonel."

We have just knocked rings, Castillo thought.

A former member of the Brigade of Midshipmen of the Naval Academy has just given his word of honor to a former member of the Corps of Cadets at West Point, fully expecting him to take it.

And the funny thing is, I'm going to do just that.

"I'll take your word," Castillo said. "Operative word, *your.* To be completely honest, you're the only one of your crew I trust."

"Some small progress is better than none at all," Hotelier said. "For your information, Colonel, we take no actions of that sort unless there is unanimity among us."

Castillo didn't reply.

"Without objection, I will continue with the toast," Hotelier said. "Ladies and gentlemen, I give you the magnificent success of Operation March Hare."

Champagne was sipped. Max took the opportunity to help himself to a bacon-wrapped oyster.

"There's liable to be a toothpick in that," Sweaty said with concern.

"Max knows who we're dealing with," Castillo said. "He looked carefully before he grabbed it. He also sniffed for cyanide."

There were a few chuckles at this.

"Very droll," Investment Banker said. "But if we are to continue working together . . ."

"And whatever gave you the idea that is even a remote possibility?" Castillo asked.

"Because we share the same objective," Hotelier said. "Of defending the United

43

States from all enemies, foreign and domestic."

"I heard somewhere that patriotism is the last refuge of the scoundrel," Castillo said. "Would you be interested in my take on You People?"

"I suspect we're going to get it even if all of us chorused, 'Hell, no,' " Annapolis said. "But I'd like to hear it."

"You started out with good intentions," Castillo said. "And I'll admit that the money you've provided to SPECOPSCOM — and I presume to the Agency and others — helped them to do things that they wouldn't have been able to do because they couldn't get the funds from Congress.

"But then — how did that Englishman put it? 'Power corrupts . . .' "

"If you're talking about John Emerich Edward Dalberg-Acton, First Baron Acton," Annapolis said, "what he said was *'All power tends to corrupt and absolute power corrupts absolutely.'* "

"Thank you," Castillo said. "Sweaty, Annapolis men always like to demonstrate their erudition."

Delchamps laughed.

"I tend to agree with the first part of that quotation," Annapolis went on. "Is that what you're suggesting happened here?"

44

"Bull's-eye, Admiral," Castillo said.

"Actually, I was a commander," Annapolis said. "All right, Colonel, we're guilty as charged. What would you have us do? Commit seppuku?"

"That'd work for you," Castillo said. "But I don't see any VFW buttons on your pals."

"What are you talking about?" Sweaty demanded.

"Seppuku, my love, also known as hara-kiri, is what defeated samurai — warriors — do to atone for their sins. It involves stabbing yourself in the belly with a sword and then giving it a twist. But only *warriors* are allowed to do that."

Delchamps chuckled.

"I don't have a VFW pin, Colonel," Radio and TV Stations said. "But I do have a baseball cap with the legend PALM BEACH CHAPTER, VIETNAM HELICOPTER PILOTS ASSOCIATION embroidered in gold on it. Would you say that gives me the right to disembowel myself?"

"Only if you didn't buy the cap at a yard sale," Castillo said.

Radio and TV Stations did not look anything like what comes to mind when the term *warrior* was used.

"I got mine after I showed them my DD 214 and gave them fifty bucks," Radio and

TV Stations said.

DD 214 was the Defense Department's form that listed one's military service, qualifications, and any decorations.

"You were a helicopter pilot in Vietnam?" Castillo asked, but even as the words came out of his mouth he knew that was the case.

Radio and TV Stations met Castillo's eyes and nodded.

"I'll be a sonofabitch," Castillo said.

"It gets better than that, Castillo," Annapolis said. "Tell him, Chopper Jockey."

"I'd planned to tell you this at some time, but not under these circumstances," Radio and TV Stations said, "but what the hell. I would guess you've heard of Operation Lam Son 719?"

Castillo nodded.

"I was shot down — and wounded — during it," Radio and TV Stations went on. "My co-pilot and I were hiding in a rice paddy, wondering if we were going to die right there — or after the VC found us and put us in a bamboo cage — when a pretty well shot-up Huey flew through some really nasty antiaircraft fire and landed next to us. The pilot and his co-pilot jumped out, threw us onto the Huey, and got us out of there.

"I later learned the pilot was a young

Mexican-American from San Antonio who had flown fifty-odd such missions before his luck ran out. He became a posthumous recipient of the Medal of Honor."

"He wasn't a Mexican-American," Castillo said. "He was a Texican, a Texan of Mexican heritage."

"You knew this man, Karl?" Berezovsky asked.

"Unfortunately, no," Castillo said.

"Don't stop there," Annapolis said. "Tell him the rest."

Radio and TV Stations considered the order, nodded, and went on: "Fast forward — what? Twelve, thirteen years? Maybe a little longer. I was in San Antone on business. I own one of the TV stations there, an English FM station, and one each Spanish-language AM and FM station.

"I found myself with a little time to kill, and finally remembering the man who saved my life just before he got blown away was from there, thought they might have buried him there in the Fort Sam National Cemetery. I called them, they said he was, so I stopped by a florist, and went to the cemetery and laid a dozen roses on the grave of Warrant Officer Junior Grade Jorge Alejandro Castillo, MOH."

47

"Your father, Carlito?" Sweaty asked softly.

Castillo nodded.

"Who, according to his tombstone had left this vale of tears when he was *nineteen* years old," Radio and TV Stations went on, "which caused me to think, what am I doing walking around with more money than I know what to do with, and this Mexican — excuse me, *Texican* — kid who saved my life is pushing up daisies?

"Inspiration struck. What I could do to assuage my guilt was throw money at his family. I even thought that might be the reason God or fate or whatever had let me make all the money, so I could do something good with it.

"So I called the guy who does security for my stations — he's an ex-cop — and told him to get me an address for Mr. Castillo's family. In ten minutes, I had it, so I told the limo driver to take me there.

"Great big house behind a twelve-foot-tall cast-iron fence. The Castillos were obviously not living on food stamps. On the lawn, a blond teenage boy and a great big fat Mexican teenage boy were beating the hell out of each other. I later realized that was probably you, Colonel."

"And my cousin Fernando, also a Texican," Castillo said.

"So I called the security guy back and got the skinny on the Castillo family. They could buy and sell me. So I told the driver to take me to the airport."

"You didn't go in the house?" Sweaty asked.

"Sweaty . . . is it all right if I call you that?"

Svetlana considered that for a full ten seconds, then nodded.

"Sweaty, I'm a coward with an active imagination. I could see myself introducing myself to Mr. Castillo's father and mother and maybe his kid, telling them their dead son had saved my life in Vietnam, and then them asking, 'So where the hell have you been for the past thirteen, fourteen years? You had more important things to do?' "

"They wouldn't have done that," Castillo said. "My father's co-pilot — my father kicked him out of his Huey just before he took off and got blown away — is practically a member of the family. He's a retired two-star."

"Like I said, Colonel, I'm a coward," Radio and TV Stations said. "What I'm hoping is that this trip down memory lane will convince you there were two of us who said 'over my dead body' when it was suggested that turning you over to Ambassador

49

Montvale so that he could turn you over to the Russians was the best solution to the Congo-X problem."

Castillo looked first at Sweaty, who shrugged, which he interpreted to mean "Maybe, why not?" and then at Delchamps, who did the same thing, and finally at Annapolis, who nodded.

"Okay," Castillo said. "Two good guys out of four. Or are there any more of you?"

"There's more," Annapolis said. "The proponents of letting Montvale turn you and Sweaty and Colonel Berezovsky over to the Russians felt their presence here today might be a little awkward."

Castillo snorted, and then asked, "How many more?"

"Well, counting Aloysius and Colonel Hamilton . . ."

"Don't count either one of us," Casey said. "Hamilton's as pissed with you people as I am. More. He was the one who let me see how you regarded us as employees."

"Does that mean you are permanently shutting down our communications?" Annapolis asked.

"It means I'm with Charley, whatever Charley decides."

"How many others?" Castillo pursued.

"In all, there are nine of us," Annapolis said.

"Which means that *five* of you wanted to throw Charley to the lions?" Mrs. Agnes Forbison asked. It was the first time she'd opened her mouth.

"Unfortunately," Investment Banker said, "five of us were considering that option."

"But were dissuaded from doing so," Agnes said. "The question then becomes, how can we be sure they can be dissuaded the next time a situation like that comes up?"

"The question, Mother Forbison," Delchamps said, "is whether or not, having indulged the Irishman by coming here in the first place, we decide we've heard enough, give these people the finger, and walk out of here."

"Is that what you want to do, Edgar?" Castillo asked.

"It was when I walked in here," Delchamps replied. "Now I'm not so sure. And neither, to judge by Mother Forbison's question, is she."

"You want to discuss this privately?" Castillo asked.

"That was the first thing that popped into my mind," Delchamps said. "But I've sort of changed my mind about that, too. Let's lay everything on the table."

"Go ahead," Castillo said.

"Giving the benefit of the doubt to the five of These People who were smart enough not to show up here today, I understand where they were coming from. They have been passing both money and information to people in the community for some time. The money was really needed and the information was more often than not useful, and the people who got it were grateful. Maybe pathetically grateful because it allowed them to do what they're supposed to do. And then the Irishman got in the act and supplied These People with better communication than anybody else has. It wasn't hard for the Evil Quintet to go from that to thinking they were really important, and thus knew what was best for the community . . . and from that to thinking they knew what was best for the country. And there's a little of *he who pays the piper calls the tune*' in that."

Castillo was surprised at Delchamps's little speech. He often thought that the veteran CIA agent was as voluble as a clam.

And Delchamps wasn't through.

"A good idea went wrong. That happens. What you do when that happens is make the necessary adjustments."

"Such as?" Castillo asked.

"Remove temptation," Delchamps said. "The information stream becomes one way. They tell us . . . only us . . . what they know, and we decide who, if anybody, also gets to know. And they don't tell anybody what we're doing unless we tell them they can. I don't think the admiral here or the chopper pilot would have any problem with that."

He paused and looked at first Radio and TV Stations and then at Annapolis, and then asked, "Would you?"

"No," Radio and TV Stations said.

"None at all," Annapolis said.

"You're not going to ask me?" Investment Banker asked.

"What you two, and especially the Evil Quintet, would have to fully understand is that whoever breaks the rules has to go."

"What do you mean, 'has to go'?" Investment Banker asked.

Delchamps shrugged. "I think you take my meaning," he said.

"My God!" Hotelier said. "Was that a threat?"

"I have never threatened anybody in my life," Delchamps said. "I'm just outlining the conditions under which we could have a continuing relationship."

Dmitri Berezovsky smiled.

They all know, Castillo thought, *that the CIA establishment refers to Delchamps and perhaps a dozen other old clandestine service officers like him as "dinosaurs."*

They were thought to be as out of place in the modern intelligence community as dinosaurs because to a man their operational philosophy had been a paraphrase of what General Philip Sheridan said in January 1869 vis-à-vis Native Americans.

The dinosaurs believed that the only good Communist was a dead Communist.

They all also know that Delchamps is alleged to have recently applied this philosophy to the SVR rezident *in Vienna and to a member of the CIA's Clandestine Service who had sold out. The latter was found dead in his car in the CIA parking garage in Langley with an ice pick in his ear, and the former had been found strangled to death with a Hungarian garrote in a taxi outside the U.S. embassy in Vienna.*

Neither the FBI nor the Austrian Bundeskriminalamtgesetz was able to solve either murder.

And maybe proving that I'm a young dinosaur, the truth is I wasn't at all upset that they had been unsuccessful.

The question then becomes how are These People going to react to Delchamps's "outlin-

ing the conditions under which we can have a continuing relationship"?

"Would you like a moment alone to discuss this?" Delchamps asked.

"So far as I'm concerned, that won't be necessary," Annapolis said. "I can accept those conditions."

"And if anyone else doesn't like it," Radio and TV Stations said, "they're out."

He looked at Investment Banker and Hotelier.

"In or out?" he asked.

"I can't remember ever having been in a negotiation before, even with the Mafia," Hotelier said, "where the options were to go along or 'go away.' "

"Is that a yes or a no?" Radio and TV Stations asked.

"I think what Mr. Delchamps has proposed is reasonable under the circumstances. I'm in."

"I always look for the bottom line," Investment Banker said. "And the bottom line here is that both parties need each other to do what we know has to be done, and that no one else can do. I accept the conditions."

"I'll deal with . . . what did you call them, Mr. Delchamps? 'The Evil Quintet'?" Radio and TV Stations said.

"That's what I call them when there are

ladies present," Delchamps said. "When you *'deal with'* them, you might mention that."

He looked at Castillo.

"Your call, Ace," he said. "You've heard the proposal. Okay by you?"

Castillo stopped himself just in time from saying, "I'm going to have to consult with my consigliere."

But he did just that, by looking first at Sweaty and then at her brother. Both nodded just perceptibly.

"Okay," he finally said, simply.

Annapolis walked to him and offered his hand. Castillo shook it. Annapolis then offered his hand to Sweaty, as Radio and TV Stations walked to Castillo with his hand extended. Wordlessly, all of Those People solemnly shook the hands of all of the Merry Outlaws.

"I think another toast is in order," Hotelier said when that was over. "More champagne, or something stronger?"

"I know not what course others may take, but as for me, give me a taste of that twenty-five-year-old Macallan," Delchamps said, pointing to a long row of whisky bottles on a bar.

"I'll go along with Patrick Henry," Agnes Forbison said.

The two waiters quickly took orders for

drinks, and quickly and efficiently distributed them.

Castillo wondered how much he could trust Investment Banker's waiters to forget what they had just heard.

Well, I think we can safely presume if they already don't know of Edgar's reputation, he'll tell them. That should ensure their silence.

"If I may," Hotelier said, raising his glass. "To the successful conclusion of difficult negotiations and our success in future operations."

Everybody sipped.

"And if I may," Castillo then said. "To full understanding of the conditions of our new relationship, and to the *long, long* time it's going to be between now and our having to put that understanding to the test."

Everybody took another swallow.

"I hate to rain on our happy little parade," Annapolis said, "but that time may be a good deal shorter than we all hoped."

When no one replied, he went on: "Just before you came in, we were watching Wolf News. We recorded it. I think you should have a look at it."

He waved at the long couch and at the armchairs around it.

There was a muted whirring and a screen dropped from under the upper-level foyer, and then another whirring as drapes slid over the windows looking down at the Miracle Strip.

When everybody had found a seat, the lights dimmed, and the stirring sounds of the fourth and final part of Gioacchino Antonio Rossini's *William Tell Overture* — sometimes known as the *Lone Ranger* theme — filled the room.

A blond, crew-cut head filled the screen.

"I'm J. Pastor Jones," the head announced. "It's five P.M. in Los Angeles, and eight in Montpelier and time for the news!"

It wasn't quite time. There followed a ninety-second commercial for undetectable undergarments for those suffering from bladder-leakage problems, and then came another ninety-second commercial for those who suffered heartburn from eating spicy pizza and "other problem-causing goodies."

This gave Castillo plenty of time to consider that he disliked TV anchors in general and J. Pastor Jones in particular. Jones reminded Castillo of the teacher's pets of his early childhood and the male cheerleaders of his high school years. J. Pastor Jones was not only from Vermont — which Castillo thought of as the People's Democratic Republic of Vermont — but had appointed himself as a booster thereof, hence the reference to Montpelier, which few people could find on a map, rather than to Boston, New York, Philadelphia, Washington, D.C., or Miami, which were also in the Eastern time zone.

J. Pastor Jones reappeared on the screen, this time sharing it with C. Harry Whelan, Jr., who was a prominent and powerful Washington-based columnist and a Wolf News contributor.

"There is bad news in the war against drugs," J. Pastor Jones announced. "Very bad news, indeed. Wolf News contributor, the distinguished journalist C. Harry Whelan, has the details. What happened, Harry?"

C. Harry Whelan, Jr., now had the entire screen to himself. It showed him sitting in what looked like a living room whose walls were lined with books.

"We don't know much," Whelan announced pontifically, "but what we do know is this: Wolf News has learned exclusively that tomorrow's *Washington Times-Post* will carry a story by the distinguished journalist Roscoe J. Danton that three American officers in Mexico to fight the drug cartels were shot to death near Acapulco at noon today. They were, according to Danton, Antonio Martinez and Eduardo Torres, both of whom were special agents of the Drug Enforcement Administration, and Chief Warrant Officer Daniel Salazar, who was attached to the U.S. embassy in Mexico City."

"Shit," Castillo said.

"According to Danton, the three murdered men were known to be traveling to Acapulco with Lieutenant Colonel James D. Ferris, an assistant military attaché of the U.S. embassy, for a conference with Mexican officials. Colonel Ferris and the embassy vehicle, a Suburban bearing diplomatic license plates, are missing, according to Danton."

"Oh, Jesus H. Christ!" Castillo said.

"Danton has declined to reveal his sources, even to me, and Roscoe and I have been friends and fellow journalists for years. He has put his distinguished reputation on the line with this story, and I believe him. Calls to the State Department, the Pentagon, and the U.S. embassy by Wolf News reporters have elicited only this response, which I quote: 'The alleged incident is under investigation.'

"Wolf News will stay on top of this story, and when we know more, you will. This is C. Harry Whelan."

The screen now filled with the head of J. Pastor Jones.

Just as Castillo was about to order that Mr. Jones be cut off, someone pushed the PAUSE button.

Castillo punched a button on his Casey-Berry, and then the LOUDSPEAKER button.

"I thought you might be calling, Charley," Roscoe J. Danton said.

"That's odd," Annapolis said. "When I tried that, I got a message, 'Not authorized.' "

He looked at Aloysius Casey.

"That was before you and Charley kissed and made up," Casey said.

"Where'd you get the Mexican story, Roscoe?" Castillo asked.

"From a lady friend in Foggy Bottom," Danton replied.

Castillo had a quick thought.

Nobody really believes the CaseyBerrys are as good as they are; we talk on them as if someone might be listening.

"You have anything more than we got from your buddy Whelan on Wolf News?" he asked.

"I talked to your old boss; he said Vic is on his way down there," Danton replied, "and about twenty minutes ago, there was an e-mail from Porky saying Clendennen will have an announcement to make tomorrow at eleven."

"Keep me in the loop, Roscoe," Castillo said.

"What about Those People?"

"Annapolis and Radio Stations are good to go," Castillo said. "I'm still making up my mind about the banker and the hotelier."

He thought: *And I'm glad Investment Banker and Hotelier heard me say that. Let that sink in a while, and then I will let them back in the tent.*

"You met with them?"

"Yeah. Just now."

"Casey told me that was going to happen. I thought maybe there'd be an AP flash: 'Mass Murder in Sin City.' "

"I *was* thinking of feeding them to the sharks in the aquarium in the Mandalay Bay. But my merciful nature took over. Thanks, Roscoe."

"We'll be in touch," Danton said.

Castillo put his CaseyBerry away.

"Well, if McNab has sent Vic D'Alessandro down there," he said, "then until we hear from him, I can't think of anything else that can be done to get Ferris back from the goddamn drug cartels."

"Carlos," Berezovsky said, "what makes you think the drug people have your friend?"

"Jesus, I never even thought about that," Castillo asked.

"Am I permitted to ask, 'Thought about what?' " Investment Banker said. "Or are you still making up your mind if my word is any good?"

"Why don't you and Hotelier think of yourselves as being in a halfway house?" Castillo said. "Where one slip from the straight and narrow will turn you into shark food?"

"What Ace didn't think about is that Dmitri's pal Vladimir doesn't like being humiliated," Delchamps said.

"And that Vladimir Vladimirovich might think a good way to get his hands on Carlos," Berezovsky picked up, "would be to grab him when he gets on his white horse and gallops into Mexico to rescue his friend from the drug people."

"Who's Vladimir?" Hotelier asked.

"His last name is Putin," Annapolis furnished.

"Carlito would have thought about Vladimir," Sweaty said loyally.

Sure I would, Castillo thought, *probably by a week from next Thursday. Jesus!*

"And now that this has come up," Sweaty went on, "we have time to think about it. Carlito is right; until we hear from Vic D'Alessandro, there's nothing we can do."

"Except remember what you and Dmitri

are always telling me," Castillo said. "Putin always has a Plan B."

"I don't follow you, Ace," Delchamps said.

"Dmitri," Castillo asked, "One, how many ex-Spetsnaz does Aleksandr have raking the sun-swept beaches at the Grand Cozumel Beach and Golf Resort? Two, how many of same would he be willing to loan me right now?"

"To do what, Ace?" Delchamps asked.

"To provide a little extra security for the people at the Lopez Fruit and Vegetables Mexico. I think Putin knows about that, too, and I don't want them getting into the cross fire."

"At least twenty," Berezovsky said. "I think Aleksandr would give you, say, ten — all that could fit into the Gulfstream — right now. More men, as soon as they could be flown up from Argentina."

"You sound pretty sure," Castillo said.

"Carlito," Sweaty said, "not only does Cousin Aleksandr love you, but he knows the best way to deal with Vladimir Vladimirovich is to — what is it Edgar says? — cut him off at the balls."

"For the record, Sweaty," Delchamps corrected her, "what I said is, 'Cut him off at the *knees.*' "

Berezovsky took out his CaseyBerry and

punched a key.

"Aleksandr, I'm with Charley in Las Vegas," he said in Russian. "Vladimir Vladimirovich has raised his ugly head again, and we need some help to cut him off at the *knees*. This is the problem . . ."

II

[One]
Yadkin and Reilly Road
Fort Bragg, North Carolina
0845 12 April 2007

The Federal Express truck pulled to the curb before a two-story brick house, and the driver, after first taking a FedEx Overnight envelope from where he had stuck it on the dashboard, got out.

He took a quick look at the envelope as he walked around the front of the truck.

The Overnight envelope, sent by the Mexican-American News Service of San Antonio, Texas, was addressed to: LTC BRUCE J. MCNAB, YADKIN AND REILLY ROAD, FORT BRAGG, NC 28307.

The FedEx driver had served in the Army, and knew that LTC meant "lieutenant colonel." And he had served long enough to know that lieutenant colonels do not live in

65

large brick homes on what was known locally as "Generals' Row."

After a moment, he decided it was a simple typo; LTC was supposed to be LTG, the abbreviation for "lieutenant general." A small wooden sign on the lawn of the house confirmed this analysis. It showed three silver stars, the rank insignia of a lieutenant general, and below that was neatly painted B. J. MCNAB.

The driver, now convinced he was in the right place, continued up a walkway through the immaculately manicured lawn toward the house.

He was almost at the door when a black Chevrolet Suburban came — considerably over the posted 25 mph speed limit — down Reilly Road, stopped and quickly backed up the driveway of the house. Doors opened. The driver, a young Green Beret sergeant in a camouflage-pattern battle-dress uniform, and a young Green Beret captain in dress uniform got out of the front seat. The sergeant quickly removed a cover from a red plate bearing three stars mounted on the bumper and then rushed to open the passenger door. He was too late. The door was opened by a Green Beret colonel in a dress uniform who marched purposefully toward the house with the captain trailing him.

The driver stood beside the passenger door.

The front door of the house opened and General McNab came through. He was in dress uniform and wearing a green beret. Both breasts of his tunic carried more ribbons and qualification badges than the driver had ever seen on one man during his military service.

Colonel Max Caruthers, who was six foot three and weighed 225 pounds, and Captain Albert H. Walsh, who was almost as large, saluted crisply and more or less simultaneously barked, "Good morning, General."

General McNab returned the salute and then turned his attention to the FedEx deliveryman.

"Far be it from me to stay a FedEx courier from the swift completion of his appointed rounds, but curiosity overwhelms me," he announced. "Dare I hope that envelope you are clutching to your breast is intended for me?"

"It is, if you're Bruce J. McNab," the courier said.

"Guilty," General McNab said.

The courier extended the clipboard for the addressee's signature.

Captain Walsh snatched the Overnight envelope from the driver, handed it to the general, and then signed the receipt on the clipboard.

General McNab ripped open the strip at the top of the envelope and took from it an eight-by-ten-inch photograph.

"Oh, my!" he said, in a tone similar to what a grandmother would use when her cake batter slipped from her hands and splattered over her kitchen floor. "Oh, my!"

He handed the Overnight envelope to Captain Walsh.

"Hold that by its edges, Al," he ordered. "Gloves would be better. It will probably be futile, but we will have tried."

"Something wrong, General?" the FedEx courier asked.

"Nothing for which you could possibly be held responsible," General McNab said. "And now, although I would rather face a thousand deaths, I must go treat with General Naylor."

The courier looked confused.

Colonel Caruthers, who recognized the remark as a paraphrase of what Confederate general Robert E. Lee had said immediately before leaving his headquarters to surrender the Army of Northern Virginia to Union general Ulysses S. Grant, failed to keep a smile off his face.

The courier started back to his delivery truck as General McNab walked toward Staff Sergeant Robert Nellis, who was standing by the open front passenger door.

"Bobby," he said, "can you find Pope Air Force Base by yourself, or would you rather that I drive?"

"I'll drive, General," Sergeant Nellis said, smiling.

"It's easy to recognize," General McNab said as he slid onto the seat. "Just look for lots of airplanes and fat people in blue uniforms."

Colonel Caruthers and Captain Walsh quickly got into the Suburban, and they drove down the driveway and turned right onto Reilly Road.

As the Suburban carrying General McNab pulled into one of the RESERVED FOR GENERAL OFFICERS parking spaces beside the Pope Air Force Base Operations building, the glass doors fronting on the tarmac opened and a half dozen Air Force officers, the senior among them a major general, came out and formed a three-line formation.

The major general stood in front. A major, wearing the silver cords of an aide-de-camp, took up a position two steps behind and one step to the left of him. The other four officers formed a line behind the aide-de-camp, according to rank, with a brigadier general to the left, then three full colonels. All stood with their hands folded in the small of their backs, in the position of parade rest.

"Seeing all that martial precision," Lieutenant General McNab announced, "I am sorely tempted to go out there and give them a little close-order drill."

His sergeant driver smiled. His aides-de-camp did not. They knew he was entirely capable of doing just that. Both were visibly relieved when McNab got out of the Suburban, walked to the corner of the building, and called, "Good morning, gentlemen. Beautiful day, isn't it?"

The major general turned toward him and saluted.

"Good morning, General," he said, and then broke ranks to go to McNab and offer his hand.

"Would you care to bet if El Supremo will be on schedule?" McNab asked.

For an answer, the major general pointed down the runway, where a C-37A — the military version of the Gulfstream V — was about to touch down.

As the sleek twin-engine jet completed its landing roll, the Air Force major general trotted back to resume his position in front of his officers.

General McNab folded his arms on his chest.

The Gulfstream V was painted in gleaming white on top, and pale blue beneath. There was no reference to the U.S. Air Force in its markings, although it carried the star-and-bar insignia of a military aircraft on its engine nacelles. UNITED STATES OF AMERICA was lettered on the fuselage above the six windows. An American flag was painted on the vertical stabilizer.

The plane stopped on the tarmac, the whine of its engines died, and the stair door behind the cockpit windows unfolded. A tall, erect officer with four stars gleaming on the epaulets of his dress uniform nimbly came down them.

He was General Allan B. Naylor, whom — to his embarrassment — C. Harry Whelan had accurately described to Andy McClarren of Wolf News as the "most important general in the world."

Whelan's argument was that since the Chief of Staff of the Army no longer actually *commands* the Army — but rather *ad-*

71

ministers it — and that since Naylor, as Commander in Chief of the United States Central Command directly *commanded* more Army and Marine troops, more Air Force airplanes, more Navy ships and aircraft, and more military assets in more places all around the world than any other officer, that made him the most important general in not only the Army, but the most important officer in uniform.

Even Andy McClarren, who had been the most watched news personality on television for ten years and counting — in large part because of his skill in being able to argue the opposite position of whatever position his guests took — couldn't disagree with that.

General Naylor exchanged salutes with the Air Force major general, and then shook hands with him and all of the officers, and finally turned to General McNab, who saluted.

"Good morning, Bruce," General Naylor said.

"Good morning, General," McNab said. "And how are things on beautiful Tampa Bay?"

The United States Central Command headquarters was on MacDill Air Force Base, Tampa, Florida.

Generals Naylor and McNab had been

72

classmates at the United States Military Academy at West Point. They hadn't liked each other as cadets, and a number of encounters between them as they had risen in rank in their subsequent service had exacerbated that relationship.

General Naylor didn't reply. Instead, with a smile, he motioned for McNab to board the Gulfstream. McNab, in turn, motioned for his aides-de-camp to get aboard. When they had done so, he followed them, and when he had done so, General Naylor followed him.

The stair door started to close as the engines started.

When the Gulfstream started to move, the Air Force general called his formation to attention and saluted. When the Gulfstream was on the taxiway, he turned to the brigadier general and softly commented, "That should be an interesting flight."

The friction between Generals McNab and Naylor was well known to senior officers of all the armed forces, and it went beyond "Isn't that interesting?" or "What a shame."

The United States Special Operations Command was subordinate to the United States Central Command, and when, at about the same time, Naylor was about to

73

be named Commander in Chief of CENT-COM and McNab to be commanding general of SPECOPSCOM, it was almost universally recognized as one of those rare situations that would see the best possible man assigned to both jobs.

It was also just about unanimously agreed that making "Scotty" McNab subordinate to Allan Naylor was going to be like throwing lighted matches into a barrel of gasoline.

General McNab took an aisle seat in the luxuriously furnished cabin. As General Naylor walked past him en route to the VIP section — two extra-large seats and a table behind the door to the cockpit, which could be curtained off from the rest of the passenger compartment — McNab held up his hand.

Naylor looked down at him.

McNab said: "General, before they start the in-flight movie, there's something I'd like to show you."

"You don't need an invitation to ride in front, Bruce, and you know it," Naylor said.

He gestured for McNab to follow him.

McNab rose, and gestured for Captain Walsh to follow him.

Reaching his seat, Naylor took it and then, when McNab had taken the opposing chair, asked, "What have you got?"

Captain Walsh extended a pair of rubber gloves to General Naylor.

Naylor looked questioningly at McNab. "Gloves?"

"I don't think they'll be able to get finger-prints off that, General," McNab said, indicating the FedEx Overnight envelope. "But they may."

Naylor took the gloves and pulled them on.

Walsh handed him the envelope, and Naylor took from it a sheet of paper and an eight-by-ten-inch color photograph.

The photograph showed a man dressed in a T-shirt and khaki trousers. He was sitting in a folding chair, holding up a copy of Mexico City's *El Heraldo de Mexico.* On each side of him stood a man wearing a black balaclava mask over his head and holding the muzzle of a Kalashnikov six inches from the victim's head.

"That's yesterday's newspaper," McNab said.

The sheet of paper, obviously printed on a cheap ink-jet printer, carried a simple message:

```
So Far He's Alive.

There will be further communication.
```

"Who is he?" Naylor asked calmly. "He looks familiar."

"Lieutenant Colonel James D. Ferris," McNab said. "The officer whom — with great reluctance, you will recall — I detailed to DEA, from which he was further detailed to be — overtly — one of the assistant military attachés at our embassy in Mexico City. Covertly, I have been led to believe, he was ordered to advise the ambassador in his relentless and never-ending attempt to reason with the drug cartels."

"I can do without the sarcasm, General," Naylor said.

"Ferris marches in the Long Gray Line beside his classmates Lieutenant Colonel Randolph Richardson, Jr., and our own Lieutenant Colonel C. G. Castillo, Retired. He has a wife at Fort Bragg and three children. Small world, isn't it?"

"Where did you get this?" Naylor asked.

"A FedEx delivery man handed it to me just now when I walked out of my quarters to come here."

"It's addressed to LTC McNab."

"I noticed. It may be a typo, or it could be on purpose. My gut feeling is that it's on purpose."

"To attract less attention?" Naylor asked.

McNab nodded.

"I've been wondering if another . . ."

"Was sent to me?" Naylor finished for him.

McNab nodded again.

"Captain," Naylor said politely, "would you ask Colonel Brewer to come up here, please?"

Colonel J. D. Brewer was Naylor's senior aide-de-camp.

"We have been cleared for takeoff," the public-address system announced. "Please fasten your seat belts."

"No FedEx Overnight envelope or other communication relative to this at MacDill, General," Colonel Brewer reported five minutes later, as the Gulfstream reached cruising altitude.

Naylor looked at McNab.

"What's the plan at Andrews?" McNab asked.

"A Black Hawk will take us to Langley; we meet the others there."

"Including Natalie?"

"I have been led to believe *the secretary of*

State will be there."

His tone made it clear that he thought General McNab should not refer to the secretary of State by her first name.

"I call her Natalie because I like her, General," McNab said. "She's my kind of gal." And then he quoted the secretary of State: " 'You miserable goddamn shameless hypocritical sonofabitch!' "

It was what Secretary of State Natalie Cohen had said to President Clendennen in the Situation Room of the White House on February 12, immediately after the President had announced that "for the good of the country, for the good of the office of the President, I am inclined to accept Ambassador Montvale's offer to become my Vice President."

It was the first time anyone in the room had ever heard her say anything stronger than "darn."

"My God!" Naylor said.

"She calls a spade a spade," McNab said. "There aren't many other people in Foggy Bottom — offhand, I can't think of one — who do that."

Naylor looked at McNab as if he were forming his words. When finally he said nothing, McNab went on:

"We can ask her at the agency if she's been

78

contacted, and I'm sure that among Lammelle's gnomes is someone who can lift any fingerprints there might be on the envelope."

Franklin Lammelle was DCI, director of the Central Intelligence Agency.

"All right," Naylor said. "And the CIA would be the most logical choice to deal with this situation, right?"

McNab didn't reply.

"McNab, you're not thinking of going down there to rescue Colonel Ferris, are you?"

"General, I would say that none of us has enough information to make any decisions on how to deal with this," McNab said. "But we can think about it while we're at Langley doing our bit to help the President get reelected."

"Is that how you think of it?"

McNab didn't reply directly, instead saying, "Having complied with Action One of the SOP by notifying my superior headquarters of the situation, with your permission, General, I will now take Action Two."

General Naylor nodded his permission.

"Al," McNab said to Captain Walsh, "would you please bring the Brick up here?"

Sixty seconds later, Walsh laid the Brick on the table. It had been provided to General McNab by the AFC Corporation free of charge. The chairman of the board of the AFC Corporation, Dr. Aloysius Francis Casey, had, during the Vietnam war, been the communications sergeant on a Special Forces A Team.

He credited that service for giving him the confidence to do such things as apply for admission to the Massachusetts Institute of Technology without having a high school diploma, and then shortly after being awarded his Ph.D. by that institution, starting the AFC Corporation, which quickly became the world leader in data processing and encryption.

"Like the jarheads say, General," he had told then–newly promoted Brigadier General McNab when he flew, uninvited, in one of AFC's Learjets to Fort Bragg, "once a Green Beanie, always a Green Beanie. And now it's payback time."

The translation was that he was willing to provide the Special Operations community with the very latest in communication and encryption equipment free of charge. When he left Fort Bragg that day, he had taken with him Brigadier General McNab's aide-de-camp — "You can call me Aloysius, hotshot," Casey had told then–Second Lieutenant C. G. Castillo — so that Castillo could not only select from AFC's existing stocks of electronic equipment but could also tell what communications abilities Delta Force and Gray Fox wished it had.

General McNab now opened the attaché case. A green LED told him the system was in STANDBY mode. He flipped a few switches and other green LEDs illuminated. One was ENCRYPTED VOICE COMMUNICATION, one ENCRYPTED DATA COMMUNICATION, and one ENCRYPTED SCAN.

General McNab removed a device about the size of a cigarette lighter from the attaché case, put it to his eye, aimed it at the FedEx Overnight envelope, and then at the photograph and message it contained.

A red LED illuminated briefly over the legend ENCRYPTED DATA TRANSMISSION IN PROGRESS, and then went out.

General McNab then picked up a telephone handset and pushed a button.

"Yes, sir?" the voice of Major General Terry O'Toole, deputy commander of SPECOPSCOM, came over the Brick's speakers after bouncing off a satellite 27,000 miles over the earth.

"Terry, I just sent you what was handed to me as I walked out of my quarters this morning," McNab said.

"I'm looking at it, General," O'Toole said.

"Load up your wife and get over to Colonel Ferris's quarters. Show her this, tell her we're working on it, and to keep her mouth shut about it."

"Yes, sir."

"Tell her as soon as I learn anything, I'll let her know."

"Yes, sir."

"I'll be in touch."

"Yes, sir."

McNab replaced the handset and closed the attaché case.

[Two]
Apartment 606
The Watergate Apartments
2639 I Street, N.W.
Washington, D.C.
0935 12 April 2007

"I would much rather drip ice water in his ear," Edgar Delchamps said as he stood beside the bed of Roscoe J. Danton. "But we're a little pressed for time."

He picked up the foot of Danton's bed, raised it three feet, and dropped it.

"You sonsofbitches!" Mr. Danton said upon being roused from his slumber.

He sat up suddenly, and then pushed himself back against the headboard.

82

"Rise and shine, Roscoe," David W. Yung, Jr., said.

"How the hell did you two get in here?" Danton demanded.

"And good morning to you, too, Roscoe," Delchamps said.

"The door was open," Yung said.

Mr. Danton's door came equipped — in addition to the locking mechanism that came with the knob — with two dead bolts, both of which Danton was sure he had set.

"How did you get through the lobby?" Danton challenged. "Or into the garage?"

"There didn't seem to be anyone on duty," Delchamps said. "Up and at 'em, Roscoe. Before we go out to Langley I want to pick up a little liquid courage at the Old Ebbitt Grill. They serve a magnificent Bloody Mary."

"I'm not going out to Langley," Roscoe said.

"And we have to talk about your million dollars," Yung said.

Danton eyed Yung. *What did he say?*

Roscoe J. Danton was a little embarrassed to privately admit that he was more than a little afraid of both men. While he didn't think David W. Yung, Jr., was capable of the sort of violence attributed to Edgar Delchamps, on the other hand, Yung's peers —

83

that was to say, others in Castillo's Merry Band of Outlaws — called him Two-Gun, and Roscoe didn't think they'd just plucked that out of thin air.

"Time, Roscoe, is of the essence," Delchamps said. "Remember to wash behind your ears."

Roscoe had some time — not much — to once again think his situation over during his ablutions.

He had come close to what President Clendennen derisively called "Castillo's Merry Band of Outlaws" in the practice of his profession, which was to say running down a story. That was a bona fide journalistic accomplishment; he was the only journalist ever to do so, and Roscoe took some justifiable pride in his having done so.

Among other things, it had resulted in a page-one, above-the-fold story in *The Washington Times-Post:*

BRILLIANT INTELLIGENCE COUP SEES MAJOR CHANGES IN WHITE HOUSE

By Roscoe J. Danton
Washington Times-Post Writers Syndicate

President Joshua Ezekiel Clendennen today chose Ambassador Charles W. Montvale, the director of National Intelligence, to be Vice President less than twenty-four hours after Secretary of State Natalie Cohen revealed that Montvale had been the brains behind the brilliant intelligence coup that saw Russia's super-secret Tupelov Tu-934A touch down at Andrews Air Force Base in Washington with American intelligence operatives at the controls.

How the aircraft — described, off the record, by senior Air Force officials as "years ahead of anything in the American arsenal" — came into U.S. possession remains a closely guarded secret, but it is known that the Central Intelligence Agency had a standing offer of $125 million for the delivery of one into its hands.

Montvale announced at Andrews that

the money would be paid to the two pilots who flew it into Andrews. They were identified only as "retired officers with an intelligence background."

Secretary of State Natalie Cohen, pointing to Montvale's long and distinguished career in public service — he has been a deputy secretary of State, secretary of the Treasury, and ambassador to the European Union — said she could think of no one better qualified to be Vice President, and hoped his selection to that office would "put to rest once and for all the scurrilous rumors of bad blood between Montvale and the President."

President Clendennen immediately nominated Truman C. Ellsworth, who had been Montvale's deputy, to be director of National Intelligence. That appointment, according to White House insiders, almost certainly was behind the resignation of CIA Director John Powell, although the official version is that Powell "decided it was time for him to return to private life."

The President announced that he was sending the name of CIA Deputy Director for Operations A. Franklin Lammelle to the Senate for confirmation as CIA Director.

Lammelle, who has worked closely with both Montvale and Secretary of State Cohen, is widely believed to have been deeply involved with Montvale in the operation that saw the super-secret Russian Tupelov Tu-934A come into American hands.

Presidential spokesman John David Parker said the President would have nothing further to say about the intelligence coup, stating that it "was, after all, a clandestine operation, and the less said about it, the better."

The problem was that Roscoe not only knew the backstory, which he had not written about, but had been part of it. He knew, for example, that the President had been known to refer to Montvale as "Ambassador Stupid, director of National Ignorance." He also knew that President Clendennen, shortly after taking office, had ordered Montvale's "Red Phone" — which provided instant access to the President and cabinet heads — shut off, and canceled Montvale's access to the White House fleet of limousines and GMC Yukons, in the hope that this would encourage Montvale to resign, so that he could appoint CIA Director John Powell — who *could,* in the President's judgment, find his ass with both hands — to replace him.

He also knew, for example, that President Clendennen had named Ambassador Montvale to be his Vice President not as a reward for the intelligence coup, or because of his admiration for him, but because the alternative had been the virtually certain indictment of the President by the House of Representatives quickly followed by an impeachment trial in the Senate.

Danton knew that the delivery of the Tupelov Tu-934A into the hands of the CIA had almost been a sideshow to what had really happened: Shortly before Clendennen had become President on the sudden death of his predecessor — an aortal aneurysm had ruptured — the United States had launched a preemptive strike on a biological warfare manufactory in the Congo.

The manufactory and everything within at least two square miles around it had been bombed and incinerated with every aerial weapon in the American arsenal except nuclear. It was believed this action had removed all of an incredibly lethal substance known as Congo-X from the planet.

This assessment was proven false when

FedEx delivered several liters of Congo-X to the Army's Medical Research Institute of Infectious Disease — the euphemism for Biological Warfare Laboratories — at Fort Detrick, Maryland. This was shortly followed by the discovery of another several liters of the substance by Border Patrol agents just inside the U.S.-Mexico border.

And this was shortly followed by the SVR *rezident* in Washington, Sergei Murov, inviting A. Franklin Lammelle, then the CIA's deputy director of operations, for drinks at the Russian embassy's dacha on Maryland's Eastern Shore.

There he proposed a deal: The Russians would turn over all the Congo-X in their possession in exchange for the former SVR *rezident* in Berlin, Colonel Dmitri Berezovsky, and his sister, Lieutenant Colonel Svetlana Alekseeva, the former SVR *rezident* in Copenhagen, who had not only defected with the assistance of Lieutenant Colonel C. G. Castillo but had also spilled the beans to Colonel Castillo about the "Fish Farm" in the Congo. The Russians also wanted Colonel Castillo.

When this proposal was brought to the attention of President Clendennen, he thought the deal made a great deal of sense, and ordered that it be concluded. When informed that Colonel Berezovsky and Lieutenant Colonel Alekseeva were not in the hands of the CIA, but in Argentina, with Colonel Castillo, who flatly refused to turn them over to the CIA, President Clendennen ordered Director of National Intelligence Montvale to send all the alphabet agencies of the intelligence community to find them and see that they were all loaded aboard the next available Aeroflot flight to Moscow.

Frederick P. Palmer, the United States attorney general, later described this action as being of "mind-boggling illegality," and suggested that if anything beyond President Clendennen's caving in to the Russians was needed to convince the House of Representatives that articles of impeachment were in order, this would do it.

And the story would have come out. The simultaneous offered resignations of Secretary of State Cohen, Director of National Intelligence Montvale, General Naylor, and even presidential spokesman Porky Parker could not be swept under the rug, even if a sense of duty might keep those resigning from making public why they could no longer serve President Clendennen.

Attorney General Palmer, however, argued that the country could not take another impeachment scandal, and that it was their duty to stay in office, with the caveats that the President appoint Montvale as Vice President, that the President ask for DCI Powell's resignation, and that he make other changes in the senior leadership that they considered necessary.

The President, having no alternative but impeachment, quickly agreed.

Roscoe Danton, running down the rumor that Lieutenant Colonel Castillo had snatched two Russian defectors from the CIA station chief in Vienna, had first encountered members of the Merry Band of Outlaws in Argentina during the time the alphabet agencies were looking for him.

Without quite knowing how it had happened, he had wound up in Mexico embroiled in Colonel Castillo's Merry Outlaws' current operation.

Castillo had learned that the Congo-X the Border Patrol had found just inside the Texas-Mexico border had been flown to Mexico in a Tupelov Tu-934A, and that the aircraft, presumably carrying more Congo-X, was on an air base on Venezuela's La Orchila Island. He launched an operation to grab both the aircraft and the Congo-X.

Roscoe J. Danton had been aboard one of the Black Hawk helicopters that landed on La Orchila Island. He had not been sure then, and was not sure now, whether he was there as a courageous journalist following a story no matter where it led, or whether he was a craven coward who believed the Merry Outlaws when they made their little joke, "Now that you know that, Roscoe, we'll have to kill you" — and actually might have done so had he not climbed aboard the Black Hawk.

Danton had managed to convince himself, before he had been so rudely awakened, that he had been more the professional journalist than professional coward. He had come to this conclusion after deciding that President Clendennen was a miserable sonofabitch for trying to swap Dmitri and Sweaty — who had also been on the Black Hawk — and Charley Castillo to the Russians.

"After the island," when he saw Castillo and Colonel Jake Torine preparing to fly the Tupelov Tu-934A to Andrews Air Force Base, he realized that he had been accepted by the Merry Outlaws as one of their own.

There were advantages to this — for example, he had been given a CaseyBerry, over which the secretary of State had given

92

him the scoop about the murders and kidnapping in Mexico — and he could see a cornucopia of other news that would come his way in the future.

But there were manifold disadvantages to his being a professional journalist that he could see as well.

As Roscoe pulled on his shorts in his bedroom, he said: "Guys, I really don't want to go out there. Why? Wolf News will carry the President's press conference from the first line of bullshit to the last."

"You're going, Roscoe," Yung said. "Charley wants you to go."

"When you get down to it, guys, I'm really not one of you."

"Charley thinks you are," Yung said. "That's good enough for the executive combat pay committee."

"For the what?"

"The executive combat pay committee," Delchamps replied. "Two-Gun, Alex Darby, and me. We're the ones who pass out the combat pay."

Yung added, "The committee asked Charley, 'What about Roscoe?' And Charley replied, 'He was on the island, wasn't he?' "

"I was on the island as a journalist," Roscoe replied. "A neutral, non-combatant observer."

But Danton thought, *Shit, I don't believe that.*

I was rooting for the good guys.

And I took the Uzi that Castillo said I might need.

"If that was the case," Delchamps said, "we'd have to kill you. You know too much."

There he goes with that "we'd have to kill you" bullshit again.

The trouble with that being I'm not sure it's bullshit.

I do know too much.

"And if we killed you, then you wouldn't get the million," Yung said.

"What fucking million?"

"I could set up a trust fund for your kids, I suppose," Yung said thoughtfully.

"What fucking million?" Roscoe demanded as he rummaged through his tie rack.

"Shooters," Delchamps said, "roughly defined as everybody who went to the island, get a million. Plus, of course, everybody who went into the Congo. Charley, Sweaty, and Dmitri opted out."

My God, they're serious! I'm being offered a million dollars!

How much would that be when the IRS was through with me?

Why am I asking?

Pure and noble journalist that I am, I'm of course going to have to refuse it.

What is this "pure and noble journalist" bullshit?

What's the difference between me taking free meals and booze from any lobbyist with a credit card and taking a million from the Merry Outlaws?

I write what I want, period.

And I was on that island, and I could have been killed.

Roscoe had a sudden, very clear flashback to what had happened several years before at the National Press Club.

Somebody had jumped on Frank Cesno, then high up in CNN's Washington Bureau — and a hell of a journalist — about the recent tendency of TV journalists to paint themselves as absolutely neutral when covering a war.

"Otherwise, both sides would think of us as spies, not journalists," Cesno had announced, more than a little piously.

Whereupon he had been shot out of the saddle by Admiral Stansfield Turner, who had been director of the CIA under Jimmy Carter.

"Frank," the admiral had said, "what do you think the Russians or the North Koreans — *or anybody* — think when they look at someone like you? Noble member of the Fourth Estate or spy?"

"David," Roscoe J. Danton inquired, "how much of a bite would the IRS take from that million?"

[Three]
Auditorium Three
CIA Headquarters
McLean, Virginia
1100 12 April 2007

Auditorium Three, unofficially known as the Director's Auditorium, was a multipurpose room which could be used as a small theater capable of hosting forty people in theater-style seating and another eight in more elegant seats in the front row, each provided with a small table and a telephone. It could also be used as a dining room capable of feeding as many as sixty people, with five tables, each seating a dozen guests.

It was secure, which caused it also to be known as the Director's Bubble, which meant that great effort was expended just about daily to ensure that nothing said or seen in the room could possibly be heard or seen anywhere else.

That sort of security wasn't a consideration today, where what was to be said by

President Joshua Ezekiel Clendennen would be heard and viewed in real time all over the world.

There was security, of course. Not only was this the headquarters of the CIA, but the President of the United States was going to be there. As were the Vice President, the secretary of State, and other very senior officials.

There are so many Secret Service guys in here, Roscoe J. Danton thought as he entered Auditorium Three, *that they're falling all over each other.*

They're competing for space with the State Department security guys — and gals — protecting Natalie Cohen, the Army security guys protecting Naylor, and the CIA's own security guys keeping an eye on both Frank Lammelle and the store in general.

Edgar Delchamps and Two-Gun Yung had dropped off Danton at the main entrance, saying they'd wait for him in the parking garage, which caused Danton to again recall the allegation — which he believed — that Delchamps had taken out a CIA traitor in the parking garage by inserting an ice pick into his auditory canal, thereby saving the Agency from the embarrassment that trying the sonofabitch would have caused.

Some of the White House Press Corps

97

filled most of the seats in the auditorium. There were far more members of that elite body than there were seats for them here today.

When Roscoe had shown his White House Press Corps credentials to the first of three security points — the "outside" one, near the main entrance — one of Lammelle's security people had handed him another credential, this one a plastic-sealed card on what Roscoe thought of as a "beaded dog tag chain." He looked at it. It held his photo and the legend PRESIDENTIAL PRESS CONFERENCE AT CIA HEADQUARTERS 1100 APRIL 12TH 2007.

"You're on the reserved-seating list, Mr. Danton," the man said.

Roscoe found this interesting, because before he had been so rudely awakened, he had had no intention of coming out here today and hadn't asked for credentials, let alone a reserved-seat reservation.

He knew the protocol for events like this, at which there would be far more seats requested by members of the White House Press Corps than were available. The "host" — in this case, Frank Lammelle — and Porky Parker would put their heads together and decide who got in. And who would have to wait outside, fuming.

Roscoe intuited that he was on the reserved-seating list because of Lammelle, not Porky Parker. While he had no problems with Porky, Porky could be expected to hand out reserved seats to the elite of the White House Press Corps, and Roscoe knew that he wasn't a member of that elite. Close, but no golden ring.

And he further intuited that it was due to his new status as a member — however uncomfortable — of the Merry Outlaws. At the beginning, Frank Lammelle had headed the CIA delegation of the alphabet agencies looking for Charley Castillo.

Lammelle even had an air-powered dart gun —

Straight out of a superhero comic book.

Jesus, that would have made a great story if I could have written it!

— with which he planned to tranquilize Castillo so that he would be amenable to being loaded aboard the Moscow-bound Aeroflot plane.

After Vic D'Alessandro — *surprise, surprise!* — had shot Lammelle with Lammelle's own Super Agent Whiz Bang air gun in Cancún — where his pursuit of Castillo had taken him — Lammelle had awakened in the middle of a desert in Mexico, at a secret airfield the Merry Outlaws had dubbed Drug Cartel International.

There, when he saw what Castillo's Merry Outlaws were doing, and compared it to what the President was trying to do to Castillo, Lammelle had changed sides. He hadn't gone to the Venezuelan island but had made a large, maybe even essential, contribution to the operation.

If I have a CaseyBerry, Roscoe thought, *you can bet your ass Castillo gave Lammelle one. And I can hear Castillo calling Lammelle on it, and asking, "Frank, can you get Roscoe into that press conference?"*

And that would neatly tie in with Delchamps and Yung — having easily slipped through the Watergate's state-of-the-art, absolutely, positively guaranteed 24/7 security system — appearing in my bedroom this morning.

Why the hell is it important to Castillo that I hear whatever bullshit our beloved Commander in Chief is going to spew today?

When Roscoe passed through two more security points and finally got into Auditorium Three, a uniformed CIA security officer took a close look at his new presidential press conference credentials and showed him to a seat where he was buried between fellow members of the White House Press Corps. He had half expected to be seated in one of the VIP seats in front. He saw that

100

Andy McClarren of Wolf News and C. Harry Whelan, Jr., had been so honored.

Roscoe glanced at the open laptop computer of his seat mate, Pierre Schiff, of *L'Humanité*, and helpfully suggested that for about ten bucks, Schiff could go to Radio Shack and buy a screen that would keep people from seeing what was on his laptop screen.

Schiff gave him a smile that would have frozen hot chocolate.

Roscoe looked around the auditorium and saw mostly what he expected to see:

There was a narrow stage holding a podium bearing the presidential seal. Against the curtain at the rear of the stage was a sea of American flags, plus the CIA flag, those of the Vice President of the United States, the secretary of State, the director of National Intelligence, the director of the Central Intelligence Agency, and two red flags, one with four silver stars on it and one with three.

To the left and right of the stage and in the rear of the auditorium, still and video cameramen — plus half a dozen guys, whatever they were called, manipulating microphone booms — were crowded together, preparing to send the images and sounds of the conference around the world.

And there was something Roscoe was surprised to see: A detachment of the 3rd Infantry — "the Old Guard" — drum and bugle corps wearing Revolutionary War uniforms. The detachment was lined up, without much room to spare, to the left of the stage, between the stage and the cameramen.

Roscoe had just enough time to wonder about them — they had never been involved in a presidential press conference that he could remember — when the lights dimmed twice as a signal that something was about to begin. The lights went up — really up, to provide lighting for the cameras — and a line of people filed onto the stage.

Vice President Charles W. Montvale came first, followed by Secretary of State Natalie Cohen. Montvale took up a position immediately behind the podium, where he would be on the right of the President when he appeared, and Cohen took up a position to the left of the podium. Next came Truman Ellsworth, the director of National Intelligence, and then A. Franklin Lammelle, the director of the Central Intelligence Agency, and finally Generals Naylor and McNab. They took up positions to the left and right of the podium.

Presidential press secretary John David "Porky" Parker stepped to the podium and announced, "Ladies and gentlemen, the President of the United States."

Everybody stood.

There came a roll of drums, and the sound of fifes playing "Hail to the Chief."

President Clendennen marched purposefully onto the stage. He was a short, pudgy, pale-skinned fifty-two-year-old Alabaman who kept his tiny ears hidden under a full head of silver hair. As he marched past the dignitaries, just how short he was momentarily was made clear; he was shorter than even Natalie Cohen. Then he reached the podium and stepped onto a hidden platform that made him appear taller than everybody.

"Good morning," the President said. "Thank you for coming."

Danton grunted softly. *Good morning, Shorty. Wouldn't have missed it for the world.*

The President's voice was deep and resonant.

I'll give him that. He sounds like what people want a President to sound like. And when he's standing on his little stool, he looks presidential.

"Most of you," the President began, "thanks to the zealous — perhaps too zealous — reporting of a distinguished journalist writing for one of our more distinguished newspapers, are aware of a tragic incident that took place yesterday in Mexico. Three of our fellow Americans were found shot to death. A fourth American is missing."

And who were these people? Did they have names? What were they doing in Mexico?

"Let me begin by stating that I have no more sacred duty as President and Commander in Chief than the protection of the lives of my fellow citizens, wherever they might be."

Aside from not getting impeached, and maybe even getting reelected.

"And let me confess, as Zeke Clendennen, private citizen, that I am as outraged as anyone in our great nation about what happened outside Acapulco yesterday. I really understand, and sympathize with, those who think — as did one of Andy McClarren's guests last night on *The Straight Scoop* — that we should send in the Marines as we did to Veracruz in 1914 and 'teach them a lesson they won't soon forget.' "

Sure you do, Zeke.

"But I am no longer Zeke Clendennen, private citizen. And as President and Commander in Chief, I have a responsibility to our great nation as a whole.

"There are parallels — as I'm sure you all know — between what happened yesterday near Acapulco and what happened in Tampico in 1914."

Most of the clowns in the White House Press Corps have no idea what happened in Tampico, or, for that matter, where it is.

"And there are considerable differences."

No shit? Give me a for-instance, Zeke.

"The nine American sailors arrested in Mexico in 1914 were not arrested by a legitimate Mexican government, but by a Mexican dictator, a self-appointed general, Victoriano Huerta. President Woodrow Wilson publicly referred to Huerta as 'false, sly, full of bravado, seldom sober, always irresponsible, and a scoundrel.'

"It should go without saying that the United States did not recognize dictator Huerta or his so-called government."

Then how come we recognize Hugo Chavez? Isn't he a dictator who's false, sly, full of bravado, seldom sober, always irresponsible, and a scoundrel?

"The exact opposite situation exists in Mexico today. The president of the United Mexican States, my close personal friend, Ramón Martinez . . ."

A close friend, Zeke, like those guys in Matamoros who grab your arm and ask, "Hey, gringo, you wanna fook my see-ster?"

". . . is a statesman recognized around the world for his lifelong dedication to the principles of freedom and honesty in government.

"When this terrible incident of yesterday came to President Martinez's attention, the first thing he did was send a senior officer from the Mexican foreign ministry to our embassy in Mexico City to inform our ambassador. Then he called his good friend in the White House — he calls me 'Zeke' — to tell me what had happened, and to apologize to the American people for what had happened. He gave me his word, officially and as a friend, that he and every branch of the government of Mexico will do everything possible not only to apprehend and quickly bring to justice those responsible for the deaths of our fellow citizens, but to locate and safely return the missing officer to his family."

Frankly, Zeke, I am not holding my breath. From what I saw in Mexico, every other cop is on the payroll of one of the drug cartels.

Castillo even bought — from the damn Federales — a Black Hawk the U.S. gave them to help fight the drug cartels. Charley used it to fly us onto the island.

I wonder what happened to the Black Hawk

after we flew it back to the USS Bataan? Charley *said that when the* Bataan *got back to Norfolk, they should say nothing; just unload the helo onto the wharf, then let the Mexican ambassador explain how it got there after the Mexican government had told us it had been totally destroyed fighting the drug cartels.*

I can't believe Natalie Cohen would go along with that, but I thought it was a great idea.

"We came very close in 1914 to going to war with Mexico . . ."

Again. I'm sure you will recall, Zeke, that we also had one with them in 1846. You know, like the Marines sing, "From the halls of Montezuma"?

". . . And we came close, as you all know, to war recently. Our late and beloved President, faced with a very difficult choice, decided it was his duty as Commander in Chief of our nation to launch a preemptive strike on what he believed was a factory in the Congo manufacturing a dangerous substance that could have been used against us."

"What he *believed* was a factory in the Congo *manufacturing a dangerous substance that* could *have been used against us"*?

Where did your late and beloved predecessor get a wild idea like that? Was he supposed to take the word of the guy who runs our biological warfare lab and personally go to the Congo to have a look?

"Like every other patriotic American, I fully supported — perhaps even cheered — his courageous decision."

I seem to recall you saying, in front of a microphone you thought had been turned off, that it was "idiotic and reckless."

"And then, when God in His infinite wisdom took our Commander in Chief from us, and I found myself in that role, I came to understand how difficult the decision he had taken was for him."

Where the hell are you going now, Mr. President?

"The President was a wise and knowledgeable man. More than anyone else, he knew how close his decision would bring us to a nuclear war, and he knew full well that could have meant the end of the world.

"I came out of my study, my appreciation, of what the President had done with two things: First, an even deeper admiration of his wisdom and character than I had had. And, second, an awareness that I was ill equipped to step into his empty shoes, and that without God's help, I simply could not do so."

Zeke baby, you finally said something I

agree with.

"So I ask you, my fellow Americans, to pray for me. Pray to God to give me the wisdom and the courage that He gave to our late Commander in Chief. Pray to God that when another problem challenges our country, He will give me the strength to not act impulsively but rather with tempered wisdom."

I hate to tell you this, Zeke, but getting God to give you tempered wisdom's going to take a lot of praying.

"I was informed just before I came up here that there are matters requiring my immediate attention at the White House. So I will not be able to take questions.

"The Vice President and others here with me today will answer any questions you may have.

"Thank you. God bless you. God bless the United States of America."

The President then stepped from behind the podium and walked quickly to the edge of the stage and down a shallow flight of stairs.

What the hell? That's it?

Before you take off, Zeke, you're supposed to wait until one of your pals in the press corps, cued by Porky Parker, cuts off the conference by saying, "Thank you, Mr. President."

The cameras followed the President and recorded Porky Parker as he fended off the White House Press Corps as they shouted questions and tried to get close to the President.

Roscoe looked at the stage and saw on the faces of the assembled dignitaries that they were as surprised by President Clendennen's sudden departure as he was.

Secret Service agents and the CIA police kept the press corps from chasing the President and Porky into the corridor. The chasing press and those who hadn't chased the President now turned their attention to the podium.

And the podium was empty.

The dignitaries looked at one another in visible confusion, until finally both DCI A. Franklin Lammelle and Vice President Charles W. Montvale at once began heading for the podium.

Lammelle deferred to the Vice President, and stepped back into line.

Montvale stepped to the podium and was under immediate assault by shouts of "Mr. Vice President!" from the press corps.

Danton shook his head at the sight of the melee, and thought, *This has turned into a*

Chinese clusterfuck!

"When everybody has calmed down . . ." Vice President Montvale began, and then stopped when he realized his microphones were not working and his voice could not be heard over the shouts asking for his attention.

He first looked at the microphones in front of him for a switch, and then, finding none, bent to look behind the podium to see if he could find a switch there.

Lammelle broke ranks again and went to the podium to help.

Unbelievable! Danton thought. *Un-fucking-believable!*

CIA functionaries, uniformed and in suits, came to the stage and the podium to help.

A moment later there came a piercing electronic scream, quickly followed by a full volume broadcast of the Vice President's voice saying, "Oh, shit!"

This served to almost quiet the room.

"As the President has left the building," the Vice President's voice came over the loudspeakers, "this press conference is over."

That's "Elvis has left the building," Montvale!

The Vice President then stepped away from the podium and walked briskly off the stage. The other dignitaries quickly followed him. CIA functionaries kept the press away from them.

The CIA can't even make their microphone work!

And since this farce is on eleven zillion television sets around the world.

Wait a minute! I'm missing something here! What the hell?

The glistening Sikorsky VH-60 White Hawk helicopter, known as Marine One when carrying the President, was waiting for the President beside the CIA headquarters building.

Supervisory Secret Service agent Robert J. Mulligan, a tall and stocky forty-five-year-old, came out of the building and quickly checked to see that everything — other Secret Service agents, a fire engine, and an ambulance — was as it should be, and then signaled to the President that he was free to board Marine One.

Mulligan had been on Vice President Clendennen's security detail, but as one of the agents, not as the supervisory special agent in charge. When Clendennen had suddenly become the President, he announced he wanted Mulligan to head his security detail. When it had been — very tactfully — pointed out to President Clendennen that there already was a supervisory agent in charge of the Presidential Security detail, the President had replied, "I don't want to argue about this. Mulligan will do it. Got it?"

President Clendennen, trailed by Porky Parker, walked quickly to the White Hawk and climbed aboard, failing to acknowledge the salute of the Marine in dress blues standing by the stair door.

Mulligan quickly followed and reached for the switch that would close the stair door.

"Leave it open," the President ordered. "And turn on the TV."

The screen showed the stage of Auditorium Three above a moving legend on the bottom, WOLF NEWS BREAKING NEWS, THE PRESIDENTIAL PRESS CONFERENCE AT CIA HEADQUARTERS, LANGLEY, VA.

The image was of assorted people, including the Vice President, trying to do something about the non-functioning microphone.

The voice of Vice President Montvale crying "Oh, shit!" filled the passenger compartment of Marine One.

"Oh, shit," presidential press secretary Parker said softly.

The Wolf News camera now turned to the VIP journalists in the front-row seats, finally settling on C. Harry Whelan, Jr., who was shaking his head in disbelief.

The voice of the Vice President announced, "As the President has left the building, this press conference is over."

The camera quickly shifted to the podium, just in time to see the Vice President march away from it. Then it shifted to a shot of the dignitaries quickly hurrying after him.

"Mr. President, I have no idea what happened," Porky Parker said. "But I'm sorry."

"You should be," the President said. "I never thought you had what it takes to be the President's press secretary."

"Excuse me?"

"You're fired, Porky. Get off my helicopter."

"What?"

"When I get back to the White House, I will announce that I have accepted your resignation."

"Mr. President, I was in no way responsible for —"

"Nobody's likely to believe that, are they, Porky? Now, get off my goddamn helicopter!"

Parker went to the door and down the door stairs.

Mulligan threw the switch that caused the door stairs to retract.

"Well, that took care of that disloyal sonofabitch, didn't it, Bob?" the President asked.

"I thought that everything went very well, Mr. President," Mulligan said.

"I owe you one," the President said. He pointed toward the cockpit. "Tell him to get us out of here."

III

[One]
Auditorium Three
CIA Headquarters
McLean, Virginia
1120 12 April 2007

Roscoe J. Danton had decided, without really thinking about it, that he was going to have to write a "think piece" about this clusterfuck, rather than just covering it. Other people, simple reporters, would cover the story. But he was, after all, a syndicated columnist of the *Washington Times-Post* Writers Syndicate; his readers expected more of him.

His biography, on the *Times-Post* website, written by some eager-eyed journalist fresh from the Columbia School of Journalism, said, "Mr. Danton joined the *Times-Post* immediately after his service in the U.S. Marine Corps."

That was true, though it hadn't happened quite the way it sounded.

Roscoe had been a Marine. He had joined the Corps at seventeen, immediately after graduating from high school. After boot camp at the Marine Corps Recruit Depot at Parris Island, South Carolina, he had been transferred to Camp Pendleton, California. A week after arriving at Camp Pendleton, a forklift had dropped a pallet of 105mm artillery ammunition on his left foot during landing exercises on the Camp Pendleton beach.

Two months after that, PFC Roscoe J. Danton had been medically retired from the Marine Corps with a 15 percent disability. He returned to his home in Chevy Chase, Maryland, and entered George Washington University as a candidate for a degree in political science.

He also secured part-time employment as a copy boy at *The Washington Times-Post*. By the time he graduated from George Washington, he had acquired a fiancé—a childhood friend he had known since they were in third grade — and decided he had found his niche in life: journalism.

This latter conclusion had been based on

his somewhat immodest conclusion that he was smarter than three-fourths of the journalists for whom he had been fetching coffee in the newsroom.

This opinion was apparently shared by the powers-that-were in the executive offices of the *Times-Post,* who hired him as a full-time reporter shortly after he graduated from George Washington.

He married Miss Elizabeth Warner two months later, shortly after she found herself in the family way. By the time Roscoe J. Danton, Jr., aged five, was presented with a baby brother — Warner James Danton — Roscoe J. Danton had not only grown used to seeing his byline in the rag, but had become one of the youngest reporters ever to flaunt the credentials of a member of the White House Press Corps.

Things were not going well at home, however. Elizabeth Warner Danton ultimately announced that she had had quite enough of his behavior.

"You have humiliated me for the last time, Roscoe, by showing up at church functions late — if you show up at all — and reeking of alcohol. Make up your mind, Roscoe, it's either your drinking and carousing or your family."

After giving the ultimatum some thought,

Roscoe had moved into the Watergate Apartments. He concluded, perhaps selfishly, that there wasn't much of a choice between the interesting people with whom he associated professionally in various watering holes and the middle-level bureaucrats with whom Elizabeth expected him to associate socially at Saint Andrews Presbyterian Church in Chevy Chase.

Alimony and child support posed a hell of a financial problem, of course, but he had a generous and usually unchecked expense account, and legions of lobbyists were more than pleased to pick up his tabs at the better restaurants around town.

And, with the lone exception of what divorce does to kids, he'd many times decided he'd made the right decision. And rising to being a syndicated columnist for the *Washington Times-Post* Writers Syndicate was just one example.

Now Roscoe understood that if he was going to write a think piece on the clusterfuck, he was going to have to find out how it had happened, and the way to do that was get to presidential spokesman John David Parker *before* ol' Porky returned from seeing the President off to reestablish some order and decorum.

Roscoe quickly got out of his seat and left

Auditorium Three.

He found Parker almost immediately. Porky was leaning against the corridor wall just outside Auditorium Three, looking, Roscoe thought, more than a little dazed.

He's probably thinking he'll soon have to face the famed wrath of Joshua Ezekiel Clendennen.

"Dare I hope to have a moment of time with my favorite presidential spokesman?"

"Make that ex–presidential spokesman," Parker replied.

"You got canned over that royal screwup? So soon?"

Parker nodded.

"They wouldn't even let me back in there," Parker said, nodding toward the uniformed CIA security people standing outside the door to Auditorium Three.

"And now you need a ride back to our nation's capital, right?"

Parker considered that a moment and then said, "Yeah, I guess I do. You have a car?"

"Indeed I do. Come on. Let's get out of here."

Roscoe just then changed his mind about covering this story as a think piece.

The head wrote itself — "Presidential Spokesman Fired" — and he had already composed the obvious lead: "In an exclusive interview with this reporter, former presidential spokesman John David Parker told . . ."

It was almost sure to make Page One above the fold.

The thing I have to do now is keep the rest of the media boys and girls away from him.

The Lincoln Town Car, with Edgar Delchamps at the wheel, was parked very close to the entrance of the garage in a slot that a neatly lettered sign announced was RESERVED FOR ASSISTANT DEPUTY DIRECTOR NUSSBAUM.

I wonder if Delchamps told the guard his name was Nussbaum, or whether the guard recognized Delchamps and, having heard the ice-pick-in-the-ear story, decided that the agency dinosaur could park anywhere he chose to.

Roscoe ushered Parker into the backseat of the car and slid in beside him.

"Get us out of here," Roscoe ordered.

"What the hell happened in there?" Delchamps asked. "We watched it on the Brick."

"My pal is about to tell us. John, say hello to Edgar and Two-Gun."

"I thought you looked familiar, Mr. Parker," Two-Gun said, turning in the seat to offer his hand.

"So the President said, 'When I get back to the White House, I will announce that I have accepted your resignation. Now get off my goddamn helicopter,' and I did," Parker finished.

"And when you went back in the building, they wouldn't let you in the auditorium?" David Yung asked.

"They even took my ID badge," Parker said.

"I don't suppose anyone cares what I think," Delchamps said, "but just off the top of my head, Roscoe, I think your pal was set up."

"Otherwise, the security guys wouldn't have been waiting for you to take your ID badge."

"So what do I do now?" Parker asked, and then answered his own question. "Go back to my apartment and lick my wounds, I guess."

"If you go back to your apartment, the press will be there for your version of what happened," Roscoe said. "And until we figure this out, no matter what you tell them, you're going to look like an incompetent who got fired for cause, or a disgruntled former employee saying unkind — and frankly hard to believe — things about our beloved President. Or both. Probably both."

And I won't have a story.

"So what do I do?" Parker asked again.

"When in doubt, find a hole and hunker down until things calm down," Delchamps said.

"Go to a hotel or something?" Parker asked.

"Or something. Roscoe, is Brother Parker really a pal of yours?"

"He's a pal of mine," Roscoe declared.

Did I say that because Porky is a good guy who's always been straight with me? Or because I can see my story getting lost?

"Problem solved," Delchamps announced.

"Meaning what?" Roscoe asked.

"You'll see."

[Two]
7200 West Boulevard Drive
Alexandria, Virginia
1255 12 April 2007

The house, which was large and could be described as a "Colonial mansion," sat on an acre of manicured lawn well off West Boulevard Drive. The landscaping on a grass-covered rise — a berm — in the lawn

122

prevented anyone driving by from getting a good look at the front door of the house.

There was a neat cast-bronze sign just inside the first of two fences:

Lorimer Manor **Assisted Living** **No Soliciting**

The first fence was made of five-foot-high white pickets. Hidden on the pickets were small cameras, and both audio and motion sensors.

The second fence, closer to the house, was of cast iron, eight feet tall, and also held surveillance cameras and motion sensors. Every twenty feet there were floodlights.

As Edgar Delchamps steered the Town Car up the drive, a herd of canines — if "herd" is the proper term to describe a collection of six enormous, jet-black Bouviers des Flandres — came charging around the side of the house.

They waited patiently for the substantial gate to open, then when the Lincoln rolled past, they followed it, gamboling happily like so many outsize black lambs.

"What's with the dogs?" Porky Parker asked.

"Clinical studies have shown that having access to dogs provides a number of benefits to elderly people, so we use them in our geriatric services program," Two-Gun Yung replied. "That makes them deductible. You have no idea how much it costs to feed those big bastards."

"They also serve to deter the curious," Edgar Delchamps added.

He stopped the Lincoln before a four-door garage, pulling it alongside one of the two black GMC Yukons parked there.

Everyone got out of the Town Car as one of the garage doors rolled upward.

A grandmotherly type in her early fifties appeared at a door in the rear of the garage. Her name was Dianne Sanders, and she was listed on the payroll of Lorimer Manor, Inc., as resident housekeeper.

The herd of Bouviers des Flandres gamboled on toward her. She put her fingers to her lips and whistled shrilly. The dogs stopped as if they had encountered a glass wall.

"Go chase a cat," Mrs. Sanders ordered sternly, pointing out the garage door.

Reluctantly but obediently the herd slowly walked out of the garage.

She looked at Delchamps and said: "Am I supposed to pretend I don't know who your friends are? In addition to inside plumbing, Lorimer Manor offers television."

"Think of that one," Delchamps said, pointing at Parker, "as a lonely stranger desperately needing the hospitality of friends. And also some lunch, if that's possible. I thought you knew Roscoe."

"Only by reputation," she said.

"You know he's one of us," Yung said.

"I heard."

"And now that you know that, Mr. Parker," Yung said, "we'll have to kill you."

Oh, Jesus, here we go again!

Porky will go bananas.

"May I ask what's going on here?" Parker asked. "What is this place?"

"Of course you can ask, but as Two-Gun just said, what you know can get you killed," Delchamps said. He smiled, then added: "Well, let's go get some lunch."

In the house, Parker looked around. Plateglass windows across the back wall offered a view of an enormous grassy area. There was a croquet field and a cabana with a grill beside an enormous in-ground swimming pool. Two of the Bouviers, their red tongues hanging and their stub tails wagging, were looking in through one of the plate-glass windows; the rest of the herd was chasing birds on the grass.

125

And Parker noted the residents: First he saw four elderly men, two in wheelchairs, three of whom looking roughly as old as Edgar Delchamps. There also was a very large — six-foot-two, 220-pound — and very black man wearing aviator sunglasses who appeared to be in his late thirties, and a woman who looked about sixty. She had a chrome walker next to her chair at a large dining table that was covered with food.

In the center of the table was a centerpiece: Two dinosaurs, each about two feet long, faced each other. There was a pink bow around the neck of one of them.

"I think everybody knows who Mr. Parker is," Delchamps announced to the residents.

Everybody nodded.

"He wants to know what's going on here," Delchamps said, "what this place is. Can I tell him?"

"Is he a friend?" one of the men in a wheelchair asked.

"Roscoe vouches for him," Delchamps said, "and Roscoe — in case you didn't know — is one of us."

"In that case, tell him."

"Sure. Tell him."

"Why not?"

The elderly lady added: "As long as he understands that if he runs at the mouth . . ."

Oh, no! Danton thought. *Not the old woman, too!*

". . . we'll have to kill him."

Another of the men, about Delchamps's age, pointed at the centerpiece of dinosaurs, and said: "That should make it quite obvious, Mr. Parker. This is where us old dinosaurs come to die."

There were grunts, and then came what appeared to Parker and Danton to be a regular war of words among the residents.

"Oh, shit, there he goes again with that crap!"

"Jesus Christ, Mac, will you knock off with that come-to-die nonsense?"

"Speak for yourself, John Alden! You've always —"

"Let me have a shot at this!" Dianne Sanders interrupted. "Mr. Parker, everybody in this room — except those two and me — is retired from the Company."

She pointed to the enormous black man and to a man who looked to be in his late forties.

"That's Dick Miller and Tom, my husband. They used to run around the block with Charley Castillo and General McNab until the Army decided they were no longer able to play Rambo, and medically retired them. I was a cryptographer, and took my retirement, too. Then came the glory days of the Office of Organizational Analysis . . . you both know what that was?"

Parker and Danton nodded.

"Charley needed a safe house here, and OOA bought this. Then Uncle Remus — you know who he is?"

Roscoe Danton knew that Uncle Remus was the politically incorrect — and some suggested racist — name that only his close friends could call Chief Warrant Officer (5) Colin Leverette, U.S. Army, Retired.

Danton nodded.

Porky shook his head.

"He's the guy who took Colonel Hamilton to the Fish Farm in the Congo," Delchamps clarified.

"One of the better snake eaters," Tom Sanders further clarified. "Dianne and I were in our happy, exciting retirement in Fayetteville, watching the mildew grow in the bathtub when Uncle Remus showed up and asked if we'd be interested in running this place. We were on the next plane up here."

"Then we thought we'd be out of a job when OOA was broken up," Dianne picked up. "But when Edgar said he needed a place to live now that he was retired, he moved in 'as a temporary measure.' "

"And then the other dinosaurs started moving in, one by one," the elderly lady offered. "We were scattered all around D.C. I was in the Silver Oaks Methodist Episcopal Ladies Retirement Community in Silver Spring. You can imagine how much I had in common with the ladies there."

"So you're also retired from the CIA?" Danton asked.

"Thirty-four years in the Clandestine Service," she said with quiet pride.

"Dinosaurs?" Porky Parker asked.

"That's what they call us at Langley," the elderly lady said. "We still believe that the only good Communist is a dead Communist, so we're dinosaurs to them."

"And, so," one of the men in a wheelchair said, "with the not inconsiderable help of Two-Gun, we formed Lorimer Manor, Inc., and bought this place from the Lorimer Charitable and Benevolent Trust. When one of Castillo's Merry Outlaws needs to use a safe house — Edgar, Two-Gun, and Gimpy stayed here last night, for example — we send a bill to the LCBF Corporation."

Gimpy, Danton thought, *must be the big black guy in the aviator sunglasses.*

"What's the LCBF Corporation?" he asked.

129

"That's who's going to pay you your combat pay, Roscoe," Delchamps said.

Porky Parker's eyebrows rose at that.

"Think of it as our basic corporate structure," Two-Gun amplified. "Providing complete financial services to our little community."

"All right, David," the elderly lady said, a little impatiently. "Now it's your turn. What the hell happened at Langley this morning?"

". . . And so the President told me he was accepting my resignation and to get off his goddamn helicopter, and then I ran into Roscoe, and he brought me here," Porky Parker concluded.

"I said, and you all heard me," one of the middle-aged men said, "that there was something phony about that failed microphone."

"What is that sonofabitch up to?" the elderly lady asked softly.

"I have no idea," Parker said. "My question is, what do I do now?"

"You stay out of sight," Delchamps said. "I already told you that. Maybe go to Mexico with us. You've got your passport?"

"My official passport is in my briefcase with my laptop," Parker said. "The last time I saw it was when I asked one of the Secret

Service guys to watch it for me backstage in Auditorium Three."

"I hoped you kissed it — *them* . . . the passport *and* laptop — good-bye," Delchamps said.

"My regular passport is in my apartment," Parker said.

"Outside of which members of the media can be counted on, sitting," Roscoe said, "burning with desire to hear your version of your surprising and sudden departure from distinguished government service."

Which will also screw up my exclusive interview with Porky.

There was a buzzing sound.

"Our master's voice," Dick Miller said as he took a CaseyBerry from his pocket and put it to his ear.

"How nice of you to call," he went on. "I just put you on conference, Charley."

Roscoe saw Delchamps and Yung quickly put their CaseyBerrys to their ears. He took out his own, found the CONF button, and pushed it.

"I didn't call to chat, Gimpy," Castillo's voice announced. "I called hoping to hear that Edgar has Roscoe in the bag and that you're about to go wheels-up. Better yet, that you're already in the air."

Danton made a face.

"Roscoe in the bag"?

What the hell does that mean?

"Ace, Roscoe is in the bag," Delchamps said.

What the hell are they talking about?

"And he brought Mr. John David Parker with him," Delchamps continued.

"What the hell is that all about?" Castillo said.

"Roscoe, would you be so kind as to tell our leader what the hell that's all about?"

"The press is looking for him," Danton said.

"Why?"

"Right about now, the President is going to announce he's accepted his resignation," Danton replied.

"Because of that fucked-up press conference?"

"Yes, but Porky didn't fuck it up," Danton said.

After a moment, Castillo replied, "Got it. And you are — what is it you say? — 'chasing the story.' "

"That's right."

"So what are you planning to do with Mr. Parker?"

"We're trying to figure that out, Charley."

"Is Mr. Parker also trying to evade the

press, Roscoe, or do you have him in handcuffs?"

"He doesn't want to see them, either."

"Okay, so bring him down here," Castillo
said.

"What?"

"Bring him down here; we'll work it out
later," Castillo said. "Got it, Edgar?"

"Jawohl, mein Führer!" Delchamps barked.

"Spare me the sarcasm," Castillo said.
"Just call me when you're wheels-up. I need
Roscoe and the Mustang down here yester-
day."

He needs me? What the hell for?

And where's "down here"?

"Jawohl, mein Führer," Delchamps repeated.

A moment later, Roscoe, seeing that
everyone had taken their CaseyBerrys from
their ears, turned his off.

"Where is 'down here'?" Danton asked.

"Cozumel," Yung replied.

Danton looked at him, and thought: *If he
says "And now that you know that I'll have to
kill you," I'll throw this goddamn phone at him.*

"And he wants me to go down there?"
Danton asked incredulously.

Yung looked at Delchamps, and said:
"Small problem. Mr. Parker doesn't have
his passport."

"I don't have my passport, either," Danton said.

"Catch, Roscoe," Delchamps said, and when Danton looked at him, Delchamps tossed him a passport.

"We've been through the 'I don't have my passport' routine with you before," Delchamps said.

"This was locked in my desk!"

"Yes, it was," Delchamps said.

"What do I need my passport for?" Parker said. "I don't want to go to Cozumel. I don't even know where that is."

"Not far from Cancún on the Yucatán Peninsula," Yung furnished.

"What's going on there?" Parker asked.

"Your call, Mr. Parker," Delchamps said. "We'll drop you anywhere you want on our way to the airport."

"John," Danton suggested, reasonably, "going to Cozumel would get you out of sight for a couple of days."

Parker considered that for a moment and then shrugged.

"Why not?" he said finally. "I don't have any other clever ideas at the moment."

Danton nodded, and thought, *Great! For a couple of days, I'll have you all to myself.*

"Back to Mr. Parker's passport problem," Yung said.

"Where do you live, Mr. Parker?" the elderly lady asked.

"The Verizon, it's at 777 Seventh, Northwest —"

"I know where it is," she said. "No problem, Two-Gun. You take your friends to BWI. By the time Gimpy has the rubber bands on the Citation wound up, we'll meet you with Mr. Parker's passport and a quick change of linen."

"How are you going to get into my apartment? Past the press?"

"Getting into your apartment would be easier, Mr. Parker, if you gave me the keys," she said. "As far as the press is concerned, it's been my experience that they pay very little attention to little old ladies who use a walker, especially little old ladies being helped into a building by a kindly member of the clergy — and accompanied by a snarling hundred-twenty-pound dog."

"Where are you going to get the kindly clergyman?" Roscoe asked.

Tom Sanders stood.

He motioned with his right hand to form a cross, then said, "Bless you, my children. Go and sin no more. And just as soon as I get my clerical collar on and load one of the dogs into a Yukon, we can get this show on the road."

[Three]
The Tahitian Suite
Grand Cozumel Beach and Golf Resort
Cozumel, Mexico
1710 12 April 2007

Vic D'Alessandro, whose barrel chest and upper arms strained his short-sleeved floral-print Hawaiian shirt, walked onto the balcony of the penthouse suite and announced, "Jesus, it must be nice to be rich!"

"It's way ahead of whatever's in second place, Vic," Fernando Lopez said agreeably. "Write that down."

Lopez, a very large man with a dark complexion, was sprawled on a chaise longue with a bottle of Dos Equis on his chest. He raised his right arm over his head without turning, and offered his hand. D'Alessandro walked to him and shook it.

Castillo got off his chaise longue and walked to D'Alessandro. They wordlessly embraced. Max sat on his haunches and thrust his paw repeatedly at D'Alessandro until D'Alessandro shook it. Lester Bradley stood behind Castillo.

"Hey, Dead Eye," D'Alessandro said.

"It's good to see you, sir," Bradley said.

Aleksandr Pevsner, Tom Barlow, and Stefan Koussevitzky, sitting on chaise longues in the shade of a striped awning, stood. D'Alessandro nodded to them, then went over and offered his hand.

"Good to see you, Mr. Pevsner," D'Alessandro said.

"And you, Mr. D'Alessandro," Pevsner replied. "This is our friend Stefan Koussevitzky."

"You can be nice to Stefan, Vic," Castillo called. "You guys went to different snake-eating schools."

"I know you by reputation, Mr. D'Alessandro," Koussevitzky said. "I'm pleased to meet you."

"You're the guy who Sweaty shot on that island, right? And call me Vic."

Koussevitzky smiled and nodded.

"I was one of them. She also shot General Sirinov in the foot. Fortunately, mine was a minor flesh wound in the leg with a thirty-two."

"Fortunately for Stefan, Svetlana always liked him," Tom Barlow said. "She was never at all fond of the general."

"So where is Charley's redhead?" D'Alessandro asked.

"She's having a bikini wax. She should be up in a minute in her bikini," Castillo said. "Lester, why don't you get Vic a Dos Equis? After which he can tell us all about

137

Acapulco."

"Lester," D'Alessandro said, "why don't you get your old Uncle Vic a double of that Jack Daniel's?"

"Yes, sir."

D'Alessandro slid onto a chaise longue in the shade of the striped awning, and sat on it.

"Is everybody familiar with the official version, the message Ambassador McCann sent to Secretary of State Cohen?" he began.

"Which she passed to Roscoe Danton, giving him his scoop," Castillo said. "Yeah, Vic, we're all familiar with that."

"Our guys in Acapulco — there's three — and the DEA guys there think that what happened is Ferris's Suburban was stopped by a roadblock manned by either Federales or people wearing Federales uniforms. They got talked out of the Suburban and the bad guys whacked everybody but Ferris. Then they loaded Ferris back into the Suburban and took off for God knows where. Or God knows why.

"Supporting this theory is that Ferris and Danny Salazar — especially Danny — had been around the block more than once, had either M-16s or CAR-15s with them, and would have offered some pretty skilled resistance to an ambush.

"Why wouldn't Ferris — and again, especially Danny — be suspicious of a Federales roadblock? Because they had good relations with the Federales, good relations being defined as sharing intelligence with them, which is further defined as they tell us only what they want us to know, and we tell them everything we know, which they promptly pass to the drug cartels."

"That bad, huh?" Castillo asked. "And Ferris went along with this?"

"How well do you know Jim Ferris, Charley?"

Castillo shrugged. "Not well. I've seen him around. People who know him well seem to respect him."

"Including me," D'Alessandro said. "He's a hell of a teacher, probably the best we have."

"But?"

"You and Ferris are different in several ways, Charley. First, you'd be a lousy teacher. You'd also be a lousy instructor, and there's a difference."

"Probably," Castillo admitted.

"Which, McNab being aware of this, is why you never found yourself at McCall teaching Snake Eating 101 to a class of would-be Green Beanies."

"I always thought it was the press of my other duties," Castillo said sarcastically.

"No. It was because McNab knew — and I knew and Uncle Remus knew — that you would set a lousy example for the new guys. You ever actually eat a snake, Charley?"

"No, and I never bit the head off a live chicken running around in the Hurlburt Field swamps, either," Castillo said.

"But — the proof being you're still alive — you performed satisfactorily in the real world, huh? And have all those medals to prove it?"

"Where the hell are you going with this, Vic?" Castillo asked more than a little testily.

"You wanted to know who Jim Ferris is. I'm telling you. He's almost exactly your opposite. He caught, killed, and ate snakes because that's what he was ordered to do. And he taught a whole bunch of people to obey orders and eat snakes, too. You went into the swamps at Hurlburt with two pounds of high-protein bars taped to your legs because you heard snake would be on the menu.

"The point being that when Jim Ferris came down here, he obeyed his orders from the ambassador to cooperate with the Mexicans. He argued with both Ambassador McCann, and the ambassador before

McCann, but he obeyed his orders.

"What you would have said, Charley, is: 'Screw this. I was sent down here to get the drug guys and that's what I'm going to do.' "

Castillo, who did not look as if he took offense to that, then said: "So you're suggesting the drug cartel had no reason to whack anybody because Ferris's people weren't causing them any trouble?"

"Yeah. And they must have known that killing three Americans and kidnapping a fourth would bring a lot of attention."

"Tell me about the drug guys," Castillo said.

"Pacific Coast operations are run by the Sinaloa cartel, which is headed by two guys, Joaquín Guzmán Loera and Ismael Zambada García. You ever hear of Los Zetas?"

Castillo shook his head.

"Loera and García needed a private army, so they bought one. They went to the Mexican army and said, 'If you come work for me, bringing along the weapons the Americans gave you, I will pay you five times what the Army has been paying you. If you don't come, we will kill you and rape your wives, mothers, and other female relatives.' "

"Shit!" Castillo said.

141

"These are really charming people, Charley, and they have very deep pockets. They have about a battalion's worth of Mexican soldiers — officers, noncoms, and privates. And all the equipment we gave them. Los Zetas are really bad guys, Charley."

"And they could have been manning the roadblock?"

"Either in Mexican army uniforms or Federales uniforms," D'Alessandro answered. "Which brings us back to why?"

"Edgar thinks it had nothing to do with the drug cartels," Castillo said, "and Alek agrees with him."

"Then what?"

"It has been suggested that Mr. Putin, on reflection, has decided that an armistice is not the way for him to go," Tom Barlow offered. "And that he's coming after Svetlana and me again."

"And after Charley," D'Alessandro added.

"And me," Pevsner said. "Not necessarily in that order."

"Jesus, I guess I should have thought of that," D'Alessandro said. "I will think about it now. Lester, I'd think better after I've had a second taste of the Jack Daniel's."

Two glistening white Yukons with the legend GRAND COZUMEL BEACH AND GOLF RE-SORT painted on their doors and a much less elegant brown Suburban with the insignia of Mexican Customs and Immigration were waiting for the Cessna Mustang when the small twin-engine jet was wanded to a parking spot.

John David Parker was relieved to be on the ground. Not only had it been his first flight in a Mustang, until today he had thought that jet aircraft required the services of two pilots. Not only had there been but one pilot — Major Dick Miller, U.S. Army, Retired — but he had seen Miller climb aboard the airplane at Baltimore Washington International — and suddenly understood why they called him "Gimpy." There clearly was something wrong with his left leg; it didn't bend as knees are supposed to.

Surprising Parker not a little, moments after Miller had boarded the airplane, the gray-haired elderly lady and "the Reverend Father" Tom Sanders had shown up with his passport, as promised. They had even

143

packed a small bag with a change of linen and his toilet kit.

Three minutes later, they were airborne. The trip was uneventful. They went through immigration at New Orleans's Louis Armstrong International Airport and then flew across the Gulf of Mexico.

Two men got out of each Yukon. One of them — a burly, fair-skinned man wearing shorts, knee-high stockings and a white jacket with the logotype of the Grand Cozumel Beach and Golf Resort on the chest — came onto the airplane as soon as the stair door was opened.

The man shook Edgar Delchamps's hand and said something in Russian.

"Hand him your passports as you get off," Delchamps ordered. "He'll take care of the formalities."

It was a five-minute ride from the airport to the Grand Cozumel, which turned out to be an enormous luxury resort complex at the center of which was a twenty-odd-story building surrounded by smaller buildings. There were two golf courses, acres of tennis courts, and, fronting the wide, white sand beach, lines of individual cottages.

Parker was not surprised that the entire property was enclosed within a substantial fence, but when they reached the main building and went down a ramp to an underground garage, he was surprised at the steel barriers that were hydraulically lowered as they reached them. They looked exactly like the barriers at the White House, through which — he had been told and he believed — an M1 Abrams tank would have a hard time crashing.

There was a line of elevators. Delchamps led them all to one marked THE TAHITIAN SUITE. In lieu of an UP/DOWN button, it had a keyboard and what looked like a small television screen or computer monitor.

When Delchamps keyed in a series of numbers, the screen lit up, showing the outline of a hand. A moment after Delchamps placed his hand on the image, there came a *ping* sound — and the elevator door slid open.

He waved everybody onto the elevator.

There were no floor numbers on the elevator control panel, just up and down arrows.

When Delchamps pushed UP, the opening bars of *The Blue Danube* came over loudspeakers. After just a faint sensation of movement, the door slid open.

Parker thought: *That was quick. We're probably only going to the second floor.*

They were on a circular foyer, off of which were eight closed doors and one open double door. A burly man in a white jacket — a twin of the man at the airport — stood next to the open doors, holding an Uzi submachine gun along his leg.

He ran his eyes among the elevator passengers and then sat down.

Delchamps walked to and through the open doors with the others following him. Parker, confused for a moment, saw that rather than being on the second floor, they were on a very high floor.

They were in a large room. There were six men. Two were playing chess while a third — a very young man, almost a boy — watched. A fourth was reading a Spanish-language newspaper, and a fifth was reading the *Wall Street Journal.* The sixth was working at a laptop computer on a glass-topped coffee table.

Through wide plate-glass doors, Parker saw two more men — one of them a very large, obviously Latino man and the other a good-looking, six-foot, fair-skinned man in his late thirties who looked American — hoist themselves nimbly out of a swimming pool and start to towel themselves dry.

A huge black dog like the ones at Lorimer Manor came trotting around the side of the pool with a white soccer ball in his mouth. He dropped it at the feet of the swimmers and then shook himself dry. It produced an explosion of water.

What the hell is it with these dogs?

A stunningly beautiful redheaded woman wearing a transparent flaming yellow jacket over a matching bikini — together, the garments left only negligible anatomical details to the imagination — rose gracefully from a chaise longue next to the pool and marched up to Roscoe Danton. She gave him a little hug and offered her cheek for him to kiss.

Then she put out her hand to Porky, and announced, "I'm Sweaty. Welcome to Cozumel. What can I get you to drink?"

That has to be a name, Parker decided, *because she damn sure doesn't smell sweaty.*

She smells as if she just took a bath in the most expensive of perfumes Chanel et Cie has to offer.

"I'll be almost pathetically grateful for anything with alcohol in it," Porky said.

A white-jacketed waiter suddenly appeared.

"Scotch, double, rocks," Porky ordered.

"Twice," Roscoe said.

I don't think ordering a double scotch was the smart thing for me to do, Porky thought. *The last thing I need to do when I have to do some serious thinking is get bombed.*

Not only do I not know what I'm doing here,

I'm not even sure where the hell "here" is.

"Well, Gimpy, I see you managed to cheat death once again," the swimmer Parker thought of as "the American" said. "Please tell me you didn't bend my nice new bird."

Gimpy gave the American the finger.

The American walked up to Parker.

"Welcome to Cozumel, Mr. Parker, you're just in time for an Argentine *bife de chorizo*, which I believe loosely translates from Spanish as 'food for the gods.' I'm Charley Castillo."

Parker knew a good deal about Charley Castillo, but this was the first time he'd ever seen him up close, and he was surprised at what he saw. It showed on his face.

Parker thought: *As a matter of fact, the only time I've ever seen him at all was on television, when he and the other guy who'd stolen that Tupelov airplane walked off it at Andrews Air Force Base.*

I guess — because of that Castillo name and because he's a Mexican-American — I expected, if not Zorro, then that Mexican-American actor, Antonio Bandana, or whatever the hell his name is.

This guy has blue eyes and lighter skin than mine, and damn sure doesn't look like a Super Spook capable of stealing a Russian airplane right from under Hugo Chavez's nose. Or, for that matter, stealing two Russian defectors from the CIA station chief in Vienna.

Oh, Jesus! That's who the redhead is!

The Russian defector, the former SVR rezident *in Copenhagen, who President Clendennen had been willing — hell, been trying desperately — to swap to the Russians.*

"Something wrong?" Castillo asked.

"No. I guess I'm a little shook up by everything that's happened."

The waiter put a glass in his hand, and Porky took a healthy swallow.

Castillo gave his hand to Danton.

"Thank you for coming, Roscoe," he said. "I know it's inconvenient, but it's important."

"Anytime, Charley," Danton replied.

He added, mentally: *I always try to oblige people who are going to give me a million dollars. And it's not as if I had much of a choice, is it?*

"Mr. Parker . . . can I call you Porky?" Castillo said.

John David Parker — who loathed being called "Porky" — heard himself saying "Certainly."

Castillo nodded, then went on: "Porky, you ever hear 'What happens in Las Vegas stays in Las Vegas'? That applies here in spades. You take my meaning?"

"I think so," Parker said.

Roscoe thought, *Porky took his meaning, all right. Castillo didn't have to say, "Otherwise, we'll have to kill you."*

Porky figured that out all by himself.

"Okay," Castillo said. "Introductions are in order. You've met Sweaty." He pointed at a man who looked very much like himself. "That's her brother, Tom Barlow. And their cousin Aleksandr Pevsner. And their uncle, Nicolai Tarasov — they answer to Alek and Nick. The fellow watching porn on his laptop is Vic D'Alessandro . . ."

D'Alessandro, without raising his head from the laptop, gave Castillo the finger.

". . . and that's my cousin, Fernando Lopez. That's Stefan — call him Steve — Koussevitzky, and last but certainly not least, Gunnery Sergeant Lester Bradley, USMC, Retired."

Roscoe knew who Stefan Koussevitzky was. The last time he had seen him was on the island. He then had been wearing the uniform of a Spetsnaz major. About the last picture Roscoe had taken on the island as the Tupelov taxied to the runway was one of Koussevitzky sitting on the ground against a hangar wall, applying a compress to his bloody leg. Sweaty had shot him with her tiny .32 Colt automatic.

150

How did he get here?
And what the hell is he doing here?

A man wearing chef's whites appeared at the door to the swimming pool and said something in what Porky recognized as Russian.

Castillo then announced, "That's Russian for 'the steaks are done,' " and gestured for everybody to go onto the balcony.

A long banquet table had been set up around the corner of the building. The man with the chef's hat and two white-jacketed waiters were lined up next to it. There was a large charcoal grill against the balcony railing, and a table loaded with bottles of wine against the building wall.

Castillo took a seat at one end of the table, and Alek Pevsner at the other. Sweaty sat at one side of Castillo, and Delchamps sat across from her. Pevsner had Tom Barlow on one side of him and Uncle Nicolai Tarasov on the other.

After everyone else filled the seats between, the waiters stood ready to pour the wine.

Pevsner picked up his glass, took a large sip, nodded his head as a signal to the waiter that it met his approval, and then watched as the waiter emptied the bottle between his, Uncle Nicolai's, and Tom Barlow's glasses. Much the same thing happened elsewhere at the table.

Then Pevsner made an announcement, or gave an order, that surprised — perhaps startled — both Roscoe and Porky.

"Let us pray," he said, folding his hands piously before him, closing his eyes, and bowing his head.

He prayed in English: "Dear Lord and Father of mankind, we thank You for the bounty we are about to receive. We thank You for the continued good health and safety of our families . . ."

Roscoe had a somewhat irreverent thought: *He sounds as if he's having a conversation with a friend who happens to be the Almighty.*

". . . and our beloved friends. We ask that You permit us to assist the Archangel Michael and the Blessed Saint George in their and Your holy war against Satan, his wicked works, and his followers. We ask their and Your help in rescuing . . . what's his name again, Karl?"

"Ferris, Colonel James D. Ferris," Castillo furnished.

". . . Colonel James Ferris from the evil men who hold him for Satan's evil purposes, and we ask that those who are about to do battle in Thy name to this end be given the courage of Saint George.

"This we ask in the name of Thy son, our Lord and Savior, Jesus Christ. Amen."

There was a chorus of amens.

What the hell was that all about? both Porky and Roscoe thought more or less simultaneously.

Pevsner went on, now icily angry: "Where the hell are the shrimp cocktails?" He then switched to Russian, and apparently repeated what he had said in English, for both waiters hurried inside the building and quickly returned with trays of shrimp cocktails.

"It doesn't get much better than this, Roscoe," Castillo announced. "The shrimp were floating around out there" — he gestured toward the sea — "not six hours ago. And the beef and the wine arrived with the ex-Spetsnaz this morning from Chile."

Parker wondered: *With the what? The "ex-Spetsnaz"? Is that what he said?*

"Charley, why was it important that I come here?" Roscoe asked.

"I'd planned to get into this after dinner," Castillo replied, "but what the hell? The thing is, Roscoe, you're one hell of a reporter . . ."

What is this, soft soap from Charley Castillo?

Watch yourself, Roscoe!

". . . and I figured it was just a matter of time before you figured out that the kidnapping of Colonel Ferris, and the whacking of the other three guys, including my old friend Daniel Salazar, probably has nothing to do with the drug trade. And I wanted to ask you to hold off writing what you learned or intuited."

Otherwise what?

"Otherwise we'll have to kill you"?

Do not pass GO.

Go directly to the cemetery and do not *collect one million dollars?*

"Are you going to explain that? If it's not connected with the drug trade, what's it all about?"

"Vladimir Vladimirovich has a problem, Mr. Danton," Pevsner said.

Who? Oh! Vladimir Vladimirovich Putin.

"That, and his ego is involved," Tom Barlow said.

"That's part of the problem," Pevsner agreed, "but his major problem is that everyone in the Russian intelligence community, and the diplomatic community, and of course within the Oprichnina —"

"Within the what?" Roscoe interrupted.

154

Pevsner flashed him an icy glance and went on as if he hadn't heard the question: ". . . is waiting for him to react. He either reacts, or . . . what is Carlos always saying? 'There goes the old ball game.' "

"Reacts to what?" Roscoe asked.

"His gross underestimation of Svetlana and her Carlitos," Tom Barlow said, and laughed.

"About sixteen months ago, Mr. Danton," Pevsner said, "Vladimir Vladimirovich thought he had the world by the tail —"

"The expression, Alek," Castillo interrupted, "is 'had the world by the *balls.*' "

Delchamps chuckled. Pevsner glared at both of them, and again went on as if he had not been interrupted: ". . . but then a series of things went very wrong for him. Again, quoting my friend Charley, 'cutting to the chase,' culminating in what happened two months ago —"

Roscoe quickly did the arithmetic and interrupted: "Exactly two months ago today, Clendennen was 'persuaded' to name Montvale Vice President. Is that what you mean?"

This time Pevsner chose to answer.

"That had a bearing on it, of course, but what I was thinking of, Mr. Danton, was what happened in the lobby bar of the

Mayflower Hotel immediately before that happened."

Danton's face showed his confusion.

Pevsner went on: "There was a meeting there between Sergei Murov, the SVR *rezident* in Washington, and Mr. Lammelle — who later that morning would be appointed as head of the CIA — and Dmitri, Svetlana, and Charley.

"The previous afternoon, as you reported on Wolf News, Charley landed a Tupelov Tu-934A at Andrews Air Force Base. On that pride of the Russian air force were the last barrels of Congo-X that Vladimir Vladimirovich and Lieutenant General Yakov Sirinov had.

"Thanks to your journalistic discretion, Mr. Danton, which we all deeply appreciate, there was no mention of the Congo-X or General Sirinov either on Wolf News or in *The Washington Times-Post.*

"But Sergei Murov, of course, knew about both, and was thus naturally quite anxious to hear what Mr. Lammelle and the others wished to say.

"Mr. Lammelle got right to the point. He informed Sergei that Secretary of State Natalie Cohen had called the Russian ambassador and told him that unless Murov voluntarily gave up his post and returned to

Russia he would be declared persona non grata and expelled within forty-eight hours."

"And I told him," Sweaty chimed in, "that when he left, I had a little present for Vladimir Vladimirovich I wanted him to take with him; a barrel of Congo-X that had been rendered harmless. And I also told him that if Stefan Koussevitzky and his family were not in Budapest within seventy-two hours —"

"She would make sure," Castillo picked up the narrative, laughing, "that every officer of the SVR would know that what Putin was doing behind closed doors when he was running the KGB in Saint Petersburg was write poetry. For some reason, I gather that Saint Petersburg poets are regarded with some suspicion vis-à-vis their sexual orientation."

Tom Barlow chuckled.

"I'm not sure that pouring salt on an open wound was wise," Pevsner said.

"I disagree," Nicolai said. "Always press an advantage, Alek. You know that."

"And it worked," Koussevitzky said. "We were on our way to Argentina via Budapest the next day."

"Which caused you to decide that Charley's offer of an armistice had been accepted," Pevsner said. "Which we now know is not the case."

He let that sink in a moment, and then went on: "It was a low point for Vladimir Vladimirovich, Mr. Danton. He had dispatched General Sirinov personally on the super-secret Tu-934A with the last stocks of Congo-X, confident that President Clendennen would happily exchange Svetlana, Dmitri, and Charley for the Congo-X.

"When Sergei — who had proposed the exchange to Lammelle — walked into the hotel bar to learn he was about to be declared persona non grata, Charley's March Hare assault on Hugo Chavez's La Orchila Island had not only already taken the Congo-X — and rendered it harmless — but also had taken possession of the Tu-934A and taken General Sirinov prisoner."

"And under those circumstances, Aleksandr," Tom Barlow said, "Svetlana was right to rub salt in his wound, and Charley was right to propose the cease-fire."

"And he accepted the cease-fire proposal, didn't he?" Pevsner countered sarcastically. "Even going so far as to permit Stefan and his family to leave Russia. Unless, of course, he did that to lull us to sleep."

"But, according to your theory," Castillo said, "in our naïveté we were already asleep. So what's the hit and kidnapping all about?

Wouldn't that wake us up?"

"I thought we were agreed, Charley," Pevsner said, "that we are all now wide awake."

"Touché," Castillo said.

"I don't *know* about any of that, Charley," Vic D'Alessandro spoke up. "But everything I heard in Acapulco — correction — *nothing* I heard in Acapulco makes me think Danny and the others were whacked because they were causing the Sinaloa cartel trouble."

"So," Tom Barlow said, "what do these people — whoever they are — want with this Colonel Ferris?"

"The last time we went down that road," Sweaty said, "we agreed we'll just have to wait and see."

"On the other hand," D'Alessandro said, "there's the possibility — which a couple of our guys —"

" 'Your guys,' Vic?" Tom Barlow said.

"The Special Forces guys in Acapulco as trainers," D'Alessandro explained. "A couple of them suggested that they snatched Colonel Ferris to exchange him for some — maybe all — of the Sinaloa cartel guys we have in jail in the states."

"And killed the others to make the point they're willing to kill Ferris if we don't go along?" Castillo asked.

"Right."

"That's possible, Vic," Delchamps said. "But I go along with Alek. I think his pal Vladimir Vladimirovich is behind this. A prisoner swap may well be part of their game plan, but my gut tells me there's more to it than that."

"And do you agree with my suggestions as to how we should deal with the situation?" Pevsner asked softly.

"I'm a dinosaur, Alek, you know that. As well as what that means."

Both Parker and Danton had sudden clear memories of what they had heard from the elderly lady with the walker at Lorimer Manor: *"Dinosaurs believe that the only good Communist is a dead Communist."*

"And you, Charley, are you in agreement?" Pevsner asked again, softly.

It took a moment for Castillo to frame his reply, and then he said, "I would really have preferred the armistice, but count me in, of course."

This time, Danton thought, *they're talking about killing people.*

And this time they're not kidding!

"So, as I understand our agreed-upon plan, we wait for Vladimir Vladimirovich's next move, in the meantime putting in place certain precautions. Need I spell them out?"

"Yeah, you do," Castillo said. "Just so everybody understands everybody else."

"Very well," Pevsner said. "I have already taken what precautions I think are called for here at the Grand Cozumel and in Argentina. What happened in Acapulco might be a diversion; and they might really start what they're up to with me.

"That said, I agree with you, Charley, that they probably are considering action against your grapefruit farm here, or even against your family — especially your grandmother — in the United States. Against that possibility, the ten ex-Spetsnaz Stefan and I brought up this morning will be flown to the grapefruit farm at first light tomorrow by Fernando and Uncle Nicolai.

"Once they are in place to his — and of course to Fernando's — satisfaction, Stefan will return here to handle the ex-Spetsnaz, another ten of them, who will arrive on the PeruaireCargo flight the day after tomorrow.

"Fernando will stay at the grapefruit farm as long as he feels is necessary or return to the United States, whichever he feels is best. I will return to Argentina tomorrow morning and see what, if anything, I can learn about Vladimir Vladimirovich's plans from

161

my sources.

"Dmitri will stay here in the Grand Cozumel. My instructions to the staff are that he speaks with my voice. You and Svetlana will go to San Antonio to satisfy yourself about your grandmother's security."

Pevsner met Castillo's eyes, and added: "Is that about it?"

"Two things, Alek. I don't care what you told your staff about Tom. He and everybody else are to understand that I'm calling the shots in Mexico. Is that understood?"

"Dmitri," Pevsner said, "is that satisfactory to you?"

"Perfectly," Berezovsky replied. "But I wonder about you. You're not used to asking anybody for permission to do anything."

"I have given my word," Pevsner said.

"That's good enough for me," Castillo said. "The agreement is that nobody takes any action — except in self-defense — until it is discussed and agreed to by Alek, Edgar, Dmitri, and me. And we're all agreed, right, that that applies to snatching Pavel Koslov?"

"You know I don't agree with that," Sweaty said angrily. "We should grab him while we have the chance."

"You made that point, my love, over and over. And you were voted down. They call that democracy."

Her brother laughed.

"Who's Pavel Koslov?" Danton asked.

"The Mexico City *rezident,*" Delchamps furnished. "I think we ought to whack him, tit for tat, if he hurts Colonel Ferris, but I agree with Charley that snatching him now is not a very good idea."

Castillo nodded, then looked around and said, "Is that it?"

"What do I tell McNab, Charley?" D'Alessandro asked. "He said he wants to see me the minute I get back."

"Tell him everything," Castillo said. "I never lied to him before, I don't want to start now, and I'm certainly not going to ask you to withhold anything from him."

"He's going to ask what you're going to want from him," D'Alessandro said. "What do I tell him?"

"I'd like whatever intel he feels he can give me. But aside from that, I'm not going to need anything from the Stockade. Except you, of course."

"Got it."

"Uncle Nicolai, you about ready to fly Vic to Mexico City?"

"No. I've been drinking. But one of my pilots is standing by."

D'Alessandro walked around the table,

shaking hands, and then disappeared past the sliding glass doors.

IV

[One]
Office of the Commanding General
United States Special Operations Command
Fort Bragg, North Carolina
0830 13 April 2007

A substantial number of liaison officers was attached to the Special Operations Command. Some of them were military — for example, the liaison officers from the Office of the Chief of Naval Operations; the Office of the Chief of Staff, USAF; the commander in chief, Central Command; the Defense Intelligence Agency; and even the XVIII Airborne Corps, which commanded the physical assets of Fort Bragg as well as the 82nd and 101st Airborne divisions.

There were also civilian liaison officers: They included a State Department liaison officer; an FBI liaison officer; and a CIA liaison officer. They all had staffs, some of them as large as a dozen deputies and clerks.

The building in which they were housed was known jocularly as "Foggy Bottom, South." Others called it "Siberia." Most liaison officers felt that Lieutenant General Bruce J. McNab regarded them as spies for their superiors, and that they were treated accordingly. They rarely saw him in person after their first brief chat with him on their assignment. They dealt with Major General Terrence O'Toole, the SPECOPSCOM deputy commander.

O'Toole had summoned Charles D. Stevens, the FBI liaison officer, to his office two days before.

"This is in connection with Colonel Ferris," he said, getting right to the point. "You're aware of the package the general received with Ferris's photo?"

Stevens had nodded. He knew about the FedEx package. He had learned of it through FBI channels, not from anyone in SPECOPSCOM.

"Neither the CIA nor your laboratory at Quantico was able to learn much — in fact, anything — from it. The fingerprints found on it were useless because it had passed through so many hands.

"The general feels that the next communication from these people will come the same way, that is via either FedEx or UPS. He would like to get his hands on that package before it is handled by everybody and his idiot brother."

"I understand, General."

"What the general would like to see the FBI do is to locate that package as soon as it enters the FedEx/UPS process. The package would then be placed, taking care to touch it as little as possible, into another envelope and then sent on its way here. Do you think the FBI can handle that, Mr. Stevens?"

"The FBI will certainly try, General."

"The general feels that it is highly likely that the address on the package will be different from the address on the original package, which itself was addressed to Lieutenant Colonel McNab, not Lieutenant General McNab, probably to avoid undue attention. So what you should be looking for is an Overnight envelope addressed accordingly, perhaps even addressed to someone in these headquarters, not the general, or to the home address of such people."

"I understand the reasoning. I'll get right on it."

"Thank you. Keep me posted, please."

FBI Liaison Officer Stevens thought: *The chances of finding that envelope among the X-many million overnight envelopes that UPS and FedEx handle every day are right up there with my chances of being taken bodily into Heaven.*

This proved to be either unduly pessimistic or a gross underestimation of the enthusiasm with which employees of FedEx or UPS would respond to a request for assistance from the Federal Bureau of Investigation.

Fewer than twenty-four hours later, Stevens received a telephone call from the special agent in charge — the SAC — of the El Paso FBI office, William J. Johnson, who happened to be an old friend.

"I'm in the UPS Store in the Sunland Park Mall in El Paso, Chuck," the SAC said. "Holding — very carefully, in my rubber gloves — a UPS overnighter addressed to Sergeant Terry O'Toole, Yadkin and Reilly Road, Fort Bragg, North Carolina. Is this what you're looking for?"

"Yadkin Road and Reilly Street is known as 'Generals' Row,'" Stevens said. "*Major General* Terrence O'Toole lives there, next door to General McNab."

"Say, 'Thank you, Bill,'" the SAC said. "You want me to open it?"

"Thank you, Bill," Stevens said. "But don't open it. General McNab wants us to just put it into another envelope and send it on its way. Anyway, I think opening it would be illegal."

[Two]

Office of the Commanding General
United States Special Operations Command
Fort Bragg, North Carolina
0530 14 April 2007

Lieutenant General Bruce J. McNab, wearing rubber gloves, carefully opened the UPS Next Day envelope and examined the two sheets of paper it contained. Vic D'Alessandro looked over his shoulder.

One of the sheets was a photograph of an unshaven Lieutenant Colonel James D. Ferris. He was sitting on a chair, holding a copy of the previous day's *El Diario de El Paso.* Two men wearing balaclava masks stood beside him, holding machetes.

"This time it's machetes," D'Alessandro said. "Is that an implied threat to behead him?"

"No more, I would guess, than the guy holding the Kalashnikov the last time was an implied threat to blow his brains out," McNab said matter-of-factly.

The second sheet of paper was the message:

> So Far He's Still Alive.
> If you would be willing to return Félix Abrego to his family we would be willing to return Colonel Ferris to his.
> Place a classified ad in El Diario de El Paso as follows for the next four days:
> "Always interested in Mexican business opportunities. Write Businessman, PO Box 2333, El Paso, Texas, 79901".

"Who's Félix Abrego, I wonder?" McNab said.

"One of the drug guys we have in the slam, seems likely," D'Alessandro replied.

"I'm sure the FBI will be able to tell us."

"Charley asked that you provide him with intel," D'Alessandro said. "Does this count as intel?"

"As you know, Lieutenant Colonel Castillo, Retired, no longer has a security clearance, Mr. D'Alessandro. However, I would suppose that one or more of his former associates in the Special Operations and intelligence communities would feel that the national security would not be seriously compromised if he somehow learned about this."

D'Alessandro nodded his understanding.

169

McNab leaned forward and pulled the red telephone connected to the Central Command circuit toward himself. He pushed 6, and then the LOUDSPEAKER button.

There was the sound of three rings, and then a somewhat metallic voice said, "General Naylor."

"Bruce McNab, General. I regret waking you at oh dark hundred, but . . ."

"What's on your mind, General?"

". . . the protocol requires that I immediately notify C-in-C CENTCOM if something of this nature comes up, and something has."

"What have you got, General?"

"There has been a second communication from the people who are holding Colonel Ferris. This one was sent UPS Next Day from El Paso, addressed to 'Sergeant' Terry O'Toole. It contained a photo of Colonel Ferris holding a copy of yesterday's *El Diario de El Paso.* And a note offering to make an exchange for him. Shall I read it to you?"

"Please."

McNab did so.

"Who is Félix whatever?" Naylor asked.

"We don't know. As soon as I can get the FBI liaison officer in here, I'm going to ask him to find out. I would guess he's someone we have in prison."

"Probably," Naylor said. "This message reached you last night?"

"About fifteen minutes ago."

"UPS delivers at . . . a little after oh-five-hundred?"

"What I did, General, was ask the FBI to see if they could intercept any new messages as soon as they entered the UPS or FedEx systems. And they were successful. Mr. Stevens, the FBI liaison officer, called last night to report that this message, this envelope, had been intercepted in El Paso. When it arrived in Fayetteville, Vic D'Alessandro was waiting for it."

"And what are your plans now, General?" Naylor asked.

"What I'm planning to do, General, is first send you photocopies of the envelope and its contents. Then I intend to get the FBI liaison officer in here, and turn the envelope and its contents over to him, so that he can send it to the FBI experts in Quantico.

"I presume you will pass the photocopies of the envelope and its contents to the chief of staff, who will presumably send copies to the secretary of Defense, the secretary of State, the director of National Intelligence, et cetera —"

"And of course the office of the POTUS," Naylor interrupted.

171

"Yes, of course. We mustn't forget President Clendennen, must we?"

"Spare me your sarcasm, McNab," Naylor snapped.

McNab didn't reply directly. After a moment, he asked: "If I may continue, General?"

"Go on," Naylor said icily.

"And that no further action by me is required at this time."

"No further action is required of you. That is correct."

"Thank you, sir. Is there anything else, sir?"

Naylor broke the connection without replying.

"Sometimes, Vic," McNab said as he reached for his Brick and opened it, "as hard as this is to believe, I don't think General Naylor likes me very much."

He checked to see if the proper LEDs were glowing, then pushed several buttons.

"Christ, McNab," the voice of DCI A. Franklin Lammelle bounced off a satellite. "Do you know what time it is?"

"I have a little gossip with which I thought you might want to begin your day," McNab said. "We have a new ally in our war against the evildoers who have snatched Colonel Ferris."

"And who might that be? Castillo?"

"Him, too, but I was speaking of Aleksandr Pevsner."

There was a moment's hesitation, then Lammelle asked, "How reliable is that?"

"From the horse's mouth, so to speak."

"What's that all about?"

"Pevsner apparently believes Putin is behind the whole thing, and is after not only Charley and the Russians again, but is against him, too."

There was another just perceptible pause.

"And you go along with that?"

"I don't dismiss it out of hand," McNab said. "Vic D'Alessandro just came back from Acapulco. He says the drug cartel there . . . what's it called, Vic?"

"The Sinaloa cartel," D'Alessandro furnished. He raised his voice. "Got you out of bed, did we, Frank?"

"Vic says the *Sinaloa cartel* had no reason to kidnap Ferris or kill the others. Ferris's people have been obeying their orders to cooperate with the Federales, which means the cartel knew what we knew."

"That's pretty good information, Vic?" Lammelle said.

"I believe it," D'Alessandro said.

"Tell him what else you learned," McNab said.

"Mr. Pevsner believes that the best defense is a good offense," D'Alessandro said.

"Oh, shit!"

"Do you think we should tell Natalie?" McNab asked.

This time there was no hesitation on Lammelle's part.

"No. Absolutely not!"

"You going to tell me why?"

"I had dinner with her, after that fiasco in Auditorium Three," Lammelle said. "She pointed out to me something I kicked myself for not realizing."

"What?"

"We no longer have the threat of impeachment we had hanging over Clendennen's head. Once we rearranged the Cabinet to our satisfaction, we lost it."

This time it was McNab who hesitated for a moment — a long moment — before replying.

"She's right," he said. "As usual."

"She says Clendennen thinks we're planning a coup. First we get him to appoint Montvale as Vice President, then we get rid of Clendennen, either by resignation or impeachment, and Montvale becomes President."

"Nice thought," McNab said, "but it never entered my mind until just now. I didn't

174

even consider Montvale becoming Vice President; that was Crenshaw's idea."

Stanley Crenshaw was the attorney general of the United States.

"And Crenshaw, being an honorable, decent man, did what you and I know better than to do: He looked in the mirror."

McNab knew Lammelle was referring to what would-be intel officers are taught often on the first day — certainly within the first week — of their training: "Never look in the mirror. Your enemy doesn't think like you do."

"Did she have anything to say about what happened at Langley?" McNab asked.

"She said that Porky Parker was the first in the long line of people Clendennen plans to knock off, one at a time. Porky's disappeared, by the way."

"Yesterday, he and Roscoe Danton were in Cozumel with Castillo."

"What's that all about?"

"I don't have a clue, Frank. Did Natalie tell you what she plans to do?"

"Yes, she did. She recommended that you and I not do anything at all that would give Clendennen a chance to fire us. She said she was going to talk with you. I gather she hasn't?"

"No. She didn't say anything about warning Montvale? Or, for that matter, Naylor?"

"I guess she figures both of them haven't been looking in the mirror. And if Truman Ellsworth has — which I doubt — Montvale will warn him. So far as Naylor goes, I get the feeling that he wouldn't be grief stricken if Clendennen relieved you."

"I can't believe General Naylor would be complicit in something like that."

"You're looking in the mirror, General. Naylor the *soldier* probably wouldn't. But above a certain level — and Naylor is *way* above it — senior officers have to be politicians and play by their rules."

McNab didn't reply.

"In this," Lammelle went on, "I'd say that both Natalie and Naylor really believe they're doing what they do — for the country; it's not a personal ego trip — better than anyone replacing them would do. And they're probably right. They want to keep their jobs for the good of the country, and will do whatever they think is necessary to keep them. Naylor thinks you're dangerous, and you know it. He wouldn't throw you under the bus, but if somebody else did, he would be able to put someone else in SPECOPSCOM he *could* control."

Again McNab didn't reply.

"I was there," Lammelle went on, "at

Drug Cartel International when Naylor suddenly decided to help. And he even told us why. If Operation March Hare failed, that would've been worse for the country than if it succeeded."

"Is that why you changed sides, Frank? For the good of the country?"

"No. I changed sides because I realized I was being used, by Clendennen, by Montvale, and — maybe especially — by Jack Powell to do something I knew was wrong. And I'm like you, I guess."

John J. Powell was the former director of the Central Intelligence Agency. Lammelle had replaced Powell when he resigned two months previously.

"What do you mean, you're like me?"

"I'm a simple soul who sees things in black or white. Sometimes I'm a little slow in making the distinction, but once I do, I try to act accordingly."

McNab didn't answer.

"Two things about Natalie . . ." Lammelle began, then added: "Why do I have a hard time using your first name?"

"It's Bruce. Use it."

"Two things about Natalie, *Bruce*. Not only does she want to keep her job, but she really believes the way to deal with Mexico — and especially with this latest outrage —

is to talk about it and keep talking about it until reason prevails.

"She was willing to resign over Clendennen's trying to swap Charley, Sweaty, and Dmitri to the Russians. But Charley waging a war in Mexico — especially with Aleksandr Pevsner — that's something that'll make her just as mad."

"So you don't think I should tell her that Charley just talked Pevsner out of snatching the Russian *rezident* in Mexico City? They decided to wait until they see if Ferris is hurt; then they'll whack him."

"Jesus Christ!"

"The trouble with what you just told me, Frank, is that it all makes sense. It just took me a little time — like a decade — to figure it out."

"Watch your back, Bruce."

"You, too."

McNab closed the lid of the Brick, and then met D'Alessandro's eyes.

"That was interesting, wasn't it, Vic?"

"The word that comes to mind is 'scary,' " D'Alessandro said.

...ies D. Stevens walked into his ...s telephone was ringing. Since his ...ry had not yet arrived, he answered ...mself.

"FBI, Stevens."

"Max Caruthers, Stevens. Where the hell have you been? The general's been looking for you since oh-seven-hundred. No answer at your house, and none at your office until now."

Stevens had a mental picture of McNab's huge senior aide-de-camp.

"I must have been driving to work," Stevens said.

"You didn't answer your cell phone, either," Caruthers accused.

Stevens decided that Caruthers would not be interested in his explanation for not answering his cell phone. Not only was talking on a cell phone while driving against the law, he regarded it as dangerous, too.

"What can the FBI do for General Mc-Nab, Colonel? Aside from getting that envelope you were asking for? That should be delivered sometime this mornin[g]

"General McNab's complimen[ts]
Stevens. The general would apprecia[te]
ing you at your earliest convenience [in his]
office," Caruthers said, paused, and [then]
finished: ". . . where we have had t[he]
envelope since oh-five-fifteen."

Chuck Stevens — who had willed himself
to walk slowly from Foggy Bottom to the
SPECOPSCOM headquarters building; *"I'm
an FBI Inspector, not some PFC who has to
run whenever his master whistles"* — arrived
five minutes later in McNab's office.

He found Colonel J. J. Tufts, the liaison
officer of the Defense Intelligence Agency,
and Colonel Christopher Dawson, the US-
CENTCOM liaison officer, already there.
And so was Mr. Victor D'Alessandro, about
whom Stevens knew very little, except that
it was rumored he had something to do with
the ultra-secret Gray Fox unit, about which
Stevens also knew very little, and that
D'Alessandro was sort of a confidant of
General McNab.

Colonel Max Caruthers was not in Mc-
Nab's office, which surprised Stevens.

"Thank you for coming so quickly, Mr.
Stevens," General McNab greeted him.
"Can we get you a cup of coffee?"

180

"No, thank you, sir," Stevens said.

"Well, here it is," McNab said, handing him a large translucent plastic envelope. "The envelope we have been looking for. I place it in your capable hands, confident that the FBI experts at Quantico will find something useful for you."

"Thank you," Stevens said.

"I have made photocopies of the contents. I didn't think to ask permission first. I hope that doesn't pose any problems."

"I don't see why it should, General," Stevens said.

"As I was just explaining to these gentlemen," McNab said, nodding toward Colonel Tufts and Colonel Dawson, "my official role in this whole affair is not much more than that of a spectator. Colonel Ferris and Warrant Officer Salazar were detached to the DEA before they were sent to Mexico.

"I can only presume that those who kidnapped Colonel Ferris are unaware of this, by which I mean they don't know that I have no authority even to reply to their messages. The only thing I can do is follow the protocol laid down by USCENTCOM to deal with matters like this. Under that protocol, I am required to immediately notify my immediate superior — that is, General Naylor — when something like this

— like the envelope arriving here — occurs. I did so immediately after opening the envelope. General Naylor ordered me to transfer the envelope and its contents to the FBI, and I have just done so. He also directed me to give copies of everything to Colonels Tufts and Dawson for their respective headquarters. And he gave me permission to retain a copy.

"Therefore, my official role in this is over, at least until General Naylor gives me further orders. On a personal note, however, Colonel Ferris is a friend of mine, and I would like to thank you personally, Mr. Stevens, for your help."

"I'm only too happy to do whatever I can, General," Stevens said.

"And, really unofficially, I'm personally curious to know who this fellow Félix Abrego is."

"I suspect, General, that he's probably in a federal prison," Stevens said. "I can find out for you. Actually, I'm curious myself. I can have that information for you probably within the hour."

"You understand that's a personal request, not an official one?"

"Understood. Not a problem. You could find out yourself by going to the Federal Bureau of Prisons website. But I think I can get the information more quickly through my channels."

"I'd really be grateful, Mr. Stevens," McNab said. "Gentlemen, unless you have something for me?"

Colonels Tufts and Dawson chorused, "No, sir."

"Then thank you for answering my call so quickly," McNab said, and stood and offered his hand.

When they had left his office and D'Alessandro had closed the door, D'Alessandro turned to McNab.

"Don't look so pleased with yourself. When Naylor and the DEA CG hear how charming and modest you've been, they're going to smell the Limburger."

"Mr. D'Alessandro, I have no idea what you're suggesting. General Naylor may even decide I have considered my wicked ways and have reformed."

D'Alessandro snorted.

McNab opened his Brick and took out the telephone handset, activated the loudspeaker function, and pushed a button.

"Aloysius? Bruce McNab."

"What can I do for you?"

"Can you set up a net within the net?"

"To do what?"

"So that I can cut Natalie Cohen out of

the loop without her knowing."

"I thought she was one of the good guys."

"She is. She's so good it's going to be a problem. I suspect she's not going to like what she might hear."

"Who do you want on the net?"

"All the Outlaws, plus Vic D'Alessandro and Lammelle."

"Just them?"

"Just them."

"And you want the other net to still function?"

"That's it. Can do?"

"It'll take me about an hour. I'll call you back when it's up."

"You will get your reward in Heaven, Aloysius."

[Four]
1700 Arizona Boulevard
San Antonio, Texas
0905 14 April 2007

Doña Alicia Castillo was waiting for Charley and Sweaty when they walked into the breakfast room. Charley's grandmother was seated at the head of the table drinking a steaming cup of *café con leche*. The table was set for four, and on each plate was a

184

grapefruit half topped with a maraschino cherry.

Max trotted over to the dignified old woman and waited for her to scratch his ears.

"Good morning," Doña Alicia said. "You slept well, I hope."

Charley and Sweaty walked over to her and kissed her cheek.

"Abuela, if she didn't snore like a backfiring John Deere, I'd have probably slept better."

His grandmother ignored him.

"Shall we wait for Lester?" she asked.

"I looked in his room," Castillo said. "He was sleeping like a cherub. Nobody was snoring in *his* room."

This earned him an icy flash from his grandmother.

"I'd forgotten how beautiful this is," Sweaty said quickly, gesturing past the windows to the garden. "What a beautiful lawn!"

"You wouldn't think it was so beautiful if you had to mow it," Castillo said.

"Carlos's grandfather believed boys should earn their allowances," Doña Alicia said.

"He paid a dollar an acre," Castillo said.

"Why don't we eat?" Doña Alicia said.

185

"We have so much to talk about. Would you say grace, darling?"

"Abuela's talking to you, my love," Castillo said. "Try to keep it under five minutes."

His grandmother shook her head.

"Dear God," Sweaty began, "we thank You for the bounty we are about to receive. We thank You for our families, and ask that You keep them safe. We ask Your protection for those who are prisoners, and ask that they be soon safely reunited with their families. We ask this in the name of Jesus Christ, thy Son and our Lord and Savior. Amen."

She turned to Charley.

"Short enough for you, my heathen?"

He made a waving gesture with his hand, suggesting she had more or less met his criteria.

"You had Colonel Ferris in mind, didn't you, Svetlana?" Doña Alicia asked.

Sweaty nodded. "Yes."

"Abuela, what do we have to talk about so much?" Castillo asked as he picked the maraschino cherry from his grapefruit and popped it into his mouth.

She gestured toward the windows.

"Well, Carlos, why don't we start with those men walking around outside the fence?"

Charley and Sweaty exchanged glances.

After a moment he said, "Oh, you noticed, huh?"

"Even before Mr. Lafferty of Gladiator Security called me and said I had no cause for concern, that there were six of them and a half dozen more could be here in less than five minutes if they were needed."

Castillo took a moment to frame his reply.

While he was doing so, Doña Alicia asked, "Have you noticed, Svetlana dear, that 'who me?' look on Carlos's face when you catch him with his hand in the cookie jar?"

"Abuela," Castillo began carefully, "think of the security guys as me just being extra-careful."

"About what?"

"Do you want me to tell her, Carlito?" Sweaty said.

"I wish you would, dear," Doña Alicia said. "I don't think you're nearly as good at getting around the truth as he is."

Castillo gestured for Sweaty to go ahead.

"We have good reason, Abuela," Sweaty said matter-of-factly, "to believe that the SVR is behind the kidnapping of Colonel Ferris and the assassinations of the other Americans. That it is a diversion in their plans to get at Carlito, my brother, our cousin Aleksandr, and me."

"And you're worried that this might involve me?" Doña Alicia asked calmly.

"Yes, ma'am," Castillo said.

"What about Billy Kocian and Otto Görner? I'd think if I were at risk, so would they be."

"We think that whatever the SVR tries," Castillo said, "it will be in Mexico. Or here. But just to be sure, Abuela, I gave Sándor Tor a call and told him what we think is going on."

"Not Otto?"

He shook his head.

"Why not?" she asked.

It was not an idle question but rather more on the order of a rebuke.

"Two reasons," Castillo replied. "After the SVR murdered that *Tages Zeitung* reporter — I forget his name —"

"His name was Günther Friedler," Doña Alicia said evenly, "and you should be ashamed of yourself for not knowing his name. He was one of your employees!"

Castillo looked at her a long moment, then nodded.

"Yes, ma'am, you're right. What I started to say, Abuela, was that after Herr Friedler was murdered, Billy arranged for Sándor Tor to take over all security for Gossinger Beteiligungsgesellschaft, G.m.b.H. He told

188

Otto that if Otto's security people had done their job, Herr Friedler would still be alive. So Otto went along.

"Anyway, I called Sándor — Billy and Sándor — and told them what we thought. Both agreed, by the way, with what we think. It probably took no more than half an hour before Sándor's people were sitting on Otto and his family."

"You didn't call Otto? Why not?"

"That's the second reason," Castillo said, pointing to a leather attaché case sitting on a sideboard. "Otto doesn't answer his Brick. He thinks the CIA listens to everything he says over it."

"Does it?"

Castillo shook his head.

"And what do you think Otto's going to do when he notices his extra security?" Doña Alicia asked. "And you know he will."

"Since Otto also believes that both the Germans and the Russians listen to his telephone calls," Castillo said sarcastically, "and since he doesn't want to use the Brick because the CIA will be listening, what he probably will do is hop in his new Mustang and fly to Budapest for a goulash lunch. Or, if the Mustang is in Budapest, invite Billy to Fulda for *Knackwurst mit Kraut*."

"Otto has a Mustang? Like yours?"

"*They* have a Mustang. Gossinger Beteiligungsgesellschaft, G.m.b.H., has had a very good year, but not good enough to be able to afford buying both of them a two-point-seven-million-dollar toy."

"I'm surprised Otto would permit something like that," she said. "He's usually very frugal."

"Oh, he protested bitterly," Castillo said. "It was as hard for me to talk him into it as it would have been for me to talk someone who's been wandering around the Sahara Desert for a month into having a glass of ice water."

She smiled.

"And how do you justify *your* two-point-seven-million-dollar toy?"

"I'd rather not tell you. You might decide that Sweaty's profligate."

"My Uncle Nicolai has one, Abuela," Sweaty explained. "He uses it to fly — 'high rollers,' right, Carlito? — back and forth to the Grand Cozumel from Mexico City and Miami . . ."

Castillo thought: *And for other purposes, such as hauling suitcases full of hundred-dollar bills out of Drug Cartel International to someplace where they can be laundered.*

". . . and when I saw the way Carlito looked at it, like a little boy watching an electric train in a store window . . ."

She mimed this by opening her eyes very wide and letting her tongue hang out the side of her mouth.

Doña Alicia laughed.

"I know the look," Doña Alicia said. "When he and Fernando were about twelve, their grandfather showed them a pair of Winchester .30-30 Model 1894 lever-actions that he said he was sending down to Hacienda Santa Maria . . ."

Doña Alicia paused when Sweaty's face showed a lack of understanding.

"The grapefruit farm," Castillo explained.

Doña Alicia went on: "The rifles were for keeping the deer from eating our grapefruit. They were to be a Christmas present for them, but they didn't know that. And both of them . . ."

She opened her eyes wide and let her tongue hang out of the side of her mouth.

Sweaty laughed, then finished: "So I bought him a Mustang."

"Grandpa told me that it was just as easy to fall in love with a rich girl as it was a poor one," Castillo said. "And I took his advice."

"I don't know how you put up with him, Svetlana dear. But, on the other hand, his grandfather was just about as bad, and I put up with him for forty-eight years before the Lord took him."

And then her face grew serious.

"Do you think the people at Hacienda Santa Maria are safe?" she asked.

Well, that's a natural transition, I suppose, from a couple of Model 94s as Christmas presents for a couple of twelve-year-olds to asking by implication if weapons are needed to protect our people at Hacienda Santa Maria.

"Fernando's down there right now, Abuela, making sure they are."

"And how is he going to do that?"

"He took some security people with him," Castillo said.

"From Gladiator Security? Was that necessary? The police chief in Oaxaca is an old, old friend of ours. And, for that matter, so is the chief of police in Acapulco. Between them, I'm sure . . ."

"Abuela, Colonel Ferris was kidnapped fifty miles from Acapulco," Castillo said.

"So you decided that people from Gladiator Security were needed?"

"Not Gladiator Security. The people Fernando took to the hacienda are Spetsnaz. *Ex-Spetsnaz.*"

"Russian Green Berets?"

"More or less. They've been protecting

Sweaty's cousin Aleksandr and his family in Argentina."

"And Fernando took them there?"

Castillo nodded.

"Then he must take this threat very seriously," she said.

"He does. You seem surprised."

"He knows it will insult our people at Hacienda Santa Maria," she said.

"Abuela, we're trying to protect them. Why should they be insulted?"

"Fernando knows — and you should — that Hacienda Santa Maria has been in the family for centuries. It was a land grant from the king of Spain. For all that time, our people there have been fighting off people who wanted to do the hacienda harm. Indians, all sorts of banditos, even French soldiers when Mexico had a French emperor. And lately these despicable drug people. They won't think they need any help."

"Well, they're wrong," Castillo said.

"And getting back to where this conversation began," she said. "Neither do I. I've been taking care of myself for a long time. I don't need more people from Gladiator than are already here."

"Wrong again, Abuela," Castillo said. "From now on, you don't go anywhere

193

without people from Gladiator. One of them will drive your car." He paused, and then added, "Which will probably cause your insurance company to heave a huge sigh of relief."

She frowned at him and looked as if she were going to reply. But then her expression changed to a smile as Lester Bradley walked into the breakfast room. He was carrying a Brick.

"Good morning, Lester," Doña Alicia said. "Did you sleep well?"

"Good morning," Bradley replied.

"Of course he slept well," Castillo said. "Nobody was snoring in his room."

This triggered a thirty-second explosion in Russian from Sweaty, which Doña Alicia could not translate but obviously understood.

Castillo put up his hands in a gesture of surrender, but did not really look very remorseful.

"Sit down, dear," Doña Alicia said, "and have some breakfast."

"Yes, ma'am, thank you," Lester said, then turned to Castillo. "Colonel, can I see you a moment?"

"Lester, we're both retired. That means I don't call you sergeant anymore, and you don't call me colonel."

"Yes, sir," Lester replied.

"Try 'Your Majesty' on for size. If that doesn't work, how about 'Charley'?"

Bradley smiled.

"I . . . uh . . ." Bradley said, and looked at Doña Alicia.

"What's up, Les?" Castillo said.

"Mr. Casey called a couple of minutes ago," Bradley said, "to tell me Net Two is up and running. If you want to use it, punch two forward slashes and then the other numbers."

"What's 'Net Two'?" Castillo asked.

"Mr. Casey said when you asked, I was to tell you to call Mr. D'Alessandro."

He laid the Brick in front of Castillo and opened it.

Castillo took out the handset.

"Two forward slashes, and then the number," Bradley repeated.

Castillo did so.

"What's up, Vic?"

"Put it on loudspeaker," Sweaty ordered.

Castillo either didn't hear her or chose to ignore her.

Their conservation was brief, essentially one-sided, with Castillo doing most of the listening and replying with short answers. Finally, he said, "We'll be in touch," and replaced the handset in the Brick.

"What is 'Net Two'?" Sweaty demanded immediately.

It took him a moment to frame his reply.

"The reason we now have two Casey networks is because we have to cut Natalie Cohen out of the original net, and we don't want her to know that she's been cut."

"That requires an explanation," Sweaty said.

"Let me tell you what she told Frank Lammelle," Castillo said. "Natalie Cohen said that President Clendennen thinks we tried, we're trying, to stage a coup d'état. First we get him to appoint Montvale as Vice President, then we get rid of Clendennen."

"My God!" Doña Alicia said.

"That never entered my mind," Castillo said. "Maybe it should have. But that's moot. Montvale and Natalie and Frank no longer have the threat of impeachment to hold Clendennen in line. So now it's his turn to get rid of people. That circus at Langley — Clendennen's press conference — was his first move. He not only got rid of Porky Parker, but he made the point to the others that he was coming after them just as soon as he could find a reason.

"Once they get the message, he hopes they will resign. They can leave his service with their reputations intact, instead of getting fired for incompetence, as Parker was. It's clear to both Lammelle and Cohen that he plans to use this mess in Mexico as the way to do it.

"So Natalie told Frank their only defense against this is to not give him any excuse at all to accuse them of either incompetence or disloyalty.

"Making matters worse, Lammelle says that Cohen — keep in mind that it was her idea to send Ferris, Danny Salazar, and the other Special Forces people down there in the first place — will go ballistic if she even suspects what Aleksandr Pevsner plans to do in Mexico."

"Which is?" Doña Alicia asked softly.

"Pevsner has decided that the best defense against what Putin has in mind for us is a good offense."

"And you, Carlos?" she asked. "How do you feel about that?"

Castillo hesitated just perceptibly before replying, "Abuela, taking into consideration both that Putin has proved — Herr Friedler was not the only man he had assassinated — that he's willing and capable of murdering everybody he thinks is in his way, I'm afraid Pevsner is right."

"You said, 'taking into consideration both.' "

"Abuela, Putin's already tried, several times, to assassinate me. There's no question that he's coming after Svetlana, and I can't let that happen. I won't let that happen."

Doña Alicia sighed. "Oh, my. We have a very bad situation on our hands, don't we?"

Castillo didn't reply for a long moment. Then he said, "We thought — naïvely thought — that we had bloodied his nose when we grabbed the Tupelov and turned General Sirinov over to the CIA. We offered him an armistice; he didn't accept it. So what we have to do now is bloody it again, hard enough this time so that he gets the message."

She considered that for a moment.

"And so what do we do now?"

" 'So what do *we* do now'?" Castillo parroted, lightly sarcastic.

His grandmother stared at him icily.

"Until you lower me into my grave, Carlos, I will continue to run this family. Never forget that!"

"Sorry," he said.

He saw Sweaty looking at her with a smile of approval.

"And what *I* am going to do now is have a

word with Señor Medina," Doña Alicia said.

She turned to Sweaty.

"Señor Medina has been running Hacienda Santa Maria for us for thirty years. And before that, his father ran it. And before him, his father."

She paused, then looked at Lester. She pointed at the Brick on the side table.

"That device, you told me, Lester, prohibits people from eavesdropping on conversations?"

"Yes, ma'am."

"And Fernando has one?"

Lester nodded.

"And you told me, Carlos, that Fernando is at the hacienda?"

"Yes, ma'am."

"Lester, would you bring that to me and show me again how to use it?"

"Yes, ma'am."

"Lester," Castillo said, "before the head of the family talks to him, you better get him on the horn and explain Net Two to him."

"Yes, sir."

Castillo looked at Doña Alicia. "And when you get Fernando on the Brick, then what?"

"I told you, I want a word with Señor Medina."

"About what?"

"I'm going to ask him to get in his car right now and go see Señor Torres . . ."

"Who is?"

"I told you before, an old and trusted friend who is commandant of the Policía Federal in Acapulco."

"Then he's probably in up to his ears with the Sinaloa drug cartel," Castillo said.

"I'll admit that possibility," she replied. "But we don't *know* that, Carlos. And he will believe me when I tell him that unless Colonel Ferris is released safely and immediately, there will be much trouble."

"You're going to threaten this guy?" Castillo asked incredulously.

"I'm going to explain the situation to him. It can't do any harm, Carlos. And if that doesn't work, I'll think of something else."

Castillo glanced at Svetlana and saw that she was once again smiling approvingly at his grandmother.

[Five]
The Situation Room
The White House
1600 Pennsylvania Avenue, N.W.
Washington, D.C.
1105 14 April 2007

Supervisory Secret Service Agent Robert J.

200

Mulligan, who in addition to being appointed chief of the Secret Service Presidential Protection Team now also seemed to be functioning as President Clendennen's personal assistant, had telephoned Vice President Charles W. Montvale, Secretary of State Natalie Cohen, Secretary of Defense Frederick K. Beiderman, Director of National Intelligence Truman Ellsworth, CIA Director A. Franklin Lammelle, Attorney General Stanley Crenshaw, and FBI Director Mark Schmidt summoning them all to a 10:45 A.M. meeting with the President in the Situation Room.

In each case he had insisted — politely but with a certain arrogance — on speaking personally with those being summoned rather than leave word of their summons with anyone else.

They all chose to arrive early, which caused a not-so-minor traffic jam in the White House driveways and in the area where the White House vehicles were parked. The Vice President, the secretary of State, and the secretary of Defense traveled in limousines, all of them preceded and trailed by GMC Yukons carrying their protection details. The others did not have limousines. Everyone but Director of National Intelligence Ellsworth — who rode in his personal car, a Jaguar Vanden Plas — traveled by Yukon, with each preceded and trailed by Yukons carrying their protection details.

By 10:40, all the dignitaries had arrived in the underground Situation Room. The President was not there, nor was the usual coffeemaker and trays of pastry.

Vice President Montvale told one of the Secret Service agents guarding the door to "see what's happened to the coffee," and the agent hurried from the door.

The coffee and pastry had not arrived when Special Agent Mulligan appeared at the door and announced, "The President of the United States."

Everyone rose as Joshua Ezekiel Clenden-nen entered the room and marched to the head of the table, trailed by Clemens Mc-Carthy, a crew-cut man who looked younger than his forty-two years, and who had been named presidential press secretary following the resignation of John David Parker.

Usually the President said, "Please take your seats" before sitting down. Today he unceremoniously sat down and said, "Well, let's get started. I've got a lot on my plate today."

After an awkward moment, the Vice President sat down and the others followed suit.

"Lammelle," Clendennen said, "I didn't find what I was looking for in my daily, quote unquote, intelligence briefing."

"I'm sorry, Mr. President. What were you looking for, sir?"

"The last developments in this mess in Mexico, Lammelle."

"There have been no developments in the last twenty-four hours, Mr. President," the director of National Intelligence replied.

"Specifically, I wanted to know if we have the bodies."

"Mr. President," Secretary of State Cohen put in, "I spoke with Ambassador McCann just before I left to come here. He told me he expects the remains to be released to us sometime today."

"And then what?" the President asked.

"Then we'll send a plane to return them to the United States," Cohen said.

"No," the President said as Clemens McCarthy stood and stepped toward him. "What we're going to do, Madam Secretary, is . . ."

He interrupted himself when McCarthy leaned over and whispered at length into his ear.

The President nodded, then went on: "McCarthy pointed out that we were about to miss a nice photo opportunity. So what you're going to do, Madam Secretary, is get on the phone to the ambassador and tell him to go to the airport — what's it called, Clemens?"

"General Juan N. Álvarez International Airport, Mr. President."

"Clemens always has details like that at his fingertips," the President said. "What you're going to do, Madam Secretary, is call the ambassador and tell him to get over to *General Juan N. Álvarez International Airport* right now. Tell him that a press plane will be coming there. Tell him to set up some sort of appropriate ceremony with the most senior Mexicans he can get together for the loading of the bodies onto the airplane . . ."

"Mr. President," Secretary of Defense Beiderman said, "in situations like this, the protocol is to have the bodies in body bags, on stretchers, with an American flag covering them. That's not a very nice picture."

"Jesus Christ!" the President said. "You tell the ambassador, Madam Secretary, to make sure that the bodies are in caskets, *nice* caskets . . ."

Clemens McCarthy whispered in the President's ear again. And again the President nodded.

"And tell him," the President ordered, "to take his Marine embassy guards with him, dressed in their dress uniforms, to carry the bodies, *in their caskets,* onto the airplane."

"You said a 'photo op,' Mr. President," Secretary Cohen said. "Do you want the ambassador to try to arrange for that?"

"I also said, Madam Secretary, if you were listening, that a press plane will be going down there. Clemens arranged it. On it will be crews from Wolf News and a couple of the unimportant ones. *And* Andy McClarren, who, as Clemens said he would, was unable to turn down a chance to have tear-filled eyes on display for his many millions of viewers."

"And does Mr. McCarthy have plans for the plane landing at San Antonio?" Secretary of Defense Beiderman asked.

"San Antonio?" the President asked.

"Yes, sir. All three men are from Texas. It is intended to bury Warrant Officer Salazar in the national cemetery there. Plans for the DEA agents have not been finalized."

"Mr. McCarthy had made all the necessary arrangements with the press for the landing of the plane at Andrews Air Force Base," the President said. "And for their interment at Arlington the day after tomorrow."

"Mr. President, I spoke with General Naylor about this. Mrs. Salazar wishes to have her husband buried in San Antonio."

"Well, call General Naylor and tell him I said for him to tell her that her husband is going to be buried in Arlington. All three are going to be buried in Arlington. And you're all going to be there. There will be a photo op. I will make remarks."

"Mr. President," Beiderman said, "I don't know what the families of the DEA agents wish with regard to their interment —"

"I just told you, Mr. Secretary, where they are going to be buried."

"— and I'm not sure that either of the DEA agents is eligible for interment at Arlington. I'm not even sure they're both veterans. And, as you know, sir, they're running out of space at Arlington."

Clendennen looked at Attorney General Crenshaw.

"Correct me if I'm wrong, Mr. Attorney General, but don't I, as Commander in Chief, have the authority to say who is eligible for interment at Arlington?"

"You have that authority, Mr. President," Crenshaw said.

"Subject closed," the President said.

He turned to the DCI.

"Lammelle, I asked you what seems like a long time ago about what new developments there are."

"Mr. President," Lammelle replied, "may I defer to the FBI?"

The President's face showed that he didn't like this answer, but he turned to FBI Director Mark Schmidt and asked, "Well?"

Schmidt handed him a large manila envelope. The President opened it, withdrew its contents, then asked, "What am I looking at?"

"Photocopies of a UPS Next Day envelope and its contents, which were delivered early this morning to General McNab at Fort Bragg."

"The address on here says 'Sergeant Terry O'Toole,' " the President said.

"*Major General Terrence* O'Toole is General McNab's deputy, sir," Schmidt said. "In the belief that another message would be sent to General McNab, possibly using an address that would not attract attention but would nevertheless reach General McNab — the first message from these people was addressed to *Lieutenant Colonel* McNab — the FBI instituted a nationwide surveillance of both FedEx and UPS overnight packages. We found that one last night in El Paso."

If Schmidt expected a compliment for the FBI's success, he was to be disappointed.

"The FBI found this last night?" the

President asked. "Then why am I getting it — why am I getting *copies* of it and not the original — now? Why wasn't I informed of this last night? Why didn't I have the whole damn thing a lot sooner than now?"

"Once we located the envelope, we notified General McNab and then put it back in the UPS delivery process."

"And then?"

"General McNab notified General Naylor of the package's arrival, and then turned it over to the FBI liaison officer at SPECOPS-COM. He notified FBI headquarters and we sent a plane to pick it up. As we speak, Mr. President, our forensic people at Quantico are examining it to see what can be learned. I ordered that a photocopy of everything be sent to me."

"What your people in El Paso should have done is sent it directly to you. The less General McNab has to do with this, the better."

"Sir, it was addressed to General McNab."

The President slammed the envelope on his desk. "No. It was addressed to Sergeant Terry O'Toole. And if you had done that, I would be looking at it a lot sooner than just now. And I'll tell you what I have learned from this, without the help of your forensic experts: These people want to swap Colonel

Ferris for" — he paused and dropped his eyes to the message — "for Félix Abrego. Who the hell is he?"

"He's a Mexican national, Mr. President," FBI Director Schmidt said, "serving a sentence of life without the possibility of parole at Florence ADMAX in Colorado."

"What did he do?"

"DEA agents intercepted a movement of drugs near El Paso — in the United States, near El Paso — during which this fellow shot and killed three agents. The DEA believes he is one of the leaders of one of the major drug cartels."

"I would suggest it's a moot point, Mr. President," Attorney General Crenshaw said.

"What?"

"The United States has a long-standing policy of not negotiating in situations like this, Mr. President."

"Policies change, Mr. Attorney General. Lammelle, has the CIA got anything to add?"

"Sir, both the DEA people in Acapulco and my man there feel there is something odd about the murders and kidnapping. The relationship between the DEA and the Sinaloa drug cartel, which controls that area, is — for lack of a better word — amicable.

Their compliance with the orders of the ambassador to cooperate with the Mexican authorities has meant that the cartel almost certainly has not felt threatened by the DEA in the area, or by the Special Forces. There is no reason for them to draw attention to themselves by doing something like this."

"Except, of course, that they want this fellow Abrego back."

"Mr. President, they could have kidnapped Colonel Ferris in Mexico City."

"Get to your point, Lammelle," the President said impatiently.

"Raw intelligence data, Mr. President, as I'm sure you know, is intelligence that has not been analyzed as to the source, and the reliability of that source. In short, it's unreliable."

"You do have a point, right?" the President asked.

"This does *not* mean that raw intelligence data is not accurate, Mr. President, just that we can't determine whether it is or not."

"Why do I suspect, Lammelle, that you're going to tell me that you have some raw intelligence data, the accuracy of which you can't determine?"

"My raw data suggests the possibility, Mr. President, that Putin — the Russians — are behind what happened in Acapulco."

"What possible interest could Putin have in Whatsisname . . . Félix Abrego?"

"My raw data suggests his interest is in Colonel Dmitri Berezovsky, Lieutenant Colonel Svetlana Alekseeva, and Lieutenant Colonel Castillo."

"Ah-ha! Well, I can understand that. Nobody likes traitors."

"Mr. President, I must object to your characterization of Colonel Castillo as a traitor," Secretary Natalie Cohen said.

"That's right," the President said with a thin smile. "He's a hero, isn't he? A well-paid hero. The Vice President and Mr. Lammelle didn't waste very much time before handing him a check for a hundred twenty-five million of taxpayers' dollars, did they?"

"Mr. President," Vice President Montvale said, "that reward for the delivery of a Tupelov was authorized by both your predecessor and by Senator Johns of the Senate Select Committee on Intelligence."

The President ignored him.

"In your opinion, Mr. Ellsworth," the President said, "presuming that Mr. Lammelle's raw and unconfirmed intelligence that Mr. Putin's wholly understandable interest in getting his hands on his two traitors is true, how is that going to affect our efforts to get Colonel Ferris back?"

"I have no idea," Ellsworth replied. "It seems to me that we're going to have to wait until we see what the Mexicans come up with. The ball, so to speak, is in their court."

"No, the ball is in our court," the President said. "They want to talk. So we'll talk."

"Mr. President," Attorney General Crenshaw said, "you're not thinking of entering into negotiations involving exchanging this fellow Abrego, are you?"

"Of course not," the President said. "I wouldn't think of violating long-standing policy. But one thought I've had running through my mind since I — finally — got a look at their message is that this fellow is a convicted murderer, not a terrorist. And I seem to recall that our policy speaks of not negotiating with terrorists. Correct me if I'm wrong."

The attorney general thought for a split second, then said, "I believe you're correct, Mr. President, but —"

"I also believe that it is within my power to show compassion. For example, if Señor Abrego were discovered to have developed a terminal illness, who could fault me for returning him to his native Mexico to live out what little remains of his life? He would then become the Mexicans' problem. And if that somehow resulted in Colonel Ferris's being released . . ."

Crenshaw glanced out the windows as he composed his reply.

"Well?" the President said.

"If you did that, Mr. President, it would have the same effect. We have fifty people like Abrego in our prisons. Once these drug cartels get the message that all they have to do to get any of them released is to kidnap —"

"We will deal with that when and if it comes up," the President said. "You don't object to this to the point where you're considering offering your resignation, are you, Mr. Attorney General?"

Crenshaw's face tightened. It was a long moment before he replied, "Not at this time, Mr. President."

"Good. It's nice to see I have at least one loyal member of my Cabinet. I think the FBI would be the best agency to establish contact with these people, whoever they are. Do you agree?"

"Yes, Mr. President."

"Now, since Mr. Lammelle has brought up the possibility that this has something to do with these Russian traitors, it might be useful to know where they are. Anyone know? There are Interpol warrants out for them, I believe. In addition to being traitors, they're accused of stealing large amounts of money from their government."

"Those Interpol warrants have been withdrawn, Mr. President," FBI Director Schmidt said. "I believe it was part of the armistice agreement Colonel Castillo made with Putin. The Russian embassy sent me a document stating that not only had a full investigation of those charges against Colonel Berezovsky and Lieutenant Colonel Alekseeva cleared them entirely, but also they had been granted permission to leave Russia, and were 'no longer persons of any interest to the Russian Federation.' "

" 'The armistice agreement Colonel Castillo made with Putin'?" the President parroted. "I thought it was illegal for an American citizen to do something like that. Could he be prosecuted for doing so?"

Vice President Montvale said, "The, quote unquote, armistice was between Castillo and Putin, Mr. President, not between the respective governments. I don't think it was even committed to paper."

"It sounds as if my Vice President approves of this 'armistice.' "

"I do," Montvale said simply.

"As do I, Mr. President," Natalie Cohen said.

"It would appear to some people that

Colonel Castillo may be angling for your job, Madam Secretary. How do you feel about that?"

"I feel that's preposterous, Mr. President."

"Speaking of the colonel and the traitors, where are they?" the President asked. When no one immediately replied, he went on, "There has been no contact with him?"

"No official contact, Mr. President," Lammelle said. "But Colonel Castillo and I are friends."

"You don't say?"

"He was recently in Cozumel, Mexico. I don't know if he's still there."

"What was he doing there? Were the traitors with him?"

"I don't know about the Russians," Lammelle said, "but he mentioned that Mr. Parker was there. And Roscoe Danton."

The President, whose face showed he didn't like that, looked as if he was going to say something, but changed his mind, and then said, "Birds of a feather, they say, flock together."

No one replied.

"Well, let me spell things out. I intend, with the cooperation of the Mexican government, to see that Colonel Ferris is released. I will do whatever I think is necessary to accomplish that, and I will not tolerate any interference from anyone, and I don't want any assistance from Castillo or his Merry Band of Outlaws.

"Furthermore, Secretary Beiderman, I want you to personally inform General Naylor that he is not even to contemplate any military action of any kind whatsoever with regard to Colonel Ferris. And tell him I personally told you to make sure General McNab is aware of this order."

"Yes, Mr. President," Beiderman said.

"That's it. I'll see you all at the interment in Arlington. McCarthy will furnish the details, just as soon as he's set them up."

He suddenly stood and, with McCarthy and Mulligan following him, marched out of the Situation Room.

The Vice President turned to the attorney general.

"Don't look so unhappy, Stan," Montvale said. "He gave you the option of resigning."

The attorney general looked at the Vice President for a moment and then gave him the finger.

"He does tend to bring out the worst in people, doesn't he?" Secretary of State Cohen said to no one in particular.

V

[One]
The Mayflower Hotel
1127 Connecticut Avenue, N.W.
Washington, D.C.
1005 15 April 2007

Mr. and Mrs. J. Herbert Kramer and Mr. and Mrs. Robert V. Dabney came out of what Herb Kramer described as "the restaurant or coffee shop or whateverthehell it is off the lobby" and took seats on two couches in the lobby, from which they had a good view of both the entrance and the bank of elevators.

Herb Kramer was pleased with his breakfast of corned beef hash topped with poached eggs.

"Most of the time you get corned beef, it's hash fresh from a can," Herb observed. "That was homemade, from real corned beef." Then he observed, "But they didn't give it away, did they?"

"What the hell, it's deductible," Bob Dabney said. "Live it up!"

Herb and Bob were in Washington to attend the annual convention of the National Association of Wholesale Hardware Dealers. Both were in that business in Missouri,

Herb in St. Louis and Bob in Kansas City. They had been pals since their days at the University of Missouri, where Bob married Kate the day after they graduated. Herb had married his Delores some years later.

They were staying at the Mayflower because of Delores. Someone had told her that the best place in Washington to see the big shots was in the lobby of the Mayflower, and Delores generally got what she wanted. She was far more interested in seeing the big shots up close than she was in seeing a bunch of old airplanes at the National Aerospace Museum, which was high on Herb and Bob's agenda for their free time while in the nation's capital.

They didn't have to wait long to learn that what Delores had been told was true.

"Look!" Delores whispered loudly as a group of ten men came down the lobby to the elevator bank. "There's Whatsisname!"

"Who?" Herb asked in a normal voice.

"The guy we see on Wolf News all the time," Delores said impatiently.

"Roger Danton," Kate furnished.

"*Roscoe* Danton," Bob corrected her. "And there's the President's press secretary."

"Ex–press secretary," Herb said. "He got canned last week."

"That's right, isn't it? What did he do?"

Bob shrugged. "Or didn't do. It sounded like incompetence."

"Well, I will be damned," Herb said. "That was them, sure as Christ made little apples."

"I wonder who the other ones are," Delores said as the men disappeared into an elevator.

Bob and Herb shrugged.

"I wonder what they're doing here?" Delores went on.

"They probably came to see Monica Lewinsky," Herb said with a straight face.

"That's right!" Delores said. "This is that place, isn't it?"

"That's how they get away with charging so much for the rooms," Herb said.

What happened next, three minutes later, was even more exciting.

Four large and muscular men strode purposefully into the lobby, looked around suspiciously — including at Herb, Bob, Kate, and Delores — and then took up positions along the corridor. One of them stood in the door of an elevator so that the door would remain open.

Then another five men entered the lobby from the street and headed for the elevators, two in front of and two behind the Vice

President of the United States. They all got in the open elevator.

"I will be damned," Herb said. "Vice President Montvale."

"He probably wants to see ol' Monica, too," Bob said, grinning at his own joke.

"Will you stop that?" Delores said. "That's the *Vice President.*"

And the parade of bigwigs was not over.

Four people — two of them women — strode purposefully into the lobby and did just about what the members of the Vice President's protection detail had done.

After looking carefully at Delores, Kate, Bob, and Herb, the men and one of the women took up positions in the lobby, beside the protection detail men already there. The second woman stood in an elevator door and kept it from closing.

Next, five people marched into the lobby, two men and two women surrounding a third, much smaller woman. They marched to the elevator and got on.

"My God, that was the secretary of State!" Kate said. "What's her name?"

"Something Cohen," Bob furnished, and then added, "Natalie Cohen. That's her name, *Natalie* Cohen."

"I'd really love to know what's going on up there," Delores said.

[Two]
Suite 1002
The Mayflower Hotel
1127 Connecticut Avenue, N.W.
Washington, D.C.
1010 15 April 2007

Suite 1002 — which consisted of a sitting room, two bedrooms, and a small kitchen — was registered to Herr Karl Wilhelm von und zu Gossinger, the Washington correspondent of the *Tages Zeitung* newspaper chain, and billed on a monthly basis to Gossinger Beteiligungsgesellschaft, G.m.b.H., of Fulda, Germany, which owned the *Tages Zeitung* chain and a good deal more.

When Herr Gossinger — who was also known as Carlos Guillermo Castillo, Lieutenant Colonel, Special Forces, U.S. Army, Retired — had called the general manager of the Mayflower the day before to announce that he not only would be checking in later that day but would require in-room late-afternoon cocktails with finger food for probably fifteen or twenty people, and possibly in-room dinner for that many people later, the GM had told Herr von und zu Gossinger not to worry, that he personally would take care of everything.

When Castillo, Lester Bradley, and Major Dick Miller arrived at about 1700, they found that the general manager — who appreciated guests who not only did not question prices but also paid promptly — had obligingly made the suite adjacent to 1002 available. The suites were identical. Hotel staff had opened the double door between the two suites and converted the sitting room of 1004 into a dining room with bar.

When the door chimes bonged, Castillo pulled the door open.

A large, middle-aged Irishman stood there.

"You're welcome here, Tom, even if I suspect you're here officially," Castillo greeted him. "Come on in. You want some coffee?"

"The Vice President's sixty seconds behind me, Charley," Supervisory Secret Service Special Agent Thomas McGuire, chief of the Vice Presidential Protection Detail, said.

"Why do I suspect I'm not going to like what he wants to tell me?" Castillo asked.

McGuire did not reply directly, instead saying: "When we heard you were in Washington, we went to the house in Alexandria. They told us you were here."

"Did you ask personally, Tom? Or in your

official capacity?"

McGuire looked uncomfortable.

"Charley, I work for him," he said.

"Yeah, I heard."

The chime bonged again.

Castillo gestured for McGuire to open the door, and he did so.

The Vice President of the United States walked into the room and looked around. He saw Roscoe J. Danton, John David Parker, Lester Bradley, Colonel Jake Torine, Major Richard Miller, and CWO5 Colin Leverette, all of whom he knew, and in the sitting room and dining room maybe ten more men he didn't know. No one was wearing a uniform, but Montvale correctly intuited they were all soldiers.

What the hell did Castillo do, Montvale thought, *bring half of Gray Fox up here?*

"Now that I think of it, Mr. Vice President," Castillo said, "I do seem to recall telling you that if you were in the neighborhood anytime, you should feel free to drop in. So welcome, welcome!"

"What the hell is going on here, Castillo?"

"Actually, we're getting ready to go to the interment of a friend. You may have heard . . ."

"What I would like to know is how you heard. Did that goddamn McNab tell you?"

"I have not had any contact with General McNab — to whom I presume you refer — for some time, now. You can ask him yourself; I presume he'll be at Arlington."

"Then how the hell —"

The chime bonged again.

"I wonder who else might be calling?" Castillo said. "Mr. McGuire, if you'd be so kind?"

McGuire opened the door. The secretary of State stood there.

"May I come in?" Natalie Cohen asked.

"Yes, ma'am. It's always a pleasure to see you," Castillo said.

She took a quick look around the room and smiled at the few people she knew.

"Let me get right to the point, Charley," she said. "You're not thinking of going out to Arlington, are you?"

"I'm going," Castillo said, and gestured around the suite. "We're all going."

"That wouldn't be a wise thing to do, Charley," she said. "Have you considered that?"

"Are you and Vice President Montvale here to try to talk me out of going to my friend Mr. Salazar's interment?"

"Is there somewhere we can speak privately, Charley?" she asked.

He indicated the door to what turned out

to be, when she and Montvale and Castillo walked through it, the master bedroom.

She closed the door, then turned to the men and said, "What is said in here goes no further. Agreed?"

Both men nodded.

"I understand you're aware, Charley, of the meeting in which it became apparent that the President thinks we have been engaged in a coup d'état that would see Charles in the Oval Office?"

Castillo nodded.

"The fact that that's absolutely untrue is really irrelevant; that's what the President believes, and it's what we have to deal with. Understood?"

Castillo nodded again.

"There was another meeting, yesterday, in the Situation Room that" — she glanced at Montvale — "with the Vice President's permission, I'd like to tell you about. All right, Charles?"

Montvale hesitated a moment and then nodded.

The secretary picked up on the hesitation, and said, "Would you prefer to tell him about it?"

"You tell him," Montvale said. "I don't think he trusts me."

"True," Castillo said.

"Well, you'd better learn to trust him, Charley," Cohen said. "If we don't stick together, the President is going to take us down one by one. He's already gotten rid of John David Parker. And what is Parker doing here?"

"As of a few minutes ago, he's director of public relations of the LCBF Corporation," Castillo said.

"What the hell is that all about?" Montvale asked.

"Keeping our names out of the newspapers and our faces off Wolf News. You were about to tell me about the meeting, Madam Secretary."

"Tell me if I leave anything out, would you, please, Charles?"

She then began to deliver a report of who had said what to whom, which ultimately lasted ten minutes.

About a minute into it, Castillo realized it was almost a verbatim report of the meeting, and moments after that, *"Almost"?*

Hell, it's not only verbatim, but with footnotes!

She's got a photographic memory!

No, that's not right. What she has is total recall. If I asked her, she could probably tell me what kind of a tie Clendennen was wearing.

Finally, she finished and looked at Montvale.

"Did I leave anything out?" she asked.

"What kind of a tie was the President wearing?" Castillo asked.

Secretary Cohen hesitated just a moment, looked confused, and then replied, "Dark blue, with what looked like crests on it. What's that got to do with anything?"

"I'm awed, ma'am, with your powers of total recall," Castillo said.

"Don't be, Charley. I was born this way." She paused. "It's the same sort of thing you have with languages. An aberration. You speak what — fourteen? — languages. And I can recall things in great detail. It's a gift, so it's nothing to be proud of. But it does give us a leg up in our professions, doesn't it?"

"Yes, ma'am, I've found that."

"Do you understand now why I think it would be unwise for you to go to Arlington? He'd see you. He hates you — he thinks you're involved in this coup d'état fantasy of his, among other things, such as you wanting my job — and seeing you there would likely set him off. The one thing none of us should do now is do anything to make him lose control."

"I want to be secretary of State?" Castillo said.

Secretary of State Cohen made a face, then nodded gently.

"Unbelievable. But what's not unbelievable is that I'm going to Mr. Salazar's interment. Everybody out there is going to it. I'm sorry if that causes any problems, ma'am."

"For Christ's sake, Castillo, didn't you hear what she said?" Vice President Montvale snapped.

"I'm sure you have your reasons," Secretary Cohen said.

"To hell with his reasons," Montvale exploded. "He's not going out there! I'll have the Secret Service confine him and the rest of them in the suite until the interment's over."

"If you do that, Mr. Vice President," Castillo said calmly, "it will be on Wolf News and on the front page of the *Times-Post.* You did see Roscoe Danton out there, didn't you?"

"Don't you threaten me, you arrogant sonofabitch! I'm the Vice President of the United States."

"Get your temper under control, Charles," Natalie Cohen said calmly. "Charley, why is this so important to you?"

"Yesterday, Mrs. Salazar telephoned me
—"

"How the hell did she know where to find
you?" Montvale demanded.

Castillo ignored Montvale.

"If I may continue, Madam Secretary?"
he asked.

"Please."

"I'll answer Mr. Montvale's question for
your background, ma'am. Special Operations, Special Forces generally, and especially Delta Force and Gray Fox — and just
about everybody outside who is or has been
one or the other or both — is like a family.
We take care of each other; we know how to
find each other when there is a problem."

"And Mrs. Salazar had a problem?" Secretary Cohen asked. "She didn't want her
husband interred in Arlington?"

Castillo nodded.

"She told me that General Naylor had
telephoned her — and now I know where
that order came from — and fed her a line
about the great honor it was for Danny to
be interred in Arlington, with the President
himself attending.

"When she told him thank you but no,
thank you — that she wanted Danny buried
in San Antonio, where she could visit and
tend his grave — Naylor told her that the

arrangements had been made, that they were sending a plane to Bragg to pick up her and the kids, and that the President would be embarrassed if she refused his kind offer to plant Danny in Arlington. So she went along.

"But after she thought it over, she went to see General McNab. General McNab told her — out of school; he's part of the family I mentioned — that he had been ordered by General Naylor not to talk to her about it, and also, incidentally, that he had been ordered to stay away from Arlington himself."

"And then that sonofabitch told her to call you, right?" Montvale said.

"No, he didn't," Castillo said evenly. "And that was the last question you get to ask, Mr. Montvale. If you open your mouth again, I'm going to have to ask you to leave."

"You can't do that!" Montvale flared.

"It's his apartment, Charles," Secretary Cohen said. "He has the right to ask you to leave."

"And if you're thinking about your Secret Service guys," Castillo added, "a scrap between them and the guys outside would be very interesting. It would also make a hell of a story for Wolf News: 'Vice President's Protection Detail Gets Their Ass

Kicked in Lobby of Mayflower.' "

Cohen said: "All right, Charley. Enough. So what happened when Mrs. Salazar called you?"

"Well, my first reaction to what she told me was to call my beloved Uncle Allan and tell him to butt the hell out of something that was none of his business. But then calm reason prevailed . . ."

The Vice President snorted.

". . . I realized that as much as I would love to embarrass the sonofabitch . . ."

"You're speaking of the President, Charley," Cohen said.

". . . who tried to turn me over to the SVR."

He met her eyes for a long moment, and then went on: "I realized there would be unacceptable collateral damage to Maria Salazar and their kids. They didn't need microphones being shoved in their faces, which would have happened if I told her she didn't have to go along with the . . . *the President's* using Danny's funeral to get himself reelected. So I told her it was indeed an honor to be buried in Arlington, as it's for national heroes. And I told her I'd see her at the interment.

"As I was telling her this, I remembered it's also an honor to be buried in the national cemetery in San Antone. My father's buried there. And then I wondered if anyone had thought to invite Colonel Ferris's wife to the interment. I knew she would want to be there.

"So I called her, and she hadn't been invited.

"So I spent the next hour or so on the telephone, setting things up. Jake Torine and Dick Miller, who are almost as pissed about this as I am, have been flying around the country picking up people who want — and have every right — to watch Danny get his military funeral. The guys — and several women — are scattered between here and the Willard.

"Mrs. Ferris and their kids are also in the Willard, about to get in the limousine that will take them out to Arlington. After the interment, they'll come here. We're going to have a few drinks, and then, later, dinner.

"So, Madam Secretary, as much as I really hate to tell you no to anything you ask of me, I'm going to be at Arlington when Danny's buried."

"I'll have you stopped at the gate to Arlington," Montvale said.

"Shut up, Charles," Secretary Cohen said. She looked thoughtful for a moment, then said, "I think it's possible that Mr. McCarthy may have considered the possibility that there are some people the President would rather not come to Arlington . . ."

"That would be another great story for Wolf News and *The Washington Times-Post*," Castillo said. " 'Brawl Mars Funeral at Gate to Arlington.' Some enterprising journalist might even dig into what it was all about."

"How are you going to move your friends out there?" she asked.

"We have four stretch limousines," Castillo replied. "In case some other friends of Danny show up out there and need a ride back here."

"And you're paying for all this?" she asked. "Sorry, I shouldn't have asked that."

"The LCBF Corporation is paying for everything. We just turned a tidy profit selling an airplane we got for a bargain to the CIA for a lot of money."

She smiled at him.

"May I ask you a question I probably shouldn't ask?" Castillo asked.

She nodded.

"What ever happened to that Mexican police Black Hawk that was 'found at sea' and then unloaded on the dock at Norfolk? Dare I hope you showed it to the Mexican ambassador and asked him how he thought it got there?"

She shook her head.

"You know I couldn't do anything like that, Charley," she said.

"So what happened to it?"

"That's not any of your business, and you know it."

"But you're going to tell me anyway, right? Is it still there?"

"Frank Lammelle wanted it for the CIA. I okayed it, but I don't know whether he's done anything about it. It's probably still covered up on the dock or in a hangar somewhere." She paused, then asked, "Charley, did you ever consider the consequences if you had been caught stealing that helicopter from the Mexican police?"

"I didn't steal it. Didn't Frank tell you?"

"Tell me what?"

"That the Mexicans reported that the helicopter had crashed — total loss — in their unrelenting war against the drug trade?"

"No," she said simply. "Then . . . how was it 'found at sea'?"

"You mean how did I get it?"

She nodded.

"I *bought* it from an officer of the Policía Federal. I think he thought I was in the drug trade and was going to use it to move drugs

234

around." He paused. "That's the question I hoped you were going to ask the Mexican ambassador. 'I thought you told us this helicopter had been totally destroyed. How do you explain its miraculous resurrection?' "

"I didn't know anything about how you acquired that helicopter," she said. "But even if I had — what I am doing is trying to build better relations with Mexico — I wouldn't have confronted him with something like that." She thought for a moment, then said, "Why in the world did you buy it?"

"I needed it to go after the Congo-X and the Tupelov," Castillo said matter-of-factly.

"I thought you used Special Operations helicopters for that," Montvale said.

Castillo gave him a dirty look, then saw on Cohen's face that she was worried he was going to throw Montvale out. He decided that would be nonproductive.

"I did. But Jake Torine and I flew the Mexican bird onto the island."

"You and Torine? Why?" Cohen asked.

"Because on an assault like that, the lead bird generally takes fire. My original idea, presuming that happened, was just to leave it on the island, which would then have had Hugo Chavez angrily asking the Mexicans

how come one of their Policía Federal chop-
pers was on his island."

"Devious," Montvale said admiringly.

"But then the Night Stalkers suppressed
the antiaircraft, and the Mexican bird didn't
get hurt, so I decided to fly it back out to
the *Bataan,* and told her captain to take it
to Norfolk."

"Where I would ask the Mexican ambassador to the U.S., 'I thought you reported
this aircraft was totally destroyed'?" Cohen
asked.

Castillo looked at her, smiled, and nodded.

"You're right, Charles, he is devious.
Maybe he should have been a diplomat, or
a politician."

"Devious and dangerous," Montvale said,
smiling.

What happened? Castillo thought. *Have
we kissed and made up?*

*No. That smile is the smile of mutual admira-
tion one shark gives to another.*

"Turning to the problem at hand," Secretary Cohen said, "which is that Charley cannot be dissuaded from going out to Arlington with all his friends, how do we deal with
that?"

"Where are those limousines you mentioned, Charley?" Montvale asked.

"In the hotel garage, waiting for me to call them. Which I am going to do in the next sixty seconds or so."

"I think you're right, Natalie," Montvale said. "McCarthy — and/or Mulligan — probably has people at the gate of Arlington to keep out people who might embarrass the President. But I think they'll just wave our convoy through."

"So we put Charley's limousines in our convoy?" she asked. "That makes sense."

Montvale walked to the bedroom door. He opened it and then looked around until he found Tom McGuire.

"Tom, may I see you for a moment?"

After the secretary of State had disappeared into the lobby elevator, nothing much happened in the next ten minutes.

Herb Kramer announced he was going to stretch his legs.

"I'll go with you," Bob Dabney said.

"Stay out of the bar," Delores said. "You don't want to go to the Ways and Means Committee smelling of alcohol."

"I'm going to go outside and have a puff on a cigarette," Herb said. "You can't smoke in here."

He pointed to a NO SMOKING sign to make his point, and then he and Bob walked down the lobby toward Connecticut Avenue.

They had just about reached the revolving door when two things happened almost at once. A burly man in a business suit stepped in front of the door to keep them from using it, and another burly man came out of one of the elevators and quickly walked down the lobby toward Connecticut Avenue.

He looked as if he were talking to his lapel.

"I'm going down there," Delores said to Kate. "Something's going on!"

The burly man who had been talking to his lapel went through the revolving door, but when Delores and Kate approached it, the burly man who had kept Herb and Bob from going outside stepped into their path.

He flashed some sort of credentials in their face. "United States Secret Service. Would you ladies please stand over there for just a minute?"

He pointed to where Herb and Bob were standing, looking through a window beside the revolving door onto the sidewalk. Kate and Delores moved beside them. After a moment, Kate tapped Herb on the shoulder, and he politely let her move in front of him so that she could get a better look.

There was a taxi stand on Connecticut

Avenue with four cabs lined up in it. A uniformed policeman gestured impatiently for them to move. When they had done so, a Yukon with red and blue lights flashing behind its grille pulled up, not into the space just vacated, but into the lane — the street — just outside it.

Then another Yukon with flashing lights pulled into what had been the taxi lane, followed by two limousines, which also had flashing red and blue lights behind their grilles.

What had been the taxi lane was now filled.

Next came another limousine, this one a stretch limousine without flashing lights. It pulled into the space reserved for vehicles discharging or picking up passengers.

A burly man spoke into his lapel, and then opened the rear door of the limousine. A moment later, a line of men came through the revolving door and quickly entered the limousine.

"There's ten of them," Delores announced. "I counted them."

"I wonder who they are," Bob mused aloud.

The burly man closed the door and the stretch limousine pulled away from the curb.

What happened next occurred so quickly

that no one but Delores could keep up with it. Limousines and Yukons kept pulling up to the curb, and then backing out of it — or going forward onto Connecticut Avenue and *then* backing up as passengers — some of them women and some of them carrying submachine guns — got into the various vehicles, and then sometimes out of them.

"You know what that looks like, Herb?" Bob said. "That automated package-distribution machine FedEx showed us in Kansas City. Except this is for people."

"You know, Bob, it does," Herb said thoughtfully.

He then gestured with his hands, miming FedEx's automated system, which had apparently impressed him with its ability to move a lot of things in different directions at the same time.

The Vice President came through one of the revolving doors and was hustled into one of the limousines with the flashing lights, and then the secretary of State came through the revolving door and was hustled into hers.

There was a wail of sirens and then it was suddenly all over. All the vehicles were gone, and so were all the Secret Service people.

"I will be damned," Herb said. "That was something!"

240

"And you didn't want to stay here," Delores said. "You said it was too expensive."

[Three]
The President's Study
The White House
1600 Pennsylvania Avenue, N.W.
Washington, D.C.
1430 15 April 2007

"When the Vice President's car reached where we were standing, Mr. President, just outside the main gate," Secret Service Special Agent Mark Douglas reported, "it stopped and the rear window went down. Vice President Montvale said, 'The four limousines are with me.' So I let them pass."

"Did you see who was in them?" President Clendennen asked.

"Yes, Mr. President. To double-check, so to speak, I stopped each one and opened the door and had a look."

"And?" the President asked impatiently.

"There were eight men, mostly Caucasian — mostly Latinos, I judged — and some Afro-Americans, in each of the first two limousines. The third one had Mr. Danton — the reporter from *The Washington Times-Post* — and Mr. Parker in it. Just them. The

241

last limo was empty."

"And then what happened?"

"The convoy moved directly to the grave site, to the road near it. And everybody got out."

"And?"

"The Vice President and the secretary of State got out and walked to where you and the other dignitaries were standing — where you were waiting for the whatchamacallit, the *caisson* with the casket, to come down the road."

"And the people in the limousines?"

"Mr. Danton followed the Vice President and Secretary Cohen."

"And Mr. Parker?" the President asked softly.

"I didn't see him there anymore. I guess he didn't get out of the limousine. I did see him later —"

"Get to later, later," the President interrupted him. "What about the people in the limousines?"

"Yes, sir, Mr. President. Well, they got out of the limos and arranged themselves in a line where they could watch what was going to happen at the grave. While they were doing that, a woman with a couple of kids walked up to them. They all knew her, and gathered around her."

"And did you learn who this woman was?"

"Yes, sir. When I told Supervisory Agent Mulligan about the limousines, he told me to find out who they were, I went there, and asked, and they said they were . . ."

He interrupted himself to consult a notebook.

". . . from the American Legion. From China Post Number One of the American Legion. The guy who told me that showed me his American Legion card."

"And did you have a chance to . . . *overhear* . . . any of their conversations?"

"No, sir. I mean, I stuck around to do that, but they weren't speaking English. Chinese, probably, I guess. But they called the woman 'Mrs. Ferris' and I put that together. She's the wife of the officer who was kidnapped in Mexico when the guy they buried got shot."

"They all spoke Chinese?"

"I'm not sure if it was Chinese, Mr. President. But it certainly wasn't English. A couple of them started speaking Spanish . . . Supervisory Agent Mulligan's orders to me were to stick around, find out where they went . . . but one of them — a guy they called 'Colonel' — pointed to me and they stopped speaking that and went back to Chinese or whatever it was."

"And when the interment was over, what happened?"

"As soon as you gave Mrs. Salazar the flag, they got in the limousines and left. Mrs. Ferris and the kids went with them."

"They didn't stay for my remarks?"

"No, sir. They got in the limousines and left. Like Supervisory Agent Mulligan told me to do, I got in one of our Yukons and followed them."

"Where did they go?"

"To the Mayflower Hotel, sir. That was where I saw Mr. Parker again. He and Mr. Danton were with them."

"And did you follow them into the hotel?"

"Yes, sir, Mr. President. They went to the tenth floor. After a while — I didn't want them to know I was following them — I went up there. They were in room — I guess suite — 1002. When a couple of waiters started rolling in carts of food, I got a look in. It was them, all right."

"Did you manage to learn who was registered in suite 1002?"

"Yes, sir, Mr. President, I got that from the waiters."

Special Agent Douglas consulted his notebook again.

"Suite 1002 is registered to a German guy. His name is Karl von und zu Gossinger.

The waiters told me he lives there. I mean, he keeps the suite all the time."

"Anything else?"

"Like Supervisory Agent Mulligan told me to, I got him on the radio, and he said to come here. That you wanted to talk to me."

"And I did indeed. You did very well, Agent . . . what did you say your name was?"

"Douglas, Mr. President. Special Agent Mark Douglas."

"Special Agent *Douglas,* would you wait outside for a moment? I may have a few more questions."

"Yes, sir, Mr. President."

Supervisory Special Agent Mulligan followed Douglas to the door and closed it after Douglas had gone through it.

"Special Agent Douglas is not a nuclear physicist, is he?" the President said. "How the hell did he get in the Secret Service?"

"He was a New Jersey state trooper, Mr. President," Mulligan said. "He's not too swift, I admit. But he's reliable."

"I was thinking he might be useful, now that we know what I suspected was going on is going on. And they don't seem to care that I know, do they? Montvale himself, that sonofabitch, and Cohen — I'm a gentleman and I won't say out loud what I think of her

— actually *took* those Special Forces people to Arlington."

He paused and shook his head as if in disbelief, and then went on: "Where they walked out before I made my remarks. An insult, and they damn well knew it. Goddamn! And they had Colonel Castillo with them. That was him, right?"

"Yes, sir, that was Castillo. And Colonel Torine was there, too."

"Mulligan," Clemens McCarthy asked, "who is this German man? What's his involvement in this?"

"His real name is Castillo, Clemens," the President answered for him. "Or maybe his real name is Goldfinger, or whatever Mulligan's rocket scientist said. As to his involvement in what's going on, he's up to his ears in it. He probably thinks President Montvale will make him director of National Intelligence. Or secretary of Defense.

"But back to my original thought. Do you agree, Mulligan, that your man, who looks to me like he has a strong back, takes orders, and can keep his mouth shut, would be useful to us?"

"Yes, I do, Mr. President."

"Well, then, get him back in here. And see if Schmidt is out there."

"Director Schmidt is out there, Mr. President," Mulligan replied. "I saw him just now. You want him to come in?"

"When I'm through with Dumbo," the President said.

"Yes, Mr. President?" Special Agent Douglas said.

"Your first name is Mark, right?"

"Yes, sir."

"Would you mind if I called you that?"

"I'd be honored, Mr. President, sir."

"Well, Mark, Supervisory Special Agent Mulligan tells me that he's had his eye on you for some time, and Mr. McCarthy agrees with me that you did a fine job today, showing high intelligence, discretion, and perseverance."

Special Agent Douglas's face colored.

"And we need someone with those characteristics around here, right around me," Clendennen said. "The first thing I require of people in my intimate circle, Mark, is loyalty. Or, phrased another way, I absolutely cannot stand disloyalty. You can have the other things I mentioned, but if loyalty is not your strong point . . ."

"I can understand that, Mr. President," Douglas said.

"Supervisory Special Agent Mulligan tells me he thinks you have that loyalty, understand the need for it. So I'm going to take a chance on you."

"Yes, sir?"

"From this moment, Mark, you are relieved of all your normal duties. You will be reporting directly to Supervisory Special Agent Mulligan, who will explain to you what your duties will be. Now — and this is important, Mark — for a number of reasons we want to keep your special assignment from becoming public knowledge. I'm sure you can understand that."

"Yes, sir, Mr. President."

Clendennen rose and offered Douglas his hand.

"Welcome aboard, Mark. We all expect great things from you."

"I will try my best, Mr. President. Thank you, Mr. President."

"Okay, Mark. You can wait for Mr. Mulligan in the outer office. And while you're out there, you can tell Mr. Schmidt he can come in."

"Good afternoon, Mr. President," FBI Director Mark Schmidt said.

"Did you see those people standing with Colonel Castillo at Arlington?" the President asked without any preliminaries.

"The ones who looked like they just might

248

be Special Forces, maybe even Delta or Gray Fox?" Schmidt replied smiling. "Yes, I did, Mr. President."

"And did you see them insult their Commander in Chief by getting in their limousines and driving off before I had finished — hell, before I had started to make my remarks?"

"No, sir, I'm afraid I didn't."

"Tell him, Clemens," the President said.

"They got into their limousines and left before the President had a chance to even begin his remarks," the press secretary said.

"Mr. President, I just don't think it was an intentional insult. I can't believe they'd knowingly, much less purposefully . . ."

"There's a good deal going on here, Mr. Director, that you'd have trouble believing if I told you. They went from the cemetery to the Mayflower, where a couple of minutes ago, they were in suite . . . what did Dumbo say the room number was, Mulligan?"

"Ten-oh-two, Mr. President."

"What I want you to do, Mr. Director, is get a team of your people over there, right now, with cameras. Movie cameras would be better, but if that can't be arranged on such short notice, the regular kind will have to do. Try not to be seen of course. I want a picture of every last one of those sonsofbitches. I want each picture to show when and where it was taken in such form that will stand up in court. And of course I want to have each of them identified. Name, rank, serial number, where they're assigned."

Schmidt looked at him in disbelief.

"Mr. President, may I respectfully suggest that you may be overreacting?"

"I don't want to argue with you about this, Mr. Director. What I want you to do is say, 'Yes, sir,' then do what I tell you to do."

"Yes, sir," Schmidt said.

"And when you have assembled all these photographs and the information, I want you to personally bring them here and give them to Mulligan."

"I'll get right on it, Mr. President," Schmidt said.

"And I don't want this spread all over the J. Edgar Hoover building. I don't want anybody who is not directly involved to know anything about it. Got it?"

"Yes, Mr. President," Schmidt said.

"Now, what have you done about El Paso? Did you place the advertisement those people asked for?"

"The FBI has a very good man in El Paso, Mr. President," Schmidt said. "The SAC —"

"The what?"

"The special agent in charge, Mr. President. His name is William Johnson. He's the man who intercepted the second message to General McNab —"

"And instead of sending it to Washington, sent it to McNab. I didn't see it until the next day. I don't want that to happen again, Mr. Schmidt."

There was a brief hesitation before Schmidt went on: "SAC Johnson placed the classified advertisement in *El Diario de El Paso,* the Spanish language newspaper —"

"Did you hear what I said about wanting any messages addressed to General McNab that the FBI discovers to be sent to me, immediately?"

"Mr. President, what I can do, should another FedEx or UPS envelope addressed to General McNab be uncovered, is immediately photocopy the envelope and its contents and send those to you."

"I don't want *copies.* I want the real thing."

"Mr. President, there is no provision in the law permitting that."

"Well, you and Attorney General Crenshaw are clever people . . . in his case, maybe a little too clever . . . and I'm sure you'll be able to find a provision."

Schmidt did not reply, having decided he

251

was going to drop this in the lap of Attorney General Crenshaw and let him deal with it.

He went on: "What SAC Johnson also did, Mr. President, is investigate the post office box — P.O. Box 2333 — mentioned in the kidnapper's first message. When he learned that it had not been rented, he rented it.

"It's possible the kidnappers knew that Box 2333 had been rented. He's looking into that . . . which postal employees would have knowledge of that. Perhaps the kidnappers intend to send further communications to P.O. Box 2333. On the other hand, it may be just a coincidence."

"Whatever means these people use to communicate with us, I want to see whatever they send immediately. You understand that?"

Schmidt nodded. "Yes, Mr. President."

"I intend to get this Colonel Ferris back, and I have no intention of letting anyone get in my way, whether through stupidity or ineptness. Or anything else."

"Yes, Mr. President," Schmidt said.

"That will be all. Thank you."

The President turned to Mulligan.

"Just as soon as the director has gone, get the secretary of Defense on the phone."

[Four]
Office of the Commanding General
U.S. Special Operations Command
Fort Bragg, North Carolina
1515 15 April 2007

When the red telephone on his desk buzzed and a red LED on it began to flash, Lieutenant General Bruce J. McNab put his hand on it.

"I wonder what message General Naylor is about to relay to me from the Deity," he said to Colonel Max Caruthers, and then he pushed the LOUDSPEAKER button before picking up the handset and putting it to his ear.

"McNab."

"I have just been on the telephone with Secretary Beiderman," General Allan B. Naylor announced without any preliminaries.

"Yes, sir?"

"General, I am not in any mood to tolerate any of your wit, sarcasm, or, more important, obfuscations. If I were you, I'd keep that in mind."

"Yes, sir. I'll keep that in mind. May I inquire into what you think I have done to displease Secretary Beiderman?"

"You will answer *my* questions, General. I

will take none from you."

"Yes, sir."

"You will recall my telling you personally, as a result of Secretary Beiderman's orders to me to do so, that you were not even to contemplate any military action with regard to freeing Colonel Ferris?"

"Yes, sir. I remember your personally telling me that," McNab parroted.

"And do you also recall that I ordered you not to attend the interment of Warrant Officer Salazar?"

"Yes, sir, I remember that very well. May I say that I have not even been contemplating any action with regard to freeing Colonel Ferris," McNab parroted, "and that I did not attend Mr. Salazar's interment?"

"Instead, you send a delegation of Delta Force and Gray Fox personnel. Does that about sum it up?"

"I did not send a delegation of Delta Force and Gray Fox personnel anywhere, General," McNab parroted again.

This time Naylor picked up on it.

"Goddamn you, McNab, don't you mock me!"

"It's hard to resist, Allan."

"Goddamn you! How dare you use my first name?"

"That's twice that you've cursed me, Al-

254

lan," McNab said. "Wouldn't you agree that's conduct unbefitting a general officer and a gentleman?"

The flashing red LED on the telephone died, indicating the connection had been broken.

McNab replaced the handset and looked at Colonel Caruthers.

"Ninety seconds," he said. "Maybe a little less."

Caruthers shook his head in disbelief. Or maybe admiration.

Sixty-two seconds later, the red telephone buzzed and the red LED started flashing.

McNab took a lot longer to pick it up than he had the first time, but finally put the handset to his ear.

"McNab."

"Please accept my sincere apologies, General McNab," Naylor said.

"I will, providing you start acting like one old soldier talking to another old soldier — and a classmate, which puts us on a first-name basis — and tell me exactly why Beiderman chewed your ass to the point where you lost your cool."

There was a long pause, and Colonel Caruthers had just about decided the LED was about to stop blinking again when General Naylor said, "Bruce, Charley was at Arlington."

"I'm not surprised. Danny Salazar was on the first A Team Charley ever commanded. But I didn't send him up there, Allan. I haven't talked to him since before these Mexican slime murdered Salazar. And I didn't send the others, either. I didn't even know they were going."

"And then they all drove away, just when the President was about to deliver his remarks," Naylor said. "And their departure was on Wolf News for the whole world to see, thanks to Andy McClarren."

"What's the President pissed off about? That they were there, or that they walked out on his speech?"

"Both. And it's worse than that. Are you alone?"

"Max Caruthers is here."

There was another long pause.

"I hope that silence doesn't mean you don't trust Max," McNab said finally.

"No offense intended, Colonel Caruthers," Naylor said. "Actually, what I was doing was rethinking whether I wanted to tell General McNab what I'm about to tell you both."

"Which is?"

"The President seems to believe that whatever happened that saw Ambassador

Montvale named Vice President was the first step in a coup d'état."

"That's absurd. I admit that it has a certain appeal, but that anyone was planning a coup is simply not true," McNab said.

"People believe what they want to believe," Naylor said. "Do I have to say whom he views as coconspirators?"

"Where did you get this, Allan?" McNab asked softly.

And again there was a long pause before Naylor replied.

"Natalie Cohen," he said finally. "And I ran it past Frank Lammelle. He confirmed it."

"He's insane," McNab said. "Not Lammelle. Clendennen."

Naylor didn't reply to that.

"What Natalie suggests is that all of us do nothing that could possibly give him a chance to ask for — demand — our resignations."

"Natalie always keeps her head."

"Natalie suggests that his plan is to get rid of us one by one, and says that John David Parker was the first one to go."

"That seems pretty clear," McNab said.

"It seems pretty clear, Bruce, that you're next on the list," Naylor said. "Beiderman made it obvious that he would support me if I relieved you at SPECOPSCOM, or even announced your retirement."

"What does he think of this coup d'état nonsense?"

"I don't know if he knows about it or not, or if he does know, his reaction to it. I think his primary motivation is to keep his job. Which brings us to, what do I tell him about Charley and your people being at Arlington, where they walked out on the President's speech?"

"To get me out of here would require that you have proof I did something I should not have done, or not done something I should have done. And my skirts are clean here, Allan.

"I have not been in touch with Charley — I told you this before — since before Danny Salazar was murdered. I did not suggest that he go to Arlington. I knew he probably would be there, sure, but I had nothing to do with his going."

"Bruce, what about the Delta Force people? How do I explain to Beiderman that fifteen or twenty of your people showed up there without your knowledge?"

"When all else fails, tell the truth. Those men — some of them commissioned officers, some of them warrant officers, and the rest senior noncoms — are not PFCs who have to knock on the orderly room door to ask the first sergeant for a pass. So long as they are available for duty — depending on their alert status — immediately, or on one hour's notice, or six hours, or twenty-four hours — they are free to go anywhere they please.

"Now, I don't know this, and you might not want to tell Beiderman this, but what I strongly suspect happened here is that after you shoved burying her husband at Arlington down Mrs. Salazar's throat —"

"That was not my idea, Bruce. The President, to use your phraseology, shoved it down Secretary Beiderman's throat, and he shoved it down mine."

"Whereupon, you obediently shoved it down Mrs. Salazar's. And after you did, I think that she called Charley. And Charley — never forget he's one of us, Allan — decided that the best thing all around — 'for the good of the service' comes to mind — was to resist what must have been a hell of a temptation for him to tell her to tell you and the President to go to hell and insist that her husband be buried in San Antonio National Cemetery.

"He probably told her he was going to be at Arlington, and that if any of the people in the Stockade wanted to go, he'd have them picked up at the Fayetteville Regional Airport by Jake Torine or Dick Miller and flown back there when the interment was over. He has several airplanes, and the wherewithal to charter more. So I suspect that the reason they left Arlington right after the funeral was to get to the airport so that they could come back here."

After a long silent moment, Naylor said, "I'll buy everything but hurrying to the airport. What they did was go to that suite Charley keeps at the Mayflower. They're having sort of a wake. As we speak, according to Beiderman, the party's still going on. And, again according to Beiderman, Roscoe Danton and John David Parker are among the mourners."

"Which will tend to convince the President even more of the coup d'état conspiracy," McNab said.

"Precisely. Well, that's what I will tell the secretary of Defense. That you knew nothing about Charley Castillo's presence at Arlington, and haven't been in touch with him since before this mess started. I don't have much hope that he'll believe me."

"Your skirts are clean, Allan. You issued the orders you were told to issue, and made sure they were carried out."

"It isn't that black-and-white though, is it?" Naylor asked thoughtfully.

"Very little is ever either black or white, Allan."

There was another pause, and then Naylor said, "You said something before . . ."

"What?"

"You suggested the President was insane."

"Oh, for Christ's sake, that was a figure of speech, and you know it."

Naylor didn't reply.

"I have, Allan, on many occasions, going all the way back to our unhappy days at Hudson High, called you chickenshit. You knew I didn't think you were really fecal matter excreted from the anus of a *Gallus domesticus*. When I accused our lunatic President of being crazy, I was —"

"What if he is, Bruce?" Naylor asked softly.

McNab took a long time to reply.

"Well, that would certainly explain a hell of a lot, wouldn't it?"

"Jesus H. Christ!" Colonel Caruthers said softly. "If you think about it . . ."

"Not only this coup d'état nonsense," McNab said. "But . . ."

"I think we had all better stop right here," Naylor said.

"That won't work, I'm afraid, Allan," Mc-

Nab said. "You've let a very ugly genie out of your bottle. He's not going to go back in."

There was another long pause, and then McNab said, "Allan, I don't think I'd mention this part of our conversation to Secretary Beiderman."

"What I think we should all do is wipe the last ninety seconds of this conversation from our minds," Naylor said.

"That won't work, either, I'm afraid," McNab said. "For two reasons. First, I don't think any of us could. Second, we've all taken an oath to defend the Constitution against all enemies, foreign and domestic. And I think a President who has done what this one has done — is doing — can be fairly characterized as a threat to the Constitution."

Another long pause ensued before Naylor asked, "For the time being, can we agree this conversation goes no further than it has?"

"Yes, sir," McNab said.

"Yes, sir," Caruthers said.

"Thank you," Naylor said.

The red LED stopped blinking.

VI

[One]
Hacienda Santa Maria
Oaxaca Province, Mexico
1515 16 April 2007

As soon as Castillo took off his headset, Lester Bradley, who was sitting with Max in the backseat of the Cessna Mustang, handed him the headset from Castillo's Brick. Castillo put it to his ear.

"Yeah, Frank?"

"Something wrong with the net? The new net?" Lammelle asked. "It took me almost four minutes to get you to answer."

"I try not to talk on a cell phone when I'm flying fifteen feet above the ocean," Castillo said. "It tends to distract me."

"Where the hell are you?"

"I just landed at the family ranch in Mexico; about fifty miles from Acapulco. What's up?"

"You free to talk?"

"Nobody here but Sweaty and Lester, and they both know all — well, almost all — of my secrets."

"I have to know. Why were you flying fifteen feet above the ocean?"

"Because that way, the radar at Xoxocotlán and Bahías de Huatulco international airports can't see me landing at the family ranch. Next question?"

"Makes sense," Lammelle said.

"My answers generally do. Now, is there something else you'd like to chat about before I get out of my airplane?"

"Mark Schmidt came to see me just now. He needed my help, he said, to identify some of the people in the pictures his intrepid agents took on the tenth floor of the Mayflower yesterday afternoon and early this morning."

"The FBI took pictures of people at the wake? What the hell's that all about?"

"The President ordered it. Schmidt is to identify everyone who was in the hotel — emphasis on the guys from Bragg — down to name, rank, serial number, and organization, and deliver same — with their pictures — to the President. Personally. And to tell no one."

"Correct me if I'm wrong, but the last time I heard, being at a private party is not against the law."

"I don't know what Clendennen is up to, Charley. The point here, I think, the reason Schmidt came to me, was not to get me to identify anybody, but to let me know what the President had ordered him to do. Follow?"

Castillo thought a moment, and then said, "I have never been able to really figure Schmidt out."

"He wanted me to know about this nutty order, but he didn't want to tell me. Anyway, I identified you and Torine and Miller and other people I would be expected to know, but I couldn't seem to recognize any of the Gray Fox or Delta guys."

"It just occurred to me that Clendennen will now have an unclassified box of pictures of about a third of the guys in the Stockade. I don't like that."

"If you can figure it out, let me know. But, speaking of pictures — this is the real reason I called — there is a new senior cultural affairs officer at the embassy of the Russian Federation in Bogotá. His name is Valentin Komarovski."

"Oh?"

"The reason they're calling him the senior cultural affairs guy is that he will supervise their cultural affairs guys in Venezuela, Panama, Costa Rica, Nicaragua, Honduras, and Guatemala."

"So who is he really, Frank?"

"Sergei Murov. I believe you know him."

"Are you sure?"

"Señor Komarovski traveled to his new duty station via Havana, on Iberia, where his picture was taken by a disaffected Castroite and passed on to our guy in the Uruguayan embassy. Our guy wondered why a senior Russian dip didn't travel Aeroflot to Miami, and make his connection there — catch the Colombian airline, Aero República — instead of waiting ten hours to catch the next Cubana flight to Bogotá. Maybe he didn't want to pass through Miami and be recognized?"

Castillo grunted.

Lammelle went on: "So by the time Señor Komarovski arrived in Bogotá, our guy at the airport there had plenty of time to make sure the lighting was in place to take pictures of him arriving. The images were here minutes later, and one of the guys in the lab recognized him from Murov's days as the *rezident* here. He brought the pics to me — 'Is that who I think it is?'

"Just to be sure, I ran them through the comparison lab. It's Murov, all right, or the Russians are now cloning people. So you have your heads-up, Charley. I don't think he likes you, and I know he doesn't like your girlfriend."

"I'm more worried, Frank, about the pictures of the guys from the Stockade getting out; I'd really hate to think I was responsible for that happening."

"You can't do anything about that, Charley. You can't stop the President from doing anything he wants to with those pictures."

"What the hell does he want them for? He's too smart a politician to try to punish a bunch of soldiers for holding a wake for one of their own. He doesn't want Roscoe going on Wolf News with a story like that."

"I don't think anyone knows what Clendennen will do next, or why," Lammelle said. "But in this case, I think maybe he'll show them to the secretary of Defense. Get Beiderman to lean on Naylor to get rid of McNab, who commands the people who (a) went to Arlington when he had made it clear he didn't want that, and (b) insulted POTUS by walking out on his speech."

"That doesn't make any sense."

"A good deal POTUS does doesn't make sense, if you think about it, Charley."

Castillo didn't reply.

"Well, as I said, you've got your heads-up about Murov. Stay in touch."

"Whoa," Castillo said. "Natalie Cohen told me she told you that you could have that Policía Federal Black Hawk that miraculously appeared on the dock at Norfolk."

"Why do I think I'm not going to like what comes next?"

"Could you move it to a secure location — not too secure — in Texas? Near San Antone, maybe?"

"What are you planning, Charley?"

"At the moment, not a thing. But life is full of surprises, isn't it? You never know what's going to happen, do you?"

"Good-bye, Colonel Castillo, Retired. Nice talking to you."

"I'll take that as a yes. Thank you, Frank."

"I'm beginning to understand why Clendennen wanted to load you on an Aeroflot flight to Moscow."

The LED stopped flashing.

[Two]
Hacienda Santa Maria
Oaxaca Province, Mexico
1725 16 April 2007

The sprawling, red-tile-roofed house with a wide, shaded veranda all around it sat on a bluff overlooking the Pacific Ocean. A circular drive led to it from the acres of grapefruit trees running as far as the eye could see to the east.

The house was known as "Don Fernando's House," but the reference was to

268

Don Fernando Lopez the Elder, rather than to the Don Fernando Lopez who now sat on the veranda facing away from the Pacific, holding a bottle of Dos Equis beer in his massive fist.

Beside him, on cushioned wicker couches and chairs, were his cousin, Carlos Castillo; Don Armando Medina, a swarthy, heavyset sixty-odd-year-old who was *el jefe* — "the boss" and general manager — of Hacienda Santa Maria; Sweaty; Stefan Koussevitzky; and Lester Bradley. They were all — except for Lester, who had a Coke — drinking wine, a Cabernet Sauvignon, from Bodegas San Felipe, which happened to be a subsidiary of Hacienda Santa Maria. Max lay beside Sweaty, gnawing on a grapefruit he held between his paws.

Fernando Lopez and Carlos Castillo were grandsons of Don Fernando Castillo, who had married Alicia Lopez. Hacienda Santa Maria had been her dowry. Don Fernando and Doña Alicia had had two children, Maria Elena, who had married Manuel Lopez — no relation — and Jorge Alejandro, who had been killed in the Vietnam War as a very young — nineteen years old — man.

Manuel and Maria Elena Lopez had three children: Fernando, Graciella, and Juanita.

Don Fernando Castillo had strained relations with the Lopez family, into which his daughter had married, but had been exceedingly fond of his grandson Fernando. He and Doña Alicia had agreed that on their deaths, Hacienda Santa Maria would go to Fernando, and everything else would be given to charity and the Alamo Foundation.

"I don't want to spend all of eternity spinning in my grave thinking of the Lopez wetbacks squandering all our money," he declared.

All of that had changed a quarter century before, when an Army officer, then-Major Allan B. Naylor, appeared in Doña Alicia's office in the Alamo Foundation building with the photograph of a twelve-year-old blond, blue-eyed boy, and said there was good reason to believe he was the out-of-wedlock son of the late Warrant Officer Junior Grade Jorge Alejandro Castillo.

Don Fernando Castillo's first reaction to this was that some Kraut Fraulein — Don Fernando had been Major F. J. Castillo of Combat Command A, 3rd Armored Division during World War II and had had some experience with Kraut Frauleins in the immediate postwar period — had learned who the Castillo family was, and intended, like the Lopez wetbacks, to get her hands into the Castillo cash box by passing off somebody else's bastard son as the fruit of their Jorge's loins.

Doña Alicia had had no such doubts. One look at the boy's eyes had been enough to convince her that she was looking at a picture of her grandson. On hearing from Major Naylor that the boy's mother was in the final stages of pancreatic cancer, she picked up the telephone and called Lemes Aviation, ordering them to ready the company Learjet so that she and Major Naylor could make the Pan American flight from New York to Frankfurt late that same afternoon.

Not two weeks later, equipped with a U.S. passport in the name of Carlos Guillermo Castillo, Karl Wilhelm von und zu Gossinger arrived in San Antonio. A week after that, his mother died, and he became the sole heir to the vast business empire known as GossingerBeteiligungsgesellschaft,G.m.b.H.

The new situation required modification of the last will and testaments of Don Fernando and Doña Alicia. Legal counsel informed them that there would be problems if Carlos were to inherit half of Hacienda Santa Maria. Mexican law did not permit foreigners to own property in the United States of Mexico.

Don Fernando was aware of this. When Maria Elena's time had come, she had flown to Mexico City, where Fernando had been born. He himself had been born on Hacienda San Dominic, the Castillo farm near Guadalajara, and Doña Alicia on Hacienda Santa Maria.

"Not a problem," Don Fernando announced. "They're like brothers; they'll work it out between them."

Carlos and Fernando had almost immediately — frankly surprising both their grandparents — become close and inseparable. Fernando called Carlos "Gringo," and Carlos called Fernando "Fatso."

Fernando and Charley were sitting with Svetlana, Stefan Koussevitzky, Lester Bradley, and Don Armando Medina on the veranda as two brown Suburbans with Policía Federal insignia on their doors kicked up a dust cloud coming up the road through the grapefruit groves to the house.

The front doors of both vehicles opened simultaneously. A trim, neatly uniformed Federale, holding a CAR-15 in his hands as if he knew what to do with it, got out of the lead vehicle.

Well, Castillo thought, *despite what Don Armando said about us being old friends, I wouldn't have recognized Juan Carlos if I'd fallen over him.*

A stout, balding man in civilian clothing, a thick black cigar clutched firmly in his teeth, got out of the second Suburban. A Colt Model 1911A1 in a skeleton holster was on his belt.

Who the hell is he?

I'll be damned! That's Juan Carlos!

Last time I saw him he looked like a model in an advertisement for men's cologne. Now he looks like . . . well, a fat Mexican cop.

Juan Carlos Pena, *el jefe* of the Policía Federal for the province of Oaxaca, waved cheerfully, and with the cigar still in his mouth, called, in perfect American English, "Carlos, you sonofabitch, how the fuck are you?"

Then he walked quickly onto the veranda, and the moment Castillo stood up, wrapped him in an affectionate hug.

Castillo saw that Fernando was smiling, and knew it was not at the display of affection but rather at Castillo's discomfiture.

"Good to see you, Juan Carlos," Castillo said.

Where the hell did he get that cologne?

And what did he do, pour it on?

"How the hell long has it been?" Juan Carlos said. "Too fucking long, that's for goddamn sure."

"How about a glass of wine, Juan Carlos?" Castillo asked in Spanish. "Or something stronger?"

"A little Jack Daniel's would go down nicely," Juan Carlos said, continuing in English. "But not until after I meet the girlfriend. You're right, Fernando, she's spectacular!"

"Swe . . . Susanna, say hello to an old friend, Juan Carlos Pena."

"Hola," Sweaty said. "Nice to meet you, Susanna Barlow."

"And this is Stefan Koussevitzky," Castillo said. "And this is Lester Bradley. My grandmother sent him down to see if he can straighten out the hacienda's computers."

Max instinctively stood up.

Sweaty laid a gentle hand on the dog's back, and in Hungarian said, "It's okay, baby."

"What the fuck is that?" Juan Carlos said. "I've ridden smaller horses."

"Meet Max," Castillo said.

Juan Carlos looked at Svetlana. "What was that language you was speaking?"

"Hungarian. I'm Uruguayan but my parents immigrated there from Hungary."

Juan Carlos nodded. "I noticed the funny accent."

"I'm surprised you don't know there's three kinds of Spanish, Juan Carlos," Castillo said. "Castilian — Spanish-Spanish; Southern Cone — the Spanish spoken in Uruguay, Argentina, and Chile; and the Spanish spoken in Mexico, Central America, and the rest of South America. Susanna speaks the Southern Cone variety."

"I heard that," Juan Carlos said. "Uruguay, huh? Is that where you two met?"

"Yeah," Castillo said.

A maid appeared, and Fernando told her to bring whiskey.

"So," Juan Carlos asked, "what brings you to Hacienda Santa Maria, Señorita Barlow?" Before she could reply, Juan Carlos added: "Barlow doesn't sound very Hungarian, if you don't mind my saying so."

"It used to be Böröcz," Sweaty said. "Which no one could pronounce, much less spell, in Spanish. So we changed it."

"You were telling me what you're doing here," Juan Carlos said.

"Stefan and I are looking at those," Sweaty said, pointing to the grapefruit grove. "When Carlos told us his family was in the citrus business — I have some pastureland I'm thinking of converting — and then that he was coming here, I imposed on his

275

hospitality. Really imposed on it. I brought a half a dozen citrus experts with me. Stefan's the expert's expert."

"I didn't know they grow grapefruit in Uruguay," Juan Carlos said.

"They don't grow much, but some. Maybe I can change that."

"And your expert's expert is another Hungarian? Koussevitzky doesn't sound like he's a native of Uruguay."

"Actually, I'm Israeli," Koussevitzky said. "Or was. Now I'm an Uruguayan citizen."

"They grow grapefruit in Israel?"

"All the citrus fruits, our — *their* — biggest market is Italy and France," Koussevitzky said.

"I'll be damned. I never heard that," Juan Carlos said, and then asked, "What were you doing in Uruguay, Carlos?"

"I was an assistant military attaché of the American embassy."

" 'Assistant military attaché,' huh?" Juan Carlos parroted. "Sounds pretty snazzy."

"It's what the Army does with officers who are not going to get promoted, and don't have enough time in to retire," Castillo said. "They send them to an embassy until they have enough time. The only good thing about it was that I met Susanna in Montevideo."

"So you're retired now?" Juan Carlos said.

The maid came to them with a bottle of Jack Daniel's and accoutrements on a tray. When she poured the Tennessee whiskey into a glass, Juan Carlos gestured for her to add more.

"Jack Daniel's is like sex," he announced. "You can never get enough."

"So is gold," Sweaty said.

Juan Carlos looked at her and smiled.

"I like her, Carlos," he said, raising his glass and taking a healthy swallow. "What I can't figure out is what a redhead like that sees in a skinny gringo like you."

"It's been a long time, Juan Carlos," Castillo said. "But I think I can still kick your ass."

Juan Carlos looked at him for a moment, and then smiled and said, "I'll bet you could. You know I'm just kidding, Red, right?"

"Carlos wasn't," Sweaty said.

He considered that for a moment, smiled, and said, "So you're retired now, huh?"

"For a couple of months."

"I was thinking that the last time I saw you was when you had just graduated from West Point. You were a second lieutenant about to go to flight school."

"I guess that's right," Castillo said.

He thought: *My ol' pal Juan Carlos didn't come here for auld lang syne.*

He came here to find out what's going on here at Hacienda Santa Maria.

He may have even heard about the ex-Spetsnaz "citrus experts."

Heard about but not seen.

Fernando flew them here onto our strip, and Stefan told them to keep out of sight, which means they did.

Which means I'm being interrogated.

Does Juan Carlos think I don't know that?

Or doesn't care if I do?

"And now you're a retired colonel."

"Retired *lieutenant* colonel," Castillo said. "I got passed over for promotion to colonel twice. That was when they sent me to Uruguay."

"So what brings you to Hacienda Santa Maria?"

"I think you know, Juan Carlos."

"I don't have a fucking clue, Carlos."

"The Army officer who was kidnapped, Jim Ferris, is a West Point classmate of mine, an old friend. I thought — Fernando told me you're the commandant of the Policía Federal in Oaxaca Province — you'd be the guy who would know. Maybe even tell me how I could help to get him back."

"You want some good advice, Carlos?"

"That's what I came here for."

"Get in your airplane and go home. Better yet, go back to Uruguay. Before you and your friends get hurt. You don't want to fuck with these people, Carlos. They're really bad news."

"So I've heard. Fernando told me. But I figured my old friend, now a heavy-duty Federale, could protect me."

"Your old friend has a tough time protecting himself," Juan Carlos said. "You saw Lieutenant Gomez, the guy with the CAR-15?"

Castillo nodded.

"There's two more guys with CAR-15s in my Suburban, and four more of them in the other Suburban. I call them the American Express, 'cause I never go anywhere without them. Don't you read the papers?"

"You're talking about the drug cartel people?"

"You bet your fucking ass I am."

"I've been in Uruguay. There's drugs in Uruguay. The cops down there don't run around with CAR-15s."

Pena looked at him as if he couldn't believe Castillo's naïveté.

Or stupidity. Or both.

"Well, Carlos, let me tell you about the drugs here," Juan Carlos said. "As opposed to in Uruguay. Where the fuck is Uruguay, anyway?"

"On the other side of the river from Buenos Aires."

Got you now, Juan Carlos, ol' buddy!

Rule Seven in the Uncle Remus List of Rules for the Interrogation of Belligerent Bad Guys: "Make them think you're stupid and then let them show you how smart and knowledgeable they are."

"Let me try to sum it up this way, Carlos," Juan Carlos said. "This stuff starts out when some *campesino* in Bolivia or wherever the fuck sticks his knife in a flower, a poppy, and collects the goo that comes out. Or boils down the coca leaf. The last stop is when some junkie in the States either sucks it up his nostrils, or sticks it in his vein. By then it's either cocaine or heroin."

"What are you telling me you think I don't know?"

Juan Carlos held his now empty whiskey glass. The maid took it.

"Put enough in it this time," he said in Spanish, and then switched back to English.

"Shut your mouth for a fucking minute, Carlos, and I'll tell you what you don't know. At every step, from processing that shit so it becomes heroin or cocaine, the price goes up, way up. You do understand that?"

"I wasn't born yesterday, Juan Carlos."

"You could have fooled me. Now, the same thing is true in every step between the fields and the junkie's nose. The price goes up. *Way, way* up by the time it gets close to the States.

"Now, the people in this business, as you can imagine, are not very nice people. Doña Alicia would not invite them to dinner — and on that subject, thank you very much, but I can't stay for dinner."

"Why not? We haven't even started walking down memory lane," Castillo said.

"I got things to do, Carlos. The only reason I'm here is to try, because we go way back, to warn you what you're fucking around with and to try to keep you alive."

"I can keep myself alive, thank you very much."

"Will you shut your fucking mouth and listen? Jesus Christ!"

Castillo hoped the look he made indicated his feelings had been hurt.

Proof that he had been successful came immediately.

"For Christ's sake, Carlos, I'm trying to help you," Juan Carlos said, almost compassionately.

"Sorry."

"Okay. Now, except for what the junkies in the States pay for their one ounce — or less — little bags of this shit, it's most valuable just before it's sent over the border into the States. By then it's in bricks, generally weighing a kilo — that's a little over two pounds.

"Some of the people taking it across the border, after buying it at a stiff price from somebody who brought it from Venezuela or Colombia, and running the risk that we'd catch them while they were moving it from south Mexico to the border, decided it would be safer and a hell of a lot cheaper to just steal it from some other trafficker.

"And the way to do that was just kill the other trafficker; let their bosses just guess who stole it. And the way to keep the police from interfering with the movement, do one of two things. Pay off the police — Carlos, you have no fucking idea how much fucking money is involved here. We grab some of these people with two, three hundred grand, sometimes more, in their pockets.

"And then they realized that it would be cheaper to kill the police who were getting close than to pay them off."

"No shit?" Castillo said wonderingly.

"No shit. So what we have is war here,

Carlos. One ground of drug movers — they call themselves 'cartels' — killing each other to steal, or protect the product, whether it's cocaine or meth or heroin, and all of them perfectly willing to kill the police.

"I don't know where it's going to end. I know the good guys ain't winning. Now, as to your friend. I heard two stories, and I don't know which one to believe. The first is that they just got in the way. By that I mean they'd been responsible for us — the Policía Federal, or the American DEA, or Border Patrol grabbing shipments. Since these shipments are worth hundreds of thousands of dollars — sometimes millions — this made them mad, so they had to be killed.

"The second story I heard is that they want to swap your colonel for a man named Félix Abrego. He's doing life without the possibility of parole in that maximum-security prison of yours . . . what's it called?"

The words *Florence Maximum* were almost on Castillo's lips when he caught himself, shrugged, and asked, "Leavenworth?"

"No," Juan Carlos said.

"Sorry, I was a soldier, not a policeman. But I do know, Juan Carlos, that it's firm American policy not to do something like that. The Taliban tried it on us in Afghanistan, and it was decided that if we —"

"Florence," Juan Carlos interrupted him. "The Florence ADMAX. It's in Colorado."

"Never heard of it."

"What they do there, Carlos, is lock you up alone, around the clock, except for one hour a day, when they let you out of your cell to exercise, alone, in what looks like a dog kennel. You get a shower every other day."

"Sounds like fun. What do you have to do to get sent there?"

"Abrego shot a few DEA agents," Juan Carlos said. "In the States. Near El Paso. They caught him."

"He didn't get the death penalty? I always thought if you killed a cop, you got the electric chair."

"Well, I'll explain to you how that works in real life, Carlos. We haven't had the death penalty in Mexico since 2005. If a Mexican in the States gets the hot seat, that's bad for our friendly relations. Mexican politicians fall all over themselves rushing up there to save him.

"And we don't extradite people — neither do the French, by the way — to any place that executes people.

"So the way it works here, if Señor Abrego had shot one of my people and got caught

— that happens every once in a while — and he got tried and convicted — that also happens every once in a while — he would have gotten life.

"And in a couple of years, after a lot of money changed hands, he would 'escape,' so to speak."

"Jesus!" Castillo said, hoping he sounded as if he was shocked to the depths of his naïve soul.

Juan Carlos nodded.

"So the way it's worked out is that your judges sentence Mexicans who deserve the electric chair to life without parole in Florence. That keeps the bad guys off the streets almost as well as the electric chair — nobody has ever escaped from Florence — and keeps Mexican politicians from making members of your Congress unhappy. Getting the picture?"

"I never heard any of this before," Castillo said.

"I *never* would have guessed," Juan Carlos said sarcastically. "Look, Carlos. There is some good news. You don't fuck with these people, they don't fuck with you. What I'm saying is there's not a goddamn thing you can do for your friend the colonel, except get yourself killed. Let whoever deals with things like swapping prisoners — the FBI maybe, or DEA? — try to get him back. You start nosing around, you're going to get yourself killed, and probably him, too. Can you understand that?"

"Yeah, I guess I can," Castillo said reluctantly. "But, Juan Carlos, if you could find out anything . . ."

"Sure. If I hear anything, I'll let you know. By mail. I suppose if I sent a letter to . . . 1700 Arizona Boulevard, San Antonio, Texas . . . I remember Doña Alicia's address; I've got a good memory for addresses and numbers, things like that . . . she'd get it to you, right?"

"I'm sure she would."

"Even with you in Uruguay? Which is really where I hope you'll be. What's your address down there, anyway?"

Shit, now what?

I don't have an address in Uruguay!

Rule One — the First and Great Commandment — in the Uncle Remus List of Rules for the Interrogation of Belligerent Bad Guys: Never ever underestimate the bad guy!

"If you're going to send a letter to Carlos down there," Sweaty said, "send it in care of me — Señorita Susanna Barlow, Golf and Polo Country Club, Km 55.5 PanAmericana, Pilar, Buenos Aires Province, Argentina."

"Wait, let me write that down."

He took a notebook and ballpoint from his shirt pocket.

Then he asked, "Argentina? I thought you said Uruguay."

"We *farm* in Uruguay," Sweaty said. "We play polo in Argentina. It's only half an hour in the plane from Uruguay."

"Polo, huh? You play polo, Carlos?"

"Frankly," Sweaty said, "he's not very good at it. Barlow is spelled B-A-R-L-O-W. You want the phone number? The country code is zero one one —"

"I won't be calling," Juan Carlos interrupted. "It probably costs ten dollars a minute to call down there."

"Closer to seven dollars, actually," Sweaty said.

Juan Carlos put his notebook back in his shirt pocket.

"Well, like I said, I have things to do," he said. He drained his glass, nodded at everybody, and then draped his arm around Castillo's shoulder.

"Pay attention to what I told you, Carlos. I really want to keep you alive."

"I know," Castillo said. "It's just that I wanted to help if I could."

"The best way for you to help is go to Uruguay. Or Argentina. Go work on your polo game in Argentina, Carlos."

Juan Carlos Pena punched Castillo painfully in the upper arm, shook Fernando's hand, nodded at the others, then quickly walked off the porch and got into his Suburban.

Ninety seconds later, both Policía Federal vehicles had disappeared in a dirt cloud down the road through the grapefruit orchards.

Castillo filled his wineglass, then said, "Comments solicited."

"A dangerous man," former SVR Major Stefan Koussevitzky said.

"But I think he really likes Carlos," former SVR Lieutenant Colonel Svetlana Alekseeva said.

"That makes him less dangerous?" Koussevitzky challenged.

"I didn't say that," she said.

"Are you interested in what I think?" Don Armando Medina asked.

"Of course," Castillo said.

"Some of the things he said were absolutely true. If you don't get in the way of the drug cartel people, they leave you alone. We have had no trouble with them."

"They aren't stealing our grapefruit?" Castillo quipped.

"One of their bricks of cocaine is worth

more than an eighteen-wheeler trailer load of grapefruit. That's another thing Juan Carlos said that's true: The amount of money involved is nearly unbelievable."

"I was hoping I could get him talking more about the people involved. He suggested everybody involved is Mexican."

"He came here to tell you as little as possible beyond 'butt out or die,' " Fernando said, "and that's just what he did."

"You think our ol' buddy is in with the drug people?"

"He's alive, isn't he?"

"Then why did he come here at all?"

"Like Sweaty said, he likes you. And he was probably curious — professionally — why you showed up here."

"And do you think I convinced him I'm just an old soldier trying to help out an old classmate?"

"Yeah," Fernando said after a moment. "Don't let this go to your head, Gringo, but that was quite a performance. You, Stefan, and Sweaty were pretty convincing."

"Looking stupid is easy for me," Castillo said. "But Sweaty? Sweetheart, I could have kissed you when he asked for an address in Uruguay and you came up with Golf and Polo."

" 'I've got a good memory for addresses

and numbers, things like that,' " Sweaty quoted. "You can kiss me later. So now what?"

"Now we get in the Mustang and go to Cozumel, and catch tomorrow's Peruaire-Cargo flight to Chile."

"Why are we going to do that?"

"I want Aleksandr to understand that whacking Sergei Murov or any of his people without asking me first is not one of his options."

"You're going to have trouble with that," Koussevitzky said. "He's convinced the best way to protect himself is to eliminate anybody Vladimir Vladimirovich sends over here."

"If he takes out anybody, Ferris will die," Castillo said.

"Stefan's right," Sweaty said. "Aleksandr will be genuinely sorry about that, but he'll think of your friend's passing as unavoidable collateral damage."

"Well, I'll just have to talk him out of thinking that way," Castillo said. "Sweetheart, your call. We either leave right now, or very early in the morning."

"Why can't we have dinner first, and then leave?" she asked.

"Because I suspect Juan Carlos is going to have the radar operators at Bahías de Huatulco International Airport report to him when any airplanes take off from here. If we take off after dark, he'll know the runway is lighted. And I don't want him to know that."

"Then dinner here, looking down at the ocean," Sweaty said without hesitation. "Afterward, we can walk on the beach, holding hands."

"Are you going to take Stefan and his 'citrus experts' with you?" Don Armando asked.

Castillo nodded. "Stefan, yes. But if you don't think the 'citrus experts' pose a danger to Hacienda Santa Maria, I'd like to leave them here. I may need them later on."

[Three]
The President's Study
The White House
1600 Pennsylvania Avenue, N.W.
Washington, D.C.
0830 17 April 2007

FBI Director Mark Schmidt, presidential press secretary Clemens McCarthy, and Supervisory Secret Service Agent Robert J. Mulligan were already in the room when Secretary of Defense Frederick K. Beiderman walked in.

Beiderman nodded at them, and said,

"Good morning, Mr. President."

"We've been waiting for you," President Joshua Ezekiel Clendennen said as he rose from his small "working desk." He walked to a library table on one side of the room. "Take a look at what we have to show you."

Clendennen gestured to Mulligan, who handed McCarthy a large manila envelope. McCarthy walked to the table, opened the envelope, and took from it a sheaf of eight-by-ten-inch color photographs. As if laying out a hand of solitaire, he laid them one at a time, side by side, in four rows on the table. When he was finished, the table was nearly covered.

Clendennen gestured for Beiderman to examine the pictures.

He did so, then raised his head and asked, "Exactly what am I looking at, Mr. President?"

"These photographs were taken yesterday afternoon outside suite 1002 in the Mayflower Hotel," McCarthy said.

"They were taken by FBI photographers, so they will stand up as evidence in court, if it ever comes to that," Clendennen amplified.

"Yes, sir. Who are these people, Mr. President?"

"Don't tell me you couldn't pick anyone

you know from them?"

"Well, sir, I of course recognize Roscoe Danton and Colonel Castillo —"

"*Retired Lieutenant* Colonel Castillo, you mean?"

"Yes, sir."

"And what about my former press secretary, Porky Parker. Did you recognize him?"

"Yes, sir, of course. But I don't recognize any of the others."

"You didn't see any of them at Arlington the day before yesterday? Maybe as they got into their limousines and drove off just as I was beginning my remarks?"

"I didn't make that connection, sir. Who are they, sir? And what were they doing at the Mayflower?"

"They're soldiers. Five of them are commissioned officers, seven of them are warrant officers, and the remaining ten are senior noncommissioned officers. They are all assigned to General McNab's Special Operations Command at Fort Bragg — to the Delta Force and Gray Fox components thereof."

"Yes, sir?"

"As to what they were doing at the Mayflower, they were having a party. The host was *Lieutenant* Colonel Castillo, Retired."

"I don't think I understand, Mr. President," Beiderman said.

"What I want you to do, Mr. Secretary," President Clendennen said, "is take these photographs to General Naylor. Tell him to show them to General McNab as proof that we know what he's up to —"

"Sir?"

"Please don't interrupt me, Beiderman," the President said unpleasantly. "Tell Naylor to show these photographs to General McNab, and to tell McNab that if he immediately applies for retirement, that will be the end of it."

"The end of what, Mr. President?"

"McCarthy thinks the less we put into words at this time, the better," the President said. "For reasons that should be obvious to you."

"I'm afraid they're not, Mr. President," Beiderman said. "Frankly, I don't understand any of this."

"I think you do," the President said icily.

"The only thing I understand is that you want General McNab to resign."

"Correct."

"Presumably in connection with this party in the Mayflower?"

"McNab will understand when General Naylor shows him these pictures, and, aware that I am repeating myself, tells him he can end this whole thing by immediately retiring, and that will be the end of it."

"The end of what whole thing, sir?"

"If you give it some thought as you're traveling to CENTCOM to see General Naylor, I'm sure it will come to you, Mr. Secretary. Call me the minute Naylor has McNab's request for retirement in hand."

Clemens McCarthy bent over the table, slid the photographs together, stacked them neatly together, and handed them to Mulligan, who returned them to the envelope and then handed the envelope to Secretary Beiderman.

President Clendennen didn't seem to notice when Beiderman left the room.

[Four]
Office of the Commander in Chief
United States Central Command
MacDill Air Force Base
Tampa, Florida
1245 17 April 2007

Colonel J. D. Brewer pushed open the door and formally announced, "General Naylor, the secretary of Defense."

Naylor was out of his chair and on the way to the door before Beiderman was halfway through it.

Beiderman offered his hand.

"Mr. Secretary, I'm a little uncomfortable not having been at the field . . ."

"Don't be silly," Beiderman said. "I told Colonel Brewer I would prefer that you not meet me. The less fuss about this, the better."

"Yes, sir. Won't you please sit down?"

"Thank you," Beiderman said, and looked askance at Colonel Brewer.

Naylor caught that, and said, "That will be all, Colonel. Thank you."

Brewer left and closed the door behind him. The implication was that SECDEF and C-in-C CENTCOM were now alone. The truth — which really made Naylor uncomfortable — was that he had ordered his senior aide-de-camp to go into the sergeant major's office and listen to and record whatever was going to happen in his office.

"Can I offer coffee, sir? Or something to eat? Or ask you to join me in my mess for lunch?"

"Thank you, no. I had a sandwich on the plane. General, let me get right to it."

"Yes, sir."

Beiderman opened his attaché case and took out a large manila envelope.

"Have a look, General," he said as he

handed Naylor the envelope. "The President gave me those just before he ordered me to come down here."

Naylor took the sheaf of color photographs from the envelope and looked at each before raising his eyes to Beiderman.

"The President desires, General," Beiderman said, "that you personally show those photographs to General McNab, tell him the President knows what he's up to, and that if he immediately applies for retirement, that will be the end of it."

Naylor didn't reply.

"I suggest the best way to accomplish the President's desires is for us to immediately fly to Fort Bragg, in separate aircraft. Once you have done what the President desires and have General McNab's request for retirement in hand, I will take it to the President and you can come back here, and that will be the end of it."

Again Naylor didn't reply.

"I will entertain your recommendations as to a replacement for General McNab at SPECOPSCOM," Beiderman said, "but I suspect the President has someone in mind for the post."

And once more Naylor didn't reply.

"Did you understand what I just told you, General Naylor?"

"No, Mr. Secretary, I'm afraid I didn't."

"What didn't you understand, General?"

"For one thing, Mr. Secretary, the photographs. Who are they of, and what are they supposed to show?"

"They were taken by FBI agents the day before yesterday in the Mayflower Hotel in D.C. They show a number of members of Delta Force and Gray Fox. They were taken after these individuals walked out on the President's remarks at Arlington. They were at a party given by retired Lieutenant Colonel Castillo."

"And what is the connection with General McNab, sir?"

"My God, Naylor! General McNab commands Gray Fox and Delta Force; he's responsible for them."

"Mr. Secretary, I have already discussed the presence of these soldiers at Mr. Salazar's interment with General McNab. He denies having anything to do with their being there. He also tells me that he has not been in touch with Colonel Castillo since before Mr. Salazar was murdered and Colonel Ferris kidnapped."

"And you believe him?"

"Yes, sir. I believe him."

"Nevertheless, the President desires that General McNab retire. Is that clear to you?"

"Mr. Secretary, may I speak freely?"

"Of course."

"Mr. Secretary, correct me if I'm wrong, but wasn't there an implied threat in what you said before? You said that if McNab asks for immediate retirement, that 'will be the end of it.' The end of what, Mr. Secretary? If General McNab declines to ask to be retired, then what?"

Beiderman didn't reply for a long moment. Then he said, "General, it is our duty to work together to get through this awkward situation."

"That doesn't answer my question, Mr. Secretary."

"Then I suppose the President will fire him."

"Mr. Secretary, did you see the photographs of Mr. Roscoe Danton in that stack?"

Beiderman nodded.

"And of the President's former press secretary, Mr. Parker?"

Beiderman nodded again.

"Mr. Secretary, do you think POTUS has considered the very real possibility that if what he desires actually occurs, then it will be a front-page story in *The Washington Times-Post* and all over Wolf News? And all over all the other media, thanks to Mr. Parker?"

When Beiderman didn't reply, Naylor went on: "Wolf News — the press generally — will have a field day with that, Mr. Secretary. 'President Clendennen Fires Top Green Beret because Green Berets Walk Out on His Remarks at Arlington Funeral.' "

Beiderman looked stricken.

"Mr. Secretary, I suggest that you and I have a duty to protect the President from something like that. Both President Clendennen personally and the office of POTUS. Wouldn't you agree?"

"Yes, of course."

"Are you open to suggestion, Mr. Secretary?"

Beiderman nodded.

"If you and I fly to Fort Bragg right now, Mr. Secretary, and comply with the President's order to show McNab these photographs, and then offer him the opportunity to immediately resign —"

"The President didn't order *me* to go to Fort Bragg, General," Beiderman interrupted. "He ordered me to come here to give *you* those goddamn pictures and order *you* to deal with General McNab."

"I beg your pardon, sir."

"You realize, Naylor, that if a story like that comes out, and since Roscoe Danton was at that goddamn party, it's a given that it will come out, then you know who the President is going to blame."

"Sir, apropos of nothing whatever, I'm sure you will agree that when people lose their tempers, they sometimes act irrationally."

"What are you driving at, General?"

"I wouldn't want to be quoted on this, sir."

"But?"

"While I can certainly understand the President's anger at having McNab's people walk out on his remarks . . . there are those who might say his reaction to the insult was a bit irrational."

"I don't like where this conversation appears to be going, General."

"Sir, when people . . . anyone . . . has a little time to think things over, to realize that when they were angry they did some things, said some things in the heat of anger, that they wish they hadn't done or said."

"Jumping to the bottom line, you're suggesting that in a day or two the President will cool off. Okay. He probably will. So what do we do today?"

"When you arrived here, Mr. Secretary, I told you that I would comply with the President's desires the moment General

McNab returned from Afghanistan, which should be in the next few days."

"McNab isn't in Afghanistan."

"He can be on his way to Afghanistan in a very few minutes."

Beiderman looked at him with his eyebrows raised.

"When you call the President, you could tell him that," Naylor said. "That General McNab is on his way to Afghanistan."

Secretary Beiderman considered that for a full — very long — thirty seconds, and then said, "Slide me the red phone."

"Sir, why don't we wait until General Mc-Nab is actually on his way to Afghanistan? That would be thirty seconds after I call him."

Secretary Beiderman considered that for another — very long — thirty seconds. Then he said, "Make your call, General Naylor."

Naylor picked up the headset of the red telephone and pushed one of the dozen buttons on its base.

"Put it on loudspeaker," the secretary of Defense ordered.

Naylor said, "Yes, sir."

Damn! he thought.

The phone was immediately answered: "McNab."

"General Naylor, General."

"Yes, sir?"

"Are you alone, General?"

"Yes, sir."

"Secretary Beiderman is with me, General."

"Yes, sir."

"POTUS sent him here with a stack of photographs of Delta Force and Gray Fox personnel at Colonel Castillo's party in the Mayflower after they walked out on the President's remarks at Arlington."

"Yes, sir?"

"Secretary Beiderman has been ordered by POTUS to order me to show them to you, General, and then inform you it is the President's desire that you immediately request retirement, and that if you do, that will be the end of it."

"The end of what, sir?"

Naylor hesitated, and then said, "I think it would be best if you heard this from Secretary Beiderman, General."

Beiderman's look of surprise — even shock — quickly turned into one of resignation — he had been had, and he knew it — and then into one of hate and loathing.

For a moment, he just sat there, and then he exhaled and leaned toward the red phone.

"General, the President seems to think

you are involved in a conspiracy that will see him resign, which would put Vice President Montvale in the Oval Office."

There was a long moment, and then General McNab said, very softly, "Mr. Secretary, would you please repeat that? I want to be absolutely sure I heard you correctly."

My God! Naylor thought. *McNab knew right away not only what's going on but how to deal with it.*

Thank God!

After a moment, Beiderman repeated, "General, the President seems to think you are involved in a conspiracy that will see him resign, and would put Vice President Montvale in the Oval Office."

Another pause, and then McNab said, "And you, Mr. Secretary, do you think I have been, or that I am, involved in a coup d'état such as you describe?"

"No, of course I don't," Beiderman snapped. "But that's what the President apparently believes, and that's what we have to deal with."

"First, Mr. Secretary," McNab said, "let me categorically deny that I am now or ever have been involved in something like that. And with equal emphasis let me say that I have no intention of requesting retirement

304

at this time. The President has — and for that matter, as you well know — you and General Naylor have — the right to relieve me of command of SPECOPSCOM at any time.

"But for me to resign under the circumstances you have laid out would be a tacit admission that I have been involved in a coup d'état. And that's treason, Mr. Secretary!"

"Now, calm down, General," the secretary of Defense said. "No one's accusing you of treason."

Naylor began: "General McNab —"

"Treason is a violation of the Uniform Code of Military Justice," McNab interrupted him with cold anger in his voice. "I demand a court-martial!"

Naylor thought, *Please, God, McNab, don't get carried away!*

"No one's talking about a court-martial, General McNab," he said.

"I am!"

"General, what Secretary Beiderman and I have been talking about is that when POTUS has a chance, over a few days, to reconsider what must be honestly described as an overreaction to what happened at Arlington and the Mayflower . . ."

"An 'overreaction'? It's insane, that's what it is!"

"Watch your choice of words, General," Naylor ordered sharply. "You're speaking of the Commander in Chief."

"Yes, sir," McNab said after a moment.

"As I was saying, Secretary Beiderman and I have been discussing the possibility that, after a few days, POTUS may reconsider and possibly even regret what can only be described as his loss of self-control."

Beiderman put in: "Get out of Dodge, so to speak, for a few days. Until this thing has a chance to blow over."

"And where should I go for a few days until this thing, this outrage, this insanity, blows over?" McNab demanded.

"If you were not at Fort Bragg, General," Naylor said, "if you were not at Fort Bragg when Secretary Beiderman and I arrived with the packet of photographs . . ."

"Go to Afghanistan, for Christ's sake," Beiderman snapped. "Confer with your people there. Just be unavailable."

After a moment McNab said, "Yes, sir, Mr. Secretary."

Congratulations, Mr. Secretary, Naylor thought. *You are now a coconspirator.*

The flashing LED on the red telephone stopped flashing.

"What the hell?" Beiderman demanded incredulously. "Did he hang up on us?"

Naylor held up his hand and then extended his arm and looked at his wristwatch.

Precisely sixty seconds later, he pushed a button on the red telephone. The LED began flashing.

"SPECOPSCOM," a new voice come over the circuit. "General O'Toole speaking, sir."

"This is General Naylor. Let me speak to General McNab, please."

"Sir, I'm sorry. He's not here."

"Where is he?" Beiderman demanded.

"Sir, he's on his way to Afghanistan."

"As soon as you can get in touch with him, O'Toole, have him call me," Naylor ordered.

"That will probably take about an hour, sir."

"As soon as possible," Naylor said, and hung up.

He met Beiderman's eyes, and said, "Done."

"And now O'Toole knows all about this," Beiderman said.

"No. O'Toole's the SPECOPSCOM deputy commander. McNab would have to tell him he was going to Afghanistan."

"Including the circumstances? *These* circumstances?" Beiderman asked. "So what

307

do we do now, General?"

"We wait to see what happens when POTUS gets his temper under control."

"And if he doesn't? If this makes him even more angry? God, Naylor, if he ever finds out what you and I just did . . ."

"If POTUS doesn't get his irrational behavior under control, which is a possibility, I'm afraid then you and I and the other rational people around him are going to have to worry about how to protect the country from that."

After a long moment, the secretary of Defense said very softly, "I've been wondering who would be the first to actually say that out loud."

[Five]
El Tepual International Airport
Puerto Montt, Chile
1945 17 April 2007

As the PeruaireCargo 777 taxied down the runway toward the refrigerator warehouses, Castillo saw that there were two other Boeings on the field. Both were identical to the aircraft on which they had flown from Cozumel — all Boeing 777-200LRs, just about the last word in heavy long-haul transport aircraft.

One bore the insignia of PeruaireCargo, and the other the paint scheme of Air Bulgaria, which Castillo could not remember ever having seen before.

But I will bet my next-to-last dime that it, too, belongs to Aleksandr Pevsner — or one of his several dozen wholly owned subsidiaries.

The Air Bulgaria freighter is about to carry a load of Argentine beef and Chilean salmon to Europe.

Maybe not to — what the hell is the capital of Bulgaria? — Sofia! — but to somewhere in eastern Europe. The PeruaireCargo 777 is almost certainly about to fly a hell of a lot of the same to San Francisco. Or to Chicago. And maybe on the way home, stop by Birmingham to pick up a load of nearly frozen Alabama chickens for the German market.

Ol' Alek seems to have a lock on the international movement of perishable foodstuffs.

And the international movement of God only knows what else that God only knows who wants moved very discreetly from hither to yon and is prepared to pay whatever it costs.

Despite his protestations that he's absolutely through doing that sort of thing.

Where the hell is the Lear?

There were no other fixed-wing aircraft on the tarmac. Castillo had expected to see

Pevsner's Learjet 45.

The only aircraft visible besides the huge cargo jets were two Bell 206L-4 helicopters, both painted with the legend CHILEAN HELICOPTERS S.A.

They were probably used to ferry the crews here from Santiago or wherever the hell else they were whooping it up between flights.

But where the hell is Pevsner's Lear?

"I don't see the Lear," Castillo said to his seatmate, who was in the process of applying lipstick, an act he found quite erotic.

They were in the small section of a dozen seats behind the bulkhead that separated them from the flight deck.

"Alek knew when we would arrive," Sweaty said. "It will be here."

The massive 777 stopped moving.

Max, who had spent just about all of the flight sound asleep, now awoke. He sat on his haunches and looked expectantly at the cabin door.

One of the crew came into the passenger compartment. There were seven men, all Russians, on the crew. All of them wore wings. Five of them wore the four-stripe shoulder boards of captains, and the other two the three-stripe shoulder boards of first officers.

The ranks didn't seem to matter, as one

of the captains functioned as the steward, cooking and serving lunch and making drinks, and the last time Castillo walked into the cockpit to see where the hell they were over South America, one of the first officers was occupying the pilot's seat.

He had come first to the conclusion that Russians did things differently, and then idly wondered what kind of passports the crew was carrying, and then decided that they more than likely had a selection of passports from which to choose, depending on where they had landed.

As a stairway mounted on a pickup truck was backed against the fuselage, the captain worked open the door.

When there was the light bump of the stairway contacting the aircraft, Max jumped to his feet, effortlessly shouldered the captain out of the way, and ran down the stairway.

"Isn't that sweet?" Castillo said. "He can't wait to see his babies."

"He's been on this plane for nine hours. I know what he wants to do," Sweaty said, then immediately stopped, realizing that she had been had.

"I better get down there before those two guys at the bottom of the steps see Max and wet their pants," Castillo said, and started to get out of his seat.

"My God," Koussevitzky suddenly said. "It's Blatov! And Koshkov!"

Koussevitzky beat Castillo to the door.

Castillo got there in time to see the two men salute, and heard one of them say, "Kapitáns Blatov and Koshkov reporting for duty, sir!"

Koussevitzky ran quickly down the stairs and the three men embraced. Castillo — moving slowly — made it all the way down the stairs before they broke apart. When they did, he saw tears running down all of their cheeks.

"Colonel Castillo, may I present Kapitáns Blatov and Koshkov, late of Vega Group Two?"

Both Blatov and Koshkov snapped to attention and saluted.

Castillo returned it, in Pavlovian response, and then put out his hand.

Koussevitzky saw the lack of understanding on Castillo's face.

"It was General Sirinov's plan, Carlos," Koussevitzky said, "that should something go wrong on La Orchila Island, a second Tupelov based in Cuba would fly in our reserve force."

"But by the time we got there, Podpolkovnik Castillo," Kapitán Koshkov said, "all we found was Major Koussevitzky resting against what was left of the hangar wall, drinking emergency liquid against the pain of the wound Podpolkovnik Alekseeva had given him."

Castillo looked at him and thought: *Emergency liquid? What the hell is that?*

"Emergency liquid?" he asked.

"Vodka, Carlos," Koshkov explained with a smile. "One knows when one has been really accepted as a Spetsnaz when the officer inspecting your equipment before a mission does not inspect your two water bottles to make sure one of them doesn't contain emergency liquid."

Kapitáns Koshkov and Blatov then snapped to attention again and raised their arms in a salute.

"Well, what have we here?" Tom Barlow asked, offering his hand. "A veterans' convention?"

"It is good to see you again, Polkovnik Berezovsky," Blatov said. And then quickly added, as Sweaty came off the stairs, "And you, Podpolkovnik Alekseeva."

Sweaty extended her hand. Koshkov and Blatov bent over it and kissed it.

Unless both of them had really been into the emergency liquid, I don't think a U.S. Army female light colonel has ever had her hand kissed by two captains.

"How did you get out?" Sweaty asked.

"It was only a question of time, Podpolkovnik Alekseeva, until they got around to deciding we were involved in the La Orchila Island disaster."

"That's not what I asked."

"We are Spetsnaz, Podpolkovnik Alekseeva," Koshkov replied. "We can do anything."

Castillo pushed back a grin as he thought: *Years ago, when I was a bushy-tailed Special Forces captain, we used to say, "Green Berets can do anything immediately. The impossible takes a little longer."*

He took another, closer look at Captains Koshkov and Blatov and decided, presuming they could speak English, they'd fit right in in the Stockade.

"Either of you speak English?" Castillo asked in English.

"About as well, Colonel," Koshkov answered in English, "as you speak Russian."

"I once studied to be a poet in Saint Petersburg," Castillo said.

Both smiled broadly.

"So, I understand, did Vladimir Vladimirovich," Blatov said. "That's the word going around."

"What are you doing here?" Koussevitzky asked.

"We're going to take you to Casa en el Bosque," Koshkov said.

"In those?" Castillo asked, indicating the Bells.

Koshkov nodded.

"They're really very nice little helicopters," he said.

"Very nice little helicopters," my ass. The factory calls them Long Rangers but they're better known as Super Rangers. High-inertia two-bladed rotors. Lots of power. Just the thing to fly through the Andes as darkness falls, presuming you have the know-how to fly them. Say a hundred hours under a good instructor.

I wonder where Alek Pevsner got them?

"How much time do you have in them, Captain?" Castillo asked.

Koshkov thought a minute, shrugged, then said, "About ten hours."

Ten hours?

Max interrupted his thought by walking up to Koshkov, sitting on his haunches, and offering his paw.

Max likes him. I'll be damned!

Koshkov stiffened; his face showed fear.

He confirmed this by announcing, "I'm not a friend of dogs."

315

"Well, you better shake that one's paw, or he'll eat you," Castillo said.

With great reluctance, Koshkov stooped and took Max's paw.

"Get in the chopper, Max," Castillo ordered, gesturing.

Max dutifully trotted to the closest helicopter and jumped inside. Koshkov was visibly relieved.

When Castillo got to the Bell, there was a man in the co-pilot's seat. A good pilot — say, one with a hundred hours under a good instructor — could fly a Super Ranger by himself, but a co-pilot, even one presumably with less than ten hours in the bird, was a nice thing to have.

"May I sit there, please?" Castillo asked politely.

The co-pilot didn't like that, but Koshkov signaled for him to give up his seat, and he did so.

Once he was seated in the co-pilot's position, a quick look at the interior of the Bell — especially at the panel — told Castillo that it was brand-new. The forward and side-looking radar screens, the GPS screen, and the radar altimeter bore the logos of the AFC Corporation, and that translated as "damn the cost, get the best."

He strapped himself in and put on the helmet that the co-pilot had reluctantly turned over to him.

"Test, test," he said through the throat microphone.

"Loud and clear," Koshkov reported. "Ready?"

"One thing, Captain Koshkov," Castillo said. "If at any time during this flight I put my hands on the controls and say, 'I've got it!' and you don't instantly take your hands off the controls, I will order Max to pull you out of your seat by sinking his teeth into your throat, and then, when we get on the ground, I will tell him to eat you, starting with your penis and testicles."

It did not produce the reaction he expected.

Koshkov smiled at him and said, "If at any time during our flight the co-pilot desires to take control of the aircraft, the pilot will be honored to turn it over to the author of *Light Helicopter Operation in Extreme Altitude and Mountainous Terrain Conditions*."

"Where the hell did you see that?"

"By Major C. G. Castillo, Chief Flight Examiner, 160th Special Operations Aviation Regiment," Koshkov finished. "I used it to teach the subject when I was at the

Spetsnaz aviation school."

"I will be damned."

"When we land, you can tell me how I did," Koshkov said. "Picking it up now."

The Bell lifted gently off. Koshkov lowered the nose, and then made a running takeoff.

VII

[One]
Casa en el Bosque
San Carlos de Bariloche
Río Negro Province, Argentina
2105 17 April 2007

At just about the moment the AFC GPS showed that they were over the estate, floodlights came on, illuminating the polo field, which was, Castillo judged, about 500 meters from the mansion.

As Koshkov brought the Super Ranger in for a smooth touchdown, with the second chopper following, Castillo saw there was a welcoming party.

Standing in front of the stable — which also served as a hangar — was a large welcoming party: Aleksandr Pevsner; his wife, Anna; and their three children, Elena, Sergei, and Aleksandr. Elena held one of

Max's pups in her arms.

Janos, Pevsner's huge Hungarian body-guard, stood where Castillo expected him to be, three feet behind Pevsner.

Standing three feet away was Berezovsky's wife, Lora, and their daughter, Sof'ya, who was holding another fruit of Max's loins in her arms. And to one side stood four women, three with small children in their arms, who had to be the wives of the pilots.

If it weren't for those dozen or more guys, all armed with Kalashnikov rifles, standing behind everybody, trying to be as discreet as possible, this would be a touching scene. If this were December, it could be Home for Christmas.

"How'd I do?" Koshkov asked as he braked the rotors.

"Not bad for someone who obviously has no natural flying talent at all," Castillo said.

Koshkov smiled and shook his head.

Max, seeing his pups, was first off the Super Ranger. With some trepidation, first Elena and then Sof'ya put their now-squirming pups on the ground. In attack mode, the dogs raced toward their father. Together, they weighed about half as much as Max.

Max instantly rolled on his back with his paws in the air, in surrender mode. The pups began to gnaw on his stomach and ears.

"I shudder to think," Aleksandr Pevsner said, as he shook Castillo's hand, "that the children's animals will eventually reach his size."

The kissing ritual began. Anna kissed Castillo. Sweaty kissed Pevsner, and then Anna. Castillo was not surprised when Anna kissed Lester Bradley — her husband was alive because Lester had put a .45 round in the forehead of Pevsner's would-be assassin, and from then on he was considered a member of the family — but he was surprised when both Blatov and Koshkov got into the line of people waiting to swap kisses with the Laird of Karinhall and his lady.

"More relatives?" Castillo asked Sweaty.

She nodded.

"Kiril and Anatoly," she replied, "are — let me see — second cousins, once removed. Aleksandr is Kiril's godfather."

"And that would make Kiril's baby what?" Castillo said. "A third cousin twice removed? Or just a second cousin twice removed?"

Sweaty considered the question seriously for perhaps thirty seconds before realizing she was being teased.

"You will pay for that, my love," she said.

"Which means they're Oprichniks in good standing?" he pursued.

"I'm getting sorry I ever told you about the Oprichnina," Sweaty said.

"Yes or no?"

"Of course," Sweaty said. "They couldn't have become Spetsnaz officers otherwise."

"Every Spetsnaz officer is an Oprichnik?"

"I didn't say that," Sweaty said.

"Yes, you did," Castillo said.

He sensed Aleksandr Pevsner's eyes on him.

"Very impressive, Alek," Castillo said, indicating the men with the Kalashnikovs. "But where's the band?"

"The band?"

"I sort of expected a brass band to welcome us. Or at least somebody playing 'The Volga Boatmen' on a balalaika."

Pevsner shook his head resignedly.

"Let's go down to the house and have dinner," he said. "Afterward, we have a lot to talk about."

"Would you like to freshen up?" the Laird of Karinhall, the perfect host, asked, "or after a drink?"

"Give me ten minutes," Sweaty said.

There was nothing in her reply, or tone of voice, that suggests she has anything more romantic — or carnal — on her mind than freshening up.

Damn!

Oh, I know. It's because I mocked the family. And the Oprichnina.

"I'll have a little of the emergency liquid, please," Castillo said, smiling at Kiril Koshkov and indicating a bottle of vodka encased in a block of ice.

"Oh, that's right, you heard about that, didn't you?" Koshkov said with a smile.

"Kiril's been telling me how undisciplined you Spetsnaz are," Castillo replied.

Pevsner was also smiling broadly as he generously poured the literally ice-cold vodka into a chilled glass.

What the hell are you smiling about, Alek? You never were Spetsnaz, and I don't think you even know what we're talking about.

Epiphany time!

You're smiling because you know that even one drink will make me one drink stupider when we have our little chat. With a little luck, I will be two — or more — drinks stupider when we have the chat.

The thing for me to remember about you, Alek, ol' buddy, is that you were SVR, and while you can take the boy out of Russia, you can't take the SVR out of the boy.

Not a problem. I will have two or more drinks

— after that flight through the Andes, I'm entitled. And we will have our little chat in the morning, not tonight.

It was fifteen minutes — during which time Castillo had two substantial belts of vodka — before Sweaty rejoined the family, and then everyone went into the dining room. Not surprising Castillo at all were both another frosty glass of chilled vodka and a bottle of Saint Felicien Cabernet Sauvignon waiting for him at his place at the enormous table.

Sweaty was seated beside him.

"I waited for you," Sweaty said quietly.

"Really? What did you want?"

She said, "It's not important." Her eyes told him carnal was off the table for tonight. And maybe for the next day, too.

What was on the table for tonight was a feast of Chilean seafood — absolutely marvelous oysters and enormous lobsters.

About half a bottle of Cabernet Sauvignon later, Castillo was watching when former Gunnery Sergeant Lester Bradley, USMC, stopped cracking the claw of an enormous lobster, pushed his chair away from the table, picked something up from the floor, and discreetly put it on his lap.

Castillo knew what had happened: When Lester rose in the morning, he stuffed a theoretically invisible flesh-colored speaker into his ear canal. When a call came to his closed Brick and there was no answer, it spoke a number into the earpiece, identifying the person who was having trouble getting through.

Castillo naturally wondered who was calling. He learned who it was only after Lester pushed back from the table, took a handset from the Brick, walked over to Castillo, and handed it to him.

The illuminated LEDs on the handset told Castillo that the Brick was in Category I encryption status and showed him the number 6.

Castillo put the handset to his ear.

"Castillo," he said.

There was a very brief period during which the system compared the digital interpretation of his voice with its database, found a 99.9 percent match, and illuminated the number 1 on the calling party's handset, telling A. Franklin Lammelle, the director of the Central Intelligence Agency, that he was now connected with Lieutenant Colonel C. G. Castillo, U.S. Army, Retired.

"Where the hell have you been, Charley?" Lammelle began the conversation. "I've been calling every five minutes for the past half hour."

"I was occupied."

"Doing what, that you couldn't answer?"

"For most of that time, I was dodging rock-filled clouds in a helicopter flown by a guy who finished flight school six weeks ago in Sevastopol. I don't take calls under those conditions."

He exchanged smiles with Koshkov.

Lester didn't think I should have gotten on the phone, either; otherwise he would have handed it to me.

"Rock-filled clouds where?"

"The Andes."

"What the hell are you doing down there? The locator's not working."

"I turned it off," Castillo replied, adding, "At the moment, eating lobster."

"Why do I suspect you've been at the sauce?"

"You're perceptive? Would that explain it?"

"Jesus Christ, Charley, the last thing I need is you smashed."

Right now, the last thing Charley needs is Charley smashed.

Whatever this is, Lammelle is excited about it.

Why the hell did I drink that goddamn vodka?

325

"Frank, calm down. Consider the possibility that I'm pulling your chain."

"You sonofabitch! You have a sick sense of humor!"

"So I have been told," Castillo said.

He saw Sweaty making an exaggerated punching motion with her index finger.

He knew what it meant — *turn on the loudspeaker function* — and ignored her.

"So are you going to tell me what's so important or not?" Castillo asked.

There was a pause, suggesting Lammelle was getting his temper under control.

"Forty-five minutes ago, I had a call from General McNab," he began. "He's on his way to Afghanistan."

"So? Half of SPECOPSCOM is in Afghanistan; he goes there all the time."

"I think maybe I should start at the beginning," Lammelle said.

"Yeah. Why don't you?"

"The people you had at Arlington — and you, too — walked out on the President's remarks."

"Actually, we got in our limos and went to the Mayflower. So what?"

"You having those Delta and Gray Fox guys at Arlington pissed the President off. And then you walked out on his remarks. That pissed him off even more. And your

326

party at the Mayflower pushed him over the edge."

"What does that mean?"

"I told you before, in the last conversation we had, that Clendennen sent the FBI to the Mayflower to take pictures of everybody there. And among those there were Porky Parker and Roscoe Danton, and that really pissed him off."

"And do you now know why he did that?"

"So that he would have proof."

"Of what? You sound as if *you've* been at the sauce."

"After FBI Director Mark Schmidt had personally identified each and every party-goer for him . . ."

"It wasn't a party, for Christ's sake. In our last conversation, you will recall, I told you it was more like a wake. We stood around drinking, telling Danny Salazar war stories —"

"I remember," Lammelle interrupted him, and then went on, ". . . he gave them to Beiderman with orders to give them to Naylor, with orders for Naylor to show them to McNab and tell him that he — the President — knew, quote, what McNab was up to, close quote, but that if McNab applied for immediate retirement it, quote, would be the end of it, close quote."

"What does he think McNab was . . . is . . . up to?"

"He apparently believes McNab is in a conspiracy to get him out of the Oval Office and Montvale into it. If I have to say this, he thinks you're a coconspirator."

"That's crazy!"

"Please remember later, if you are asked under oath, that I did not introduce that word into this conversation. You did."

"Jesus Christ," Castillo muttered, then exhaled audibly, and said, "The first thing that comes into my mind — unwilling as I am to accept crazy — is that he's into the bottle. A secret tippler. Was our beloved Commander in Chief sober when he did all this?"

"Yes, he was. He's a teetotaler. The boozers in his family are his mother and mother-in-law."

"Where are you getting all this, Frank?"

"General McNab made the point to me that he has not spoken with you since before Salazar and the others were murdered and Colonel Ferris kidnapped . . ."

"He hasn't," Castillo confirmed.

". . . which of course suggested to me that he wanted me to bring you into the loop especially in view of the fact that the other players are not liable to."

"The other players being?"

"Thus far, Naylor and Beiderman. So, after speaking with General McNab, I spoke — separately — with both General Naylor and Secretary Beiderman."

"They agree with your crazy theory?"

"I don't have a crazy theory, Charley. Write that down. In blood. On your forehead."

"They agree with the 'he's out of his mind' theory?"

"They talked around it. But, yeah, they're worried."

"What happened when Beiderman or Naylor told McNab the President wanted him to retire?"

"It didn't get that far. Beiderman told McNab to get out of Dodge before he had to show him the pictures. He did."

"For McNab to retire would be an admission that he was involved in this nutty coup d'état scenario. He wouldn't — couldn't — do that. He'd demand a court-martial."

"That's precisely what McNab told them just before Beiderman told him to go to Afghanistan before he could show him the pictures and deliver the 'retire now' ultimatum. Both Beiderman and Naylor are hoping the whole thing will pass when Clendennen has a couple of days to cool off."

"That looks to me like pissing into the wind, Frank."

"Yeah. Agreed."

"Did my name come up when you talked with Naylor and Beiderman?"

"Oh, yes."

"Either one of them think I'm involved in this conspiracy?"

"No. But when your name came up, the phrase Beiderman used was 'loose cannon,' in the phrase 'the one thing we don't need in these circumstances is a loose cannon like Castillo.' "

"And Naylor didn't rush to my defense?"

"No. He didn't."

"So what happens now?"

"We wait to see if this coup d'état theory of the President goes away when he's had a few days to cool off."

"And if it doesn't?"

Lammelle was silent a long moment. Then he said, "I don't know, Charley."

Then, when Castillo didn't reply for maybe thirty seconds, Lammelle asked, "Any questions?"

"Just one. Where's my helicopter?"

"I'm not sure I should tell you."

"Come on, Frank."

Lammelle took another long moment of silence before he said: "Okay, Charley. In a move I regretted before I finished hanging up the phone, I ordered it loaded onto a truck and taken to Martindale Army Airfield at Fort Sam for indefinite storage."

"Despite what everybody says about you, Frank, on certain occasions, you can be a good guy."

"I'm not asking what you're going to do with it, because I don't want to know."

The green LED on Castillo's handset went out.

"So long, Frank," he said to the dead headset. "It's always a pleasure to hear from you."

He handed the headset to Lester, picked up his lobster fork, then glanced around the table. All eyes were on him.

"Anything wrong, Charley?" Aleksandr Pevsner asked with a smile. "You looked very unhappy while you were talking."

"Nothing I can't handle in the morning, Alek, when time will have taken the emergency liquid out of my system."

"Excuse me?"

"I thought you knew that I never discuss serious things when I've been drinking."

"Not even with family?"

"*Especially* not with this family," Castillo said.

That earned him smiling lips and icy eyes

331

from Pevsner.

When he looked at Sweaty, he knew she wouldn't be smiling, and he expected to get the same icy glare from her blue eyes.

Instead, he got a faint smile — of approval, he realized with some surprise after a moment — and then, as he moved a chunk of lobster from a bowl of melted butter to his mouth, she groped him tenderly under the tablecloth.

The feeling of euphoria — or at least carnal anticipation — lasted until they were in their room. Castillo had waited maybe a second after Sweaty had gone into the bathroom before getting naked and under the sheets. He had been lying on his back with his fingers laced behind his head, waiting for her to join him, when his world crashed around him.

Epiphany!
Stop thinking with your dick, James Bond.
What you thought about good ol' Alek is also true of Sweaty.
You can take the girl out of Russia, but only a fool thinking with his little head would believe you could take the SVR out of former Podpolkovnik Svetlana Alekseeva.
The most important thing to any of them is

family. And/or the Oprichnina.

And you are not family. And certainly not an Oprichnik.

They told me — and I believe it — that the way they've survived since Ivan the Terrible is by doing whatever was necessary. The translation of that is being as ruthless as necessary.

And she's smart. God, is she smart! When Juan Carlos Pena wanted my nonexistent address in Uruguay, she came up with the Golf and Polo Club in the next breath.

Which means she had no trouble at all figuring out that I'm likely to pose problems in their current battle with their former comrades in the SVR. I told her I was going to make it clear to Pevsner that I wasn't going to let him whack anybody without my permission. And when I got into it with Pevsner just now . . .

"I never discuss serious things when I've been drinking."

"Not even with family?"

"*Especially* not with this family."

. . . it had to be obvious to her that I was not going to be a good little boy and do whatever Wise ol' Uncle Alek thinks I should do.

So what to do about that? They can't whack me — although that remains a possibility for the future — because right now they need me.

She knew that I was talking to Lammelle on

the phone, even from the one side of the conversation I let her hear.

So, just as fast as she came up with the address for Juan Carlos, when she saw that I was already challenging Pevsner's authority, she decided the way to deal with the situation was in bed. She could control me there.

And why shouldn't she think so?

Less than twenty-four hours after we first met, she was in my bed — and has been leading me around by the wang ever since.

So she grabbed hold of it under the table here.

And I can't even get really pissed off at her. She is what she is, and what she is is a fourth — hell, maybe sixth — generation Soviet spook.

Can I be pissed at me — James Bond Junior?

Sure.

Because James Bond Junior is acting not like even a junior spook — one six months out of Fort Huachuca or the Farm — but like some seventeen-year-old with raging hormones who just got laid for the first time and is convinced there has never been love like this since Adam screwed Eve in the Garden of Eden.

And because it's humiliating having to face proof of my gross stupidity.

■ ■ ■ ■

Sweaty came out of the bathroom, holding a towel by its edges.

"Showtime!" she said, and dropped the towel.

That has to be the most beautiful woman in the world.

She walked on her toes to the bed quickly and with exquisite grace and got in beside him.

She laid her body half across Castillo, making him think that she had the most wonderful breasts he had ever encountered by any standard he could think of.

"You play the fool so well," she said, "that sometimes I forget that you're not a fool at all."

He could feel her breath against his ear.

"Flattery will get you everywhere," he said. "But what specifically do you have in mind?"

"Aleksandr's face, when you told him you never discuss business when you're drinking, especially with *this* family, was priceless."

Well, here it is. The schmooze starts.

"Beware of Russians bearing booze is my motto, baby."

"And why didn't you tell me you're a legend?"

"Who said I was?"

"Kiril. When I said, 'Thank you for letting Carlos fly as your co-pilot,' he said, 'I was glad to have him. I don't think anyone knows more about flying in the mountains than he does. He even wrote a book about it. He's a legend in the American army.' Why didn't you tell me?"

"Modesty."

She pinched his nipple.

Well, she's a good schmoozer. I almost believe her.

"Can I ask you a personal question?" he said.

"No."

"What kind of don't-get-pregnant medicine do you take?" he pursued, then thought: *Where the hell did that come from? Did Alek put a little sodium pentothal in that vodka?*

"I should have known . . ." she said with a sigh.

"You're not answering the question."

"You really want to know?"

"I really want to know."

Why not? Like it says on the CIA's wall in Langley, "Ye shall know the truth and the truth shall make you free."

336

"When I stopped living with Evgeny, I stopped taking those once-a-day pills."

"You were on that stuff when you were married to Evgeny? Why?"

"I didn't want his baby, obviously."

Charley thought: *And since you certainly don't want mine . . .*

He said: "And now?"

"When I knew Dmitri and I were going to try to get out, I went to a Danish gynecologist and she gave me a shot."

"What kind of a shot?"

"I don't know what it was called, but she said it would keep me from getting with child for a year . . ."

In case you just happened to meet somebody who could be useful if you let him into your pants, right? Like me?

". . . which was enough. I didn't mind dying, but I didn't want the bastard child of an SVR interrogator . . ."

"What?"

"The first step when breaking down a senior female traitor is to rape her," Sweaty said matter-of-factly. "Multiple times, different men, over a forty-eight-hour period. I could handle that, but I didn't want a child coming into the world that way. If they shot me, it wouldn't have been a problem, but they could have — probably would have —

just kept me in prison, where I would wind up giving birth to the bastard child. So I got the shot from the Danish doctor."

Update on the epiphany: She's not making this up.

Jesus H. Christ!

"Two weeks later I met you," Sweaty went on. "And sure enough, the shot kept me from being with child for a year. Actually for fourteen months."

"So what are you going to do now?"

She met his eyes, and after a moment said: "In seven months, we're going to have a baby. I told you I was going to give you a son. *Sons.* Didn't you believe me?"

He stared into her ice blue eyes, now genuinely warm, and thought: *Calling Charley Castillo a miserable lowlife sickly suspicious sonofabitch is the monumental understatement of all time.*

Then, taking him absolutely by surprise, his chest started to heave and his eyes teared.

"Oh, God!" he said in anguish. "Oh, Sweaty!"

"I thought you'd be happy?" she said, confused.

"Sweetheart, I am so happy I think I'm going to have a heart attack."

The Breakfast Room
Casa en el Bosque
San Carlos de Bariloche
Río Negro Province, Argentina
0815 18 April 2007

Aleksandr Pevsner, Tom Barlow, Nicolai Tarasov, Stefan Koussevitzky, Kiril Koshkov, and Anatoly Blatov were sitting around the long table when Castillo and Svetlana walked in, holding hands, trailed by Lester Bradley, his arms full with two laptops and a Brick. Janos was in his usual place, sitting in a chair against the wall.

A maid and one of Pevsner's ex-Spetsnaz waiters were clearing away the breakfast dishes.

I knew Alek was going to play King of the Hill sooner or later, and that just won't work. Better settle it once and for all right now.

"Sweaty, I don't think the *Reichsmarschall* plans to feed us," Castillo said in English. "Do you think we could possibly have annoyed him in some way?"

"The *Reichsmarschall*," Pevsner replied sarcastically, "didn't know how long it would be before — or even if — Romeo and Juliet could bear to be torn apart. So we decided we'd better start without you."

339

Castillo looked around the table. Tom Barlow was smiling. The others were stone-faced.

"Nice try, Hermann, but no brass ring," Castillo said. "Starting without me would be what Kiril, Anatoly, and I would call really flying blind, and you know it. Or you should."

Pevsner stared at him icily but didn't reply.

Castillo turned to the waiter and, switching to Russian, ordered: "Set places for us. Put me at the head of the table, where Mr. Pevsner is now sitting. Podpolkovnik Alekseeva will sit to my right, and Mr. Bradley to my left."

The waiter looked at Pevsner for direction. He got none.

"Your house, Alek, your call," Castillo said. "You either stop behaving like you think you're Ivan the Terrible and I'm a second lieutenant of your household cavalry, or we're out of here."

"*We're* out of here?" Pevsner parroted sarcastically.

"ETA of Jake Torine and the Gulfstream at San Carlos de Bariloche International is twelve fifteen," Castillo said. "Unless you agree that I'm the best man to deal with our mutual problem, I'll just get on it and leave you here to deal with your problem by yourself."

"Then get on your goddamn airplane and go," Pevsner said.

"Where Carlos goes, I go," Svetlana said.

Pevsner shot back: "Then *both* of you get on the goddamn airplane and go. I will deal with the problem this family faces."

"Aleksandr," Nicolai Tarasov said, "I think you should listen to what Podpolkovnik Castillo has to say."

Pevsner looked at him in disbelief.

"I'll go further than that," Tom Barlow said. "You *have* to listen to what Carlos has to say."

"Or what?" Pevsner snapped.

"Or when Carlos's airplane leaves, Lora, Sof'ya, and I also will be on it. Presuming of course Carlos will take us."

"Of course we will," Svetlana said. "You're family."

"Family? Family? What it looks like to me is that my family is betraying me and taking the side of this goddamn American."

Svetlana snapped: "You goddamn fool! You are alive because of this 'goddamn American.' "

Castillo thought: *She sounds like an SVR lieutenant colonel.*

"And if not for Carlos," Tom Barlow added, "Svetlana, Lora, Sof'ya, and I would never have gotten out of Vienna. And you really would be handling this family problem by yourself."

"Before this family starts doing to each other what Vladimir Vladimirovich wants to do to us," Tarasov said, "can we at least listen to what Podpolkovnik Castillo has to say?"

Pevsner glared at each of them.

"I'll listen," he said after a moment.

"How gracious of you," Castillo said, his tone dripping sarcasm. "May I presume that I have the floor?"

"I should have killed you on the Cobenzl," Pevsner said evenly.

"I guess I don't," Castillo said.

"Yes, you do," Tom Barlow said. "Aleksandr, I just figured your odd behavior out. You just can't face the fact that Carlos can deal with this problem better than you can. Carlos was right — again — to say that you think you're Ivan the Terrible and we're in Russia. You're not, and we're not. I say, thank God for Carlos."

"So do I," Anna Pevsner put in.

Castillo snapped his head around. He had been unaware she'd come into the room.

"What?" Pevsner snapped.

"Will anyone join me in giving thanks to the Lord for bringing Carlos into the family?" Anna said as she bent her head and put her hands, fingertips touching, together in prayer.

Castillo thought that Svetlana would be agreeable to involving the Deity, but he was genuinely surprised when Nicolai Tarasov and Stefan Koussevitzky got to their feet, bowed their heads, crossed themselves, put their hands together, and waited for Anna to continue.

And really surprised when Aleksandr Pevsner did the same thing.

Ninety seconds later, after everyone had joined Anna in saying "Amen," Castillo suddenly found himself facing an expectant audience.

And so I have the floor . . .

"The way I'm going to do this is with what the U.S. Army calls a staff study," he began. "If we can get laptops in here for everybody, Lester has my staff study on a thumb drive . . ."

"You heard Podpolkovnik Castillo," Aleksandr Pevsner barked at the waiter. "What are you waiting for? Bring the goddamn laptops! And immediately serve their breakfast, as was ordered."

[Three]
The Oval Office
The White House
1600 Pennsylvania Avenue, N.W.
Washington, D.C.
0830 18 April 2007

"Go see who's out there, Douglas," President Clendennen ordered. "I called this meeting for half past eight, and that's what time it is."

"Yes, Mr. President," replied Secret Service Special Agent Mark Douglas, who now saw himself as the guardian of the President's door. He went through the door into the outer office.

The President pointed at Clemens McCarthy, the presidential press secretary, and at Supervisory Secret Service Agent Robert J. Mulligan — both seated on simple chairs against the wall — and motioned them toward the armchairs and couches to which senior officials felt entitled.

"We don't want these disloyal bastards to feel too comfortable in here, do we?" the President asked rhetorically.

Douglas came back into the office and announced, "The secretary of State, the attorney general, and the FBI director are out there, Mr. President."

"Look at your watch, and in precisely five minutes let them in," the President ordered.

"Yes, sir. And the secretary of Defense, Mr. President, and General Naylor are out there."

"I didn't send for them," Clendennen said.

"Secretary Beiderman said he is aware he doesn't have an appointment, Mr. President," Douglas said. "He said he will await your pleasure."

Clendennen considered that a moment, and then said, "Let them in with the others."

"Yes, sir."

Five minutes later, Secretary of State Natalie Cohen led Attorney General Stanley Crenshaw, FBI Director Mark Schmidt, Defense Secretary Frederick K. Beiderman, and CENTCOM Commander in Chief General Allan Naylor into the room.

"Since I didn't send for you, Secretary Beiderman," the President said, "what's on your mind? Let's get that out of the way first."

"Mr. President, I regret to have to tell you that General Naylor was unable to speak with General McNab as you requested."

"Why not?"

"General McNab was on his way to — by

now is in — Afghanistan," Beiderman said, and waited for the explosion.

It didn't come.

Clendennen didn't say anything at all.

Beiderman went on: "It was our intention, Mr. President — General Naylor's and mine — to speak with General McNab together. But when General Naylor called, General O'Toole, the deputy SPECOPSCOM commander, reported that General McNab was on his way to Afghanistan."

The President considered that for a moment, and then said, "Well, we'll just have to deal with that issue at a later time, won't we?"

"Yes, sir," Beiderman said.

"And the photographs?"

"I have them right here, Mr. President."

"Give them to Mulligan," the President said. "We wouldn't want them to disappear, would we?"

"Yes, sir," Beiderman said. "I mean, no, sir, we wouldn't."

Still standing, and thus somewhat awkwardly, he opened his attaché case, took out the manila envelope that held the photographs, and handed it to Supervisory Special Agent Mulligan.

"Will that be all, Mr. President?" Beiderman asked.

"No. Stick around. I think you should hear what we're going to do about Colonel Ferris. You, too, General Naylor."

"Yes, sir," they replied, speaking on top of each other.

Natalie Cohen, although she had not been invited to do so, sat down in one of the armchairs. After a moment, Attorney General Crenshaw sat on one of the couches, and a moment later FBI Director Schmidt sat beside him. Beiderman and Naylor remained standing.

"So where do I start?" the President asked rhetorically, and then answered his own question. "With you, Schmidt."

"Yes, sir?"

"How are things going in El Paso? Has that classified advertisement our Mexican friends have asked for been published yet?"

"Yes, sir. Yesterday. The first time, yesterday. It will run for four days."

"And when do you think there will be a reply. Today? Or when?"

"Mr. President, my SAC there — William Johnson — I told you about him, sir. He's one of my best —"

"That's nice to hear, but it doesn't answer my question," the President interrupted.

"I was about to say, sir, that SAC Johnson has determined that the average time for

347

delivery of a letter deposited in a post office to be delivered to a post office box in the same building is a minimum of six hours, and may take as long as twenty-four."

"You're telling me it takes our postal service at least six hours to move a letter from the in slot to a box?"

"Yes, sir. And that's presuming the letter would be placed in a mail drop slot in the post office building itself. If it were placed — as it very likely would be — in one of the drive-past post boxes outside the post office, that could add as much as two hours to that time. Mail is collected from the outside boxes every two hours from eight A.M. to midnight. It is collected only once from there from midnight until eight A.M.

"And of course if a letter were deposited in a mailbox not immediately outside the main post office, that time would be further increased, as the mail is picked up from there usually only twice a day. And if it were mailed in Ciudad Juárez — right across the border from El Paso — that would add at least another twenty-fours to the time. And if it were mailed in, say, in San Antonio, it —"

"I get the picture, Schmidt," the President said, cutting him off. "There is a very unlikely possibility — on the order of a miracle — that if our Mexican friends went to the main post office in El Paso yesterday, their reply could be in our box right now. If that isn't the case, we have no idea when we'll hear from them."

"If a letter had been deposited in Post Office Box 2333, Mr. President, we'd know about it. SAC Johnson has agents all over that post office," FBI Director Schmidt announced, more than a little proudly.

"Not only are there surveillance cameras inside and outside the building," Schmidt went on, "but agents, male and female, are constantly rotated through the lobby. Additionally, there are agents in the working area of the post office physically checking each piece of mail as it is dropped in a slot. Other agents go through mail coming into the post office from all sources."

Then Schmidt suddenly got carried away with his recitation of SAC Johnson's accomplishments: "Mr. President, the FBI has got that post office covered like flies on horseshit."

President Clendennen did not seem very impressed.

He said: "So what happens if somebody drops a letter addressed to box . . . whatever . . ."

"Box 2333, Mr. President," Schmidt furnished.

". . . and an agent sees him do it? Or someone comes into the post office and goes looking in Box 2333? What then?"

"In the first case, Mr. President, two things will happen. The envelope will be opened, and the contents photocopied, sent to the FBI's San Antonio office, and immediately forwarded to the J. Edgar Hoover Building, where agents are standing by to bring it here. Meanwhile, the letter dropper will be surveilled to see where he goes. Same surveillance will be placed on anyone going to Box 2333."

"What if he heads for Mexico?" the President asked.

"He will be arrested if he tries that, Mr. President."

"No," President Clendennen said. "He will not be arrested."

"Sir?"

"And you tell your SAC that if this happens, and the person being surveilled even looks like he suspects he is being surveilled, your SAC will be fired. Got it?"

"Yes, sir."

"I'm going to get this Colonel Ferris back," the President said. "And this is how I'm going to do it. First step: Get on the phone right now, Schmidt, and tell your SAC what I just said — that he is not to arrest anybody without my permission, and if anyone he is surveilling in this situation even suspects we're watching him, you will transfer him to Alaska."

"Yes, sir."

"Go do it," the President ordered as he pointed to the door to the outer office.

"Mr. President, I can contact SAC Johnson on my cell phone; it has encryption capability."

"Well, then take your cell phone with its encryption capability in there and call him."

He waited until Schmidt had reached the door and then turned to Secretary of State Natalie Cohen.

"Has Ambassador McCann proved to be as capable as I thought he would be, Madam Secretary? More important, how close has he managed to get to President Martinez?"

"Ambassador McCann is both highly capable, Mr. President, and has already established a good relationship with President Martinez."

"I want you to get on the horn to Mc-Cann, Madam Secretary, and tell him to see Martinez right now, and get him to send me a letter."

"Sir?"

"Give it to her, Clemens," the President said.

McCarthy handed Cohen a sheet of paper.

"Or words to this effect," the President said. "Read it aloud, Madam Secretary, so everybody will be on the same page."

Cohen took the sheet of paper, glanced at it, and began, "This is apparently a draft," and then read the letter aloud:

---

draft draft draft draft draft draft draft draft draft draft

{This would be better on Martinez's personal, rather than official, stationery}

date
My dear friend Zeke,

I come to you to ask for an act of Christian charity and compassion.

As a devoted father and family man yourself, you know that once in a while — perhaps more often than we realize — every family produces a worthless son, even a murderer.

Such is the case with the Abrego family, a thoroughly decent family who work a

---

small farm in Oaxaca State. They have had two daughters and a son, Félix. According to Bishop (need a name) a truly wise and Christian man, whom I have known for years, and who brought this to me, Félix started to go bad when he was twelve, and despite every prayerful thing his mother and father and his priest tried to do for him, kept moving ever faster on the path to hell.

Bishop (Whatsisname) knows this, because earlier in his career he was the Abrego family priest. And as a wholly honest man, Bishop (Whatsisname) is as willing as I am to admit that, guilty as charged, Félix Abrego fully deserves the punishment laid upon him by an American court for brutal acts of murder. He is currently imprisoned, for life, without the possibility of parole, in your federal prison in Florence, Colorado.

Señora Abrego, his sixty-seven-year-old mother, has been diagnosed with a particular nasty cancer (get a name for the cancer?) and has less than four (two? three?) months to live. She is confined to her bed, and can get around only in a wheelchair.

Obviously, she can't travel to Colorado, and she wants to see her son for a last time before she dies. I'm imploring you to help me arrange that.

What I propose is this:

There are at least a half dozen "open" Policía Federal warrants involving Félix Abrego. They have not been actively pursued because it was reasoned that since he is already confined without the possibility of parole, it would be a waste of time and money to try to convict him of something else.

I have been told there is a provision in U.S. law whereby a prisoner like Félix Abrego may be released from prison into the custody of the U.S. Marshal Service and taken for interrogation to a foreign country, such as Mexico.

In this case, if you would use your good offices to approve a request from the Policía Federal to bring Abrego to Mexico for interrogation, your Marshals would transport him to the Oaxaca State Prison, where they would turn him over to prison authorities.

This would permit the Policía Federal to interrogate him. And it would also permit

Señora Abrego to visit her son for the last time before her death. Once that inevitably happens, Abrego could either be returned to the United States to complete his confinement or, alternatively, tried here. In this case, there are so many charges against him here that he would almost certainly be sentenced to spend the remainder of his life in a Mexican prison.

If in your good judgment something can be worked out, please call me at your convenience and we can work out the details.

With warm regards,

Your friend
Ramón

"Well?" the President asked when she had finished.

"Mr. President, what is it you wish me to do with this?" Secretary Cohen asked.

"I told you. Get it to McCann and have him take it to President Martinez."

"Mr. President," Attorney General Crenshaw said, "the long-standing policy of the United States has been never to negotiate with terrorists."

"Who's negotiating with terrorists?" Clemens McCarthy replied for the President. "What President Clendennen is going to do is send a convicted criminal for interrogation in Mexico, which has the added benefit of permitting a terminally ill woman to see her son for the last time. If that also results in the release of Colonel Ferris, what's wrong with that?"

"It's bullshit, McCarthy, that's what's wrong with it," Crenshaw said.

"There's a lady present, Mr. Attorney General," the President said. "Watch your mouth!"

"I beg your pardon, Madam Secretary," Crenshaw said.

"Obviously, Mr. Attorney General," the President said, "you have some objections to my plan to secure the release of Colonel Ferris."

"Yes, sir, I have a number of —"

"I'm not interested in what they might be, Mr. Attorney General. This is the plan of action your Commander in Chief has decided upon. My question is whether your objections will keep you from carrying out my orders to see that what I want done is done."

"That would depend, Mr. President, on what orders you give me."

"Fair enough," the President said. "If I

ordered you to have this fellow Abrego moved from his present place of confinement to the La Tuna Federal Correctional Institution, would your conscience permit you to carry out that order?"

"Mr. President, are you aware that Abrego has been adjudicated to be a very dangerous and violent prisoner requiring his incarceration in the Florence maximum-security facility?"

"So Clemens has told me."

"And that La Tuna is a minimum-security facility? What they call a country club for the incarceration of nonviolent white-collar offenders?"

"Are you going to be able to obey my orders or not?"

The attorney general looked at the secretary of State and saw on her face and in her eyes that she was afraid he was going to say no.

"Mr. President, if you order me to move Abrego from Florence ADMAX to the La Tuna minimum-security facility, I'll have him moved."

"Good. I like what the military calls 'cheerful and willing obedience' to my orders to my loyal subordinates."

President Clendennen turned to Secretary of State Cohen.

"I presume that you are also going to cheerfully and willingly obey my orders to you, Madam Secretary, vis-à-vis having Ambassador McCann deliver Clemens's brilliant letter to President Martinez?"

"I will take the letter to Ambassador McCann, Mr. President, but I'm not sure he will be willing to take it to President Martinez, and I have no idea how President Martinez would react to it if he does."

"McCann will do it because he works for you, Madam Secretary — although actually, since I appointed him, he's *my* ambassador extraordinary and plenipotentiary and knows who butters his bread — and Martinez will go along with it. What my good friend Ramón wants to do is not antagonize the drug cartels any more than he has to. And to keep the tourists and retirees — and all those lovely U.S. dollars — going to Acapulco and those other places in sunny Mexico. My plan will allow him to do both."

He turned to Defense Secretary Beiderman and General Naylor.

"Now, as far as you two are concerned, I presume that you two, as loyal subordinates of your Commander in Chief, will both cheerfully and willingly obey this direct order: I don't want any involvement by the military in this. Period. None. Either of you have any problems with that?"

"No, sir," Beiderman said.

"No, Mr. President," Naylor said.

"Okay," the President said. "That's it. Thank you for coming in. Douglas, show them out."

"Yes, Mr. President," Special Agent Douglas said.

Attorney General Crenshaw caught up with Secretary of State Cohen as she was about to get into her limousine in the driveway.

"Natalie, we're going to have to talk."

"Not now," she replied as she slid onto the backseat. "I tend to make bad decisions when I am so upset that I feel sick to my stomach."

"We can't pretend this didn't happen," he insisted.

"Give me twenty-four hours to think it over," she said, and then pulled the limousine door closed.

[Four]
United States Post Office
8401 Boeing Drive
El Paso, Texas
1005 18 April 2007

A very short, totally bald, barrel-chested

man in a crisp tan suit leaned against the post office wall, puffing on a long, thin black cigar while reading *El Diario de El Paso.*

A man in filthy clothing — with an unshaven and unwashed face, and sunken eyes — sidled up to the nicely dressed man. If profiling was not politically incorrect, he might have caused many police officers and Border Patrol officers to think of him as possibly an undocumented immigrant or someone suffering from substance abuse or both.

The wetback junkie looked around as if to detect the presence of law enforcement officers, and then inquired, "Hey, gringo, you wanna fook my see-ster?"

"Your wife, maybe," the well-dressed man replied. "But the last time I saw your sister, she weighed three hundred pounds and needed a shave."

The junkie then shook his head, smiled, and with no detectable accent said, "You sonofabitch!"

"There's a Starbucks around the corner," the well-dressed man said.

"Dressed like this? Where's your car?"

"In the next parking lot," the well-dressed man said, and nodded across the street. "Walk down the street. I'll pick you up."

The well-dressed man walked away to the

left, and the junkie to the right.

Five minutes later, sitting with the junkie in a rented Lincoln parked five blocks from the post office on Boeing Drive, Vic D'Alessandro punched the appropriate buttons on his Brick, and fifteen seconds later was rewarded with the voice of A. Franklin Lammelle, the director of the Central Intelligence Agency.

"And how, Vic, are things in scenic El Paso?"

"Pics coming through all right?"

"I'm looking at them now," Lammelle said. "Who am I looking at?"

"That's the guy who dropped a letter addressed to Box 2333 into the slot in the post office."

"The FBI told you that?" Lammelle asked.

"No," the junkie offered. "But when, thirty seconds after this guy dropped his envelope into the slot, half a dozen FBI guys inside the lobby started baying and going on point like so many Llewellin setters, we took a chance."

"Hey, Tommy, how are you?" Lammelle said.

"Very well, Mr. Director, sir," CIA Agent Tomás L. Diaz replied. "How are things in the executive suite, Mr. Director, sir?"

"You don't want to know," Lammelle said. "So what happened next?"

"He walked back to his car, more or less discreetly trailed by the aforementioned Llewellins and a dozen unmarked vehicles, including, so help me God, Frank, a Model A hot rod."

"Jesus," Lammelle said. "So he cleverly deduced he was being followed?"

"I'm sure he expected it," Diaz said. "He didn't try to lose anybody until he was in Mexico, and then he became professional. He didn't have to. The FBI stopped at the border."

"But you didn't lose him?"

"It's been a long time since I did this, Frank, but it's like riding a bicycle. Once you learn how . . ."

"You didn't lose him," Lammelle pursued.

"He changed cars three times. I don't know about the first two, but you'll notice the dip plate on the Mercedes."

"I noticed. You get a gold star to take home to Mommy, Tommy."

"These aren't drug guys, Frank. This is too professional."

"SVR?"

"Who else? Mexican intelligence is an oxymoron. Maybe Cuban, maybe even some of Chavez's people. But I'd go with SVR."

"Castillo thinks this whole thing is an SVR operation," Lammelle said, and then asked, "Tommy, did the FBI make you?"

"No. They were too busy falling all over each other to look for something like that."

"I'd love to know what was in that envelope," Lammelle said.

"So would I," D'Alessandro said. "But once it went into the slot, it was firmly in the clutch of the FBI; we couldn't get close, and I didn't think I should ask for a look. Can you find out?"

"I'll try. Where are things now?"

Diaz said: "Vic's got half a dozen guys standing by in Juárez —"

"Who, Vic?" Lammelle interrupted.

"China Post. On Castillo's dime. He — we — didn't want to use anybody from the Stockade."

Lammelle knew that American Legion China Post #1 in Exile enjoyed among its membership certain retired special operators. And he knew that Castillo often hired the highly skilled warriors.

"And what are they doing now?"

"Things that I could not do without getting my cover blown," Diaz said. "And now we have both the dip license plate and the photos of the people — all of the people, not just the letter dropper. If we can get a positive ID on any of them —"

Lammelle put in: "The dip plate — I got this just now — goes on a Venezuelan-embassy Toyota Camry assigned to their consulate in Juárez."

"That's where it was," Diaz said. "So we will — because we don't have anything better — radio the code word 'Hugo' to the China Post guys, and they will start sitting on the Venezuelan consulate. Two questions."

"Shoot."

"How soon can you ID the letter dropper?"

"Those pics are being run through comparison now. No more than an hour; probably less."

"My work would be a lot easier if I had some better radios."

"We're trying to keep McNab out of this, so that means no equipment from the Stockade, and you'll understand, Tommy, that it would be just a little awkward for me to walk into domestic operations here and check out something you could use."

"I can hear the chorus of whistles blowing," Diaz said. "Well, then, how about a couple of Bricks like Vic's?"

"Castillo's working on getting you something — it won't be Bricks, but maybe CaseyBerrys. As soon as we can get them to you, we will."

"I'd really like to have a Brick, Mr. Director, sir."

"Talk to Castillo. I'll call you as soon as I have a positive ID on the letter dropper."

[Five]
Office of the Director
Federal Bureau of Investigation
The J. Edgar Hoover Building
935 Pennsylvania Avenue, N.W.
Washington, D.C.
1205 18 April 2007

"An unexpected pleasure, Frank," FBI Director Schmidt said as he offered his hand to DCI Lammelle. "What can I do for you?"

"How do you turn off the recorder, Mark?"

"Excuse me?"

"Turn it off, Mark. I don't want this recorded for posterity."

After a just perceptible hesitation, Schmidt pointed to a door. "I've got sort of a bubble in there," he said.

"Fine, providing you swear on your honor

365

as an Eagle Scout that the recorder in there is shut off."

Lammelle then held up his right hand, palm outward, center fingers extended, thumb and pinky crossed over the palm, in a gesture signifying Scout's honor.

"Frank, I don't think mocking Scouts is funny. I was an Eagle Scout."

"I know. I know a lot about you, Mark. And so that you know a little more about me than you apparently do, I was also an Eagle Scout. Is that recorder going to be turned off, Scout's honor?"

"The recorder will not be turned on," Schmidt said.

Lammelle wagged the hand that made the Scout's honor and raised his eyebrows.

Schmidt sighed, then made the sign with his right hand, and said, "Scout's honor."

As they both put down their hands, Schmidt asked, "What's this all about?"

"Why don't we wait until we get in your bubble?"

Schmidt waved him through the door into a small, windowless room equipped with a library table, four chairs, a wall-mounted flat-screen television, and an American flag. There were two telephones on the table, one of them the red instrument of the White House telephone network.

When Schmidt had closed the door behind him, Lammelle laid his attaché case on the table, opened it, then sat down and took from it a manila envelope.

"Beware of spooks bearing gifts, Mark."

Schmidt took the envelope, removed a stack of photographs, and examined them.

"This is the guy who dropped the letter in the post office in El Paso," Schmidt said. "Two hours ago. How the hell did you get this?"

"A friend gave it to me. Do you know this guy's name?"

"No. Not yet. I'm working on it. Is that why you're here? You want to know his name?"

"His name is José Rafael Monteverde," Lammelle said. "He's the financial attaché of the embassy of the República Bolivariana de Venezuela in Mexico City."

"You sound pretty sure."

"I am sure. And how about a little tit for tat? Show me what was in the envelope."

"I shouldn't even be talking to you about this. And you shouldn't have been nosing around El Paso. Christ, you could have blown the FBI surveillance!"

"I hate to tell you this, Mark, but my friends said your surveillance guys were about as inconspicuous as two elephants

367

fornicating on the White House lawn. Not that it mattered, because they didn't follow Señor Monteverde across the border into Juárez" — Lammelle pointed at the photographs — "where most of those were taken."

Schmidt's face had tightened at the fornicating-elephants metaphor, and now he appeared to be on the verge of an angry reply. But then he shrugged and instead said, "The 'don't follow anybody across the border' order came from the President."

"He does have a tendency to micromanage, doesn't he?"

"He's determined to get Colonel Ferris back from the drug cartels. I can't fault that."

"The drug cartels don't have him, Mark." Lammelle pointed at the photograph of José Rafael Monteverde. "There's the proof."

"This guy could be tied to the cartels."

"Before he joined the Venezuelan foreign service, he did three years with the Cuban Dirección General de Inteligencia."

"Even if that were true . . ."

"It's true, Mark."

". . . how could I go to the President with that? I think he'd want to know where I got my information."

"Don't go to the President with it. Just face the real problem."

"Which is?"

"You know exactly what I'm talking about. Are you going to close your eyes to it?"

Schmidt met his eyes but didn't reply.

"And I've had this further discomfiting thought," Lammelle said. "Maybe he's right. Maybe Montvale does want to move into the Oval Office."

"Have you heard anything?"

Lammelle shook his head. "But one way for him to get there would be to allow Clendennen to get a lot of egg on his face trying to swap Félix Abrego for Ferris."

Schmidt didn't reply directly. Instead, he said: "The President has ordered the attorney general to move Abrego from Florence to a minimum-security prison, La Tuna, which is twelve miles north of El Paso."

"You've already heard from the, quote unquote, drug people?" Lammelle asked.

Schmidt went to his desk, worked a combination lock, opened a drawer, and took from it a folder. From that he pulled out a single sheet of paper and a photograph and handed both to Lammelle.

The photograph showed Colonel Ferris much as the first two photos of him had. He was sitting in a chair. Two men with Kalashnikov rifles stood next to him. Ferris's beard showed that he had not shaved. He was holding a day-old copy of *El Diario de El Paso* in front of him.

Lammelle read the message, which, like the first two messages, had been printed on a cheap computer printer:

Delighted that we can do business.

To prove that Señor Abrego has been moved from Florence, please arrange for El Diario to publish a photograph of him taken in an easily recognizable location near El Paso from which he can be quickly moved to the exchange point, which will be made known to you once we have examined the photograph.

"Clendennen has his own channel to these people?" Lammelle asked.

"That came in *after* the President ordered Abrego moved," Schmidt said.

"Where is Abrego now?"

"I don't know. I don't think there's been time to move him to La Tuna."

"Find out for me," Lammelle said. "I want to know where he is minute by minute."

"Why?"

"Because when the Merry Outlaws launch their plan to rescue Ferris, Abrego's location is intelligence Castillo has to have."

"The President doesn't want Castillo anywhere near this."

"I know. Which means you're going to have to make up your mind whether you're going along with Clendennen's — how do I put this? — *logically challenged* notions of how to deal with this, which will probably result in Ferris's being dead, the President really going over the edge, and Vice President Montvale convening the Cabinet to vote on Clendennen's, quote unquote, temporary incapacity, requiring him to assume the presidency, or going along with Castillo."

"Castillo has a well-earned reputation for leaving bodies all over."

"Do you really care how many SVR bodies or drug cartel bodies Castillo leaves anywhere?"

Schmidt considered the question for a long moment, as if it confused him, and then he said: "Frank, when I consider the option of Montvale taking over, I have to admit that I don't."

VIII

The Lobby Lounge
Llao Llao Hotel and Spa
Avenida Ezequiel Bustillo
Bariloche
Río Negro Province, Argentina
1225 18 April 2007

Castillo, Sweaty, Bradley, Tom Barlow, Kiril Koshkov, and Stefan Koussevitzky were sitting around an enormous round table with a wood fire burning in its center when a white-jacketed bellman pointed them out to the four men he'd just brought from the airport.

They were Colonel Jacob Torine, U.S. Air Force (Retired); Major Richard Miller, U.S. Army (Retired); former Captain Richard Sparkman, U.S. Air Force; and CWO5 Colin Leverette, U.S. Army (Retired).

Castillo stood and addressed Torine: "Good afternoon, Colonel, sir. I trust the colonel had a nice flight?"

Torine eyed him suspiciously.

"Why am I afraid of what comes next?" Torine asked, then went to Svetlana and kissed her cheek.

"I believe the colonel knows Colonel Ber-

372

ezovsky," Castillo went on. "And he may remember Major Koussevitzky . . ."

"Indeed, I do," Torine said. "How's the leg, Major?"

"It only hurts when I move, Colonel," Koussevitzky replied. "Good to see you again, sir."

"And this is Kiril Koshkov, late captain of the Spetsnaz version of the Night Stalkers," Castillo went on. "Kiril, Stefan, these distinguished warriors are Colonel Jacob Torine, Captain Richard Sparkman, and Mr. Colin Leverette."

The men shook hands.

"I'm afraid to ask," Torine said, "but why arc wc being so military?"

Max walked to Torine, sat beside him on his haunches, and thrust his paw at Dick Miller until he took it.

"Max, I hate to tell you this," Miller said, "but as I came through the door there was a sign in at least four languages that says NO DOGS."

"Not a problem. Max knows the owner," Castillo said.

"You were telling me, Colonel," Torine said, "why we are being so military."

"I spent the morning playing general," Castillo said. "I gave a PowerPoint presentation of a staff study that I am forced, in all

373

modesty, to admit was brilliant."

Svetlana shook her head in resignation.

"How so?" Torine asked, smiling.

"Don't shake your head at me, Podpolkovnik Alekseeva," Castillo said. "Did I, or didn't I, convince Ivan the Terrible Junior that his plans for this problem wouldn't solve it?"

"What were his plans?" Torine asked.

"They did have, I'll admit, the advantage of simplicity," Castillo said. "What he wanted to do was whack anyone who he suspected was SVR. I finally managed to convince him that Vladimir Vladimirovich has more SVR operators than we have bullets, and that a wiser, less violent, solution was called for."

"Which is?" Torine asked, smiling as he beckoned to a waiter.

"I'm still working on that," Castillo said. "Little problems keep popping up."

"You managed to talk Pevsner out of whacking everybody in sight and letting God sort it out," Leverette asked, incredulously, "without having a Plan B?"

"I was impressed," Tom Barlow said. "That's just what he did. I didn't think he was going to get away with it."

Castillo smiled at Svetlana, and said, "Pay attention to your big brother, Sweaty."

"What makes either of you think you really got away with it?" Sweaty replied.

"No plans at all, Charley?" Leverette asked.

"More questions than plans," Castillo said.

He pointed at the laptop in front of Bradley.

"Lester, show Uncle Remus, Uncle Jake, and Gimpy the letter that the President wants President Martinez to send to him."

The three bent over the laptop and read the letter.

"Where'd you get this?" Torine asked.

"What is it?" Miller asked.

"That's the letter the President ordered Natalie Cohen to give to Ambassador McCann, so that McCann can go to President Martinez with it, and have Martinez send it back. She sent it to Lammelle, and he sent it to me."

"So?" Torine said. "He wants to swap the guy doing time in Florence for Ferris. We knew that."

"Uncle Remus has that pained look on his face that shows he's thinking," Castillo said. "That, or he smells a rat."

"Both," Leverette said.

"Go on."

"The President wrote this himself?" Leverette asked.

"The President told Natalie that Clemens McCarthy wrote it," Castillo said. "He told Natalie he thought it was brilliant."

" 'L . . . your Marshals would transport him to the Oaxaca State Prison, where they would turn him over to prison authorities,' " Leverette quoted.

"I, too, found that interesting."

"I don't understand," Torine said.

Castillo nodded, then said: "Question one: Why would the President be specific about where Abrego was to go to be exchanged? Question two: Why the Oaxaca State Prison? It's way south, not near the U.S. border. There must be a state prison near our border."

"Oaxaca is closer to Venezuela?" Uncle Remus asked.

"That may — probably does — have something to do with it. I have no idea what, but there is a reason."

"You just said McCarthy wrote the letter," Miller said.

"Same questions," Castillo said.

"Where are you going with this?"

"I don't know; I just started thinking about it," Castillo said. "Okay, here goes. A lot of people are beginning to realize that Clendennen is losing, or has lost, his marbles. That's what everybody — including me — thought when we heard his paranoid suspicions that we were staging a coup d'état to get him out of the Oval Office, and Montvale in.

"There's considerable proof that he's not playing with a full deck. For example, he staged that business at Langley and fired Porky Parker for disloyalty. Then he went bananas because we walked out on his speech. And then he started this swap-Abrego-for-Ferris business."

"But?" Leverette asked.

"The possibility exists that he's not being paranoid about a coup d'état."

"Jesus Christ!" Miller said.

"Who would be behind that, Charley?" Torine asked dubiously, and then had an additional thought and incredulously asked, "Montvale?"

Castillo nodded.

Miller said, "Jesus Christ! Are you serious, Charley?"

"I may be wrong. I hope I am wrong. But, yeah, the more I think about it, the more serious I become."

"How long have you had this dangerous idea?" Miller asked.

"When I smelled something wrong in that letter — where the President wanted Martinez to tell him where he wanted Abrego to be sent. What the hell is that all about?"

"He didn't," Torine argued. "McCarthy wrote that letter."

"Even worse," Castillo said. "How could McCarthy know about the Oaxaca State Prison? He's been on the job only a couple of days."

"So where did he get it?"

"Supervisory Secret Service Agent Mulligan probably knew about it."

"You're suggesting Mulligan had a hand in writing that letter," Leverette said.

"Yeah, I am. When Montvale was director of National Intelligence, he had the secretary of Homeland Security in his pocket. And the Secret Service is part of Homeland Security. I don't think it's much of a stretch to wonder if he had this Mulligan character keeping an eye on Clendennen for him. And if Mulligan did slip Oaxaca State Prison into that letter — why would he do that unless Montvale told him to?"

"Why, Charley?" Torine asked.

"Try this scenario on for size," Castillo said. "Abrego is taken to this prison in the middle of nowhere in Mexico by U.S. Marshals. I don't know whether they're planning to exchange him for Ferris or 'allow him to escape.' It doesn't matter, the plan blows up. Abrego gets away and Ferris is whacked.

"They find him with his head cut off, or hanging from a bridge overpass in Acapulco, or both. The press starts to run down the story. The letter from Martinez is leaked —" He paused in thought, then went on, "Going off on a tangent, Clendennen is pushed over the edge at this point. He publicly accuses Crenshaw and Cohen of betraying him. Since they haven't betrayed him, they deny it. Clendennen starts looking like a lunatic.

"By this point, the press is hot on the story. They learn from the Bureau of Prisons that they were ordered by the attorney general to take Abrego from Florence to the Oaxaca State Prison — something that is against long-standing U.S. policy and has never been done. The attorney general says Clendennen ordered it over his objections and that Natalie Cohen not only was there when he did it, but was also given a letter by him — this letter — which set up the whole thing.

"At this point, either Clendennen resigns or impeachment proceedings start in the Congress, or — and I think this is what Montvale is shooting for — Clendennen really starts frothing at the mouth, which will cause whatever authorities make decisions like this — the Cabinet? — to conclude that his mental condition is such that he cannot discharge his duties as POTUS, whereupon . . ."

Jake Torine finished: "Whereupon the Vice President steps forward and says he is forced to assume the President's responsibilities until such time as the poor man recovers his faculties."

"And what happens then?" Leverette asked.

"Uncle Remus, we can't let it get that far," Castillo said.

"So how do we stop it?" Leverette asked.

"We follow that military adage of 'When you don't know what to do, doing anything is better than doing nothing.' "

"Are you going to translate that, Charley?" Leverette asked.

"All I can think of is snatching Ferris or Abrego or both of them, before, during, or after the exchange, escape, or whatever at Oaxaca State Prison and then wait to see who — beside the Mexicans — comes out of the woodwork looking for them."

"And how are you going to do that?" Torine asked.

"And how does all this tie in with your scenario that the whole Ferris business is an

SVR plot to get you and the other Russians?" Leverette added.

" 'The other Russians'?" Castillo parroted sarcastically.

"You know what I mean," Leverette said.

"Uncle Remus, I don't know how it fits in. I don't even know if the SVR is really after me and the other Russians. And I can't explain the business about the Oaxaca State Prison. Truth to tell, I'm flying blind."

"Okay," Leverette said. "So now that we know that, what's the plan?"

Torine laughed.

Castillo then said, "I recently ran into an old acquaintance, Juan Carlos Pena, *el jefe* of the Policía Federal for the province of Oaxaca. He came to Hacienda Santa Maria — the grapefruit farm — and out of the goodness of his heart told me to get the hell out of Dodge before I got hurt. These drug people, Juan Carlos told me, are very dangerous."

"And you suspect he might be pals with them?" Leverette asked.

"That thought has run through my mind," Castillo said. "I think I'd better have another talk with him."

"A nice talk? Or the other kind?" Leverette asked.

Castillo didn't reply directly. He instead

said, "What I hope I can do is get Juan Carlos, for auld lang syne, to (a) tell me all he knows about the involvement of the Venezuelans — which means the SVR — in this, and (b) keep me up to date on the plans for Señor Abrego at the Oaxaca State Prison."

"That's a tall order, Charley," Torine said.

"Yeah, I know."

"Okay," Leverette said. "Let's say that works. You know that Abrego is going to be at the prison at a certain time. Then what?"

"Then I offer whoever was going to let Abrego go more money than the Venezuelans are offering, and grab him. And/or grab Ferris, when they take him to Oaxaca State Prison."

"And there you are, near this prison in the middle of nowhere, with either or both of them," Leverette said. "What are you going to do with them?"

"Load them on my Black Hawk," Castillo said.

Leverette looked askance at Castillo. "Before I ask you where you're going to take them in your Black Hawk, where in hell are you going to get a Black Hawk?"

"I already have a Black Hawk," Castillo said. "By now . . . or certainly by tomorrow . . . it will be at Martindale Army

Airfield at Fort Sam."

"The one you stole from the Mexican cops?" Leverette asked.

"The one I *bought* from the Mexican cops," Castillo said. "Natalie Cohen didn't want to embarrass the Mexican ambassador by asking him to explain its miraculous resurrection from the total destruction he said it suffered in the war against the drug cartels — complete with its weaponry and Policía Federal markings intact — so she gave it to Lammelle and asked him to get rid of it. While making up his mind about the best way to go about it, he had it trucked from Norfolk to Fort Sam for storage."

"Did he just do that, or did you ask him to?" Torine asked.

"I asked him."

"Then his neck is on the line," Torine said.

"All of our necks are going to be on the line with this, Jake," Castillo said. "I'm not going to line everybody up and ask for volunteers to take one step forward, but I'll understand if —"

"Come on, Charley," Dick Miller interjected. "You damn well know better than that."

Castillo met his eyes, then started to say something but apparently couldn't find his voice. He offered his hand to Miller, who shook it.

Then Castillo stood up and wrapped his arms around Miller.

"I'll let you hug me, too, Charley," Leverette said. "But if you think I'm going to kiss you, don't hold your breath."

[Two]
Office of the Warden
United States Penitentiary Administrative
Maximum Facility (ADX)
Florence, Colorado
1605 18 April 2007

J. William Leon, warden of the Florence ADMAX facility, was a large (six-three, 225 pounds) red-haired man known behind his back to his staff as "Willy the Lion" or sometimes simply as "the Lion."

He was generally recognized within the federal prison community as the most senior of all prison wardens. In the United States there were 114 federal incarceration facilities, which the Federal Bureau of Prisons, part of the Department of Justice, called "institutions."

Leon's status as the most senior warden was de facto, if not de jure. He ran Florence ADMAX. That said it all.

He was de jure subordinate to a number of people in the Bureau of Prisons bureaucratic hierarchy but de facto answered only to Harold M. Waters, the director of the Bureau of Prisons. Howard Kennedy had begun his executive career working under Leon when Leon had been the assistant warden of Federal Correctional Institution, Allenwood, in Montgomery, Pennsylvania. He often said that everything valuable that he had learned about the incarceration business he had learned from Willy the Lion, and that Willy the Lion was the best warden in the bureau. Period.

Leon had joined the federal prison system as a trainee shortly after graduating from college, and the first time he had ever been inside a prison was the day he reported for work. He had needed a job, and his decision to join the incarceration profession had almost been as a lark — "What have I got to lose? It might be interesting."

Ten years into his career — then a captain at the United States Penitentiary in Leavenworth, Kansas — Leon had been offered a chance to move into the administrative side of the bureau — in other words, out of working with prisoners and into an office in Washington. A bright future was foreseen for him, and everybody thought he had made a mistake when he turned down the job offer.

He had decided — this time not impulsively — that he liked working with prisoners a good deal more than he would have liked working at a desk in the Bureau of Prisons headquarters in Washington.

What he meant by "working with prisoners" was the challenge he faced making them behave. The Lion had believed that the question of whether anyone belonged in prison or not had been decided in the courtroom and was none of a warden's business. And he quickly decided that rehabilitation was mostly bullshit.

Willy the Lion had concluded that a warden's business was confining a prisoner in decent conditions in such circumstances that he (or she) did not pose problems for the guards, fellow prisoners, or him- or herself. And the way to accomplish this was simple: Establish rules that were fair and made sense, and then see that they were obeyed.

His rise through the warden hierarchy was slow at first, but grew quickly as his superiors came to realize that he was not only good at running a prison, but even better at straightening out a prison in trouble. And trouble in prisons was not caused only by the inmates; the staff also contributed. Willy the Lion earned the reputation among them of being fair and reasonable, but not a man to cross.

No one was surprised when the Lion was first named assistant warden at Florence ADMAX facility, or a year later when he was named warden, after it had proved too much to handle for its first warden.

Once he took over, there had been no further problems. Period.

And shortly after that happened, he demonstrated that he had another skill, one that no one suspected, and one that surprised even him.

Willy the Lion could handle the press . . . from the handwringers convinced that the Bureau of Prisons spent most of its time figuring out ways to violate the civil rights of the prison population to the heavy hitters from the television news networks who had long known that covering bloody prison riots attracted as many millions of viewers as did the sexual escapades of movie stars and politicians.

Once Willy the Lion's skill at handling the press became known to the upper brass of the Bureau of Prisons, whenever there was trouble — a riot or allegations of guard brutality or corruption — that was likely to draw the national press to the gates of a prison, when the Fourth Estate showed up they very often found that Willy the Lion, the warden of the toughest prison in the world, had "coincidentally" been there when the trouble started.

Willy the Lion was a story by himself, so they dealt with him, and he was truthful with them, and they learned that he neither coddled the prison population nor made any effort at all to cover up malfeasance on the part of the warden or his guards.

With rare exceptions, the press left the site of the story convinced that the Federal Bureau of Prisons had one hell of a tough job to do, and most of the time did it well, and in those few instances where somebody fucked up, there were a large number of people — like Willy the Lion — standing ready to make things right.

Director of the Bureau of Prisons Harold M. Waters sometimes thought that Willy the Lion's public relations role was almost as important as his proven skill at running Florence ADMAX.

No one — not even Director Waters — knew that for the past nine months Willy had a personal problem with one of the prisoners in Florence ADMAX, one Félix Abrego, register number 97593-655.

A federal court in Houston, Texas, had convicted Abrego on three counts of first-degree murder. The victims were all special agents of the Drug Enforcement Administration. And one of the three was Willy the Lion's eldest sister's youngest boy, Clarence, who had been twenty-two years old and on the job just over a year when Félix Abrego had stood over him and fired four shots into the groin area of his body, and then a fifth shot into his face.

Abrego had been sentenced to life imprisonment without the possibility of parole. The sentencing investigation had turned up his record as a hit man for the Mexican drug cartels and that he had been sent to Florence ADMAX from the Federal Detention Center, Houston, immediately after his trial.

This caused Willy the Lion for the first time in his adult life to consciously violate the regulations — which of course have the force and effect of law — of the Federal Bureau of Prisons.

For obvious reasons, a warden should not be in charge of the incarceration of a prisoner to whom he is related, or who has committed a crime against the warden, or a member of the warden's family.

Ordinarily this poses no problem. Such a

prisoner is assigned to a prison where the warden has never heard of him.

The problem here for Willy the Lion was that if ever anybody deserved to spend twenty-three hours of every day for the rest of his life in a cell furnished with a poured-concrete bed, a sink and toilet, a television screen providing educational and religious channels only, and windows that permitted a limited view of the sky, it was the miserable Mexican sonofabitch who had murdered Clarence.

Sending Félix Abrego to any other prison would give him a better life, and he did not deserve a better life.

On the other hand, if Abrego were incarcerated at ADMAX, Willy the Lion would have to leave. He could not see the justice in that. Why should he have to give up being warden of Florence ADMAX? Not only had he earned that job, no one could handle it better than he could.

So he said nothing.

If he got caught, he would watch Abrego being sent in shackles somewhere else, or he would retire.

And until something happened, Abrego would be treated exactly like every other prisoner a judge had sentenced to life without the possibility of parole and sent to

Florence ADMAX.

Assistant Warden (Administration) Kurt Grosch, a stocky, nearly bald fifty-five-year-old, stood in the open door of the warden's office and waited to be noticed.

Willy the Lion finally looked up from a thick sheaf of paper on his desk, saw Grosch, and raised his eyebrows.

"I've got something I thought I better show you, Warden."

Leon waved him in.

"What have you got, Dutch?" Leon asked.

What Grosch had was an Order to Transfer Prisoner, signed by Kenneth L. Brackin, deputy director, U.S. Bureau of Prisons, ordering the transfer of Félix Abrego, register number 97593-655, from Florence ADMAX to La Tuna Federal Correctional Institution in Anthony, Texas.

"This has got to be a mistake, Dutch," Willy the Lion said. "La Tuna is a country club."

"I know. So what do I do?"

"Nothing. I'll call Brackin and get him to tear this up before Waters hears about it. Waters would shit a brick, and Brackin's a pretty good guy."

"What do I tell the Marshals?"

"What Marshals?"

"There's four of them, and they more or less politely ask that we hand this guy over to them as soon as we can fit that into our busy schedule. Like right now."

"Today's Wednesday," Leon said. "The next JPATS flight is next Monday, right?"

The Department of Justice operated several Boeing passenger jets to move prisoners between Bureau of Prisons institutions and — primarily — illegal aliens about to be deported to the border. It was commonly known by the acronym JPATS.

"The Marshals aren't using JPATS. They have a DOJ jet, a little one" — he searched his memory — "a Gulfstream. At Butts."

Butts Army Airfield served Fort Carson, Colorado, a short distance from Florence ADMAX.

"What the hell is going on here, Dutch?"

"I was hoping you'd tell me."

Willy the Lion reached for his telephone and punched in a number from memory.

"Director Waters, please, Warden Leon calling."

After a moment, Waters came on the line.

"Good afternoon, Mr. Director . . .

"I'm fine, thank you. Yourself? Dorothy and the kids?

"I'm really sorry to bother you, but something has come up. Four Marshals have shown up here in a DOJ Gulfstream with a transfer order signed by Ken Brackin moving a life-without-parole prisoner named Félix Abrego to the La Tuna facility in Texas . . .

"Is there a problem? Yeah, there's a problem. This guy Abrego murdered three DEA agents. Why is he being transferred to one of our more comfortable country clubs?

"Because the attorney general said so? Jesus Christ, Harry, what's he thinking?

"I understand. Well, if it's out of your hands, it's out of mine. I'll send Mr. Abrego on his way."

He put the handset into its cradle and looked at Grosch.

"You heard that, Dutch?"

Grosch nodded.

Leon shook his head in disgust. "Waters said, 'The question is not open for debate,' and that this is one of those times when I have to smile and say, 'Yes, sir.' "

"Jesus, what the hell?"

"Give Abrego to the Marshals, Dutch, as soon as you can."

"Yes, sir."

Leon watched as Grosch left the office, and then rose from behind his desk and walked to the door, called "No calls, Doris" to his secretary, and then closed the door.

He knew what he wanted to do but had learned it was always better to think things over for two or three minutes when he was really pissed.

He took off his wristwatch and laid it on the desk in a position where he could see the sweep of the second hand. He watched as the hand made three revolutions.

Then he went to his laptop computer, clicked on his address book, found the name he wanted, and punched the number in his personal cell phone.

"Roscoe," he said into the phone a moment later, "this is Bill Leon, the warden of the ADMAX prison in Colorado. Do you remember me?"

[Three]
Apartment 606
The Watergate Apartments
2639 I Street, N.W.
Washington, D.C.
1615 18 April 2007

Roscoe J. Danton, of the *Washington Times-Post* Writers Syndicate, and John David Parker, the newly appointed director of public relations of the LCBF Corporation, had tested their theory that the President's firing of his press secretary was now old news and that it was therefore safe for Porky to move about Washington without having to dodge the White House Press Corps by having a drink at the Old Ebbitt Grill.

There had been half a dozen members of that elite body in the bar refreshing themselves after Mr. Clemens McCarthy's afternoon briefing. Only two of them had even acknowledged Porky's presence with so much as a nod.

Porky was indeed yesterday's news.

That test had told them that it was safe for Porky to go back to his apartment in the Verizon, which had the added benefit that he would no longer be Roscoe's roommate.

It wasn't that Roscoe didn't like Porky. Surprising to both of them was the fact that they had become quite close since President Clendennen had ordered Porky off his helicopter and Roscoe had offered him a ride home from Langley. But Porky's presence in the apartment obviously prevented Roscoe from entertaining overnight female guests.

As Roscoe thought of it, he was a lover, not an exhibitionist.

So after having a second Bloody Mary in the Old Ebbitt, they had taken a cab to Roscoe's apartment in the Watergate so that Porky could pick up his things.

The phone was ringing when they walked in.

"What the hell was that all about?" Porky asked when Roscoe had hung up.

"I was about to say I'd tell you, but then I'd have to kill you."

"That would be a lot funnier if I hadn't heard it before," Porky replied.

"But then I realized you're sort of a probationary member of the Merry Outlaws," Roscoe went on, "so I guess you get a pass. That was J. William 'Willy the Lion' Leon. He's the warden of the ADMAX prison in Colorado."

"And?"

Roscoe told him what Willy the Lion had told him.

"So what are you going to do?"

Roscoe consulted his cell phone's address book and dialed a number.

"Roscoe J. Danton of the *Times-Post* for the attorney general . . .

"Well, I'm sorry he's not available at the moment. When he becomes available, will you be good enough to tell him I tried to call him before I went on Wolf News to tell J. Pastor Jones's three million viewers the attorney general's version of the story I've got that he personally just moved a guy doing life without parole in Florence ADMAX for killing three DEA agents to a country club in Texas . . .

"Yeah, I'll hold for a minute."

Roscoe met Porky's eyes.

Porky grinned knowingly as Roscoe, then said: "And how are you this afternoon, Mr. Attorney General?

"What have I got? I'll tell you."

He did so.

"You know I can't tell you where I got that, Mr. Attorney General. That would be what they call revealing a source. I don't do that . . .

"Whether you find it hard to believe or not, Mr. Attorney General, I know it's true. I even have the prisoner's name. One Félix Abrego . . .

"Will I do you a favor? That depends on the favor . . .

"Yeah, as a favor, you've always been straight with me, I can sit on this for a couple of hours — say, until Andy McClarren's *Straight Scoop* goes on Wolf News at nine — while you get to the bottom of this. Let me give you my cell phone number."

He broke the connection and turned to Porky Parker.

"Whatever it is, Porky, I just touched a nerve."

"Do you have to call me 'Porky'?"

"If I didn't, I'd have to kill you," Danton said.

"Oh, shit," Parker replied.

[Four]
1625 18 April 2007

"Warden Leon."

"This is Stanley Crenshaw, Warden Leon. I'm glad I caught you."

"You just barely did, Mr. Attorney General. I was about to call it a day."

"Warden, have you been talking to Roscoe Danton?"

"To who, Mr. Attorney General?"

"Roscoe Danton. Roscoe J. Danton. The *Washington Times-Post* reporter. The one who's always on Wolf News."

"Oh, yeah. I know who he is."

"You have been talking to him?"

"No, sir, Mr. Attorney General. I was trying to say I know who he is. Has he been trying to talk to me? I've been in the office all afternoon. Is something wrong?"

"What do you know about the transfer of Félix Abrego from Florence ADMAX to the La Tuna facility in Texas?"

"Oh. Now I understand. So there was a mix-up."

"Excuse me?"

"When that transfer order came in, I thought there was something not quite kosher, transferring someone like Abrego from here to a country club like La Tuna, so I called Director Waters and asked him. He assured me that everything was hunky-dory, that you had personally authorized the transfer, so I told my assistant warden to turn the prisoner over to the U.S. Marshals you sent out here."

"And when will this prisoner actually be transferred, Warden Leon?"

"He's on his way to the La Tuna facility as we speak, Mr. Attorney General."

"Warden Leon, if Mr. Danton or any other journalist calls you out there, don't be available. Refer them to me. You understand?"

"Yes, sir."

"Don't answer any questions. Don't say anything at all."

"Yes, sir, Mr. Attorney General."

[Five]
1635 18 April 2007

The attorney general began his conversation with the director of Central Intelligence with no preliminaries whatsoever.

"Frank, Roscoe J. Danton just called me, and after I was very nice to him — damn near groveled at his feet — he gave me until five minutes to nine to explain why Félix Abrego is being transferred from Florence ADMAX to that country club prison in Texas. Otherwise, at nine tonight he goes on Wolf News — on Andy McClarren's *Straight Scoop* — with what he's got."

"I wonder how he found out," the DCI mused.

The attorney general of course had already given that question a good deal of thought. After talking with Warden Leon, he had decided it wasn't Leon.

Then who?

His suspicions finally settled on the U.S. Marshals he had sent to Florence ADMAX. For one thing, since they were transferring Abrego, they knew about it. For another — the U.S. Marshal Service was the oldest federal law enforcement agency; it had been founded in 1789 and its members had an unfortunate tendency to regard themselves as the Knights Templar of federal law enforcement — they often tattled to the attorney general on what they thought of as less than pure activities of other agencies. Since they couldn't tattle on the man himself who had ordered Abrego's very questionable transfer — the attorney general — they had gone to Roscoe J. Danton.

Who would certainly recognize a damn good story when one was dumped in his lap.

"I have no idea," Stanley Crenshaw said. "All I know is that he knows, and is about to go on Wolf News and tell the world. What do I do?"

"I just had a thought," Frank Lammelle said. "I'm not supposed to know that Abrego is going to be swapped for Ferris. The President told you and Natalie Cohen, and maybe Schmidt, but I guess he doesn't think I have the need to know. That raises the question 'Did he tell Montvale or Truman Ellsworth?' Keep that it mind when you're talking to him."

"Okay, so I'm telling you now. And now that you know, what should I do?"

"Are you sure you want to tell me, Stanley? Clendennen's liable to consider that a breach of trust."

The attorney general considered that for a moment.

"Okay, I didn't tell you. Who did tell you?"

"If I answered that, that would be a breach of trust."

"Shit," the attorney general said, and broke the connection.

"The President's line, Agent Mulligan."

"This is Stanley Crenshaw, Mulligan. Is the President available?"

"Does the President expect your call, Mr. Crenshaw?"

"Please tell the President I have to speak to him."

"I'll see if he's free."

A moment later, there was another voice on the line.

"This is Clemens McCarthy, Mr. Crenshaw. The President is not available at the moment. He asked me to take a message, and he'll try to get back to you."

I'm the attorney general of the United States. When I call the President, I want to speak to him, not his goddamn press agent.

"Actually, McCarthy, we might not have to bother President Clendennen with this. This is really in your area of responsibility."

"What would that be, Mr. Crenshaw?"

"Roscoe J. Danton called me just now and gave me until five minutes of nine to tell him why Félix Abrego is being transferred from Florence ADMAX to the La Tuna facility near El Paso. Otherwise he says he's going on *The Straight Scoop* with Andy Mc-

Clarren at nine with what he's got."

"And what does he think he has?"

"That the convicted murderer of three DEA agents is being transferred to a minimum-security institution."

"How does he know that?"

"I have no idea. I'm just telling you what I know, and asking what I should do about Mr. Danton."

"Just a moment, please."

Twenty seconds later, the President of the United States barked: "What the hell is going on, Crenshaw?"

The attorney general told him.

"I want to know who told that sonofabitch Danton about the transfer!"

"I have no idea, Mr. President."

"Well, some disloyal sonofabitch obviously did, and I want to know who."

"Mr. President, I have no idea."

"Goddamn it, you should! You're the attorney general; you're in charge of the FBI. I don't care what you or Mark Schmidt have to do, just find out what disloyal sonofabitch did this to me."

"Yes, sir. And what would you like me to say to Mr. Danton, Mr. President?"

The President considered the question for a long moment.

"I'm going to let McCarthy handle that,"

he said finally. "But you and Schmidt get your asses over here right now. McCarthy might need you."

The President hung up.

[Seven]
1650 18 April 2007

"Good afternoon, Madam Secretary," the DCI said. "And how were things in sunny Meh-hee-co?"

"Why does your ebullience worry me, Frank?" Natalie Cohen replied.

"The problem of swapping Colonel Ferris for Félix Abrego may be solved. I just got off the phone with Stanley Crenshaw. He is probably at this moment telling the President what he told me."

"Which was?"

"Roscoe J. Danton gave him until five minutes to nine tonight to explain why ol' Félix has been transferred to the La Tuna Country Club, otherwise he goes on *The Straight Scoop* with Andy McClarren and tells the world."

Cohen didn't reply.

"I take back all the unkind things I ever said about devious diplomats," Lammelle said. "That was pure genius."

"What are you talking about?" she said.

"Well, Clendennen can't send Abrego to Mexico now, can he?"

"How did Danton find out?" she asked.

"What is that, 'credible deniability'? Your secret is safe with me, Natalie."

"I didn't tell Danton, if that's what you've been thinking."

"Then who the hell did? That's a very interesting question, Natalie. Who knew besides Stanley and me? And possibly Mark Schmidt?"

"I was not taken into the President's confidence in this matter. I heard it from Schmidt. Do you think Schmidt told Roscoe?"

"No. That would be committing career suicide," he said. "And he likes being director. That leaves Stanley, and that doesn't make sense. Did Montvale know? Or Truman Ellsworth?"

"I've learned from painful experience that Charles Montvale often knows more than one presumes he does," the secretary of State said. "And that's equally true of Mr. Ellsworth. Who would actually move Abrego? The FBI? The Bureau of Prisons?"

"The U.S. Marshals," Lammelle said. "And when Montvale was director of National Intelligence, he was over the Marshal Service."

"But why would Montvale tell Roscoe Danton? To embarrass the President?"

She was silent a moment, then offered: "Montvale would tell Danton — but *after.* If something went wrong, then, to embarrass the President, he'd leak it to him after."

"So, we're back to: Then who?"

"I don't know, Frank. But I think it behooves us to make a serious effort to find out. I wouldn't be surprised if there was a connection with the coup d'état business."

"I'll see what I can find out."

[Eight]
1655 18 April 2007

"Mental telepathy, Frank," Charley Castillo said. "I was just this moment thinking of calling you."

"To tell me, a little late, that you told Roscoe that Clendennen's moving Abrego to the La Tuna facility outside El Paso?"

"No shit? I didn't know that. Who the hell told Roscoe?"

When Lammelle didn't answer, Castillo said: "Well, what I was going to ask is what I should tell the cops if I'm arrested stealing my Black Hawk back?"

"What?"

"Before, I thought it might be nice to have

406

in case I needed it; now I know I have to have it, preferably late tomorrow afternoon, when I get back to the States."

"Why do you have to have it?" Lammelle said, and immediately regretted it.

What I should have said is: "Sorry, Charley, forget that helicopter."

"Frank, I don't think you really want to know. Do you?"

"Yes, I do, Charley."

"Why don't you tell me what's on your mind? Who told Roscoe what?"

"Roscoe called the attorney general about an hour ago and gave him until five minutes before Andy McClarren goes on Wolf News tonight to explain why Félix Abrego is being transferred from Florence ADMAX to a minimum-security prison near El Paso."

"Okay, I'll ask again: How the hell did Roscoe hear about that?"

"Until just now, I thought maybe you told him."

"Not me. Natalie Cohen?"

"No. The suspect right now is Montvale, but why would he do that?"

"If that story gets out, Clendennen can't send Abrego to Mexico," Castillo said thoughtfully.

"Because it would be irrational, right? Think that through, Charley."

"Jesus!" Castillo said, and a moment later asked, "Frank, that letter Clendennen wants President Whatsisname of Mexico . . ."

"Martinez," Lammelle furnished. "Notice what? Natalie and I aren't quite sure what to think about it."

"Didn't either of you think there was something strange in Clendennen wanting *Martinez* to tell him *he* wanted Abrego sent to the Oaxaca State Prison?"

"That went right over my head," Lammelle said after a moment. "And Natalie's, too, or else she would have said something. What's that all about? What's so special about the Oaxaca State Prison? For that matter, where is it?"

"In the middle of nowhere in Oaxaca State. Not anywhere near the U.S.-Mexican border. But not far from the Guatemalan border."

"Where there is a new cultural affairs officer of the Russian Federation . . ."

"Valentin Komarovski, aka Sergei Murov," Castillo furnished.

"Which means what?"

"Somebody's planning for something to happen at that prison."

"Who? What?"

"There are three — at least three — things going on here, Frank. One is that the drug

408

people want their guy Abrego back, and kidnapped Ferris so they can swap him. We don't know if they're doing that by themselves or whether it's being orchestrated by the Russians. It's possible that there is some sort of coup d'état going on. Natalie said that McCarthy, the President's new press secretary, wrote that letter, and we don't know if the President was responsible for the 'send Abrego to Oaxaca' clause, or whether that was put in by McCarthy. Clendennen either didn't see it or did see it and didn't smell the Limburger. But who told McCarthy to put that in, and why? It could've been Sergei Murov, but that's a stretch. Or maybe Montvale, which also is a stretch.

"But one scenario there has that whatever is going to happen at that prison will go wrong, that the letter will be leaked to the press, and Clendennen will be in trouble.

"And that raises the question of who told Roscoe and why. That seems to point at Montvale."

"Natalie said he'd do that *after* something goes wrong, not before."

"And since she is smarter than you and me combined, she's probably right."

Lammelle grunted his agreement, then said: "And while all this is going on,

Schmidt and the FBI are dealing — or are about to deal — with the drug cartels, if they are the drug cartels — and not the Russians."

"Curiouser and curiouser."

After a moment, the DCI said, "Charley, do you really believe the Russians are after you and your friends?"

"Absolutely."

"And where do they plan to do you in?"

"My scenario there is even more vague than anything else. I would suspect that it would happen around the Oaxaca State Prison. But so far my name hasn't come up, so how do they get me to Oaxaca? Is that a diversion, so that they can whack Aleksandr Pevsner and company here in Argentina?"

"Interesting. So what are you going to do, Charley?"

"Go with what I've got. I'm going to put people on the ground near the prison. I'm going to have another talk with an old friend — delete that — old *acquaintance* who just happens to be the chief of the Federales in Oaxaca State to see what he knows. What I'd like to do is grab either Abrego or Ferris, or both, when they show up at that prison and see who that brings out of the woodwork."

He paused and then added, "What I really would like to do is get my hands on Sergei Murov."

When Lammelle didn't respond, Castillo went on: "And to do any of the foregoing, I'm going to need that Black Hawk."

"And how would you suggest I let you have that Black Hawk without finding myself in jail?"

"I've been thinking about that," Castillo said. "What I need is either a set of CIA credentials — better yet, a CIA agent who knows his way around and can be trusted to keep his mouth shut."

"And what could a CIA agent who knows his way around and can be trusted to keep his mouth shut do?"

"He goes to Martindale Army Airfield at Fort Sam, asks for the rotary-wing maintenance officer, waves his credentials at him, says the U.S. of A. is going to give the Black Hawk to the Mexican cops, and he would really appreciate it if they could fuel it and have an auxiliary power unit standing by when the pilots come to pick it up for a test flight."

"And then you show up and fly away with it?"

"Dick Miller does. He and a guy named Kiril Koshkov."

"Who the hell is Koshkov?"

"Ex-Spetsnaz," Castillo replied. "And when the Black Hawk is at Hacienda Santa Maria, Dick will call you, and then you call your guy and he calls Martindale and tells the maintenance officer it flew so well that they decided there was no point in bringing it back to Fort Sam, so they took it to Mexico. And thanks so much for your courtesy. Since that Black Hawk was destroyed in the war against drugs, and Natalie Cohen told you to get rid of it —"

"What's Hacienda Whatever-you-said?"

"A grapefruit farm that's about thirty-five minutes Black Hawk flight time from the Oaxaca State Prison. It belongs to my family."

"And what makes you think you can — or Miller and your Russian buddy can — fly a Black Hawk across the border and then all the way to your grapefruit farm — Jesus Christ, a grapefruit farm? — without being seen by either the Border Patrol and five thousand Mexicans, many of them wearing police uniforms?"

"Because the flight will be at night and nap-of-the-earth. That means just off the ground, Mr. Director."

"Miller can do that?"

"Before he dumped his Black Hawk in

Afghanistan — actually he didn't dump it; they took an RPG hit — he was very good at it. And Kiril, with whom I just flew through the Andes at night, is just as good — maybe better."

"This sounds insane, Charley, even coming from you. You realize that?"

"The other option is Dick and me sneaking onto Martindale at night and just stealing it. The odds against getting caught are better if you have some spook you can loan me. Or, maybe, make up a set of CIA credentials for Miller and me and FedEx them to me —"

"One question, Charley," Lammelle said, cutting him off. "Have you been talking to Vic D'Alessandro lately?"

"No. Why?"

"Is that the truth?"

"Boy Scout's honor. Why?"

"Because Vic is in El Paso watching the post office with the help of a Clandestine Service guy named Tomás L. Diaz. General McNab does not know that Vic is there, and I don't know that Tommy Diaz is there. Getting the picture?"

"I think so."

"He'll be expecting to hear from you."

"You will get your reward in heaven, Frank."

"Will that be before or after we both go to Leavenworth? Leavenworth, hell, Florence ADMAX." He chuckled. "This is not the sort of excitement I thought I'd get when I joined the CIA."

Then he hung up.

[Nine]
The President's Study
The White House
1600 Pennsylvania Avenue, N.W.
Washington, D.C.
1730 18 April 2007

"You sure took your own sweet time to get here," President Clendennen said to Attorney General Crenshaw and FBI Director Schmidt when Secret Service Agent Douglas had passed them into the President's study.

"I didn't think it would be wise to come here with sirens screaming, Mr. President," Crenshaw said. "I thought it would make people wonder what's going on."

The President glared at him but didn't reply directly.

"Let's start with you, Director Schmidt. What's going on in El Paso?"

"SAC Johnson is standing by at the La Tuna prison, Mr. President, waiting for the

414

Marshals to deliver Abrego. Once he arrives and is taken into the prison — in other words, comes under the authority of the Bureau of Prisons again — he will be outfitted in civilian clothing and taken to the Magoffin Home —"

"What the hell is that?" the President interrupted.

"It's the former home of the Magoffin family, Mr. President. Now a museum. It's a large adobe structure —"

"A well-known El Paso landmark, in other words?" President Clendennen interrupted again.

"Yes, sir."

"Then why didn't you just say that? I don't need the Chamber of Commerce bullshit."

"Yes, sir. Photographs of Abrego shaking hands with SAC Johnson will be taken —"

"What the hell is that all about?"

"SAC Johnson will be identified — under another name — as an officer of the Magoffin Home Foundation, and Abrego — also under another name — as a contributor to the Magoffin Home Foundation. SAC Johnson has arranged for the photo to be published in tomorrow morning's *El Diario de El Paso*. This, SAC Johnson — and I — feel will satisfy the cartel's requirement, quote, to publish a photograph of him taken in an easily recognizable location near El Paso, close quote. The next move will be up to them."

"Okay," the President said, "so who told that sonofabitch Roscoe J. Danton that we're moving Abrego to Texas?"

"Mr. President, I have no idea."

"Neither does the attorney general," President Clendennen said, looking at Crenshaw. "So I have the director of the FBI and the attorney general telling me that they have absolutely no idea of the identity of the treasonous sonofabitch whose meddling is interfering with the foreign policy of the President of the United States. Would either of you find it hard to understand why I find that unacceptable?"

Crenshaw cleared his throat, then said, "Mr. President, I have begun an investigation —"

"Somehow that doesn't reassure me," the President snapped. "So tell me what you have on this sonofabitch Danton."

"Excuse me?"

[Ten]
Apartment 606
The Watergate Apartments
2639 I Street, N.W.
Washington, D.C.
1735 18 April 2007

"How the hell did you get in here?" Roscoe J. Danton demanded of Edgar Delchamps and David W. Yung when they walked into his kitchen. Danton and John David Parker were sitting at the kitchen table sharing a pizza.

"The door was open," Delchamps said. "I didn't think you'd mind."

"I locked that door very carefully," Danton said.

"How they hanging, Porky?" Delchamps said, ignoring the challenge.

"What the hell do you want?" Danton demanded.

"Charley wants to talk to you," Two-Gun Yung said.

"Then why doesn't he call?"

"He said it would be better if Edgar and I were here when you had your little chat," Yung said. "So we could clear up any misunderstandings that might come up."

"Can I have a slice of that?" Delchamps asked as he reached for the pizza.

417

Yung took his CaseyBerry from his pocket, punched a number, and then handed the instrument to Danton.

"Leave it on speakerphone," he ordered.

Danton held up the cell phone.

"Danton," he said.

"My favorite journalist," came Castillo's voice from the speakerphone. "How are things in our nation's capital?"

"What's going on, Charley?"

"In the very near future — in the next couple of minutes, probably — you will get a telephone call from the White House. Unless they've already called?"

"The White House has not called. I expect them to."

"Well, when they do, they're going to ask you not to go on *The Straight Poop* with Andy McClarren . . ."

"That's *Straight Scoop*," Roscoe corrected him in a Pavlovian response.

"Forgive me. As I was saying, they are going to ask you not to go on Mr. McClarren's widely viewed program tonight with the story of the attorney general ordering the movement of Félix Abrego from Florence ADMAX to the La Tuna facility. Or they are going to threaten you with all the terrible things they will do to you if you do."

"How the hell do you know about that?"

"The question, Roscoe, is, who told you about it?"

"A confidential source," Danton said, again responding in a Pavlovian reflex.

"First, Roscoe, we'll deal with what you say when the White House calls. Handle it any way you want — enjoy yourself and make them grovel, whatever — but in the end you will agree that you will not go on *The Straight Scoop* tonight. Got that?"

"The hell I won't. Nobody tells me what to write or what to say on the tube."

"Wrong. I can, and in this case I have to. Edgar, is Porky there?"

"Sitting right across from Roscoe," Delchamps replied.

"Roscoe, if I told you that your going on *The Straight Scoop* tonight would probably get Colonel Ferris killed, would this change your mind?"

"I can't believe you're serious," Danton replied.

"Two-Gun, you have the CIA's Whiz Bang Super Duper air pistol?" Castillo asked.

Yung went into his attaché case and came out with what looked like a Glock semi-automatic pistol, except that the slide was perhaps twice as large.

"Got it," Yung said.

"You're not actually going to threaten me

419

with that gun," Danton said.

"Two-Gun, shoot Porky," Castillo ordered.

Yung raised the pistol and squeezed the trigger.

There was a *pfffffft* sound.

John David Parker suddenly screamed: "Ouch! Shit!"

He looked down at his shirtfront. A plastic thumb-size dart had penetrated the shirt pocket and then his skin. The dart's feathers hung limply on his chest.

"Sorry, Porky," Castillo said. "Don't worry. You'll wake up in about fifteen minutes. I had to make the point to Roscoe that I am about as serious as I ever get, and I just don't have the time to get into an esoteric philosophical argument about journalistic ethics with him."

John David Parker, now with a dazed look on his face, suddenly slumped forward, his upper torso landing on the kitchen table with a *thump.*

Two-Gun Yung bent over Porky and removed a slice of pizza from under Parker's forehead.

"We're not playing games here, Roscoe," Castillo said evenly. "Am I getting through to you on that?"

"Jesus Christ, Castillo!"

"Do you understand what you're to do when either the attorney general, or Clendennen's press agent, or maybe Clendennen himself calls?"

"Yeah, I understand."

"Good. Now, back to my original question: Who told you about Abrego getting moved by the attorney general? It's important that I know."

"And if I refuse to reveal my source?"

"Then I will be very disappointed in you, and you will wake up in the basement of Lorimer Manor, where Edgar will sooner or later get you to tell us. I need the name."

Danton didn't immediately reply.

"I presume, Two-Gun, that you're locked and cocked?" Castillo said. It was more an order than a question.

"Two-Gun," Delchamps put in helpfully, "wait until I move the rest of the pizza out of the way."

Danton's eyes widened considerably.

"Willy the Lion Leon," he said quickly.

"Who the hell is he?" Castillo said.

"Warden of Florence ADMAX."

"Why did he tell you?"

"One of the three DEA guys Abrego shot was his nephew."

"Did he know why Abrego was being transferred?"

"No."

"Roscoe, when the White House calls, you can get on your journalist's high horse and refuse to divulge your source. Let's keep them guessing."

"Yes, sir," Danton said sarcastically.

"That's more like it," Castillo said. "Once you take the king's shilling, you're supposed to 'yes, sir' to the man in charge."

"King's shilling? What the hell are you talking about?"

"You took a lot more than a shilling, Roscoe," Edgar Delchamps said. "Don't tell me you forgot."

Danton looked at Delchamps and thought, *Jesus Christ!*

When he and Two-Gun waltzed in here, past the famed impenetrable security of the Watergate the day of the presidential press conference at Langley, they said I was going to get a million dollars in combat pay for going to the island with them.

I thought it was more of their bullshit, and then completely forgot about it.

How the fuck could I forget a million dollars? No wonder they're pissed.

"Would you believe I completely forgot about that?"

"That would be a stretch for me," Castillo said.

"For me, too," Delchamps said, "even though I'm willing to believe just about anything about someone in your line of work."

"I believe him," Two-Gun said.

"Tell me why," Castillo said.

"There was a stack of mail on a little table by the door when he came in. My FBI training took over. One envelope, which Roscoe had not yet opened, was his bank statement."

"And there's a million-dollar deposit?" Danton asked.

"It shows that deposit and a wire transfer to the IRS of three hundred ninety-five thousand dollars. Taxes. I thought it best to take care of that for him. Prompt payment of one's taxes tends to keep the IRS off one's back."

"Your call, Edgar," Castillo said. "Do we scratch up Roscoe's initial lack of co-operation to his being an ungrateful prick, or consider him a bona fide outlaw with a mind-boggling disdain for a million dollars?"

After what Roscoe considered a very long moment, Delchamps said, "My sainted mother always told me even the worst scoundrel deserves a second chance."

"Okay, stick around until the White

House, or Crenshaw calls, and then let me know how he handled it."

"You got it, Ace," Delchamps said as he looked at the passed-out Porky Parker, then glanced at his watch. "We've even got time to order a couple more pizzas. Porky's no doubt going to wake up more than a little groggy and hungry."

[Eleven]
The President's Study
The White House
1600 Pennsylvania Avenue, N.W.
Washington, D.C.
1735 18 April 2007

"Somehow that doesn't reassure me," the President said. "So tell me what you have on this sonofabitch Danton."

"Excuse me?"

"Schmidt, I am in no mood to hear a recitation about the purity of the goddamn FBI. As you damn well know, J. Edgar Hoover was the most powerful man in this town because he kept dossiers on the character flaws of everybody of importance. Don't ask me to believe that the FBI has stopped doing that. Now, tell me what you know that we can hold over the head of this goddamn Roscoe J. Danton to keep him off

Wolf News tonight."

The director of the FBI looked uncomfortable for a full thirty seconds.

"As a matter of fact, Mr. President, just before I came over here, I asked to see what we know about Mr. Danton . . ."

"And?"

"Actually, sir, Mr. Danton doesn't seem to have many character flaws. He's not homosexual, so far as we have been able to learn, and the affairs he does have are with single women."

"I don't believe that sonofabitch is a saint, Schmidt."

"There is only one thing, and I don't know what to make of it," the FBI director said.

"Tell me what it is, and I'll decide what can be made of it."

"The day of your press conference at Langley, Mr. President, there was an unusual deposit to his bank account."

"How unusual?"

"It was a wire deposit, Mr. President, of one million dollars."

"Who wired it?"

"The LCBF Corporation, Mr. President."

"Who are they?"

"I don't know, Mr. President. The wire was from their account in Liechtenstein.

And the same day of the deposit, there was a wire transfer to the IRS of three hundred ninety-five thousand dollars."

"And what do you make of this?"

"The wire transfer to the IRS was a tax payment, Mr. President. It suggests to me that he wants to keep the IRS from getting curious."

"I can run with that, Mr. President," Crenshaw said. "I'll get Mr. Danton on the phone, and tell him that unless he wants the IRS investigating not only this suspicious million dollars but everything else, to stay off Wolf News tonight."

"Why don't you give Mr. Danton a call, Mr. Attorney General?" the President ordered.

IX

[One]
Hacienda Santa Maria
Oaxaca Province, Mexico
0930 20 April 2007

The two brown Policía Federal Suburbans drove rapidly up the road through the grapefruit orchard to the big house. Two policemen got out of the lead vehicle, carrying Kalashnikov rifles at the ready. They looked around suspiciously and, seeing nothing more threatening or suspicious than *el jefe*'s gringo friend, the gringo's girlfriend, and several other gringos on the veranda, signaled that it was safe for *el jefe* to get out of the second Suburban.

Juan Carlos Pena, commander of the Policía Federal for Oaxaca State, did so, and walked quickly to the veranda.

"What the hell are you still doing here, Carlos?" he demanded.

"Good morning, Juan Carlos," Castillo replied. "Can I offer you a cup of coffee?"

"I don't want a fucking cup of coffee. I want to know what the fuck the emergency is you called me about. And why the fuck you're still here."

Castillo shrugged. "You might as well have some coffee. You're going to be here for a while."

He gestured toward the orchard.

There was a line of a dozen men walking out of the orchard toward the house. They were wearing black coveralls, their faces were covered with balaclava masks, and they were all armed with Kalashnikovs.

"What the fuck?" Juan Carlos exclaimed, and turned back to Castillo. He now saw that another half dozen men, similarly clothed and armed, had come onto the veranda from inside the house.

"Your American Express is outgunned, Juan Carlos," Castillo said. "I think you'd better tell them to lay down their weapons. I don't want to kill them, but that's your other option."

Pena thought: *"Your American Express is outgunned"?*

He wouldn't dare try killing my bodyguards!

He said: "What the fuck is going on here?"

"The weapons, please, Juan Carlos," Castillo said. "And then we can have our little chat."

"You're not actually threatening me? You know who I am."

"You're the man who's going to tell your men to put their weapons down, because otherwise they'll be dead."

"You're out of your fucking mind if you think I'm going to let you get away with this," Pena said, and then switched to Spanish and ordered his bodyguards to lay down their weapons.

Castillo then issued an order in Russian to the men in the balaclava masks.

Pena looked at him with wide eyes.

"That was Russian, Juan Carlos," Castillo said. "What I did was tell them to restrain your men. That means they will put your men in plastic handcuffs, take them to the back of the house, sit them on the ground in a circle, and then handcuff them together. I have no intention of hurting them — as a matter of fact, I'm hoping we can become pals — but for the moment, that's what's going to happen."

A maid appeared from inside the house, pushing a wheeled cart holding a coffee service toward a table where Svetlana sat in one of the upholstered wicker chairs.

"Ah, and here's our coffee," Castillo said.

Pena watched in furious fascination as his visibly terrified bodyguards were efficiently cuffed and led around the side of the house.

"You will not be harmed," Pena called out to them in Spanish.

His bodyguards appeared anything but convinced.

Four of the black-clad men then gathered the Policía Federal weapons, took them to one of the Suburbans, unloaded and disassembled them, and then put roughly half of the parts in the second Suburban. Then they emptied the magazines of their cartridges, left the magazines in the first Suburban, and put the cartridges in the second.

Castillo issued a second, somewhat shorter order in Russian.

Pena looked at him.

"What I told them to do now was go in

the kitchen and get lemonade and give it to anyone who is thirsty," Castillo said. "And I suspect most of them will be. When the Russians were in Hungary, I learned from the Államvédelmi Hatóság — the Hungarian secret police; probably the best interrogators in the world, better even than the Mossad — that terror causes unusual thirst. And your American Express certainly looked terrified just now, wouldn't you agree?"

Pena barked: "You're going to spend the rest of your life in the Oaxaca State Prison, you realize. If you live long enough . . ."

"Think that through, Juan Carlos. Are you really in a position to threaten anyone? The guys with the guns get to do the threatening. You might want to write that down."

"I don't scare, Carlos. You might want to write that down."

"I really hope that's true," Castillo said.

Two of the men in black got into the Suburbans and drove them out of sight into the grapefruit orchard.

"Speaking of the truth . . ." Castillo began, and then interrupted himself. "But before we get into that, why don't you sit down and drink your coffee?"

"Fuck you and your coffee," Pena said.

"Are you saying that because you don't

like coffee, or to prove you're not terrified and aren't thirsty?"

"Fuck you," Pena repeated — but couldn't restrain a slight smile.

"Go on, have some coffee," Castillo said, taking a seat beside Sweaty. "We used to be pals, and, who knows, maybe we can be again."

"Oh, for Christ's sake," Pena said. He sat in one of the upholstered wicker chairs across from Castillo and Svetlana, and reached for the coffee.

Max walked up to him, sat on his haunches, and thrust his paw at him.

Pena shook it.

"What's a nice dog like you doing hanging around with a crazy gringo?" he asked.

Castillo thought: *Max, you better be right! Please, God, let Max be right!*

"I have a confession to make, old buddy," Castillo said. "I have not been exactly truthful with you."

"No shit?" Pena said, as he scratched Max's ears.

Castillo gestured with his coffee cup at Koussevitzky.

"The last time you were here, I told you that my friend Stefan Koussevitzky here is an Israeli citrus expert. Actually, he's not an Israeli, and he really doesn't know much

431

about citrus."

"No shit? Then what is he?"

"He's a businessman, associated with the LCBF Corporation. And before that, he was a major of Spetsnaz." He gestured toward the black-clad men. "You know about the Spetsnaz, Juan Carlos, right?"

"I've heard the term," Pena said.

"And I told you that Señorita Barlow owns an estancia in Uruguay. That's true, but before she bought the estancia, she was known as Svetlana Alekseeva, and she was an SVR *podpolkovnik.* That's a lieutenant colonel, Juan Carlos."

Pena studied her, then said, "You won't mind, Red, if I find that *very* hard to believe."

"I won't mind, but you'd be a fool if you didn't," she said.

"And, finally, I told you that Lester here is a computer expert. That's also true, but what I didn't tell you is that he's my version of your American Express."

"This kid is your American Express?" Pena said.

Castillo smiled. "Looks can be deceiving, *mi amigo.* Say hello to Gunnery Sergeant Lester Bradley, USMC, Retired."

Pena shook his head, then eyed Lester.

"He's your bodyguard?" he said, incredulously. "Come on, Carlos! You don't really expect me to believe that."

"You'd better. If we were keeping score, it would be Lester six, SVR zero."

"I'm dying to know why you're trying to lay all this bullshit on me," Pena said.

"I'm hoping that now that I'm telling the truth, you'll tell *me* the truth."

"First, why don't you tell me the truth about you? What the fuck is this all about?"

"Well, first why don't *you* tell me the truth about yourself? Think carefully before replying, Juan Carlos. When you came here the first time and told me to get the hell out of Dodge before I got hurt by the drug cartels, what was that all about?"

"Meaning what?"

"Okay. Did they send you? Or maybe you're part of — maybe even running — one of the cartels, and decided it would be smarter to get me out of town than to kill me, which would cause all sorts of public-relations problems?"

"Fuck you!" Pena exploded.

"You expect me to believe that you're one of the two honest cops in Mexico?" Castillo pursued.

"Goddamn you! We've been friends since we were twelve," Pena said, coldly furious.

"How could you even ask me something like that?"

"Héctor García-Romero" — Castillo paused until Pena acknowledged the name — "he's been Doña Alicia's lawyer for thirty years, maybe longer, and he's in the drug business up to his ears. Why not you?"

Pena met Castillo's eyes and was quiet a long moment.

"How the hell did you learn that about García-Romero?" Pena then demanded.

Castillo shrugged, signaling that Pena was not going to get an answer.

"Okay, you sonofabitch," Pena said. "I came here the first time to keep you alive. I didn't think — I still don't — that you knew what the hell you were getting yourself into."

"I take that as meaning: 'Yeah, I'm one of the two honest cops in Mexico.' "

"There's a few more than two of us. Now you tell me what the hell's really going on around here."

"Take a look at this, Juan Carlos," Castillo said, and handed him a copy of *El Diario de El Paso*. It was folded so that page 5 was exposed.

"What am I looking at?"

"What do you see?"

"A picture of some guy who laid a bunch of money on the Magoffin Home," Pena said, then looked at Castillo. "Is that what you mean?"

"You didn't recognize Félix Abrego?"

"I'll be goddamned," Pena said after a second look.

"The other guy is the FBI SAC in El Paso," Castillo said. "The people who whacked the DEA agents and my friend Danny Salazar and kidnapped Colonel Ferris . . ."

"Your *friend* Danny Salazar?"

Castillo nodded. "We went back a long way."

"So you were Special Forces, too? Not a military attaché?

"You said, 'too,' " Castillo said, smiling. He shook his head, then asked, "How did you know Danny was Special Forces?"

"After we became friends, he told me."

"You were friends?"

"Yeah. We were friends. Is that so hard to believe?"

Castillo hesitated a moment before saying, "Now that we're now telling each other the truth, no."

"Danny understood how things work here."

"And how do they work here?"

"Like I told you the first time I was here, the bad guys are winning. Anybody who

435

thinks the drug cartels can be defeated is a fool. The best that me and people like me — and the other three or four honest cops — can do is fuck them up from time to time. Danny and I hit it off right away, when I first met him . . ."

As Pena spoke, Castillo glanced at Max and thought: *How could I ever have doubted your infallible ability to judge human character?*

". . . and believed me when I told him how things are. After that, from time to time, I used to slip him information. Between us, we caused the bad guys to lose a lot of money."

They locked eyes for a moment.

I believe him.

"One of the reasons I wanted you out of Dodge, Carlos — aside from keeping you alive — is that I didn't want you getting in the way of my dealing with the guys who whacked him."

Castillo's eyes narrowed. "You know who the sonsofbitches are?"

Pena nodded. "The Zambada cartel. They used to be in our special forces. The cartel's run by a really nasty guy named Joaquín Archivaldo. I was surprised that Joaquín was in on the whack/kidnapping — he likes to keep his distance — but he was, and I think

I know why. And so was his number two, another nasty guy by the name of Ismael Quintero."

"How are you going to deal with them? More important, if you know who they are, why haven't you locked them up?"

"Because if I did, they would escape within two weeks and then come after me with even more enthusiasm than they are coming after me now."

"So how are you going to deal with them?"

"How do you think, Carlos? Just as soon as I can set it up so that somebody else gets the blame."

When Castillo didn't reply, Pena said, "Am I shocking you, Carlos?"

"He's wondering what will happen to Colonel Ferris," Svetlana put in, "after you eliminate these people."

"That, too, sweetheart," Castillo answered, "but also why Juan Carlos wants to take these people out."

"Because Danny trusted me, and because he did, now he's dead. Somehow Archivaldo found out what Danny and I had going — I may have done something stupid, or he just put two and two together — and decided to whack him. And once he decided to do that, he figured, 'What the hell, I'll try to get my old pal Félix out of Florence while I'm doing that. And then I will go after Juan Carlos Pena.' I'm not going to let him get away with either one."

Castillo exchanged glances with Svetlana.

"Tell him, Carlito," she said.

"Tell me what, Red?" Pena asked.

"Everything," Svetlana said. "Tell him everything, Carlito. Or I will."

Castillo looked at her for a long moment.

I don't have any choice.

I know both that look and that tone of voice.

She's made her decision that Juan Carlos is telling the truth — and that he has to be told.

Told everything.

And right now what I think about doing that doesn't matter.

Why?

Epiphany: Because when he made that crack, "The best that me and people like me — and the other three or four honest cops — can do is fuck them up from time to time," he sounded like the Mexican chapter of Oprichnina International.

That's the way "the good Russians," the Christians, have dealt with every vicious bastard from Ivan the Terrible to Vladimir Vladimirovich: They fucked them up from time to time.

She's decided that Juan Carlos is a kindred soul.

Please, God, let her be right.

"You have the floor, Podpolkovnik Alekse-eva," he said finally.

It took Svetlana about five minutes to tell Juan Carlos everything. At first there was a cynical expression on Pena's face — "I recognize bullshit when I hear it" — but it changed as she spoke, and when she was finished, he nodded, as if in approval.

"Okay, Red," he said. "I now believe you were an SVR colonel."

She nodded but didn't say anything.

"Which leaves us where?" Juan Carlos asked. "What do you want from me?"

"To make up your mind whether you're going to help us or not," she said.

"It looks like I don't have much choice, do I?"

"I hope that's because you think we're right," she said.

"As opposed to what?"

"Knowing your other option is you and your men being found as Carlito's friend and the DEA agents were found, and having this man Joaquín Archivaldo try to figure out who did it."

Pena looked between Castillo and Svetlana for a moment.

He said: "And because I'm willing to

believe Red is ex-SVR, I guess I'm willing to believe she's capable of doing exactly that. Where the hell did you find this woman, Carlos?"

"Actually, my brother and I found *him,*" Svetlana said, matter-of-factly. "It didn't turn out the way we expected. We planned to eliminate him, and almost did."

"What happened?"

"God showed us another path," she said.

"Somehow I don't think you're being sarcastic," Juan Carlos said.

"I'm not."

"I'll be damned," Pena said. "I was beginning to think I was the only Christian left on earth except for the Pope."

"There's a few of us Christians left," she said. "And I'm working on Carlito."

"Good luck with that," Pena said. "Which brings us back to my original question: Where are we?"

"As my heathen Carlito would put it, Juan Carlos, are you in or out?"

"You already know the answer to that, don't you, Colonel?" Pena said.

Svetlana raised her voice and issued an order in Russian. One of the Spetsnaz popped to attention, saluted, and motioned to two of his men, who followed him as he trotted around the side of the house.

"He's going to free your men," she explained, "and bring them here. After you have explained the change in the situation, we'll give them their weapons, and then Carlito will show you the helicopter and ask your suggestions vis-à-vis how it should be used."

"What helicopter?" Juan Carlos asked.

"A Policía Federal Black Hawk," Castillo said simply, and sipped his coffee as he watched Pena's face change expression.

[Two]
The Oval Office
The White House
1600 Pennsylvania Avenue, N.W.
Washington, D.C.
1005 20 April 2007

Supervisory Secret Service Agent Robert J. Mulligan pushed open the door and announced, "Mr. President, His Excellency Raul Vargas, ambassador of the United States of Mexico to the United States, and Secretary of State Natalie Cohen."

President Clendennen rose from behind his desk and with a cordial smile and his hand extended walked toward Vargas — a tall, olive-skinned, elegantly dressed man with a carefully trimmed pencil-line mus-

441

tache — and the secretary of State.

"How nice to see you again, Mr. Ambassador," he said.

"The pleasure is entirely mine, Mr. President," Vargas replied.

"Secretary Cohen tells me you're carrying a letter for me?"

"Yes, I am, Mr. President," Vargas said.

He took a business-size envelope from his jacket pocket and handed it over.

"Please have a seat, Mr. Ambassador, while I read what my friend Ramón has to say."

He indicated one of the couches, turned to Clemens McCarthy, and ordered, "Get the ambassador some coffee, McCarthy."

McCarthy in turn gestured more than a little imperiously to Mulligan, who in turn gestured, even more imperiously, to Special Agent Douglas.

"May I sit, Mr. President?" Secretary Cohen asked.

Clendennen waved in the general direction of the couch as he sat down at his desk but did not otherwise respond. The President then tore open the envelope, took out the letter it contained, and began to read it:

Ramón Manuel Martinez
Mexico City D.F. 19 April 2007

My Dear Joshua:

Ambassador McCann was kind enough to personally deliver your letter of 18th April, and I hasten to reply.

I am of course anxious to do what I can to see that Colonel Ferris is returned safely to his family. I fully agree with your belief that interrogation of Félix Abrego by Mexican law enforcement authorities will be quite helpful in identifying those responsible for his kidnapping and the murder of the other American officers.

To this end, I have instructed the Oaxaca State Prison officials to be prepared to receive Félix Abrego when he is delivered there by your Marshals, and to make him available for interrogation by Mexican officials.

Further, as soon as I can contact — at the moment, he's not available — Señor Juan Carlos Pena, chief of the Policía Federal for Oaxaca State, I will direct him to call Ambassador McCann to coordinate with your Marshals the moving of Abrego

> to the Oaxaca State Prison, and to personally supervise his interrogation.
>
> If there is anything else I can do, please let me know.
>
> With warm personal regards,
>
> Ramón

When Clendennen had finished reading the letter, he looked at Ambassador Vargas and started to say something.

The secretary of State, who had seen President Martinez's letter, thought, *He's about to lose control.*

"Mr. President," Vargas spoke first, "there is something else — another message."

"Really?" Clendennen asked coldly.

"Yes, sir. President Martinez thought it best under the circumstances that it be delivered privately and verbally, rather than commit it to paper."

"Privately?" Clendennen asked, then said, "Madam Secretary, would you give us a moment in privacy?"

"Mr. President," Vargas said, "Secretary Cohen is familiar with the contents of the message. President Martinez suggested that she be with me when I deliver it, to assure you of its accuracy."

"Well, then, Mr. Ambassador, why don't you deliver the message President Martinez doesn't want committed to paper?"

"Yes, sir. Quote. I am sure you will understand that what I propose is the best I can do under the circumstances at this time. End quote."

Cohen thought: *If he didn't lose control a moment ago, he will now.*

He didn't.

President Clendennen considered that calmly for a moment, and then politely asked, "Madam Secretary, is that the message you understand President Martinez wanted the ambassador to verbally deliver?"

"Yes, it is, Mr. President," Cohen replied.

"Thank you, Mr. Ambassador," the President said. "There's no point in keeping you from the press of your duties any longer. Please be good enough to pass to President Martinez both my gratitude and my best wishes."

"It will be my pleasure, Mr. President," Vargas said.

"Madam Secretary," Clendennen asked politely, "may I have a few minutes more of your time?"

"Yes, of course, Mr. President."

The President waited until the door had closed behind Vargas, and then stood up, holding Martinez's letter.

"Have you seen this fucking thing?" he asked furiously.

"Yes, sir, I have," Cohen said.

"May I see it, Mr. President?" Clemens McCarthy asked.

The President threw it at him. McCarthy tried and failed to catch it in the air. It fell to the carpet in front of the President's desk, and then floated out of sight under the left pedestal of the desk.

McCarthy got on his hands and knees and tried to retrieve it.

"That is not the letter I asked that sonofabitch to send me," the President said.

"No, sir, it is not," Cohen agreed.

"What happened to my letter? The one I wanted him to send me?"

"I delivered it to President Martinez, sir," she said, "and told him what you were asking."

"I told you to have Ambassador McCann do that," the President said.

"Ambassador McCann thought it would be best if I went with him, and I agreed."

She remembered exactly what McCann had said: *I am not going to Martinez with that crazy letter. Is Clendennen out of his mind, thinking that he can push Martinez around like that? I'll go with you, but that's it. Otherwise,*

446

you can have my resignation."

"And?" Clendennen pursued.

"President Martinez asked us to wait . . ."

"Mulligan," Clemens McCarthy interrupted, "get me something so I can get this goddamn letter."

"What should I get, Mr. McCarthy?"

"An umbrella, a ruler . . . just something that'll reach the fucking letter!"

The President looked from McCarthy to Cohen: *"And?"*

". . . *and* about forty-five minutes later, he called us back into his office, and gave us the letter Ambassador Vargas gave you. He then told us Ambassador Vargas was on the telephone. He told Vargas that I was going to bring a letter he wished Vargas to give to you, and that verbal message. Then, almost as an afterthought, he asked me if I would accompany Ambassador Vargas here to verify the verbal message."

"But you have seen the letter?"

She glanced at McCarthy on his knees digging for the letter, then looked back to Clendennen. "Yes, sir. Ambassador Vargas showed it to me on our way here from the Mexican embassy."

"That miserable, ungrateful sonofabitch!" Clendennen exploded. "After all I've done for him! Millions of dollars in aid! *Ten* fucking Black Hawk helicopters! Pretending I don't know what's going on at the border. Not one word about his being blind to that secret drug cartel airport! And all I wanted him to do was provide me a little cover in case something goes wrong."

Cohen didn't reply.

"And what is this bullshit about taking this Abrego character to a prison . . . the Ox something . . ."

He looked to where now both McCarthy and Mulligan were on their hands and knees, trying with a letter opener to get the letter from under the desk.

"Just pick up the fucking desk and move it out of the way, for Christ's sake!" the President ordered.

They immediately tried. It proved too heavy for both of them.

"Jesus Christ!" the President said. "Douglas, get them some help. I want that goddamn letter!"

Special Agent Douglas went to the outer office and returned with the two Secret Service agents who guarded the outer office.

As Mulligan, Douglas, McCarthy, and one of the latter took a grip on the desk, one of the outer-office Secret Service agents fashioned a hook from a wire clothes hanger and, as they lifted, he managed to stab the letter with it, then pull it out from under the desk.

He extended it to the President, who snatched it, tearing it on the makeshift hook of the clothes hanger.

The President looked at the letter and found what he wanted.

McCarthy walked quickly to him and read over his shoulder.

"What's this business about taking Abrego to the . . . how the hell do you pronounce this prison?"

Secretary Cohen furnished the correct pronunciation of Oaxaca to the President.

"Never heard of it," the President said. "Or anything about us taking Abrego there. Thus, I know goddamn well it wasn't in my letter to Martinez."

He looked at McCarthy.

"Was it?" he asked.

"No, Mr. President, it wasn't," McCarthy said.

Cohen thought: *Yes, it was. What's McCarthy up to? I read the draft letter aloud right here in the Oval Office!*

"Then where the hell did it come from?"

"Possibly from the FBI?" McCarthy asked innocently.

"That's probably it, Mr. President," Su-

449

pervisory Special Agent Mulligan chimed in. "No telling what the FBI said to those people, or vive-ah-versa."

Secretary Cohen thought: *That's vice versa, you cretin, not vive-ah-versa.*

Then she thought: *So Mulligan's part of whatever is going on here.*

What the hell is going on here?

And then she noticed that McCarthy was looking at her carefully, as if he expected her to say, *"I'm sorry, but in the letter I took to President Martinez — the one he said you wrote, Mr. McCarthy — there were specific references to taking Abrego to the Oaxaca State Prison."*

She said nothing.

"Get Schmidt and Crenshaw in here," the President ordered. "Right now. I want to know what the hell is going on."

"You don't want to talk to them on the telephone, Mr. President?" Special Agent Douglas asked.

"If I did, Douglas," the President replied sarcastically, "I would have said, 'Get Schmidt and then Crenshaw on the phone.' "

"Yes, sir," Douglas said, and walked to a telephone on a sideboard to summon Schmidt and Crenshaw.

The President turned to the secretary of State.

"You don't know anything about this Oaxaca Prison?"

Cohen was aware that McCarthy seemed very interested in what her reply would be.

"Just what I've heard and seen here, Mr. President," she said.

"Then I don't see any point in taking any more of your valuable time, Madam Secretary. If I need you later, I'll call."

"Thank you, Mr. President," Cohen said, and stood up and walked out of the Oval Office.

When the door had closed, the President asked, "McCarthy, do you think she's telling the truth?"

"I have no reason to believe she's not, Mr. President," McCarthy said. "But I just thought it might be wise to ask her to keep what she heard here to herself."

"Yeah," the President said.

"Should I bring her back in here, Mr. President?"

"No. You can tell her as well as I can that she goddamn well better keep what she just heard in here to herself."

McCarthy caught up with the secretary of

451

State as she was about to get in her limousine.

"Madam Secretary!" McCarthy called. "A moment, please."

She turned to face him but didn't speak.

"The President asked me to tell you he hopes you understand that what took place in the Oval Office just now has to be kept between us."

Cohen nodded but didn't reply.

"And let me say I appreciate your wisdom in not getting further into the business of what was and what was not in the letter you took to President Martinez," McCarthy said.

Again she didn't reply. But her eyebrows rose in question.

"None of us want him to go off the deep end just now, do we, Madam Secretary? Now would be a very bad time for something like that to happen."

"Now?" she asked, and then before he had a chance to reply, said, "Good morning, Mr. McCarthy," got into the limousine, and gestured to the State Department security officer who was holding the door open to close it.

[Three]
The Oval Office
The White House
1600 Pennsylvania Avenue, N.W.
Washington, D.C.
1055 20 April 2007

"It took you two long enough to get here," President Clendennen greeted Attorney General Stanley Crenshaw and FBI Director Mark Schmidt as they walked into the Oval Office.

"Mr. President," Crenshaw said, "we quite literally dropped what we were doing when we got Douglas's call saying you wanted to scc us right away."

"And what exactly was it that you quite literally dropped when Douglas called?"

"A discussion of the latest development in El Paso."

"Let me get this straight," Clendennen said. "Schmidt, there has been a development in El Paso that you were discussing with Crenshaw?"

"Yes, Mr. President."

"Weren't you listening when I told you I wanted to hear immediately of anything that happened?"

"Mr. President, I work for Attorney General Crenshaw," Schmidt said, uncomfortably.

"You work for me, goddamn it!" the President said, furiously.

"Mr. President, I'm responsible," Crenshaw said. "I told Director Schmidt to make me —"

"Well," the President interrupted, "what *is* this latest development that you were going to tell me about when you finally got around to it?"

"It's this, Mr. President," Crenshaw said, and handed him a sheet of paper.

The President took it and read it:

Transfer Instructions

At 0830 21 April put your guest and no more than two U.S. Marshals aboard an El Paso police helicopter at El Paso International.

File a local aircraft test flight plan and take off no later than 0845.

At 0900 contact Ciudad Juárez International with the message "Necessary to make a precautionary landing."

Your aircraft will be met on landing, and the exchange of your guest for ours will be accomplished at that time.

Your aircraft will then be free to return to the United States.

"What the hell is this?" the President asked. "Where did it come from?"

"According to SAC Johnson, Mr. President, it was handed to one of the FBI agents on stakeout in the El Paso post office," Schmidt said.

"Which suggests to me that the FBI agent didn't succeed in being inconspicuous," the President said. "Who handed it to him?"

"May I see that, Mr. President?" Clemens McCarthy asked.

The President handed him the letter.

"Try to keep it from going under the desk, McCarthy," the President said, and then turned his attention to Schmidt. "I'm waiting."

"A boy, Mr. President. A boy, twelve years old, Latino, handed it to one of the FBI agents. He said that a man gave him five dollars and told him to hand that — it was in an envelope addressed 'To the FBI' — to him. I mean, he indicated to whom the boy was to hand the envelope."

"And that man? Do we know who he is? Is it too much to hope that he was detained for questioning?"

"By the time they started looking for him, Mr. President," Schmidt said, "the man had gone."

"A regular James Bond, huh?" the President said with a snort, and then asked, "Do either of you have any idea what's going on here?"

"I don't understand the question, Mr. President," Crenshaw said.

"That doesn't surprise me at all," the President said.

"Schmidt and I were discussing how to deal with the exchange when you called."

"What do you mean by that?"

"We were thinking of sending FBI agents — instead of Marshals — on the helicopter for the exchange."

"Jesus H. Christ!" the President exploded. "Let me tell you what would happen if you sent FBI agents on that helicopter. They would land at that airport and be greeted by, say, a dozen Mexicans, all armed to the teeth, who would relieve them of this fucking Mexican murderer and then wave byebye. They would not get Colonel Ferris, who is probably five hundred miles from Ciudad Juárez. I know what they think of your intelligence, but I'm surprised they think I'm also that stupid."

Neither Crenshaw nor Schmidt replied.

"What we are going to do, gentlemen, is go along with President Martinez, that ungrateful sonofabitch. He wants Abrego turned over to this Mexican cop — what's his name, McCarthy . . . ?"

"Pena, Mr. President," McCarthy furnished. "Juan Carlos Pena, chief of the Policía Federal for Oaxaca State."

". . . for interrogation, which means to be turned loose," the President picked up. "So we're going to do just that. We're going to take this goddamn murderer to the Oaxaca State Prison and exchange him for Ferris. He'll be taken there, gentlemen, not by U.S. Marshals, not by the FBI, but by as many of those super Green Berets — what do they call them, McCarthy?"

"The Delta Force, Mr. President?" McCarthy asked, his confusion evident in his voice.

"No, goddammit! I said *super* Green Berets."

"Gray Fox, Mr. President?" Attorney General Crenshaw asked, and his confusion was equally evident in his voice.

"Right," the President said. "*Gray Fox*. As many of those Gray Fox people that'll fit on three Black Hawks. They'll either get Ferris back when they get there or they'll bring the goddamn Mexican back and throw him in his Florence cell. I don't think a goddamn Mexican cop is going to want to get in a fight with twenty, twenty-five Gray Fox guys. Get General McNab on the phone."

"General McNab is in Afghanistan, Mr. President," McCarthy said.

"Then get his deputy, that Irishman, what's his name? McCool? Something like that."

"O'Toole, Mr. President. Major General Terrence O'Toole," McCarthy said.

"Well, get Major General Terrence *O'Toole* on the phone and tell him to get up here. And while you're at it, get Naylor and Beiderman in here, too. I'll teach that bastard Martinez he can't fuck with Joshua Ezekiel Clendennen."

[Four]
Office of the Director
Central Intelligence Agency
McLean, Virginia
1110 20 April 2007

"An unexpected pleasure, Madam Secretary," DCI A. Franklin Lammelle said. "If I had known you were coming, there would have been a brass band."

"Can we dispense with the clever repartee, Frank?" Natalie Cohen replied. "I'm really in no mood for it."

"I tend to hide behind clever repartee when I have problems," Lammelle said. "What's yours?"

"Recording devices turned off?"

He nodded. "I usually turn them on only when the enemy is at the gates," he replied, then realized that might qualify as clever repartee, and added, "Sorry."

She nodded, accepting the apology.

"I just came from the Oval Office," she said. "With the unnerving suspicion that there may be something to President Clendennen's conspiracy theory."

He raised his eyebrows, made a "give it to me" gesture with his hands, and said, now quite serious, "Tell me all about it."

"Martinez didn't buy that draft letter . . ." she began.

". . . And after I had been dismissed," she concluded, "McCarthy caught up with me as I was getting in my car in the portico, told me the President had sent him to tell me to keep my mouth shut, and then said,

459

quote, 'I appreciate your wisdom in not getting further into the business of what was and what was not in the letter you took to President Martinez,' end quote. When I didn't reply, he added, quote, None of us want him to go off the deep end just now, do we, Madam Secretary? Now would be a very bad time for something like that to happen, end quote."

"So now you're willing to buy in on the coup d'état theory?" Lammelle asked.

"I'm not sure I'm willing to go that far, but something very unsavory is going on here, Frank."

"Would you say the situation is desperate?" he asked.

"I'm not sure I'd go that far, either. But I — we — have to get to the bottom of it."

"Time to get off the fence, Natalie."

"What does that mean?"

"The situation is, or is not, desperate. This is not one of those times when you can put off making that decision."

"Why am I getting the idea that you know something I don't?"

"Maybe because I'm the DCI? We have a reputation for knowing things and doing things that other people don't know about."

"Or don't want to know about," Natalie said after a moment. "Where are you going with this, Frank?"

"You haven't answered my question. Is this situation desperate? Desperate enough to require taking desperate action?"

She considered that for a long moment, and then said, "I'll listen to what you have to say."

"Not quite good enough, sorry."

"What is it exactly you want from me, Frank?"

"Your word that after I offer my suggestion, and tell you what I know, that you won't take any action of which I disapprove."

"That's too much to ask."

"Then good luck with your problem, Natalie."

"I don't like this at all."

"I didn't think you would."

"I'm the secretary of State. You are required by law to provide me with any intelligence you have that I might find useful in the discharge of my duties."

"Spoken like a true dip," Lammelle said. "Big words meaning nothing in real life. You want to walk that scenario through? You go to Truman Ellsworth — do you really want to go to Ellsworth? — and you tell him I'm not giving you information you're entitled to by law. He tells me to give you what you

461

want, and I tell him I don't have any idea what you're talking about. So he goes to President Clendennen — do you really want Ellsworth going to President Clendennen about this? — and he says Lammelle . . ."

She held up her hand to shut him off.

"Tell me again what it is you want me to give my word about," she said.

"That after I tell you what I know, you won't go any further with it — that's sort of moot, because if you did that, I'd deny it — and also that you take no action of any kind without my approval."

"I don't know why I'm surprised," she said. "You didn't get to be DCI by being a nice guy, did you, Frank?"

"I got here by doing what I had to, in what I thought were the best interests of the United States."

"What was it that Samuel Johnson said, Frank, on that April night in 1775? Something about patriotism?"

"Now I get the history lecture," Lammelle said, chuckling. "He was talking about *false* patriotism, Natalie, when he said it was the last refuge of the scoundrel, not the real thing. False is when it doesn't cost you anything. My kind is expensive. You can be disgraced. You can go to prison. You can even lose your life."

"Are you feeling just a little self-righteous, Frank, after doing something you know you shouldn't have done?"

"Okay. Conversation over. Is there anything else I can do for you before you go?"

The secretary of State was in deep thought a moment, then said, "Okay, you have my word."

When he didn't reply, she said, "Maybe you should have gone in the Foreign Service, Frank. You're really a tough negotiator."

"I have your word?" he asked.

"I said that you did."

"All right. What Charley Castillo plans to do is grab Abrego — and, he hopes, Ferris — when either of them shows up at the Oaxaca State Prison, and see who that brings out of the woodwork."

"How could he possibly manage that? The President has personally ordered General Naylor to see there is absolutely no U.S. military involvement . . ."

"At last count, he's got about forty ex-Spetsnaz."

"Where did he get ex-Spetsnaz?"

"From Aleksandr Pevsner, who believes that this whole kidnapping business is connected with Vladimir Putin's plan to take out him and his family. Pevsner's original reaction to hearing that the new Russian cultural affairs officer for Venezuela, Panama, Costa Rica, Nicaragua, Honduras, and Guatemala is Valentin Komarovski — who of course is really our old pal Sergei Murov, the SVR *rezident* here — was to whack anybody Pevsner even suspected was SVR until Putin got the message."

"Oh, my God!"

"Castillo has managed to talk Pevsner out of this for the time being — which means until Castillo's able to snatch Abrego and/or Ferris at the prison, and then see what the interrogation of whoever comes out of the woodwork turns up.

"We know the Venezuelans are involved. The guy who dropped the kidnapper's letter in the post office slot in El Paso is José Rafael Monteverde, the financial attaché of the embassy of the República Bolivariana de Venezuela in Mexico City."

"How do you know that?" Secretary Cohen asked.

"A friend of mine happened to be in the El Paso post office when he did it."

"I will refrain myself from commenting that the CIA is expressly forbidden by law from operating within the United States," she said.

"Anyway, Charley's got people from China

464

Post sitting on this guy. I think they're going to want to talk to him."

"China Post? The mercenary employment agency?"

"Charley prefers to think of them as former comrades in arms," Lammelle said.

"Where's he getting the money to pay for all this?" she asked, and then quickly added, "Don't tell me. I think I know. 'Those People'?"

"So far, I think he's picking up the tab himself. Or Aleksandr Pevsner is. But that Las Vegas money is going to be available if he asks for it."

"If Castillo kidnaps this Venezuelan diplomat, President Martinez —"

"What? Won't like it? Won't let him get away with it?"

"Both, and you know it."

"So what if he doesn't like it?" Lammelle said. "He's done nothing, and you know it, to get Colonel Ferris back, or get the people who murdered Salazar and the DEA agents. And as far as not letting Castillo get away with what he's doing, how is he going to do that? With the Policía Federal? Come on, Natalie."

"Frank, you don't really expect me to look the other way at any of this?"

"I expect you to do what you can to

465

prevent a coup d'état. We don't know who's behind that. The only ones I'm sure are not are Generals Naylor and McNab. And we can count on their help once we find out who's behind it. But we have to find out who's behind it, whether the Russians, or Montvale, or Truman Ellsworth . . ."

"You think that Ellsworth might be involved?"

"I think it's possible. The only thing I know for sure is that the only one who can find out is Castillo, and if he breaks a few laws finding out, I have no problem with that."

She considered that a moment, and then said, "Don't interpret this as a sign that I'm considering going along with any of this, but as a practical matter, how is he going to . . . I guess 'kidnap' is the word . . . Ferris and/or Abrego from the Mexican authorities, or the kidnappers, or for that matter, the U.S. Marshal Service?"

"I told you, he has the ex-Spetsnaz he got from Pevsner and the people from China Post — plus, of course, the Merry Outlaws."

"And how, as a practical matter, Frank, is he going to move them around Mexico with the entire Policía Federal — plus the kidnappers, the drug cartels, and possibly even the SVR — looking for them?"

"Well, he has the helicopter. That'll help."

"You're not talking about that Black Hawk?"

He nodded.

"You actually turned that helicopter over to him?"

"Persons representing themselves as officers of the CIA went to Fort Sam and flew it away," Lammelle said. "They told Fort Sam officials they were returning it to Mexico."

"You actually sent your people to Fort Sam to steal that helicopter for Castillo?"

"What I said was 'people representing themselves as officers of the CIA.' And it was never stolen. Though there wasn't exactly a bill of sale, Charley did buy it for a million plus, so it could be argued it's actually his chopper."

"My God! You're insane!"

"Natalie, you're the one who told me that the Mexicans reported that Black Hawk was destroyed in President Martinez's war on the drug cartels. How can you steal something that doesn't exist?"

She shook her head in disbelief.

"Anyway, apparently these persons have gotten away with their deception. There have been no reports to anyone about anything unusual happening at Fort Sam."

"And how does he plan to get the Black Hawk into Mexico?"

"It's already there. As we speak, he's showing it to a man he describes as one of the four honest cops in Mexico. I was just talking to him. I hung up" — he pointed to the Brick on his desk — "as you were coming through the door."

"Does this honest cop have a name?" she asked.

"I'm sure he does."

"But you're not going to tell me?"

"Castillo's going to do what he's going to do, Natalie. What you have to decide is whether you're going to help him or not. Whether, in other words — this is the choice Naylor had to make when he knew there was nothing he could do to stop Charley from going to La Orchila Island — Charley's failure would do more harm to the country than his success."

"Get him back on the Brick," she said.

"He may not want to talk to you."

"Why not?"

"I think he's as much afraid that your high moral standards will demand that you do 'the right thing,' as you're afraid he's about to start a war with Mexico."

"You're saying he doesn't trust me? I don't believe that."

"I'm saying he thinks you have a different agenda, one probably in conflict with his." He paused, then went on: "Natalie, I'm betraying a confidence when I tell you this, but I think you should know there are now two nets on the Brick. The old one, which you have on your Brick, and the new one. You're not on the new one. Neither are Those People. Charley doesn't entirely trust them, either."

"So where does that leave us?"

"I just realized it puts me in a somewhat uncomfortable position," Lammelle said. "What the hell!"

He reached for his Brick, took out the handset, put his index finger in front of his lips as a signal to Cohen, and then pushed one of the direct connect buttons and the SPEAKERPHONE key.

"Yeah, Frank?" Castillo's voice came over the loudspeaker.

"What would you say if I told you that Natalie Cohen knows what you're up to and wants to talk to you about helping?"

"I'd say you have a dangerously loose mouth and have been smoking an illegal substance. What the hell is this all about?"

"I thought you liked Natalie and trusted her."

"I like her very much. Do I think she

wants to help? No. If she knows what I'm doing and wants to talk to me, it's to talk me out of what I'm doing. And goddamn you, Frank, if you did tell her."

There was a buzzing sound.

Cohen and Lammelle looked at each other until they realized the buzzing was coming from the secretary of State's Brick.

"Hold one, Charley," Lammelle said.

Cohen opened the leather attaché case and took out the handset. She saw which number was illuminated, and mouthed, "Crenshaw."

"See what he wants," Lammelle said.

"See what who wants?" Castillo demanded impatiently. "Who are you talking to, Frank?"

Lammelle cut the connection.

"Natalie Cohen," she said.

"If there was ever any question in your mind that the President is acting irrationally, forget it," the attorney general said.

"What are you talking about?"

"Schmidt and I just left the Oval Office," Crenshaw said. "The President just decided to send three Black Hawks loaded with Gray Fox operators to the Oaxaca State Prison to exchange Abrego for Ferris. And from his attitude, I don't think he cares if there's a firefight with the Policía Federal.

470

In fact, I think he's hoping for one."

"Why would he want . . . oh."

"The word is 'irrational,' Natalie, and that's a euphemism."

"Let me get this straight, he's going to send Gray Fox to deal with this Policía Federal officer?"

"Juan Carlos Pena," Crenshaw said.

"That's going to take him at least twenty-four hours, maybe forty-eight, before they can leave, right?"

"McNab is in Afghanistan, so Clendennen sent for McNab's deputy, General O'Toole. And for Beiderman and Naylor. That'll take some time, of course."

"Let me get back to you, Stanley," she said. She met Lammelle's eyes and added, "I realize this is a desperate situation, requiring desperate measures. Let me see what I can do."

She broke the connection.

"You say this no longer works to talk to Castillo?"

"You still can talk to him on it. You just won't know what's being said on what we're calling Net Two."

She punched a number on her handset.

"Hello, Madam Secretary," Castillo's voice came over the loudspeaker.

"Charley, what do you know about a

Policía Federal officer named Pena? Juan Carlos Pena."

"Rude question, but necessary," he replied. "Why do you want to know?"

"Because the President is about to send three Black Hawks loaded with Gray Fox special operations to exchange Abrego for Ferris at the prison this man operates in Oaxaca State."

"He doesn't operate the prison. He's the head of the Policía Federal for Oaxaca State."

"So you do know him?"

"Yeah, I know him," Castillo said. "Why don't you go back to the beginning with this, so I know what you're talking about."

"All right," she said. "This is the problem."

X

[One]
Andrews Air Force Base
Prince George's County, Maryland
1125 20 April 2007

General Allan B. Naylor was walking from the VIP waiting room in the Base Operations building towards his C-37A — the military designation for the Gulfstream V —

when Colonel J. D. Brewer, his senior aide-de-camp, who was walking beside him, took his Signal Corps Brick from his tunic pocket.

He glanced at it to see who was calling, and then handed it to Naylor.

"Secretary Beiderman, General," he announced.

Naylor stopped walking and put the device to his ear.

"General Naylor, Mr. Secretary."

"Where are you, Allan?"

"At Andrews, about to get on my plane."

"Brussels and NATO are going to have to wait," Beiderman said. "Mulligan called me just now, and said the President wants to see you and me right away."

"Okay," Naylor said.

"He also wanted to know when McNab will be back from Afghanistan. I told him I'd have to ask you."

"As I recall, we told McNab to get out of Dodge and stay there until the President got his temper under control. Does this mean that hasn't happened?"

"I don't know," Beiderman confessed.

"Well, if the President has ordered him back . . . Do you want me to handle that?"

"I already have. He'll be leaving over there as soon as he can get on a plane."

"You realize, I hope, that he was dead serious when he said if he is relieved over that nonsense at Arlington, he'll demand a court-martial?"

"Can he do that? Demand a court-martial? He's not going to be punished, reduced in rank, or anything like that; just relieved."

"I don't know. It would depend on the circumstances. What he could do — what he probably *will* do — is go to Roscoe Danton and argue his case in the court of public opinion. In other words, on the front page of *The Washington Times-Post* and the television sets tuned to Wolf News. And the President will lose that battle; Danton loathes the President and thinks McNab walks on water."

The secretary of Defense grunted, and then said, "Wouldn't it be nice if we could say, 'Screw him. Let him make an ass of himself like that!' "

"But we can't, can we? We're in the uncomfortable position of having to defend the presidency against the luna—"

Naylor heard what he was about to say and stopped midword.

"You can say it, Allan," Beiderman said. "We have to defend the presidency against the lunacy of the President."

"Have you got any good ideas on how we can do that?"

"No. But I'll try to think of some on my way over there."

"There? Where's there? The White House?"

"Andrews. I'll pick you up in ten, fifteen minutes."

"You don't have to do that."

"What I don't want to do is walk into the Oval Office all by myself."

"Are you going to have room for my people? Colonel Brewer and —"

"Mulligan said the President wants to see you and me only," Beiderman said.

"I've got a car. Why don't I just meet you at the White House?"

Beiderman considered that, then said, "Okay. But if I get there before you, I'll wait. Come now."

"Done," Naylor said, and broke the connection.

[Two]
The President's Study
The White House
1600 Pennsylvania Avenue, N.W.
Washington, D.C.
1225 20 April 2007

When Secret Service Agent Mark Douglas showed Beiderman and Naylor into the room, Supervisory Special Agent Robert J. Mulligan, Press Secretary Clemens McCarthy, and the President were standing before a map board. It held a map of Mexico.

"What the hell is McNab doing in Afghanistan?" the President greeted them less than warmly. "I need him here now."

"As you know, Mr. President," Naylor responded, "a substantial portion of General McNab's command is in Afghanistan. He spends a good deal of his time there."

"What about this other Special Forces guy, McCool? Is he any good?"

"If you are referring to General McNab's deputy, General O'Toole, Mr. President —"

"Okay. *O'Toole.* Is this *O'Toole* any good?"

"General O'Toole is a fine officer, Mr. President," Naylor said.

The President looked between Beiderman and Naylor, and said, "I'd rather have Mc-

Nab, but you go with what you've got, right?"

"Yes, sir," Naylor and Beiderman said almost simultaneously.

"I had Clemens call *O'Toole* and tell him to drop everything and get up here," Clendennen said. "When's he due, Clemens?"

"He should already have landed at Andrews, Mr. President," McCarthy said.

"Well, while we're waiting for him, let me bring you up to speed on what's going on around here and how I'm going to deal with it," the President said.

The sound of helicopter rotors penetrated the sound-insulated walls of the White House.

"That has to be him," the President decided out loud. "We'll wait. I hate to explain things over and over."

Major General Terrence O'Toole was shown into the President's study. He was wearing a somewhat mussed camouflage-pattern battle-dress uniform.

He saluted and said, "Pardon my appearance, sir."

"You look, General," the President said, "as if you're ready to go to work. No apologies are necessary."

"So that's the plan, gentlemen," the Presi-

477

dent said. "What do you think?"

"Mr. President, I think it's brilliant," Clemens McCarthy promptly said.

"What you think, McCarthy," the President immediately shot him down, "is irrelevant. You're a press agent. What is it they say? 'You might want to write that down.' "

"Mr. President," General Naylor said, "with all possible respect, sir, I have a few questions. Possibly because I missed some things as you laid out your plan."

"I expected you and McCool here to have questions, General. I'm the Commander in Chief, but I'm not a soldier. What didn't you understand?"

"As I understand the situation, Mr. President, there are two sites for the exchange of this fellow Abrego for Colonel Ferris."

"No. There's only one. At the Oaxaca State Prison."

He turned to the map. Using a ruler as a pointer, he aimed it at the map.

"Here," Clendennen said. "It's apparently in the middle of goddamn nowhere."

Naylor said: "Excuse me, sir, but I thought I understood you to say that there has been a message from the kidnappers stating they wanted the exchange to take place at the Juárez International Airport."

"And I thought I had made it perfectly

478

clear that if we did that, we'd play right into their hands. The helicopter would land there, the two U.S. Marshals on it would find themselves outnumbered by Mexican banditos, who would take this man Abrego from them, and then either wave bye-bye or kill them, too." As he looked around the room at everyone, he added, "The exchange will take place at the Oaxaca State Prison. Clear?"

"Yes, sir," Naylor pursued, "but may I respectfully suggest that these people do expect the helicopter to appear at the Juárez airfield at oh-nine-hundred tomorrow. If — when — it does not, then what?"

"Then they will figure out that they haven't made a sucker out of Joshua Ezekiel Clendennen."

"That may put Colonel Ferris at risk, Mr. President," Naylor said, carefully.

"He's already at risk, isn't he, General?" Clendennen responded. "You ever hear what Patton said, General? Or was it Mac-Arthur?"

"I'm afraid I don't follow you, Mr. President."

" 'Never take counsel of your fears' is what one of them — now that I think about it, it was MacArthur — said. You never heard that?"

"I'm familiar with it, sir," Naylor said.

"Mr. President, may I make a suggestion?" General O'Toole asked.

"That's what you're here for, General," the President said.

"As I understand your plan, sir, it is your intention to send U.S. Marshals to establish contact with the Mexican police chief Pena."

The President nodded, and gestured for O'Toole to get to his point.

"I think it might be best to send a special operator to do that, sir. In addition to setting up the schedule for the exchange, he would be able to reconnoiter the terrain. That would be valuable in case there was trouble."

"Presumably, you have a specific special operator in mind, General?"

"Yes, sir," O'Toole said, looked at Naylor, then went on: "I don't know if General Naylor would agree with sending a special operator, or with my recommendation of who that should be."

"That's moot, General," the President said. "I'm making the decisions here. I think sending a special operator instead of a Marshal is a good idea — hell, send in *all* of Gray Fox. Now what you have to do is convince me that the man you want to send is the right one."

"I was thinking of Mr. Victor D'Alessandro, Mr. President."

"*Mister* D'Alessandro? That sounds as if he's a civilian. I don't want anybody from the goddamn CIA involved in this. Or from the DEA or any other place like that."

"He's a retired chief warrant officer, Mr. President, now a DAC — a Department of the Army civilian employee — working for SPECOPSCOM."

"And in your opinion he would be the best man to send?"

"Yes, sir."

"I concur, Mr. President," Naylor said.

"Well, that's nice to know," the President said, sarcastically. "We've really had entirely too much dissension in the ranks around here lately."

Clendennen let that sink in, and then went on: "Okay. Then this guy D'Alessandro goes. Mulligan, get Secretary Cohen on the phone. Tell her . . . Hell, tell her to get over here. She can't be kept out of this; she already knows too much."

Mulligan picked up the red presidential circuit telephone.

"But that's all," the President said. "I don't want every idiot and his twin brother involved in this. Nobody else is to learn of it unless I personally clear it." He looked

481

around the room again. "Everybody got that?"

"Mr. President," Naylor said, "do I correctly infer that you don't plan to tell the DCI what you're going to do?"

"Correct."

"And the director of National Intelligence, Mr. Ellsworth?" Naylor pursued.

"Correct."

"And Vice President Montvale?"

"Especially not Montvale!" Clendennen flared. "And you damn well know why."

"I'm afraid, sir, that I don't know what you're talking about," Naylor said.

"The hell you don't!" the President snapped.

"Sir, I don't."

Both Naylor and Beiderman were about convinced that Naylor had just pushed the President over the edge.

Clendennen's face tightened and whitened, and he opened his mouth as if to speak and then changed his mind. When he finally spoke, he apparently had himself under control.

"I don't know why I'm arguing with you about this, General," the President said. "The decision whether to involve the Vice President in this is mine — and mine alone

— to make. I have decided not to tell him. Clear?"

"Yes, sir."

"There is a precedent," Clendennen then said, reasonably. "I don't think anyone would argue that my trying to get Colonel Ferris back from those who hold him captive is anywhere near as important as the atomic bomb. Still, President Roosevelt didn't think Vice President Truman had the need to know we had the atom bomb and elected not to tell him. And I don't think Vice President Montvale has the need to know about what we're about to do, and I have elected not to tell him. Any questions, General?"

"No, sir," Naylor said.

"Okay. Now let's get to the nuts and bolts of this operation. How are we going to get this civilian, what's his name again?"

"D'Alessandro, Mr. President," O'Toole furnished. "Victor D'Alessandro."

"How are we going to get this man *D'Alessandro* from where he is — and by the way, where is he? Shouldn't he be here? — to the Oaxaca State Prison?"

After a moment, O'Toole realized the President's question was not rhetorical.

"Sir, I would recommend the use of a Black Hawk to get Mr. D'Alessandro from where he is — El Paso — to the prison," O'Toole said.

"Why not fly him there in a regular airplane?" the President challenged. "There's an airport right by it."

He picked up the ruler again and pointed at the map with it. "Right here. How the fuck do you pronounce that again?"

Clemens McCarthy correctly pronounced *Xoxocotlán* for the President.

"What is that, Inca? Incan?" the President asked.

"That's certainly what it sounds like, Mr. President," McCarthy said.

The President turned to O'Toole.

"I'm waiting, General."

"Sir?"

"For you to tell me why Whatsisname is better off flying to the prison in a helicopter instead of using an airplane to fly to the airport with the unpronounceable name."

"Yes, sir. Sir, for the same reason I gave before. It will permit him to reconnoiter the area; he can do that better in a Black Hawk."

"Yeah, I suppose he can," the President conceded. "Now, where are we going to get the helicopter?"

"I would suggest, sir, that since we're going to use Night Stalker birds to carry the Gray Fox —"

" 'Night Stalker birds'?" the President interrupted. "What the hell are they? Is that?"

"It's how we refer to the rotary wing aircraft — the helicopters — assigned to the 160th Special Operations Aviation Regiment, sir."

"I see that I'm going to have to get used to the terminology you people use. I'm the Commander in Chief, and I should know it, but sometimes I think you and General Naylor are speaking a foreign language."

"I can see where it might be a little confusing, sir," O'Toole said.

"Okay. I've got several questions. What kind of a helicopter are we talking about?"

"UH-60Fs, sir. They're specially modified Black Hawks for missions like this."

"And they have the range to fly to this prison from El Paso?"

"Yes, sir. I believe they do."

"You believe they do? Don't you know?"

"I always like to consult the experts, Mr. President," O'Toole said.

"Who would that be?"

"Colonel Arthur Kingsolving, sir. The 160th Regiment's commander."

"Well, why isn't he here?"

Naylor offered: "We can have Colonel Kingsolving here in flight time from Fort

Campbell, Mr. President."

"See, that's what I mean," the President said. "I sometimes think you're speaking a foreign language. What the hell does 'flight time from Fort Campbell' mean?"

"Colonel Kingsolving can be here, sir," Naylor said, "in the time it will take him to fly from Fort Campbell. The 160th is stationed at Fort Campbell, sir."

"Why aren't they stationed at Fort Bragg, with SPECOPSCOM?" the President asked. "What the hell are they doing way out in Kansas?"

"Fort Campbell is in Kentucky, Mr. President," Naylor said.

"The President knows where Fort Campbell is, General," McCarthy said.

"Answer the question, General," Clendennen snapped.

"I wasn't privy to the decision to station the 160th at Campbell, sir," Naylor said. "It was made by the chief of staff."

"And he didn't even ask you, or O'Toole here, where you thought such an important organization should be stationed?"

"No, sir. He did not."

"Did you — or General O'Toole — complain when the chief of staff put this organization in the middle of *Kentucky* instead of Fort Bragg, where it should be?"

"No, sir."

"Why not?"

"It was in the nature of an order, sir. Soldiers are expected to obey their orders, not protest them."

"An admirable philosophy," Clendennen said. "I wish I knew how to instill it in the people around me." He paused. "Okay. So where are we?"

"We were talking about getting Colonel Kingsolving here, Mr. President," Naylor said.

"No. That's already been decided. The question is how. Is there any reason he couldn't come here in a Black Hawk?"

"No, sir. The flight time would be longer, sir," O'Toole said.

"I'd already figured that out, General, believe it or not," the President said. "Get him on the phone and tell him to come here in a Black Hawk. I'd like a good look at one. Mulligan, clear it for him to land on the West Lawn."

"Yes, sir."

"Mr. President," Naylor said, "I would recommend having a Black Hawk sent to El Paso from Fort Campbell to take Mr. D'Alessandro to the prison."

"Do it," Clendennen ordered.

"And that would raise the question of Mr.

D'Alessandro's orders, sir. How is he to deal with this Mexican police chief?"

"If this fellow is as good as you and O'Toole say he is, he should be able to figure that out himself, wouldn't you say?"

"Sir, as General O'Toole pointed out, he will have two missions. The first, he will have to know about that. That is, the arrival of Abrego at the prison. That's the overt mission. The covert mission is to determine the best way of liberating Colonel Ferris. How much do you want O'Toole to tell him about that?"

The President gave that question thirty seconds of serious consideration.

"I was about to say, leave that to General O'Toole's good judgment. He has experience in these matters. But then I realized I want General O'Toole here with me to answer the questions about this and that, ones that will inevitably arise. So, what I think we should do, General Naylor, is have you go to El Paso to give this man D'Alessandro his marching orders."

"General, my appearance at Fort Bliss would raise questions . . ."

"Who said anything about Fort Bliss? I want you to go to El Paso."

"Sir, Fort Bliss abuts El Paso. There is an Army airfield there, Biggs Army Airfield. If

I went into El Paso International instead of Biggs, questions would be raised."

"Well, you don't have to travel in that Gulfstream of yours — going there on a regular airline would be one way of avoiding attention, wouldn't it?"

"Yes, sir. If you think it's best, I can go commercial."

"No," the President then said. "There would be questions about that, too; why you weren't traveling in your Gulfstream. Besides, it will be quicker going and coming, if I need you back here. So here's your marching orders, General: Get down to El Paso. General O'Toole will have this man D'Alessandro waiting for you, and he will have arranged for a Black Hawk to take him to meet this Mexican cop. You will give D'Alessandro his marching orders, and as soon as he's on his way to Mexico, you come back here. Got it?"

"Yes, sir. And after Mr. D'Alessandro meets with the Mexican policeman, what should I tell him to do?"

"Tell him to go back to El Paso and await further orders. We'll cross that bridge when we get to it."

"Yes, sir. I'll leave right away."

"Yeah," the President said. "Have a nice

flight, General."

"Thank you, sir."

[Three]
Office of the Director
Central Intelligence Agency
McLean, Virginia
1310 20 April 2007

"And what can the CIA do for the most important general in the world today?" A. Franklin Lammelle answered his telephone.

"You know I don't think that's funny, Frank," General Allan B. Naylor said.

"It was a perfectly serious question."

"You can tell me where I can find Vic D'Alessandro."

"Two questions," Lammelle said. "What makes you think I would know, and why do you want to know?"

Lammelle held the commander in chief of the United States Central Command in the highest possible regard in terms of ability and integrity. But he didn't like him very much — and sometimes not at all.

Naylor was deeply into the West Pointer's creed of duty, honor, country. And while that was certainly commendable, Naylor,

Lammelle had decided over the years, just went too goddamn far with it.

The best example of this was Naylor's relationship with Charley Castillo. He had known Charley since he was a child. Charley and Naylor's son had been a year apart in a private elementary school in Germany when Charley's mother, suffering from terminal cancer, announced her desire to find Charley's father. She had told Mrs. Naylor, her friend, that she'd been impregnated at seventeen by a dashing nineteen-year-old Army chopper jockey, who'd then disappeared. Mrs. Naylor pressed her husband, then-Major Naylor, to find the boy's only living relative.

Naylor had been happy to do it. He was a highly moral man who really loathed officers who knocked up young German women and never made the slightest effort to meet their responsibilities vis-à-vis their love child.

Castillo's father hadn't been hard to find. He was buried in the Fort Sam National Cemetery beneath a headstone onto which had been chiseled a representation of the Medal of Honor.

Charley's status changed from that of a poor German bastard who had been shamefully treated by a U.S. Army officer —

whose ass Naylor intended to burn — into the son of an officer who had been awarded the nation's highest award for valor on the battlefield.

The first thing Naylor had done was set in motion the legal wheels which would keep Charley's substantial inheritance from being squandered by his newfound family. When that hadn't proved to be necessary — Charley's father's family turned out to be as well off — stinking rich, to put a point on it — as his mother's, "Uncle Allan," as Naylor had quickly become, now turned his efforts into getting Charley into the Long Gray Line. His father's Medal of Honor gave him a pass into West Point, and at West Point he would be imbued with the duty, honor, country philosophy which had guided Naylor all of his life.

A. Franklin Lammelle knew that that had almost — but not quite — turned out the way Naylor had planned.

Charley had graduated from the Military Academy toward the top of his class and been commissioned into Armor. Five generations of generals named Naylor had been Cavalry and then Armored officers.

The Naylor plan for Carlos G. Castillo was working. Most of Naylor's plans for anything worked; he was by then already a three-star general, and serving as General "Stormin' " Norman Schwarzkopf's operations officer for Desert Storm.

But then the plan went off the tracks.

Some publicity conscious brass hats had decided it would be good public relations if the son of a MOH helicopter pilot also flew as a helicopter pilot in the upcoming Desert War I. A training slot at Fort Rucker "was found" for him, and Castillo was sent there to learn how to fly the Bell HU-1 helicopter. On his second day at the aviation school, it was learned that not only did Castillo already know how to fly but had more than 230 hours as pilot-in-command of the twin-engine version Huey. One of the subsidiaries of Castillo Enterprises was Castillo Aviation, which serviced oil wells in the Gulf of Mexico. Castillo had begun flying for Castillo Aviation as soon as he acquired his commercial rotary wing pilot's license, which he had done when he was sixteen and a high school junior.

The brass had regarded this as a fortuitous circumstance. The hero pilot's son could go into Operation Desert Storm, once he finished transition training, flying the Army's glamour machine, the Apache AH-64 attack helicopter.

Once he got to Arabia, and realizing the

twenty-one-year-old second lieutenant was not qualified to fly the Apache, the brass did the best thing they could think of to keep him alive. He was assigned as co-pilot to the most skilled and experienced Apache pilot in the unit.

That plan went awry, too.

Two hours into Desert Storm, the Apache, on a mission to take out Iraqi antiaircraft weapons, was struck, the pilot blinded, and Castillo wounded. Castillo was faced with the choice of landing the shot-up helicopter and waiting for help, or trying to get the pilot medical attention. He flew the smoking and shuddering Apache, at fifty feet above the desert, back two hundred miles.

General Naylor learned for the first time that Second Lieutenant Castillo was not where he was supposed to be — at Fort Knox, undergoing Basic Officer's Course training — when Castillo was marched into Desert Storm headquarters so that he could receive the "impact awards" — in other words, get the medals immediately — of the Distinguished Flying Cross and Purple Heart medals from the hands of General Schwarzkopf himself.

Appropriate counseling was given to the officers who had put Castillo in the cockpit of an Apache he was clearly unqualified to fly, but that left the problem of what to do with Second Lieutenant Castillo. Loading him on the next airplane for Fort Knox would suggest that Castillo had done something wrong, and that was clearly not the case. And so would taking him off flight status.

Checking the roster of units assigned to Desert Storm, Naylor thought he had found just what he needed: the 2303rd Civil Government Detachment. It was commanded by Colonel Bruce J. McNab, a classmate of Naylor's. He hadn't liked McNab at West Point, thought him to be an inferior officer, and was not surprised that he was still a colonel commanding an insignificant civil government unit. But the roster showed that the 2303rd had half a dozen Hueys assigned to it.

Naylor called McNab and told him the story and said he was sending Castillo to him, and McNab was expected to keep the young officer out of harm's way.

"Just have him fly you around, McNab. Nothing more."

McNab had said, "Yes, sir."

The next time Naylor saw Castillo was just after the Iraqi surrender, when Colonel McNab showed up at Desert Storm headquarters with Castillo at the controls of Mc-

Nab's heavily armed Huey.

They were there to personally receive from the hands of General Schwarzkopf impact awards of the Distinguished Service Cross (McNab), Silver Star (Castillo), and Purple Heart (both) medals. McNab also had the star of brigadier general and Castillo the Combat Infantry Badge pinned to their tunics by General Schwarzkopf.

Naylor had learned only then that the "Civil Government Detachment" part of the 2303rd's unit designation was disinformation. Its actual role in Desert Storm had been the direction, under the Central Intelligence Agency, of covert Special Operations.

Naylor had been quietly furious that he had been kept in the dark, even more furious that Castillo had not been kept out of the line of fire, and had almost — but not quite — lost control when McNab told him he was taking Castillo, whom he described as a "natural warrior," with him to Fort Bragg as his aide-de-camp.

As far as A. Franklin Lammelle was concerned, what McNab "had done" to Castillo — turned him over the years into a legendary special operator — was the real source of the friction between McNab and Naylor. There was something in Naylor's makeup that made him hate unconventional warfare and its practitioners.

And, in Lammelle's judgment, it was Naylor's close personal relationship with Castillo that made Charley unwilling on two significant occasions to accept that his Uncle Allan had been perfectly willing to throw him under the bus when ordered to do so.

The first instance had been when Castillo, by then an Army lieutenant colonel heading up the President's secretive Office of Organizational Analysis, had embarrassed the CIA by flying two senior SVR defectors out of Vienna to Argentina under the noses of Vladimir Putin and the CIA station chief in Vienna.

Charles W. Montvale, then the director of National Intelligence, was not interested in Castillo's explanation that he had done so because the Russian defectors had good reason to believe the SVR was waiting to grab them in Vienna's Westbahnhof station, and that he had been unaware the CIA station chief in Vienna had been trying to set up their defection for some time.

What concerned Montvale was that the CIA station chief had gone to syndicated columnist C. Harry Whelan, Jr., with the story that the President was illegally operating his own private CIA headed by Castillo, and that Presidential Agent Castillo had snatched the defectors.

Montvale's solution to that potential embarrassment to the President and the CIA was simple: Castillo would be retired from the Army for psychological reasons — that would explain his erratic behavior — and then turn the defectors over to the CIA.

General Naylor, seeing the protection of the President as his primary duty, had gone along with Montvale. Castillo, the unconventional warrior molded by Bruce McNab, had to be shut down, and he sent one of his Adjutant General Corps colonels to Buenos Aires with Montvale to order Castillo: *"Sign here. You're now retired. Don't let the doorknob hit you in the ass on your way out."*

Castillo refused. The Russian defectors had told him that the SVR and others were operating a biological weapons laboratory and factory in the Congo — what the CIA had dismissed as being only a "fish farm." Castillo saw it as his duty to prove, or disprove, what the Russian defectors said, and managed to convince McNab, by then a lieutenant general commanding SPEC-OPSCOM, that the allegations deserved to be investigated.

McNab put his own career at risk. He arranged for a Gray Fox team to secretly infiltrate the "fish farm" in the Congo, taking with them the Army's preeminent expert in biological warfare, Colonel J. Porter Hamilton, MC.

Hamilton reported to the President that the situation was even more dangerous — he called it "an abomination before God" — than the Russians had said.

The President immediately launched a preemptive strike against the fish farm, using every air-deliverable weapon in the U.S. arsenal except for nuclear weapons. That solved the problem of the incredibly lethal substance called "Congo-X."

But it did not solve the problem of Presidential Agent C. G. Castillo.

The political damage of having the world learn that the President had brought the nation to the cusp of a nuclear exchange on the word of a lowly lieutenant colonel would destroy his presidency. So he gave Castillo a final order: *"Go fall off the edge of the earth, and don't ever be seen again."*

Castillo had barely arrived in Argentina when word came that the President had suddenly died of an aortal rupture.

Castillo had just begun to adapt to his new status of having fallen off the edge of the earth when he learned that the Army's biological warfare laboratory had received — via FedEx — a container of Congo-X.

While that development was being evaluated, the SVR *rezident* in Washington invited the CIA's deputy chief for operations — A. Franklin Lammelle — for drinks at the Russian embassy compound outside Washington. There he offered a deal. If the Americans turned over to Russia the two Russian defectors and Lieutenant Colonel C. G. Castillo, then the Russians would turn over what stocks of Congo-X they had, and give their solemn word that was all of it, and none of it would ever appear again.

The new President, Joshua Ezekiel Clendennen, thought this to be a satisfactory solution to the program, and ordered Director of National Intelligence Montvale to start looking for Castillo and the Russians and then load them on an Aeroflot plane for Moscow. He also ordered General Allan Naylor to participate in the search and exchange.

A. Franklin Lammelle knew all this because the CIA director also ordered him to assist Montvale — and by the time Lammelle found Castillo, he had decided that what Clendennen was trying to do to Castillo was unconscionable. He wanted no part of it.

And this became the second time that Lammelle found Naylor blindly prepared to throw Castillo under the bus.

When Naylor finally found Castillo — and was prepared to order him to return to the United States, there to hold himself in readiness to obey what orders the President might have for him — Castillo and his Merry Band of Outlaws had already learned how the Congo-X had reached the United States and were in the final stages of planning an ad hoc assault on a Venezuelan island where the remaining stock of Congo-X could be found.

Despite this, Naylor delivered his orders, whereupon Castillo very politely placed him under arrest. Lammelle had witnessed the surreal exchange — and what followed.

Naylor — concluding that the assault's failure would be more damaging to the United States than its success — finally decided to help. He provided a Navy helicopter carrier and three 160th Black Hawks that probably guaranteed the success of the assault.

Naylor's change of heart had nothing to do with Castillo attempting the obviously right thing to do in the circumstances. And it certainly had nothing to do with their personal relationship. Lammelle understood that Naylor's decision could easily have gone the other way.

Lammelle had then decided that it was a case of not if, but when, they faced another situation where Castillo was going to try something of which Naylor might not approve and Naylor would decide not to help.

Or, worse, that Naylor's duty was to prevent Castillo from doing what he planned to do — thus once again throwing him under that proverbial bus.

This was one of those times, Lammelle now decided, when he didn't like General Allan B. Naylor at all, and that meant he wasn't going to tell him anything at all that might in any way hurt Charley Castillo.

When Naylor did not immediately respond to Lammelle's questions about why he thought Lammelle would know where Vic D'Alessandro was, and why did he want to know, Lammelle asked a third: "Why don't you ask Terry O'Toole where he is? Vic works for him."

"General O'Toole doesn't know where he is. That's why I'm asking you, Lammelle."

"That brings us back to my original question: Why do you want to know?"

"We have a mission for him. An important

mission. I'm sorry, but that's all I can tell you."

"That's all you want to tell me, Allan. And that's not enough."

"POTUS made it clear that he doesn't want the CIA involved in any way in this mission."

"Which is?"

When Naylor didn't immediately reply, Lammelle went on: "I'm sure you find this distasteful, General, but once in a while you have to disobey an order. Particularly an order from Clendennen, who we are agreed is not playing with a full deck."

"You're speaking, Lammelle, of the President of the United States."

"Yes, I am."

There was a long pause.

"I was going to begin this by saying this has to go no further," Naylor finally said. "But that would be a waste of my breath, wouldn't it?"

"General, what I try to do is live up to my oath to protect the U.S. from all enemies, foreign and domestic."

Naylor ignored that. He said: "The original communication from the kidnappers ordered us to take this fellow Abrego by helicopter from the La Tuna prison to Juárez International Airport, just across the border, accompanied by two U.S. Marshals. This was to be tomorrow morning. The exchange was to take place then. The President feels that if this plan were followed, they would be met by an overwhelming force who would relieve them of Abrego and — the phrase he used was 'wave bye-bye' — with the result being they would have Abrego and we would not have Colonel Ferris."

"That makes sense. So what's Plan B?"

"This is what the President does not want the CIA involved with in any way."

"Involved with what?"

"President Martinez sent him a letter saying that Abrego should be taken to the Oaxaca State Prison for interrogation by the chief of the Policía Federal for Oaxaca State, a man named Juan Carlos Pena."

"And he's going to do this?"

"Martinez said contact should be established with this man Pena."

"And you want to send Vic to make contact?"

"Yes. Now, where is he?"

Lammelle was quiet a moment, then said: "I don't think you're telling me everything, Allan. Why should Clendennen be worried about me knowing about something as simple as sending Vic to see this cop?"

"That's all I can tell you," Naylor said. "I've already told you more than I should."

"But not as much as you're going to tell me if you want me to put you in touch with Vic."

"So you do know where he is?" Naylor snapped.

"I'm the head of the CIA, Allan. I know everything. What else have you got to tell me?"

Lammelle could hear Naylor exhaling audibly before Naylor said, "When Abrego is taken to the prison, after we establish that Ferris is there, the President is sending three Black Hawks loaded with Gray Fox operators with him. They will free Ferris."

"Gray Fox?" Lammelle asked, incredulously.

"He's set up a command post in his study," Naylor said. "General O'Toole is there with him. Colonel Kingsolving has been sent for."

"And once they grab Ferris, how are they going to get him out of Mexico? That prison is in southern Mexico, almost to the Guatemalan border."

"Why do I think you know more than you're telling me?"

"Allan, Vic is in the El Paso Marriott, on Airport Boulevard, registered as José Go-

505

mez. If you've got a pencil, I'll give you the number."

"If you know something I should, Frank . . ."

"The area code is 915 . . ."

"Hold one," Naylor said. "Okay. Give me that number again."

Lammelle gave it to him, and then said, "Give me five minutes, Allan, and I'll call him and tell him you'll be calling."

"What have you got him doing down there?"

"It's always a pleasure to talk to you, Allan," Lammelle said, and hung up.

[Four]
Hacienda Santa Maria
Oaxaca Province, Mexico
1345 20 April 2007

"Well, Frank, life is full of surprises, isn't it?" Castillo said over the speakerphone of his Brick. "The last I remember is Clendennen trying to think of some way to stand Gray Fox against a wall for walking out on his speech at Arlington."

"I'm having a little trouble remembering who knows what," Lammelle said. "What did you tell Natalie Cohen about your pal Pena?"

506

"I told her that Juan Carlos Pena wasn't too smart, but from what I heard, he was reasonably honest."

That caught the attention of Juan Carlos Pena. He was sitting opposite Castillo and Svetlana on the veranda of the Big House. He had a bottle of Dos Equis resting on his stomach. He turned to Castillo and gave him the finger.

"And what should I tell Vic?"

"That Juan Carlos is not too smart but may be honest. The one thing we can't afford is for anybody to even suspect we're pals. You may have heard that the more people that know something, the sooner everybody does."

"You got the satellite photos of the prison?"

"Yeah. Thanks. I wouldn't like to be a guest of that place. We just flew over it. Juan Carlos and I have been talking about grabbing Abrego and Ferris. Conclusion: Make sure Ferris is there, then grab him quick before anybody knows what's happening."

"What about Abrego?"

"In the best of all possible worlds, getting the both of them would be nice. And if we can't get Ferris, then we'll grab Abrego and see who that brings out of the woodwork. In addition to his drug cartel pals, I mean."

"You can do that with only a dozen ex-Spetsnaz?" Lammelle asked, doubtfully.

"Plus Uncle Remus," Castillo said. "It'll be like old times."

"When I talked to Vic just now, he told me your China Post guys have lost José Rafael Monteverde."

"How lost?"

"They were sitting on his apartment in Mexico City. They saw him go in, saw the lights go out when he presumably went to bed, sat on all possible points of egress and access to the place all night, and waited for him to go to work in the morning. When he didn't appear, they went and had a look. He was not in his apartment, and there were no signs of anything that looked suspicious."

"I don't like that, Frank," Castillo said.

"Well, nobody I know has ever accused the Cuban Dirección General de Inteligencia — or former members thereof — of being incompetent."

"It sounds as if he knew he was being surveilled," Castillo said.

"Yeah," Lammelle said. "It does."

"So, what are they doing about it? Did anybody think about the Venezuelan embassy?"

"According to Vic, they were of course sitting on the Venezuelan embassy. I will not tell Vic that you asked that question."

Castillo grunted. "I guess what I'm supposed to say now is, 'Well, these things happen . . .' "

"Yeah, you are. So, what happens now is that Naylor is en route to Fort Bliss — El Paso — to give Vic his marching orders. At least one — redundancy, you know — Black Hawk is by now en route from Fort Campbell to El Paso to take Vic to meet Pena. And as soon as Natalie gets to the White House, I think it reasonable to presume she will be ordered to have Ambassador Mc-Cann ask where that meeting will take place. Or will be told to do that herself."

"Yeah," Castillo agreed. "And what's going to happen tomorrow morning when Abrego doesn't show up at Juárez International?"

"I suppose we'll just have to wait and see."

"I was asking: 'What do you think they'll do to Ferris?' "

"Same answer. Except that, dealing with these people, he may already be dead. We could demand proof of life before the exchange."

"I don't think he is," Castillo said. "And as long as he's alive, he's a bargaining chip in what they are really after, whacking Pevsner."

"And C. Castillo and his girlfriend," Lammelle said. "We'll just have to wait and see. Speaking of Pevsner, where is he?"

"So far as I know, hunkering down on the shores of beautiful Lake Nahuel Huapi."

"That doesn't sound like him," Lammelle said.

"Well, the one thing you can safely say about Aleksandr Pevsner is that you never know what he's up to."

"That brings us back to 'we'll just have to wait and see,' doesn't it? I'll be in touch, Charley," Lammelle said, and broke the connection.

Castillo looked at Svetlana.

"Frank's right, my darling," she said. "Doing nothing is not how Aleksandr operates."

"But he promised to do nothing without asking me first," Castillo said.

"What he promised was to do nothing without *telling* you," she countered. "There's a big difference."

Castillo raised an eyebrow. "Well, baby, at the risk of repeating the phrase, I guess we'll just have to wait and see, won't we?"

[Five]

The President's Study
The White House
1600 Pennsylvania Avenue, N.W.
Washington, D.C.
1930 20 April 2007

"General Naylor called while you were gone, Mr. President," Clemens McCarthy said as the President led Colonel Arthur Kingsolving and Secret Service Supervisory Special Agent Mulligan into his study.

The President held up his hand to silence him as he walked to the window, pushed the drape aside, and watched as the MH-60K Black Hawk lifted off from the White House lawn.

"You seem perfectly comfortable in turning your 'Night Stalker bird' over to your co-pilot, Colonel," the President said.

Kingsolving recognized the statement as a question.

"Every 160th pilot is fully qualified as an MH-60 pilot-in-command, sir," Kingsolving said.

General O'Toole put in: "Having said that, Mr. President, Major Humphreys will now crash that one into the Washington Monument on his way to Andrews."

The President considered that for a mo-

511

ment, and then laughed.

"You people are really something," he said. "I guess it comes with the territory. Well, let me tell you: I'm really impressed with that helicopter, and I thank you for the ride."

"It was my privilege, sir," Kingsolving said.

"The only thing I didn't like about it is that it made me realize the secretary of State talked me into giving a half dozen of them to the goddamn Mexicans," the President said.

"Sir," Kingsolving said, "the Mexicans didn't get that one, the MH-60K. That's a special configuration for the 160th."

"How specially configured?" the President asked.

"Among other things — state-of-the-art avionics, for example — it has an in-flight refueling probe," Kingsolving began.

The President held up his hand to silence him and turned to McCarthy.

"Well?" he demanded.

"Sir?"

"You said General Naylor called while we were gone."

"Yes, sir, he did."

"And did he call just to say 'howdy' or did he have more on his mind than that?"

"General Naylor said that he has established contact with D'Alessandro; explained the situation to him; that the helicopter from Fort Campbell was expected momentarily and that as soon as we tell him where D'Alessandro is supposed to go, he'll send him on his way."

"Where is D'Alessandro and the helicopter that's expected momentarily?"

"In El Paso, sir."

"What's the status of that?" the President asked.

"The status of what, sir?"

"Finding out where my friend Martinez wants D'Alessandro to meet the Mexican cop?"

"I don't know, sir. We haven't heard from Secretary Cohen about that."

"Well, Clemens, how about getting her on the phone and asking her?"

"Yes, sir."

"On second thought, Douglas, you call her," the President ordered. "Clemens here seems to be having trouble keeping up with all this."

"Yes, sir."

"If she hasn't heard from my friend Martinez, tell her to call the sonofabitch."

"Yes, Mr. President," Special Agent Douglas said.

"I want to get this show on the road, and

I don't want any surprises," the President said. "And I've got a couple of questions, which occurred to me as we were flying over the Pentagon. Has it ever occurred to anyone else that the more you're told, the more you learn, the more questions come up?"

"I've had that experience, Mr. President," General O'Toole said.

"Okay. Now, Colonel Kingsolving told me that while the Night Stalker birds can make it from El Paso to this prison, they don't have the range to make it back without being refueled. Okay. Tell me how that's going to happen."

"There are several options, Mr. President —" O'Toole began to answer for Kingsolving.

"I was asking Colonel Kingsolving," the President cut him off.

"Sorry, sir."

"The first option, sir, is the simple one," Kingsolving said. "They will refuel at Xoxocotlán airfield, which is the closest airfield to the Oaxaca Prison."

"I was just starting to be awed by your all-around knowledge," the President said. "That answer just blew that. I can see a number of problems with that, starting with how do we know there would be enough fuel at Xoxocotlán airfield to fuel four Black Hawks, even if they were willing to do so?"

"That is a problem, sir, obviously. We don't."

"Other options?"

"In-flight refueling, sir. Have one or more KC-130J tankers rendezvous with the Black Hawks shortly before they reach Oaxaca-Xoxocotlán. The Black Hawks then would have full tanks on landing, and be prepared to fly back to the States."

"That strikes me as almost as stupid as Option One," the President said. "What do you think the goddamn Mexicans are going to think when they see one or more . . . what's the nomenclature of that tanker?"

"KC-130J, sir."

"That's that great big airplane with propellers, right? Not jet engines?"

"That's correct, sir."

"What do you think the goddamn Mexicans are going to think when they see four Black Hawks — instead of the one they expect — flying over their country with a couple of great big aerial gas stations? Jesus, I'm glad I brought this up!"

"Another option, Mr. President," O'Toole said, "if I may?"

"Let's hear it."

"Another option would be to refuel the

Black Hawks, before or after the exchange, using a Navy assault vessel, such as the USS *Bataan,* in international waters — say fifty miles out — off the coast. This is what Castillo did when he made the assault on La Orchila Island . . ."

General O'Toole's face flushed as he heard what he had just said.

The President looked at him coldly.

"That's what Lieutenant Colonel Castillo, Retired, did before he almost got us in a war with Venezuela?"

"Yes, sir."

"I'd like to know who authorized the use of that vessel," the President said. "Was that you, General O'Toole?"

"No, sir. But under the circumstances, it was, in my judgment, the right thing to do."

"Fortunately you are not in a position to make decisions like that. If it wasn't you, who was it? That mustachioed idiot McNab?"

"I don't believe General McNab was involved, Mr. President. And certainly not able to give orders to the captain of a Navy vessel."

"Well, that narrows it down somewhat, doesn't it? McCarthy, make a note for me to discuss this with General Naylor at the earliest opportunity."

"Yes, sir."

"And with Secretary Beiderman. And incidentally, where the hell is he?"

"He's at the Pentagon, sir," Mulligan said.

"Get him on the phone and get him over here," the President said.

"Yes, sir."

"Well, since we will not be using a U.S. Navy vessel operating fifty miles off the Mexican coast to fuel the Black Hawks, does that mean we're out of options? Jesus H. Christ! Talk about going off half cocked!"

"There is one more option, sir," O'Toole said. "A submarine. It would rendezvous with the Black Hawks off the Mexican coast . . ."

"A *submarine?*" the President parroted incredulously.

"Yes, sir. We have been experimenting with the technique. In our tests a Black Hawk can be refueled on the high seas in about ten minutes, sir."

The President did not reply.

O'Toole said, "One problem with using a sub —"

"Go on, O'Toole, drop the other shoe. What's the problem with this option?"

"I'm not sure a submarine could be equipped with the necessary equipment in time for this operation."

"I'll tell you this, General," the President said. "A submarine will be equipped in time for this operation, or we'll have a new secretary of Defense, a new secretary of the Navy, and a new chief of naval operations."

"Yes, sir."

XI

[One]
Hacienda Santa Maria
Oaxaca Province, Mexico
2105 20 April 2007

"With all possible respect, Señor Diputado Procurador General," Juan Carlos Pena said, with a smile in his voice, "you don't really want to know what I'm going to do tonight. I'll meet you in the Diamante at nine, and I promise not to ask what you did tonight."

He laughed at the deputy attorney general's response, and then hung up.

"What's the Diamante?" Castillo asked.

"Will he trace the call here?" Svetlana asked.

"Oh, she is a professional, isn't she?" Pena observed. "He might, Sweaty, and I will handle that by walking into the restaurant tomorrow morning with a case of Hacienda

518

Santa Maria's finest grapefruit for him. He will then conclude that I was here checking your security, which means to pick up the envelope."

"What envelope?" Svetlana asked.

"The envelope containing the small token of Don Armando's appreciation for my keeping the bad guys away from Hacienda Santa Maria," Pena said.

Don Armando Medina, the general manager of Hacienda Santa Maria, chuckled.

"Don Armando, you're actually paying protection money to the Federales?" Castillo demanded.

"Jesus Christ, Carlos!" Pena replied. "I can't believe you actually asked that."

"Does that mean we're paying you or not?" Castillo pursued.

"It means, my naïve old buddy, that it's important that people such as Manuel José Guzmán, Diputado Procurador General de la República, think you're paying me. Otherwise, Manuel José might suspect that I'm honest, and we certainly couldn't have that, could we?"

"Sorry," Castillo said.

"Carlos, I knew Doña Alicia, called her Tia Alicia, long before I met you."

"I said I was sorry," Castillo said. "I wasn't thinking."

"That's a problem for you, isn't it?"

"Juan Carlos," Svetlana said. "He said he was sorry. What did this man have to say?"

"Unless I'm wrong — and I very seldom am, that's why I'm still alive — at nine tomorrow morning in the restaurant of the Diamante — full title Camino Real Acapulco Diamante, one of the better hotels in Acapulco — he will explain to me when and how Félix Abrego will manage to escape from the Oaxaca State Prison. And then, because he knows how ashamed I will be because of Señor Abrego's escape from my custody, he will give me an envelope to assuage my pain."

"The deputy attorney general is working for the cartels?" Castillo asked, surprised.

"*With,* I would say, not *for.* Abrego has many friends, Carlos, and most of them have lots of money."

"If nobody has anything more to say," Castillo said, "I think I will have a little grape before we have dinner. It's been a busy day, and it's long past my normal wine time."

As if on cue, someone had something to say.

Castillo's Brick buzzed.

"Hand me the sonofabitch, please, Lester," Castillo said. "And we'll see who is trying to keep me off the sauce."

Bradley handed him the handset. Castillo looked at it.

"It's your Cousin Aleksandr, Sweaty," Charley said, then put the handset to his ear. Sweaty stood up and leaned over the Brick and pushed the LOUDSPEAKER button.

"And how are things on the shores of picturesque Lake Nahuel Huapi, Aleksandr?" Castillo asked in Russian.

"Speak English," Sweaty ordered.

"Yes, ma'am," Castillo said, glancing at her.

"Are you alone?" Pevsner asked.

"Clearly no. And Svetlana wants you to speak English."

"What's that all about?" Pevsner asked, in English.

"I can only guess that she wants her new buddy to hear what you have to say, and he doesn't speak Russian."

"Who's her new friend?"

"Juan Carlos Pena, chief of the Policía Federal for Oaxaca State."

"Have you been drinking?"

"Not yet. But make whatever this is quick, will you please? I'm about to start."

"I gave you my word that I wouldn't take any of several actions until I first told you."

"Without my permission is the way I remember that."

"I'm not in the habit, as you are well aware, of asking anyone for permission to do anything."

"Why don't you tell me what's going on down there on the shores of Lake Nahuel Huapi?"

"I'm in Cozumel. How soon can you get here?"

"If you can convince me this is important and nothing happens between now and, say, nine tomorrow morning, I can be there in time for lunch."

"I mean tonight."

"Tonight's out of the question. I can't take off from here without letting the local airport — and this means the Policía Federal — know my airfield is capable of night operation. And I don't want to throw away that tactical advantage."

"I thought that you were friends with the local police?"

"Stand by a moment, Aleksandr," Svetlana said. She motioned for Castillo to give her the handset, and when he had, she held it against her breast to muffle the microphone.

"You understand Carlito's concern, Juan Carlos?" she asked.

He nodded.

"Who besides you would learn the field is capable of night flight if Charley were to take off right now?"

"Nobody," Juan Carlos replied.

"And you can keep it that way?"

Pena nodded.

She moved the handset from her breast to her ear.

"If I have your word that you'll do nothing until Carlito approves," Svetlana said, "we can take off from here in about fifteen minutes."

"You have my word that I will take no action until I tell him what I am going to do, and why," Pevsner said. "And, Svetlana, remember who you are. How dare you talk to me that way."

"I'll tell you who I am, Aleksandr," Svetlana said. "The woman who will tell my Carlito to fly over there. Or to stay here. And if we stay here, you will be free to do whatever you wish, and I can only hope that you will realize that you will be doing it alone."

There was a long silence.

"What's his name?" Juan Carlos asked.

"Aleksandr," Castillo furnished.

"Can you hear me, Aleksandr?" Pena asked, raising his voice.

"I can hear you," Pevsner said. "The policeman?"

"Actually, I'm a little more than a policeman," Pena said. "But I used to be, and when I was, I learned that there are some women you just don't fuck with, and your Cousin Sweaty is one of them. I wouldn't cross her if I was you."

"Pay attention, Aleksandr," Castillo said, laughing.

There was a twenty-second pause.

"Then I will expect to see you in a little over three hours," Pevsner said. "During which time you have my word that I will take no action that could possibly displease either my friend Charley or you, my dear Svetlana."

The LEDs on the Brick went out; Pevsner had ended the call.

"Why do I think Aleksandr is annoyed with us?" Castillo asked rhetorically, then said, "You going to Acapulco tonight, Juan Carlos? Or do you want to spend the night here?"

"Neither. I'm going with you," Juan Carlos said. "I've been hearing about that sonofabitch for years. Not only do I want to hear what he's got planned, and for who, I want a look at him."

"I can assure you, Juan Carlos," Svetlana

said, dead serious, "that Aleksandr's parents were married. You are speaking of my mother's sister, and she was not a bitch."

"I'll keep that in mind, Sweaty," Pena said. "No offense intended."

"Watch your mouth in the future."

"Sí, señorita," Juan Carlos said, contritely.

[Two]
The Tahitian Suite
Grand Cozumel Beach & Golf Resort
Cozumel, Mexico
0005 21 April 2007

When they had landed at Cozumel International, Castillo had seen "the other" Cessna Mustang, the one used to fly high rollers to the Grand Cozumel casino, and drug money to be laundered out of Mexico. So he was not surprised to find former SVR Colonel Nicolai Tarasov sitting on the balcony of the twenty-third-floor penthouse suite beside former SVR Colonel Aleksandr Pevsner.

Max, delighted to see Pevsner, ran out onto the balcony, reared on his hind legs, draped his paws over Pevsner's shoulders, and affectionately lapped his face.

"Can't you control your goddamn animal?" Pevsner demanded.

"He likes you," Castillo said. "Be grateful.

His other mode is 'rip your throat out.' "

"Very interesting," Juan Carlos said. "Maybe you're not the all-around son . . . bas . . . *evil* person everybody says you are."

Castillo laughed when he saw that Juan Carlos was applying his *"when meeting someone cutthroat, attack to put them on the defense"* theory of how best to deal with dangerous people who expect to be treated differentially.

Sweaty said, "You're learning, Juan Carlos."

"You're the policeman, obviously," Pevsner said.

"Carlos has been telling me that Max is an infallible judge of character," Juan Carlos said. "I tend to agree. We hadn't known each other ninety seconds when he was begging me to scratch his ears."

"And if I may be permitted to say so, Señor Pena," Pevsner said, "I am not at all surprised that you and Karl are friends. You share not only a very odd sense of humor but a complete inability to take things seriously."

"That's it!" Svetlana snapped. "Stop."

She walked to her Uncle Nicolai and allowed him to kiss her cheek.

"Introduce me to your friend, Svetlana."

"Juan Carlos, this is my Uncle Nicolai,"

Sweaty said. "Nicolai Tarasov, Juan Carlos Pena. I'd forgotten. You know Lester, don't you?"

"How could I forget Mr. Bradley?" Tarasov said, and patted Lester on the back.

Tarasov and Pena shamelessly examined each other as they shook hands.

"And tell me what brings the chief of the Policía Federal for Oaxaca State so far from home?" Tarasov said.

"Well, not much was happening at Hacienda Santa Maria," Pena said, "so I thought I might as well come over here and arrest somebody."

Castillo chuckled.

"I said stop that and I meant it!" Svetlana said. "All right, Aleksandr, what's so important that you couldn't tell us on the Brick?"

"Before we get into that, do you suppose I could have a glass of wine?" Castillo said.

"It would be better if you were sober when I tell you what I have to tell you."

"I said a glass, Aleksandr, not a damn bottle. Humor me."

That's unusual. He usually tries to feed people he's dealing with all the booze he can get into them.

What the hell is this all about?

A waiter — whose starched white jacket did not entirely conceal the mini Uzi on his hip — appeared.

"Bring wine, some of that Cabernet Sauvignon, for my guests," Pevsner ordered. Then he turned to Castillo. "The reason I didn't open this subject on the Brick is I didn't think you'd believe me."

"What makes you think I'll believe you now?"

"Get to it, Aleksandr," Svetlana ordered.

He looked at her and nodded.

"Vladimir Vladimirovich doesn't want to exterminate us," he said. "Unless of course that should prove to be convenient while he's doing what he set out to do in the first place. It took me a long time to figure that out."

"Of course he wants to exterminate us!" Svetlana said. "For all the reasons you know."

"Listen to me carefully, Svetlana," Pevsner said. "If he can eliminate us while he's *doing what he set out to do in the first place,* he'd be pleased. But eliminating us is not his highest priority."

Castillo looked at Pevsner. *Where the hell is he going with this?*

"Then what is?" he said.

"We misjudged him. We thought of him as what we think he is, rather than what he believes he is."

528

"Which is?" Castillo asked.

"Tsar of all the Russias. Vladimir the Terrible. Cast in the mold of Ivan the Terrible. Chosen by God to restore Russia to its former magnificence."

"You're serious, aren't you?" Castillo asked.

There was not a hint of sarcasm in his voice.

"Perfectly. Absolutely," Pevsner said.

"Where did this come from, Aleksandr?" Castillo asked. "Your notion that Putin thinks of himself as . . . Ivan the Terrible reincarnate?"

"The first time I thought of it — and dismissed it — was during the funeral."

"The imperial family's funeral?"

Pevsner nodded.

The waiter pulled the cork from a wine bottle with a *popping* sound, and poured a little for Castillo to taste.

I probably shouldn't take this.

But what the hell?

"You know Saint Petersburg?" Pevsner asked.

Castillo nodded, and Pevsner went on: "Renamed Petrograd from Saint Petersburg in 1914, then renamed Leningrad in 1924, and then back to Saint Petersburg in 1991, after the Soviet Union became the Russian

Federation."

Castillo vaguely remembered seeing photographs of the funeral. He hadn't paid much attention to it.

"On July 17, 1998, eighty years to the day after the Tsar and his family were executed by the Bolsheviks, they were interred — as 'The Royal Martyrs Tsar Nicholas II and his beloved family' — in the Royal Vault of the Cathedral of Saints Peter and Paul.

"His Holiness Patriarch Alexis came from Moscow to preside, and President Boris Yeltsin represented the government of the Russian Federation.

"The arrangements — moving what was left of the bodies from where they had been tossed down a well in Yekaterinburg, some nine hundred miles east of Moscow, and DNA examination of the remains to prove it was indeed the Tsar and his family, were handled by one Vladimir Vladimirovich Putin, then the KGB's man in Saint Petersburg . . ."

"Now, that's interesting," Castillo interrupted.

". . . who was very visible during the interment," Pevsner finished.

"Yeah," Svetlana said. "That caught my attention, too. I thought he was being blasphemous."

"And that was my initial reaction, too," Pevsner said. "But then, as I said, I dismissed it, deciding that either possibility was improbable."

"Either possibility?"

"That he was being blasphemous, as Svetlana thought, or that he had gone back to the Lord."

"But?"

"I began to think of it again a few days ago in San Carlos de Bariloche," Pevsner said. "When I was trying very hard, and failing, to see how Vladimir Vladimirovich's intention to eliminate us tied in with the kidnapping of Colonel Ferris. When I finally realized it had nothing to do with that — the kidnapping had nothing to do, except possibly as a diversion, with eliminating us — everything suddenly began to be clear."

"Tell me how," Castillo said.

"Who is Vladimir's greatest enemy? I don't think anyone would argue it's not the United States. Can he engage in a war against the United States? No. If he could, he would. Can he, at virtually no cost to himself, cause the United States trouble? Weaken it? Yes, he can. And is."

"And that's what he's up to?" Castillo asked.

Pevsner nodded. "Mexico is the battlefield. For one thing, the Mexicans hate the United States. The United States took most of the Southwest away from Mexico in the war of 1848, and the Mexicans have never forgiven them for that. Mexicans by the millions illegally enter the United States while the Mexican government not only looks the other way but actively encourages them. If those people aren't in Mexico, not only don't they have to be fed and hospitalized and educated but they send money — billions and billions of dollars — to their families in Mexico."

"That seems a little far-fetched, Aleksandr," Castillo argued.

"It won't if you give it some thought," Pevsner said. "But illegal immigration isn't the point here, and neither is the drug traffic — both of which weaken the U.S., which is fine with Vladimir Vladimirovich, but what he's really after is the destruction of the United States government."

"And how does he plan to do that?"

"Off the top of your head, friend Charley, tell me what were the greatest threats to the stability of the United States government in your lifetime?"

"I don't know," Castillo admitted. And then after a moment, asked, "You're talking about Nixon?"

"Before Nixon resigned, there was rioting in the streets. You needed armed troops to protect the Pentagon."

"And later the impeachment of Clinton," Castillo added thoughtfully.

"And now you have a President who should be in a room with rubber walls," Pevsner said.

"Who told you about that?" Castillo asked. "And what makes you think Putin even knows about it?"

"Oh, he knows," Pevsner said, and issued an order in Russian: "Put two chairs there," he said, pointing. "And bring them out."

Two folding chairs were set up and then two men — stark naked, showing signs of having been severely beaten — shuffled onto the patio, their hands and their ankles bound together with plastic ties. Janos, Pevsner's Hungarian bodyguard, brought up the rear of the procession.

I wondered where Janos was.

The waiter offered Castillo more of the Cabernet Sauvignon.

"No, thank you," Castillo said, politely. "I've had quite enough for the time being."

"You've met Sergei, I understand," Pevsner said. "But I don't think you've met José Rafael Monteverde."

Both men looked at Castillo. Monteverde

looked terrified. Murov, Castillo decided after a moment, seemed resigned to his fate, whatever that might turn out to be.

"Untie their hands, Janos," Castillo ordered in Hungarian. "Lester, get them water and a cigarette if they want one."

Janos looked at Pevsner for guidance. Pevsner nodded.

Lester went to the wet bar for water.

"Where is Colonel Ferris?" Castillo asked.

Neither man replied.

"I don't know about you, Mr. Monteverde," Castillo said in Hungarian, "but you're a professional, Mr. Murov. You know what options you have. You either answer my questions or Janos will slowly beat you to death."

Castillo looked at Janos. "What have you been using on him?"

Janos flicked his wrist and a telescoping wand appeared in his hand. He flicked it back and forth. It whistled.

"That's the one with the little ball of shot at the end?" Castillo asked.

Janos extended the wand to show Castillo the small leather shot-filled ball at the end of his wand.

"Very nice," Castillo said. "It's been some time since I've seen one."

"As one professional to another, Colonel

Castillo, can we get this over with quickly?" Murov asked, in Russian.

"Do you speak Hungarian, Mr. Monteverde?" Castillo asked, in Hungarian.

Monteverde's face showed he did not.

"Pity," Castillo said, in Russian. "Hungarian seems to have become the *lingua franca* of interrogations like this. Now you won't know what Mr. Murov and I are talking about, will you?"

Monteverde's face showed he understood this.

Castillo then said in Hungarian: "As a matter of personal curiosity, Mr. Murov — though it doesn't really matter — when did you become aware of President Clendennen's mental instability? Before or after he became President?"

"It wasn't much of a secret, was it, Colonel?" Murov replied.

"Lester, where's the cigarettes I asked for for these gentlemen?" Castillo asked.

Janos gave a quick order in Hungarian, and the waiter walked to Lester and handed him a package of Sobranie cigarettes.

Bradley looked at them dubiously.

"Those are Sobranie, Les," Castillo explained. "I don't know whether those are Russian made or the ones they make in London."

"Huh?" Lester said.

"Cigarettes are very bad for your health, Lester. I wouldn't smoke one of those, if I were you."

"No, sir, I hadn't planned to," Bradley said.

Everyone on the patio — including Murov and Monteverde — looked askance at the exchange.

Lester walked to Murov and Monteverde, handed them cigarettes, then lit them for them.

"Thank you," Monteverde said.

"Beware of either Americans or Hungarians bearing gifts," Castillo said in Hungarian. "Especially counterfeit Russian cigarettes."

Pevsner and Tarasov smiled and shook their heads.

Monteverde eyed his cigarette suspiciously.

"It's soaked with sodium pentothal, of course," Castillo said, in Spanish. "My protocol is to use that before pulling fingernails and doing other things like that."

Monteverde's face showed that he was perfectly willing to accept that.

I think I've got him.

"Tell me, Señor Monteverde," Castillo then went on in Spanish, "when you were in Cuba, did you happen to run into Major Alejandro Vincenzo?"

Monteverde's face showed that he had, and was surprised that Castillo knew of the Cuban Dirección General de Inteligencia officer.

"No," he said.

"He got in a gun fight with Lester in Uruguay," Castillo said, conversationally. "Right out of the O.K. Corral. Lester put him down with a head shot, offhand, from at least one hundred yards. That's why we call him 'Dead Eye.' "

Monteverde looked at Castillo as if he couldn't believe what Castillo had just said.

"Well, those things happen in our line of business, don't they?" Castillo said. "Sometimes people just don't make it."

He let that sink in for a moment, and then said, "Lester, why don't you take Mr. Monteverde back where he came from? What we're going to do next is see if Colonel Alekseeva and Chief Pena can't talk Señor Monteverde into making the right decisions tonight, before things get unpleasant."

He paused.

"You heard me, Monteverde. Stand up!" he ordered, unpleasantly.

Monteverde did so, and then as he was again suddenly aware he was naked, he put his hands over his crotch.

"Not necessary, Señor Monteverde," Castillo said. "Colonel Alekseeva is also a professional. That's not the first ding-dong she's ever seen, although I don't think she's ever seen one quite that — how do I say this? — *unappealing.* You have an accident or something or is that the way it usually looks?"

Flushing from his forehead to halfway down his chest, Monteverde allowed himself to be led, shuffling in his plastic ankle ties, off the patio. Pena and Svetlana walked after him.

Castillo waited until Monteverde was out of hearing, and then turned to Murov.

"Well, what brilliant psychological weapon do I use on you, Sergei? Threaten to have 'Saint Petersburg Poet' chiseled on your tombstone?"

Pevsner and Tarasov chuckled.

Despite himself, Murov smiled.

"Now I know, Aleksandr," Murov said, "why you wanted him here. He's a master at this, isn't he?"

"No, I am but a simple novice sitting at the feet of Master Pevsner," Castillo said. "But this much I know, Sergei: When you get over your humiliation at being grabbed by Aleksandr's people, you will decide yourself that you don't have any choice but to tell me everything I want to know."

"Or Janos will beat me to death with his wand?"

"Or I'll leave you tied up on the steps of the Russian embassy in Mexico City and let Vladimir Vladimirovich decide how painfully you should die."

He looked around and caught the waiter's eye.

"Yes, thank you, I will have another sip of that lovely Cabernet Sauvignon while I'm waiting."

Ten minutes later, Svetlana came back onto the patio and somewhat imperiously signaled to the waiter for a glass of wine. When he delivered it, Castillo held up his glass.

"How much of that have you had?" she challenged.

Castillo caught her eye. "Try to get this straight. You may ask that only *after* we're married. And if you keep asking now, your chances of that happening diminish exponentially."

She glared at him but did not respond.

"Well?" Castillo asked. "How did you do with Señor Monteverde?"

"He'll be out in a minute," she replied. "He's cleaning himself up. When Juan

Carlos was dangling him from the balcony, Monteverde threw up all over himself."

" 'Dangling from the balcony'?" Castillo parroted.

"Juan Carlos hung him by his foot from the balcony," she said, "using a sheet for a rope. When he was swinging back and forth" — she demonstrated with her hands — "Juan Carlos took another sheet and ripped it. It made a sound loud enough for Monteverde to hear. Then Juan Carlos let the sheet rope drop another couple of feet. Monteverde thought he was about to die."

"It would then be safe to presume that Señor Monteverde is going to be co-operative?"

"Oh, yes," she said. "Your Colonel Ferris is being held in Retainhuled, Guatemala. It's about fifty miles from the border."

"Who's holding him?" Castillo asked.

"Venezuelan drug traffickers under the direction of the SVR," she said, matter-of-factly. "Which brings us to the senior officer of the SVR involved in this. What are we going to do with you, Sergei?"

"I'd say that's in the hands of God, wouldn't you, Svetlana?" Murov replied.

"Actually, it's in my hands," Castillo said, "and I'm not nearly as nice as God."

"Don't blaspheme, Carlito," Svetlana said,

and then added, "He pretends to be a heathen, Sergei. But he's really not."

"You want to take a chance betting on that, Sergei?" Castillo asked. "Let's start over, before I tell Janos he can start up again with his flyswatter. Here's where we are: Monteverde is going to tell me everything he knows, and you know that. But what he doesn't know, and what I want from you, is the names of the people you have in the Oval Office, and I will do whatever I have to find out."

"And you know I can't tell you that," Murov said. "I have given my vow to God, and whatever happens to me is in his hands."

"Whatever happens to you in is *my* hands," Castillo said. "But I digress. I want those names. And will do whatever I have to do to get them. That includes guaranteeing you asylum in the United States, or anywhere else you'd like to go, and a hell of a lot of money. Opening bid, one million."

Murov shook his head. "How could I shave in the morning, Colonel Castillo, looking out on some Caribbean beach, knowing that the price of my being there was my family in the basement of the Lubyanka prison?"

"Just as soon as Vladimir Vladimirovich

finds out you fucked up again, that's where Vladimir Vladimirovich is going to put them, and you know that, too."

"The matter is in God's hands," Murov repeated doggedly.

"Jesus Christ, you people make me sick! Are you listening to yourself, Murov? You sound like a character in a very bad Russian novel. In the first place, committing suicide is not noble. I'm not sure, but I strongly suspect, in this religion all of you keep spouting, it's also a sin."

"I'm not committing suicide," Murov said.

"What would you call it? And you're the one who put your beloved wife and kiddies in a Lubyanka cell, Murov. *You.* Don't try to hang that on Vladimir Vladimirovich. That's the rules of this game we play, and you damn sure know them as well as I do."

Murov was silent.

"Okay, Murov. For the sake of argument, after Janos literally beats you to death with that thing of his, you nobly refuse to tell me what I want. You pass out. You open your eyes, and there you are, inside the pearly gates. Saint Peter looks down at you.

" 'Tell me, my son, why the fuck didn't you at least try to get your beloved wife and kiddies out of Lubyanka?' What are you going to say, Sergei? 'Nothing I could do, Pete.

It was in God's hands.' Jesus!"

"Carlos, you're blaspheming," Svetlana said.

"Butt out, Sweaty!" Castillo snapped.

"You just don't get people out of Lubyanka, Colonel, and you know that," Murov said.

"Maybe not, but a man — particularly a Christian — would fucking well try for his family," Castillo fumed. "And what are you going to say when good ol' Saint Pete asks —"

"Carlos, stop!" Svetlana said.

"Stay out of this, Svetlana," Nicolai Tarasov said, sharply.

"He's blaspheming," she said.

"I don't think so," Tarasov said. "What it looks like to me is that he's trying to save Sergei's soul."

The support came as a shock to Castillo. He forgot what he had been saying.

"Where the hell was I?" Castillo said aloud. "Okay. So, what are you going to say to Saint Peter, Saint Sergei, when he asks, 'Why the hell wouldn't you tell Castillo what he wanted to know? I know he's a heathen, but what was he doing wrong? Were the Americans about to nuke Moscow? Maybe drop a couple of barrels of Congo-X on it? Did you really believe, as well educated as you are, as widely experienced, that the Americans were planning to attack Holy Mother Russia? For that matter, anyone?"

"Fuck you, Colonel Castillo," Murov said. "And may God forgive you!"

Castillo saw that Svetlana had tears running down her cheeks.

"I am still in charge here, Aleksandr," Castillo said, but it was a question.

Pevsner nodded.

"Janos," Castillo then ordered, "put some clothes on him, and take him back where you found him. And leave him."

"You're still going to interrogate him?" Svetlana asked.

"No, my love, I'm through interrogating him. He wouldn't tell me the truth anyway; you heard him, God is on his side. And I won't give the miserable bastard the satisfaction of having Janos beat him to death. Three'll get you ten he's already into self-flagellation. Get him out of my sight, Janos."

Janos, Castillo noticed, did not look this time to Pevsner for permission to carry out the order.

Janos went to where Murov was seated, pulled him to his feet, and started marching him out of the room.

"Hand me the wine, my dear, and spare me your comments," Castillo ordered.

Svetlana complied docilely.

"Colonel Castillo," Murov called.

Castillo looked. Murov and Janos were at the door. Janos had his arms wrapped around the struggling naked man.

Castillo made the sign of the cross.

"Bless you, my son," he called. "Go in peace, and sin no more. Amen."

"Carlos!" Svetlana said, in almost a whine.

"It's Clemens McCarthy, Colonel Castillo," Murov said. "And a Secret Service agent named Douglas."

[Three]
The President's Study
The White House
1600 Pennsylvania Avenue, N.W.
Washington, D.C.
0805 21 April 2007

Secret Service Special Agent Mark Douglas pushed the door open and announced, "Mr. President, the secretary of State."

"Well, show her in," President Clendennen ordered.

"Good morning, Mr. President," Secretary Cohen said.

"Dare I hope, Madam Secretary, that you have heard from that miserable sonofabitch Martinez?" Clendennen asked.

"Actually, Mr. President, I've just spoken with Ambassador McCann," she replied. "President Martinez called him with the information we've been waiting for. I took the call from the ambassador just now in my car."

"And?"

"Mr. D'Alessandro is to meet with a Mexican deputy attorney general, a man named Manuel José Guzmán, at one o'clock this afternoon in the Camino Real Acapulco Diamante in Acapulco. Señor Guzmán will have the police chief, Pena, with him."

"The where?"

"The Camino Real Acapulco Diamante, Mr. President. The literal translation is 'Royal Road Acapulco Diamond.' What it is is one of the better hotels in Acapulco."

"Does this man D'Alessandro know how to find it? Where is he? How's he going to get from where he is to Acapulco?"

Secretary Cohen said: "I understand that Mr. D'Alessandro is with General Naylor in the El Paso Marriott."

"You heard that, Douglas," the President ordered. "Get this man or General Naylor on the phone."

"D'Alessandro may be registered as José Gomez, Mr. Douglas," the secretary of State said.

"What the hell is that all about?" the President demanded.

"I don't know, sir," she said.

"Well, goddammit, don't you think you should?"

"General Naylor told me that, sir," she said. "I have no idea why Mr. D'Alessandro might be registered under another name. I was just trying to be helpful to Mr. Douglas."

"I have General Naylor for you, Mr. President," Douglas said, extending the handset of the red presidential circuit telephone to him.

"We finally heard from the goddamn Mexicans, General," the President began the conversation. "Are you in contact with this man D'Alessandro?"

The telephone was not set on loudspeaker; only the Washington end of the conversation could be heard by others in the presidential study.

"Put him on, please."

"This is the President, Mr. D'Alessandro," Clendennen said. "Let me make this clear from the beginning. If you fuck this up, you're not going back to Fort Bragg. If I can't figure out some way to fire you, you're going to find yourself counting envelopes in the Nome, Alaska, post office. You clear on that, Mr. D'Alessandro?"

"Okay. We've heard from the goddamn Mexicans. You're to meet a deputy attorney general . . . what's his name, Madam Secretary?"

Secretary Cohen furnished the information.

"By the name of Manuel José Guzmán," the President went on. "In the Diamond hotel in Acapulco at one this afternoon —

"Yes, the *Camino Real Acapulco Diamante,*" the President confirmed impatiently. "He's going to have this cop, Pena, with him. Can you make it down there in time?

"Okay. By the time you get there, these people will have figured out that they didn't make a fool of me at the Juárez airport this morning. So let them know I'm mad. Tell them we're not going to produce this Mexican bandito Abrego until we have proof we're about to get Ferris in exchange for him. Like that photograph they wanted of Abrego standing outside somewhere recognizable in El Paso. Tell them to take a picture of Ferris standing outside the Oaxaca State Prison holding a copy of that day's newspaper —

"How the hell am I supposed to know what newspaper? Find out what it is, and

548

tell them to use that. And tell them to give the photo to somebody from the embassy. Hold one."

The President turned to Secretary Cohen.

"How do we do what I just said?" he asked.

"I suppose I could ask Ambassador Mc-Cann to send an embassy officer to Deputy Attorney General Guzmán's office," she said, after a moment's thought.

"Ask him, hell," the President said. "*Tell* him. D'Alessandro, the embassy's going to send an officer to Guzmán just as soon as Secretary Cohen tells him to. Have Guzmán, or this cop, give him the picture. He'll send it to me. When I see it, we'll move Abrego down there. Got it?

"And as soon as you do this, you get back to El Paso and stand by. Got it?

"Don't fuck this up, D'Alessandro," the President said, and handed the handset to Agent Douglas.

"Give it to the secretary, Douglas," the President ordered. "She's going to call Ambassador McCann."

Camino Real Acapulco Diamante
Carretera Escenica Km 14
Acapulco, Mexico
1315 21 April 2007

Vic D'Alessandro walked out of the lobby with Juan Carlos Pena and two of Pena's bodyguards following.

Immediately, two Policía Federal Suburbans pulled up under the portico to where they were standing.

"Why don't you get in the back, Mr. D'Alessandro?" Pena suggested.

"You don't have to do this, chief," D'Alessandro said. "I can take a taxi."

"You never heard of Mexican hospitality?" Pena asked. "Get in."

One of the Policía Federal officers opened the right doors.

"Slide over to the middle, Mr. D'Alessandro," Pena ordered, "so my men can get in on each side of you."

D'Alessandro obeyed. He found himself sitting between two large Policía Federal officers.

The Suburbans moved out from under the portico.

D'Alessandro felt something hard and cold against the base of his neck, and had just decided whatever this was, they weren't going to kill him, at least not here and now, when a voice inquired, "Hey, gringo, you wanna fook my see-ster?"

Juan Carlos Pena laughed out loud, surprising D'Alessandro, for Pena hadn't so much as cracked a smile during the meeting with Guzmán.

"She gives a discount for undersized penile apparatus," the voice said, now without a Mexican accent. "Like yours."

"Charley, you sonofabitch!" D'Alessandro said.

"Welcome to Sunny Meh-hee-co," Castillo said. "How did things go with Guzmán?"

"Slick," D'Alessandro said. "He should be a used-car salesman. And, obviously, I misjudged Señor Pena."

Pena turned from the front seat and offered D'Alessandro his hand.

"Call me Juan Carlos when no one's looking, Vic," Pena said. "Carlos — Charley — and I go back a long way. He says nice things about you, which may or may not be a good thing."

"You are going to tell me what's going on here, right?" D'Alessandro asked.

"On our way to General Juan N. Álvarez International we're going to plan how to snatch Ferris from the bad guys," Castillo said. "That's presuming Guzmán went along with having Ferris's picture taken standing in front of the Oaxaca State Prison."

"How the hell did you hear about that?"

"I have a lady friend in Foggy Bottom," Castillo said. "Well, did he?"

"Yeah. You know where Ferris is?"

"Yeah. All Juan Carlos had to do was dangle Señor Monteverde from the twenty-third-floor Tahitian Suite of the Grand Cozumel Beach and Golf Resort on a bedsheet and he quickly volunteered to tell us Ferris is being held by drug guys working for Venezuelans under the direction of the SVR —"

"You're talking about Murov? He's disappeared, too."

"Didn't your mommy tell you it's not polite to interrupt people?" Castillo asked, then went on: ". . . in Retainhuled, Guatemala, which is a small town about fifty miles from the border. Now, their plan, Murov, Juan Carlos, and I think —"

"Murov?" D'Alessandro interrupted. "You know where he is?"

"He's in the Suburban behind us."

Involuntarily, D'Alessandro turned to look. All he could see was the darkened windows of the following Suburban.

"He's in *that* Suburban?" D'Alessandro asked, incredulously.

"All right, we'll go down that road. Ol' Sergei has had a religious experience. He has seen the light, and is now prepared to fight the good fight against the forces of evil. When you get back to Biggs Army Airfield, Frank Lammelle will be there to meet him with open arms and a briefcase with one million dollars in it, which I'm sure Sergei will count carefully on his way to wherever Frank intends to stash him."

"You turned Murov for a million dollars? That's peanuts! Jesus Christ, Charley! He's Putin's number two!"

"*Was* Putin's number two," Castillo said. "But then he had the religious experience I mentioned, which caused him to examine the downside of committing suicide."

Castillo let that set in for a moment, and then went on: "As I was saying before I was so rudely interrupted — we'll get to the few remaining loose ends when I finish — Sergei, Juan Carlos, and I are agreed that their most likely plan is to take Ferris to the prison and then — when you and Abrego arrive — whack everybody."

"That scenario occurred to me," D'Alessandro said drily.

"So, what we are going to do is grab Ferris before that; as he's being transported from Retainhuled to the prison."

"Who's *we?* And how?"

Castillo told him.

"Pity you won't be there, Vic. It will be like old times."

"Tell me about the 'few remaining loose ends,' " D'Alessandro said. "Offhand, I can think of, say, fifty, but I'd rather hear them from you."

"Well, for example, I haven't made up my mind about the million dollars. Whether I should let the CIA pay it or Those People."

"That's not what I meant, Charley."

"And I haven't made up my mind how we should handle the two SVR people looking over Clendennen's shoulders."

"You know who they are?"

Castillo nodded. "What I haven't decided is who I should tell, if anybody, or what to do about them."

"I'm not anybody, Charley," D'Alessandro said evenly.

"No, you're not. And I haven't figured out how to get Ferris out of Mexico after we grab him."

"That's what they call changing the subject," D'Alessandro said.

"Yeah," Castillo agreed. "I guess it is."

"Well?"

After a brief moment, Castillo said: "Clemens McCarthy and a Secret Service agent named Douglas. I never heard of him."

"Clendennen calls him 'Dumbo,' " D'Alessandro said. "You're sure?"

"I got it from Murov. Who said this whole exercise is designed to prey on Clendennen's instability. To create another impeachment crisis. Nixon and Clinton."

D'Alessandro considered that a moment.

"Have you told Frank?"

Castillo shook his head.

"Sometimes, Charley, despite the old saw that any action is better than none, the best thing to do is nothing. At least, for a while."

"We're almost at the airport," Juan Carlos said. "How do you want to handle this?"

"We'll load Murov and Vic on their Black Hawk," Castillo said. "And wave bye-bye, and then Lester and I will get in the Mustang."

"Lester's here?" Vic said.

"Sitting on Sergei," Castillo said, jerking his thumb toward the following Suburban.

"I thought you said Murov had seen the light?"

"I don't want him committing suicide by Policía Federal. I'm sure he's figured out that we can't let him go free. So he knows if he runs, he gets shot."

"How are you going to stop him?"

"Juan Carlos has told his guys not to shoot, and I gave Lester an old Winchester pump .22 of mine, with which he will shoot Sergei in the leg. Or legs. I figured if that proved necessary, he wouldn't bleed to death before you got him to the States. He's in pretty bad emotional condition."

"Don't tell me remorse."

"Thinking of his wife and family in Lubyanka."

"That'll do it," D'Alessandro said.

They pulled close to the U.S. Army UH-60F sitting in a remote corner of the airfield.

"Charley, I didn't mention this before because it's lunacy on its face. Clendennen's got everybody running around getting a submarine ready to refuel the 60Fs he plans to send to the shoot-out at the prison."

"If we snatch Ferris, there won't be a need to send 60Fs to the prison," Castillo said.

"I don't think freeing Ferris will stop that mission. Clendennen is now in love with Gray Fox."

"Find out where the sub will be, and when, and get me the radio call signs."

"That may be a tall order, Charley. Naylor will want to know why I want to know.

And he doesn't know what you're up to. Do you want him to?"

"No. Tell him nothing," Castillo said. "But see what you can find out about the submarine, please."

[Five]
KM 125.5 National Road 200
Near Huixtla
Chiapas State, Mexico
0915 22 April 2007

The small convoy that had crossed into Mexico at Tapachula a little after eight consisted of a somewhat battered Suburban, a Mercedes S550 that appeared nearly new, a Suburban in better shape, a Mercedes C230, and a Ford F-150 pickup truck.

The Policía Federal roadblock they encountered — no surprise on that stretch of road — consisted of a Suburban and a Ford F-150 pickup. It was near the crest of a small rise.

When it became visible to the passenger in the front seat of the large Mercedes, he leaned over and sounded the horn, and then motioned the driver to pass the Suburban in the lead.

The Federales would know who he was, he reasoned, and they could get through the roadblock quickly, especially if he handed to whoever was in charge a sheaf of United States hundred-dollar bills. He did not want the Federales to start asking for identification.

When he got close, he saw that the man in charge was a Policía Federal second sergeant who would, he thought, be more grateful for the little gift he was about to give him than a more senior policeman — say, a first sergeant or even a *comandante* — would be.

He was a little annoyed when the second sergeant didn't immediately walk — or trot — to the Mercedes, as he expected him to do.

But finally, the second sergeant came from the barrier and walked to the Mercedes, trailed by a dozen other Federales. They walked to the vehicles behind the Mercedes and took up positions on either side of them.

"Good morning," the passenger in the front seat of the Mercedes said.

"Would you step out of the car, please?" the second sergeant asked politely.

"What for?"

"This is a check for drugs," the second sergeant said.

"Do I look like a drug dealer?" the man asked.

"No, sir, you don't. This won't take a minute, señor."

The man got out of the front seat, forced himself to smile, and handed the second sergeant the sheaf of U.S. hundred-dollar bills.

"A little something for the wife and kids," he said.

The second sergeant examined the money, smiled, and tucked it into his shirt pocket.

The man, convinced that the nonsense was now over, turned and started to get back in the Mercedes.

When he did, the second sergeant raised the muzzle of his Heckler & Koch MSG90A1 and fired two rounds into the back of the man's head. Then he leaned forward, and as the driver took an Uzi from the floorboard, put two rounds in the driver's head just above the ear. He then turned his attention to the rear seat, and shot, in their faces, the two men sitting there.

Much the same thing happened, more or less simultaneously, in the other vehicles in the convoy, except that in addition to killing just about everybody inside the nearly new Suburban, its rear door was opened and a visibly terrified man — the sole survivor — was pulled out over the rear seat and onto the road.

The second sergeant, now walking quickly, just shy of a trot, went to the man who had just been pulled out of the SUV. He gestured with the muzzle of his Heckler & Koch that the man was to walk toward the Suburban and the Ford pickup at the crest of the rise.

The sole survivor had almost reached the vehicles when he heard the familiar sound of Black Hawk rotor blades. He looked and saw that the noise was indeed coming from a UH-60, specifically from one painted in the color scheme of the Policía Federal.

The helo settled in for a landing. The pilot's door opened, and a Policía Federal officer ran toward them.

"Close your mouth, Jim," the man said. "You look like you're catching flies."

After a moment, the survivor said, "*Castillo?* Charley Castillo?"

"In the flesh. Come on, buddy. Let's go home."

He started to propel him toward the open door of the Black Hawk.

Another man appeared. He was a fat man in civilian clothing.

"I'm going with you," he announced in English.

"You didn't tell me you were going to do

this, goddamn you," Castillo said, gesturing at the convoy.

Colonel James D. Ferris looked where Castillo had pointed. Policía Federal officers were administering what in a polite society was known as the *coup de grâce*.

"Was this necessary?" Castillo pursued furiously.

"Dead men tell no tales, Charley. You never heard that?"

They were now at the open side door of the Black Hawk.

Hands reached to help Ferris inside.

"Good to see you, Colonel," the face behind the hands said.

"You remember Uncle Remus, I'm sure," Castillo said. "You want to lie down, Jim?"

"I'm all right," Ferris said.

"Go, Dick!" Castillo shouted.

The sound of the engines changed as Dick Miller advanced the throttles and prepared to make a running takeoff.

[Six]
Pope Air Force Base, North Carolina
1530 27 April 2007

In the Presidential Compartment of Air Force One, Joshua Ezekiel Clendennen was having what those close to him thought of

561

as another shit fit.

"Where the hell is McCarthy? That sonofabitch has a remarkable ability to disappear just when I need him the most!"

The door to the compartment swung open and Defense Secretary Beiderman stepped in.

"I suppose it's too much to hope that you know where McCarthy is," the President snapped. "Nobody else seems to have a clue."

"Sir, I'm afraid that I do," Beiderman said.

"What do you mean, you're afraid you do?"

"Mr. President, I just got the word. I'm sorry to inform you that Mr. McCarthy and Special Agent Douglas were killed about an hour ago en route to Andrews."

"What do you mean, killed? You mean dead? Who killed them?"

"There was an accident, sir. The vehicle in which Agent Douglas was driving Mr. McCarthy to Andrews collided with a propane truck, and there was an explosion, sir. The Beltway is just about shut down, they tell me."

"Sonofabitch!" the President said. "Dumbo was no nuclear physicist, but I liked him. He was loyal."

"Dumbo, sir?"

"Douglas," the President said. "I called Douglas 'Dumbo.' It was a term of endearment, for Christ's sake."

"It's a tragedy, sir," Beiderman said.

"So, what do I do now?" the President asked.

"About what, sir?"

"About every idiot in the press and his retarded brother out there," the President said, gesturing out the window. "There's at least a hundred of them, waiting for Naylor to arrive with Colonel Whatsisname."

"Ferris, sir," Supervisory Special Agent Mulligan said. "Colonel James D. Ferris."

"Right. What am I supposed to say to them?"

"Sir, may I make a suggestion?" Mulligan asked.

"Why not?" the President said.

"Don't say anything at all," Mulligan said. "Just be standing there waiting when General Naylor's plane lands. General Naylor will get off first and salute you, and then Colonel Ferris, and he will salute, and you say, 'Welcome home, Colonel. We're glad you're back.' And that's all."

Joshua Ezekiel Clendennen considered that a long moment. "I'll be goddamned if I don't think he's right. I don't have to say anything. The people will see me there, seeing me welcome Harris —"

"Ferris, sir," Mulligan corrected him.

"— welcome *Ferris* home. As Commander in Chief. Nobody would pay attention to anything I had to say anyway. What'll stick in their minds is Colonel Ferris saluting the Commander in Chief. Set that up, Beiderman."

"Yes, Mr. President."

ABOUT THE AUTHORS

W. E. B. Griffin is the author of six best-selling series: The Corps, Brotherhood of War, Badge of Honor, Men at War, Honor Bound, and Presidential Agent. He has been invested into the orders of St. George of the U.S. Armor Association and St. Andrew of the U.S. Army Aviation Association, and is a life member of the U.S. Special Operations Association; Gaston-Lee Post 5660, Veterans of Foreign Wars; China Post #1 in Exile of the American Legion; the Police Chiefs Association of Southeast Pennsylvania, South New Jersey, and Delaware; and the Flat Earth Society (Pensacola, Florida, and Buenos Aires, Argentina, chapters). He is an honorary life member of the U.S. Army Otter & Caribou Association, the U.S. Army Special Forces Association, the U.S. Marine Corps Raider Association, and the USMC Combat Correspondents Association.

William E. Butterworth IV has been an editor and writer for more than twenty-five years, and has worked closely with his father for several years on the editing of the Griffin books. He is the coauthor of the bestselling OSS Men at War novels *The Saboteurs* and *The Double Agents*; *Death and Honor, The Honor of Spies,* and *Victory and Honor* in the Honor Bound series; *The Traffickers* and *The Vigilantes* in the Badge of Honor series; and *The Outlaws* in The Presidental Agent series. He lives in Texas.